Praise for Anne Bishop's

Daughter of the Blood

"Anne Bishop has sco... *Daughter of the Blood*. Her poignant s... only by her flair for the dramatic and her deft characterization . . . a talented author."
—*Affaire de Coeur*

"[Bishop] has a unique voice—the writing is so rich and lush . . . [the] characters are so dark and compelling."
—*American Bookseller*

"A fabulous new talent . . . a uniquely realized fantasy filled with vibrant colors and rich textures. A wonderful new voice, Ms. Bishop holds us spellbound from the very first page."
—*Romantic Times* (4½ stars)

"Lavishly sensual . . . a richly detailed world based on a reversal of standard genre cliches."
—*Library Journal*

"Mystical, sensual, glittering with dark magic, Anne Bishop's debut novel brings a strong new voice to the fantasy field."
—Terri Windling, coeditor of
The Year's Best Fantasy and Horror

"*Daughter of the Blood* is among the most intense novels I've ever read. Erotic, violent, and imaginative, Bishop's book infuses fantasy with raw passion. This one is white-hot."
—Nancy Kress, author of *Maximum Light*

"Bishop's *Daughter of the Blood* is a unique vision of hell and darkness, love and hope [that] transcends the seductive intricacies of Anne Rice's vampire series."
—Lois H. Gresh, coauthor of *The Termination Node*

continued on next page . . .

Heir to the Shadows

"Daemon, Lucivar, and Saetan ooze more sex appeal than any three fictional characters created in a very long time . . . features a fascinating world consisting of three realms amply peopled with interesting and nearly always dangerous characters."
—*The Romance Reader*

"The fabulous talent of Anne Bishop is showcased in *Heir to the Shadows*. . . . Ms. Bishop's striking magical concepts and powerful images are wonderfully leavened with unexpected dash and humor, creating an irresistible treat for fantasy fans."
—*Romantic Times*

". . . [M]any compelling and beautifully realized elements. It's a terrific read, and I highly recommend both it and *Daughter of the Blood*."
—*The SF Site*

Queen of the Darkness

"The smashing conclusion of the *Black Jewels Trilogy*. . . . A storyteller of stunning intensity, Ms. Bishop has a knack for appealing but complex characterization."
—*Romantic Times*

"A powerful finale for this fascinating, uniquely dark trilogy."
—*Locus*

THE INVISIBLE RING

ANNE BISHOP

A ROC BOOK

ROC
Published by New American Library, a division of
Penguin Putnam Inc., 375 Hudson Street,
New York, New York 10014, U.S.A.
Penguin Books Ltd, 80 Strand,
London WC2R 0RL, England
Penguin Books Australia Ltd, 250 Camberwell Road,
Camberwell, Victoria 3124, Australia
Penguin Books Canada Ltd, 10 Alcorn Avenue,
Toronto, Ontario, Canada M4V 3B2
Penguin Books (N.Z.) Ltd, 182–190 Wairau Road,
Auckland 10, New Zealand

Penguin Books Ltd, Registered Offices:
Harmondsworth, Middlesex, England

First published by Roc, an imprint of New American Library,
a division of Penguin Putnam Inc.

First Printing, October 2000
10   9

ROC REGISTERED TRADEMARK—MARCA REGISTRADA

Printed in the United States of America

PUBLISHER'S NOTE
This is a work of fiction. Names, characters, places, and incidents either are the
product of the author's imagination or are used fictitiously, and any resemblance
to actual persons, living or dead, business establishments, events, or locales is
entirely coincidental.

for
Merri Lee and Michael Debany

ACKNOWLEDGMENTS

My thanks to Jennifer Jackson, for her continued enthusiasm and support of my work; to Laura Anne Gilman who, among her many other talents as an editor, has the ability to turn a phrase in a way that makes me laugh—even when she says that terrifying word, "clarify"; to Pat York and Lynn Flewelling for their insights; to the Circle, who understand what it means to dance with the Muse; to Kandra, webmaster extraordinaire; to Vince and Felicia for all the wonderful dinners sent over the fence; and to Pat and Bill Feidner for just being there.

JEWELS

White
Yellow
Tiger Eye
Rose
Summer-sky
Purple Dusk
Opal*
Green
Sapphire
Red
Gray
Ebon-gray
Black

*Opal is the dividing line between lighter and darker Jewels because it can be either.

When making the offering to the Darkness, a person can descend a maximum of three ranks from his/her Birthright Jewel.

Example: Birthright White could descend to Rose.

Blood Hierarchy/Castes

Males:

landen—non-Blood of any race

Blood male—a general term for all males of the Blood; also refers to any Blood male who doesn't wear Jewels

Warlord—a Jeweled male equal in status to a witch

Prince—a Jeweled male equal in status to a Priestess or a Healer

Warlord Prince—a dangerous, extremely aggressive Jeweled male; in status, slightly lower than a Queen

Females:

landen—non-Blood of any race

Blood female—a general term for all females of the Blood; mostly refers to any Blood female who doesn't wear Jewels

witch—a Blood female who wears Jewels but isn't one of the other hierarchical levels; also refers to any Jeweled female

Healer—a witch who heals physical wounds and illnesses; equal in status to a Priestess and a Prince

Priestess—a witch who cares for altars, Sanctuaries, and Dark Altars; witnesses handfasts and marriages; performs offerings; equal in status to a Healer and a Prince

Black Widow—a witch who heals the mind; weaves the tangled webs of dreams and visions; is trained in illusions and poisons

Queen—a witch who rules the Blood; is considered to be the land's heart and the Blood's moral center; as such, she is the focal point of their society

PROLOGUE

Lord Krelis, the new Master of the Guard, tried not to fidget as he watched Dorothea SaDiablo slowly pace the length of her private audience room. If she'd been any other woman, he might have openly admired her slender body, might have wondered if the black hair gracefully coiled around her head felt as silky as it looked, might have dared to run a hand over the brown skin that wasn't covered by her long red dress. He might have enjoyed the way the dress swished in counterrhythm to her swaying hips. He might have wondered if the way she caressed her chin with that large white feather was a subtle invitation for other kinds of caresses.

But Dorothea SaDiablo was a Black Widow, a member of the Hourglass, the most dangerous and feared covens in the Realm of Terreille. Black Widows specialized in poisons and journeys of the mind, in shadows and illusions, in dreamscapes that could ensnare a man and leave him locked in an endless nightmare.

She was also the Red-Jeweled High Priestess of Hayll. Since there were no Queens in the Hayllian Territory who could match the psychic strength that Jewel signified, and since no weaker Queen who wanted to stay whole and healthy challenged her authority, Dorothea ruled as she pleased—which was something no male in Hayll dared to forget.

"Have you seen your predecessor lately?" Dorothea purred as she swished past him. Her coquettish smile didn't match the vicious pleasure in her gold eyes.

"Yes, Priestess," Krelis replied, trying to keep his voice neutral. When he and a troop of men had gone into the slums of Draega, Hayll's capital, to round up some of the dregs for expendable labor, he had seen his former commander stumbling out of a filthy alleyway.

The former Master of the Guard was now a maimed, tortured mockery of the man he'd been. Worse, his inner web, that intimate core of Self that made the Blood who and what they were, had been shattered so that he could no longer wear the Jewels, could do no more than basic Craft, if even that. The keen tactical mind that had protected Dorothea for so many decades had been split open like a melon and scraped clean. But not completely. If the haunted eyes in the scarred face were any indication, enough thought had been left for him to remember what he had been. And who had done this to him.

Dorothea swished past Krelis again. Sweat beaded his forehead as he blanked his mind and prayed to the Darkness that she wouldn't sense anything that would make her want to open his inner barriers and sample his thoughts.

"I gave your predecessor an important task, and he failed me." Stopping in front of him, Dorothea smiled as she brushed the feather against his cheek. "Now he belongs to the Brotherhood of the Quill."

Krelis shuddered. Mother Night! To be shaved of all the organs that made a man a man. To need one of those large quills to . . .

"Are *you* going to fail me?" Dorothea purred, leaning close to him.

"No, Priestess," Krelis stammered. "Tell me what you wish of me, and I'll do it."

"A wise man." She tickled his lips with the feather before turning away. "You know of the Gray Lady?"

Had he failed already? Oh, he'd heard vague whispers a few months ago, but he'd still been a Third Circle guard at the time—and commanders weren't in the habit of telling their men more than was necessary. Feeling sick, he swallowed hard, and managed to whisper, "No, Priestess."

Dorothea flashed a malicious, amused look at him before resuming her leisurely pacing. "She's a dangerous enemy, a Gray-Jeweled Queen who rules the Territory called Dena Nehele on the other side of the Tamanara Mountains. She's been a thorn in my side since she set up her court forty years ago, and she continues to fight my attempts to bring the Realm of Terreille under the beneficent guidance of Hayll."

Krelis said hesitantly, "Since she's not from one of the long-lived races, surely she must be old by now."

"But still strong," Dorothea snapped. "As long as she continues to live, Dena Nehele will be able to resist being drawn into Hayll's shadow, and the Territories bordering it will be strengthened by that resistance. Even if she died tomorrow, it would still take at least one of their generations to eliminate her influence."

"You intend to declare war on this Gray Lady?"

Dorothea's gold eyes turned hard yellow. "Hayll does not lower itself to such barbarities as war. What would be the point of acquiring a Territory that had been savaged by the kind of war the Blood fight?" She tapped the feather against her chin. "There are subtler ways of making a Territory ripe for the plucking. But that doesn't concern you."

Krelis stared at the floor. "No, Priestess."

"Your task is to eliminate the Gray Lady."

He didn't think before he blurted out, *"How?"*

She looked disgusted. Was she regretting savaging the old Master and losing that tactical mind? Then her expression changed.

"Poor boy," she murmured, gently stroking his cheek. "I've been cruel to you, haven't I? No, darling"—she pressed her fingers against his lips—"you needn't deny it. There's no reason why you would know that bitch's habits." She stepped back and sighed. "Grizelle is too well protected in her own Territory for you to reach her there. However, over the past few years, she's come out of her lair twice each year for the slave auctions at Raej."

"Slave auctions." Krelis's gold eyes lit up.

Dorothea shook her head. "Raej is considered neutral ground. If a Queen were killed there for any reason, others might hesitate to visit, and then how would everyone sell the toys they're ready to discard and buy new ones?"

"A slave could be replaced with a loyal servant and then—"

"She doesn't buy anyone from Hayll, and there are no loyal servants outside of our own people. Sometimes not even within our own people."

Krelis leashed his frustration. This was the first important task she'd given him since he became Master of the Guard a few months ago. He wouldn't fail. He wouldn't. "Then what should I do, Priestess?"

Dorothea stopped pacing. "Lord Krelis, you're the Master of the Guard. How you accomplish this is entirely up to you." Her expression softened. "However, if you wish me to, I'll use my particular Craft to assist you in whatever way I can."

He breathed a sigh of relief. "Thank you, Priestess."

Dorothea studied him for just a little too long. Then she smiled. "I knew I'd made the right choice in my new Master of the Guard. I made the same offer to your predecessor, but he didn't want my help. Since the bitch escaped his trap rather easily, that was reason enough to doubt his loyalty, don't you think?"

Remembering what the former Master's face looked like now, Krelis shivered. "Yes, Priestess."

"I'm not going to have to worry about *your* loyalty, am I?"

"No, Priestess."

Dorothea walked up to him and wrapped her arms around his neck. "You know, darling, I'm very generous with a male who pleases me." She rubbed her breasts against his chest, kissed him thoroughly, then purred, "That's to remind you of the rewards that come from serving me well. And this"—she tucked the large white feather into his belt—"will remind you of the penalties of failure."

CHAPTER ONE

*N*othing that had been done to him over the past nine years had hurt as much as the harsh truth that he had brought this on himself. With one error in judgment, the eighteen-year-old boy he had been, that young strutting buck who had been so sure of himself, had sent him down this pain-filled road. A road that would soon end in the brutality that waited for men in the salt mines of Pruul.

Over the past few days, while he had waited to be brought to the slave auction, he had tried very hard to forgive that boy for ignoring the uneasiness his friends had felt and the warnings the older Warlords had given him when that witch had walked into the inn. He had tried to forgive him for not looking beneath the surface, for not sensing the rot that existed beneath the beautiful face and lush body, for grabbing that musky bait with such enthusiasm. He had tried to forgive him for believing the whispered words that had promised a forever filled with nighttime romps, for being so caught up in the pleasure between his legs that he'd let her put that gold ring around his cock because she'd poutingly told him about all the naughty things she wanted to do with him and for him—but not until he wore a Ring of Obedience because she needed a little control over his passion.

She'd played with him for a day before he learned just how cruel the Ring of Obedience could be when it was used by someone who enjoyed inflicting pain.

Having been a pleasure slave for the past nine years, he couldn't remember why he'd ever wanted to get into bed with a woman.

And he blamed that boy, bitterly. With the salt mines of Pruul waiting for him, oh, yes, he blamed that boy.

*   *   *

"What's a Red-Jeweled Warlord doing in *this* pen?" one of the slaves whispered. "They don't usually put the likes of *him* down *here.*"

Another slave spat. "Don't matter what Jewels a slave wears."

"True enough, but . . . I remember seeing him before. I thought he was a pleasure slave."

"He was," a third man answered, "until he became a Queen killer."

"A Queen killer!"

Queen killer. Queen killer.

Jared remained in the corner of the slave pen he had claimed for himself, ignoring the whispers that swirled around him, pretending he didn't see the way the other men avoided him. Even here, in the vilest slave pen, Blood males who were now considered unmanageable for anything but the meanest labor didn't want to be contaminated by a man who had a Queen's blood on his hands.

He understood that. When the blinding rage had faded enough for him to see the bodies of the Queen and her Prince brother, he had been horrified by what he'd done.

His breath hitched as emotional pain ripped through him again, threatening to tear him apart.

One part of himself had been horrified, that was true enough—the part that had learned the Warlord's code of honor from his father, the part that had been raised to serve the distaff gender. But another part, a savage part that he hadn't known existed, had howled in triumph.

The pain eased, again, while that wild stranger inside him prowled the edges of his mind and heart.

He didn't trust that stranger, even feared its presence. *It* wasn't *him.* But he would use its savagery one more time for just one reason: He wanted, *needed,* to get home just long enough to see his mother and take back the words he'd had years to regret saying. After that . . .

There was no point thinking there would be anything after that. But it would be enough. *Had* to be enough.

Which meant he had to escape tonight. Tomorrow, Raej's autumn slave auction would begin. The witches who came to this island to buy and sell would be on the auction grounds accompanied by hired guards, and the guards watching the pens would be too edgy, too quick to react to *anything* a slave did.

So tonight he would find a way to get close enough to the official landing place outside the fairgrounds and catch one of the Winds, those webs of psychic roadways that allowed the Blood to travel through the Darkness. He would catch one and ride it all the way back to Ranon's Wood.

The decision made, Jared watched the sun set and the quarter moon rise while he thought about his mother, his father and brothers, his home . . . and the boy he used to be.

CHAPTER TWO

Krelis closed the small wooden box Dorothea had given him, then used Craft to vanish it.

All the plans were made. There was nothing he could do but wait.

Staying in the Master's office made him feel too confined, so he left the building that housed the First Circle guards and began walking aimlessly across the practice fields.

Thank the Darkness Dorothea hadn't demanded his presence at dinner tonight. While his bloodlines could be traced to two of Hayll's Hundred Families, his family on both sides was from minor branches. He'd grown up in a small village, and he still wasn't comfortable in the jaded, glittering aristo society that made up the social power of Hayll. A man on guard duty during one of these functions could watch the seductions and the games, could listen to the double-edged conversations, could observe the dance of wealth and power without having to participate. But the Master of the Guard was one of the three most important males in a court, and, when required, he was expected to socialize with the people who gathered around his Lady. He was expected to talk with the other men and dance with the women, was expected to flirt just enough not to give offense, without flirting so much that servicing the woman would be required.

He'd already sweated through a couple of smaller functions. He didn't need to dance on the knife edge tonight.

Leaving the practice fields, Krelis followed a bridle path until he reached a small reflecting pool. Sitting on a stone bench near the pool, he watched the still water.

Either the former Master of the Guard had become arrogantly foolish or he'd turned traitor. That was the only way Krelis could explain the failed attack on the Gray Lady when she was returning to Dena Nehele after the spring auction at Raej.

It wasn't strange that the Master hadn't led the attack. Along with the Steward and the Consort, the Master seldom left the court unless he was accompanying his Lady. His duties were no longer in the field. But one of those duties was to choose the right men for an assignment.

The old Master had sent a handful of lighter-Jeweled, Fifth Circle guards and a small band of marauders to destroy a Gray-Jeweled Queen and the escort waiting for her at the Coach station. There had been no time to overwhelm the escort before the Gray bitch's arrival. There had been no backup force to attack her if she tried to escape on the Winds. There had been nothing.

Only one of those lighter-Jeweled Hayllian guards had returned to report the failure.

One was all Dorothea had needed.

Well, he hadn't made that mistake. He had tame marauder bands waiting at the Coach stations the Gray Lady would most likely use on her return from the auction. They would eliminate any escorts waiting for her and send a messenger to Lord Maryk, his second-in-command. Maryk, along with carefully selected, experienced First and Second Circle guards, would arrive at the station just ahead of the Gray Lady to finish the kill. If that ambush wasn't completely successful, and Maryk and the men were killed, he still had a way to keep track of the bitch and leave a trail the marauder bands could follow. The hunt would continue until the Gray Lady was destroyed.

Krelis fingered the Master's badge on his left shoulder.

With the spells Dorothea had woven for him, his strategy would bring down her most dangerous rival. That would prove to the aristo bastards in the First and Second Circles that he wasn't some upstart Third Circle guard who had gained a coveted position in the court by using his cock.

Of course, he didn't know any male who wouldn't use sex in order to achieve his own goals.

It hadn't always been like that.

He remembered that night so many, many years ago. He'd been permitted to stay up when some of his father's friends had come to the house for their weekly chess games and male conversation. The evening had grown late and he'd been dozing on the couch when his father, who had a strong interest in Hayll's history, especially where it pertained to the Blood, had gently voiced his concern about some of the changes that had taken place in their society over the past few centuries. Olvan had made no accusations, had named no names, had merely pointed out some differences in the way males who didn't serve in a court were treated.

The next day, when he and Olvan were taking a rambling walk along one of the country lanes near their village, the Queen of the Province and twelve of her guards came riding up. The Queen had snapped a few questions at Olvan, becoming more and more enraged with his respectful replies.

A few minutes later, Olvan dangled from a tree branch. The spelled ropes around his wrists had prevented him from using Craft to undo the knots or sever the ropes. Even if he'd managed to free himself, his Jewels weren't dark enough to challenge the combined power of the Queen and her guards.

They let him hang there while he pleaded with the Queen to tell him how he had displeased her. When the pleading finally stopped, six of the guards uncurled their whips.

The force of the blows swung Olvan back and forth, back and forth.

There had been no sympathy in the guards' faces, no mercy in the strong arms that wielded the whips. If anything, there had been a hint of fear in their eyes, as if coming in contact with a male who didn't understand obedience would taint them somehow and make them less desirable to the Queen they served.

Through it all, another guard had held Krelis and made him watch.

When they rode away, they left his father hanging there, half-dead.

Krelis still remembered running desperately to the nearest house for help, still remembered sitting next to his father's bleeding body during the ride back home, still remembered the Healer's reluctance to do anything.

And he still remembered the moment, years later, when he realized that the whipping had nothing to do with the courteous answers his father had made to the Queen and everything to do with Olvan's oldest and most trusted friends never once coming back to the house or inviting his father to any of theirs.

That was the moment he decided to train to be a guard.

That was the moment he understood that how males were treated in the past didn't matter. The only thing that mattered to a young Hayllian male was surviving the way things were *now*. And the only way to do that was to serve in a strong court.

Krelis stood up and stretched.

So here he was just beginning his sixteenth century—a young man by the standards of the long-lived Hayllian race—and he was already the Master of the Guard of the strongest court in Hayll. An important goal in itself, but now just a stepping-stone toward the other things he wanted.

He had worked too long and too hard to let some Gray-Jeweled bitch who would die in a few decades anyway spoil his plans.

CHAPTER THREE

*H*e had almost made it, had almost gotten close enough to catch one of the Winds. If he'd had a few more seconds before the auction steward had used the Ring of Obedience to pull him down and make him easy prey for the guards and their whips, he would have been home by now.

He would have had those seconds if he had killed the guard keeping watch on the slave pen. But at the last moment, when that wild stranger inside him had surged forward intent on the kill, he had seen the same fear and knowledge in the guard's eyes that had been in the eyes of the Queen just before her blood had covered his hands . . . and he had yanked that savagery back. His attack had stunned the guard long enough for him to escape from the pen, but the man had recovered too quickly, had been able to sound the alarm too soon.

There would be no other chance. Not after last night.

I'm sorry, Mother. I'm sorry.

"Don't look so pretty now, do ya, twat-licker?"

Pain and the guard's sneering words brought Jared back to the present. He looked at the man—a vicious brute whose Yellow Jewel was as grimy as the rest of him—and said nothing.

The guard hawked and spat. "All you pretty boys, prancing around in your fancy clothes, acting like you was better than other men, *real* men, who know what to do with their spears. Well, no one's going to want to play with you now, are they, pretty boy? 'Cept the Queens in Pruul, and everyone knows what kind of games *they* like to play." The guard grinned, showing a black hole where a couple of teeth were missing.

Jared watched the guard warily. He'd been brought back to this slave pen at dawn, forced to his knees, and then tied so securely to the four waist-high iron posts he couldn't move at all, not even his head. He'd had no food or water since yesterday afternoon's ration. The auction steward in charge of the controlling ring connected to his Ring of Obedience had been sending low-level pain through the Ring since his capture last night. His genitals were so tender that even a fly walking across his balls made him grit his teeth to keep from screaming.

The flies were an additional torment, buzzing around the lash wounds on his back and belly that had reopened when the guards had pulled his hands behind his back and yanked his arms up to tie the straps to the back posts.

One fly landed on Jared's cheek. He closed his eye before the fly could reach it.

The guard stared at him for a moment, then cursed savagely. "You son of a whoring bitch, are you winking at me?" Grabbing Jared by the hair, he used Craft to call in a knife, then slowly turned the blade until all Jared could see was the sharp edge. "Well, slut, you don't need two eyes to dig salt."

Jared panted as the blade came closer, closer. Explaining wouldn't help him. Neither would pleading. If he used Craft to protect himself, all the guards would be down on him and, by the time it was over, he'd end up losing more than an eye.

Just before the blade came close enough to cut, the guard jerked, stumbled back a step. He shook his head as if to clear it, then rubbed the small of his back with a fist. When he turned around, he froze and let out a soft whimper.

Jared blinked rapidly, not sure if it was tears or sweat blinding him. Didn't matter. The guard was between him and whatever had caught the man's attention.

During those long seconds when the guard stood frozen, Jared became aware of the silence. All the usual, small noises inside a slave pen had stopped, as if slaves and guards alike were afraid to do anything that might call attention to themselves.

Finally, the guard vanished the knife and moved away slowly, awkwardly, as if his legs had become unsteady.

No longer blocked by the guard's body, Jared looked straight into Daemon Sadi's cold, golden eyes.

If pleasure slaves were the aristos in the slave hierarchy, then Daemon Sadi was as far above the rest of them as they were to the slaves used for hard labor. Looking at his broad-shouldered body and beautiful face or listening to his deep, sexy-edged voice was enough to arouse most women—and quite a few men, regardless of their preference. He could seduce anything that breathed.

They called him the Sadist because he was as cruel as he was beautiful. Owned by Dorothea SaDiablo, he'd been a pleasure slave for centuries and wore the Ring of Obedience. He was also a strong Warlord Prince, and people who annoyed Sadi had an odd way of disappearing.

Jared sighed in relief when Daemon finally looked away, the bored expression on that beautiful face betraying no thoughts, no feelings. But the voice that reached Jared on a Red psychic spear thread held sympathy and understanding.

So. You finally couldn't stomach it anymore.

Jared thought of the last Queen who had owned him, and the kinds of bedroom games she and her Prince brother had wanted to play. He shuddered. *No, I couldn't stomach it anymore,* he replied. *I couldn't stomach them.*

If Daemon hadn't taken an interest in him eight years ago when they'd been in the same court, he wouldn't have survived this long. Pleasure slaves tended to become emotionally unstable after a few years of serving in the bed. Daemon's lessons had helped him stay detached from what he was ordered to do, or what was being done to him.

Even that detachment hadn't been enough that last time.

The bitch deserved to die, Daemon said, as if killing a Queen was so commonplace it wasn't worth more than a casual remark. Which, for Sadi, was probably close to the truth. Then his tone changed, and he sounded like a teacher who was mildly annoyed with a favorite student. *But you could have been more subtle.*

The woman next to Daemon tugged on the sleeve of his black, tailored jacket. She seemed confused to find herself so far away from the amusements and the merchant booths. Compared to Daemon's looks and Hayllian coloring—golden-brown skin, glossy black hair, and gold eyes—she looked bleached and plain. She mumbled something and tugged again.

Daemon ignored her.

Jared couldn't hear the words, but he heard the whine in her voice. His muscles tensed. He held his breath.

She spoke again, but her whining was cut off by Daemon's low, vicious snarl. She quickly stepped away from him. Once she was safely out of reach, she raised her voice. "I could use the Ring."

Daemon smiled, a cold, brutal smile.

The guards exchanged nervous glances and shifted their feet.

It seems my Lady requires some entertainment, Daemon said. There was something beneath the bland tone that made Jared wonder if the Lady wasn't going to be very sorry she'd made that threat.

May the Darkness embrace you, Lord Jared, Daemon said as he offered his arm to the Lady and started to walk away.

And you, Prince Sadi, Jared replied.

They were out of sight when Daemon's last words reached him. *That guard's going to come down with a mysterious fever. He'll recover, but he'll never regain enough strength in his limbs to resume his duties. What use do you think a man like that will have in a place like Raej?*

Jared shuddered, grateful Sadi had already broken the link between them. He owed Daemon a great deal, but there were things about the Sadist he preferred not to know.

Another fly landed on his cheek.

Jared closed his eyes, and tried not to think. Tried not to remember. And failed.

* * *

When he opened his eyes again, the day had waned to dusk. At any moment, the bell that signaled the end of that day's auctioning would ring. The Blood Lords and Ladies who came to buy preferred to do so in harsh sunlight that didn't hide flaws that wouldn't be as apparent when a naked slave was displayed in muted candle-light or, better yet, flickering torchlight.

He saw the guard standing outside the pen, watching him. Not one of the usual brutes. The badge on the clean uniform jacket indicated that this was one of the guards who hired out as an escort. It was a fixed rule at the auction; Ladies were required to hire two of Raej's guard escorts to help with any slaves they might purchase. Since the man was alone, his partner was probably guarding the slaves that had already been purchased.

Which still didn't explain why the man was wandering around near the pens that held the most-condemned males. It still didn't explain why the bastard was staring at . . .

Something crept through the air. Something tantalizing. Something intriguing. A psychic scent that made his heart speed up and his muscles quiver. A scent that made the wild stranger inside him strain toward it, wary and eager—and hungry.

A Queen's scent.

Jared looked at the empty space beside the guard escort. Except it wasn't empty.

Despite feeling certain of what he would see, he looked straight at her and still almost didn't see her. She was gray, and stood so still she blended into the dust and the waning light and the taste of despair.

No. *No!* Not *that one.*

He began hoping, desperately, that the auction bell would ring. Then, maybe, if the Darkness was kind, she wouldn't return in the morning, wouldn't come back to stare at him with those hard gray eyes.

There were a few courts where being a slave was almost tolerable. There were others where every command abraded a man's soul.

In the slave quarters, stories and rumors were fearfully

whispered in the dark. Warnings and advice were passed along. Because of that, the slaves had a saying: the bite of a lash was better than being owned by Dorothea SaDiablo; being owned by Dorothea was better than dying in the salt mines of Pruul; but dying in the salt mines was better, far better, than being touched by Grizelle, the Gray Lady.

No slave who went into her Territory ever came out again. No slave survived being owned by the Gray-Jeweled Queen who was standing outside the pen, so silent and so still, looking at him.

Fear swelled inside him until it overwhelmed all the rest of the day's torments. Tied to the iron posts, he couldn't turn away, couldn't even look down since the wide, tight leather collar kept him from moving his head. Isolated, he couldn't blend in with the other slaves who clustered on the other side of the pen. He was pinned, alone, physically and emotionally naked beneath that gray stare.

She terrified him. The only advantage he'd ever had was that the Queens who had owned him hadn't worn Jewels that could threaten his inner web. But the Gray Jewels were darker than the Red, and a Queen who could tear apart his inner barriers and shatter his inner web as easily as she could tear apart his body wasn't a woman he wanted to get close to. In any way.

But the wild stranger, that beast that had been so angry and so eager to kill, now wanted to crawl to her and expose its belly in an act of complete submission.

That terrified him even more.

"Lady, there's nothing here of interest. These males are unmanageable, unfit for anything but hard labor."

Hearing the undercurrent of worry in the man's voice, Jared focused on the guard escort standing next to Grizelle. The man had reason to worry. A hired escort who failed to protect the Lady in his charge would probably find himself on the auction block the next morning.

Ignoring the escort, Grizelle withdrew one hand from her robe's wide sleeves and pointed at Jared. "That one."

Jared's chest clenched so hard he couldn't draw a breath. Hell's fire! Even her *voice* was gray!

And she wanted him.

No no no no no!

"*That* one?" The escort sounded shocked. "Lady, that one killed the last Queen who owned him and attacked a guard last night, trying to escape. He's going to the salt mines unless someone buys him for a killing sport."

Listen to him, Jared thought fiercely, trying to make her feel the words without risking a direct link. *I'm tainted, twisted, past any hope. I'll fight you with everything I am for as long as I can, and I'll hate you long after that.*

The finger didn't waver. The gray eyes didn't blink.

As he focused on the finger pointing at him, nine years of pain and fear began to crystallize into deadly, chilling hatred. He'd once believed in service and honor. Now all he believed in was cold hatred and rage. He was a Red-Jeweled Warlord from Shalador. He was Blood. He'd fight her, and die in the fighting. That was better than cringing and cowering while she tore him apart piece by piece.

The wild stranger howled in distress and desire, fighting against the very rage it should have embraced, shattering it almost before it formed.

"That one," the Gray Lady said again.

You will not have me, Jared thought as he watched the reluctant approach of the auction steward who had been summoned. *I will not yield to you. Even if I can't do anything else, I can still do that much. Will do that much.*

When a price was finally agreed upon, the steward bowed to Grizelle, then gestured to two of the guards inside the pen. "We'll clean him up for you, Lady," he said. His pompous smile died beneath that steely stare. "I'll have him and the papers ready in . . . an hour?"

"Thirty minutes."

The steward paled. "Of course, Lady. I'll see to it personally."

Offering no response, Grizelle and her unhappy escort walked away.

They gave him no chance to fight. Not that he could have with the way his cramped legs screamed when the guards hauled him to his feet. They attached two chains to the wide collar and kept his hands tied behind his back. With a prissy smile, the steward increased the level of pain coming through the Ring of Obedience until Jared's already unsteady legs buckled and breathing took all of his concentration.

The short walk to the small building where lower-class slaves were delivered to their new owners took forever and ended too soon.

The wash-down room contained a pump and half barrel, a wooden table that held a large chest, and two iron posts positioned on either side of a drain.

Pain shot through the Ring at the same moment the guards untied his hands. By the time Jared could think again, his wrists and ankles were cuffed to the posts. One guard pumped water into the half barrel while the one who'd wanted to cut his eye rummaged through the chest. Jared's gorge rose when the guard turned around and held up a wide strip of leather that had buckles on the ends and a leather ball sewn to the center.

"Open your mouth, pretty boy," the guard said with a sneering smile as he came toward Jared. "You know how to do that."

Jared clenched his teeth.

Vicious pleasure filled the guard's eyes as he held the gag in front of Jared's mouth. "Open your mouth, or I'll break your teeth."

The steward appeared in the doorway between the rooms and huffed with annoyance. "We've no time for this. She'll be here soon. Besides, he's already bought. If there's any fresh damage, the bitch will demand compensation." His voice shook a little, leaving no doubt about the kind of compensation the Gray Lady would demand.

Another flash of pain came through the Ring of Obedience. Jared kept his teeth clenched and tried to ride it out, but it didn't end, didn't end, didn't end until he opened his mouth in a breathless scream.

With a satisfied grunt, the guard shoved the gag into his mouth and buckled the straps behind his head.

The wide leather collar was too thick and stiff to yield to the pressure of bone, so opening his mouth had forced his head back. His tongue worked relentlessly to keep the leather ball from sliding too far back. His stomach twitched, threatening to respond forcefully if he choked. And his mind . . .

It was during his third year as a pleasure slave, serving in a Black Widow's court. She wasn't Hayllian, but she'd been a protégée of Dorothea SaDiablo and had relished the lessons on how to cripple the male spirit. He remembered what it felt like to lie on his back, tied hand and foot to the bed, wearing a gag like this one. Already dosed with *safframate,* a vicious aphrodisiac, he'd had no control over his body's merciless need. He'd lain there, helpless, while she played with him and rode him until he screamed.

Something had twisted inside him that night, and he'd felt the first flash of savagery. But it had taken six more soul-killing years before his father's training and the ingrained honor and respect Blood males felt for the feminine gave way to hatred strong enough to let him fight back. Six years between that night and the night that savagery had broken free and he killed the Queen and her Prince brother. But two years ago, he'd secretly rejoiced when he'd heard that that Black Widow had played one game too many with the Sadist—and had lost.

A slap on the belly brought him back to the wash-down room and the current source of pain.

The guard bared his teeth in a smile. "Since you ain't going to the salt mines now, the least we can do is bring a little of the salt mines to you."

The other guard grinned as he opened a large sack and poured coarse-grained salt into the half barrel of water. Using Craft, he raised the half barrel and guided it across the room.

Jared closed his eyes as the half barrel floated toward him. He ignored his quivering body.

He would make a brutal dive down into the abyss until he reached the full strength of his Red Jewels. He would gather every drop of strength he had. And as he dove, he would place a Red circle around the building to form a psychic boundary. Then he would unleash all the power he had gathered. That Red strength would hit that boundary and turn back on itself. Even if someone survived the initial unleashing of that much dark power in a small space, the

backlash would finish the destruction. They would all die—
and so would he, because he wasn't going to hold back any
of that Red strength to shield himself.

I'm sorry, Mother. I'm sorry.

He dove into the abyss.

The wild stranger rose to meet him, smashed into him,
stopping his descent.

Damn you, LET ME DIE! Jared screamed as he tried
to slip past the part of himself that had become his enemy
and reach his Red strength. *Let me—*

The half barrel of salty, frigid water flooded over him.
Jared's muscles locked around his lungs. The open lash
wounds burned. He couldn't think, couldn't breathe.

With a scream of rage, the wild stranger dove back into
the abyss, going so deep he could no longer feel it, could
no longer find it.

Sagging, Jared felt the pull in his shoulders as his arms
took his weight. The plan he'd had a moment ago to destroy himself became less than a memory. The past nine
years of slavery pressed down on him until he thought his
shaking body would snap under the weight.

He wasn't broken. His psychic power was still there, but,
somehow, the wild stranger had taken away the will to
use it.

I'm a Shalador Warlord. I am Blood.

The words sounded pathetic and empty now.

The guard removed the gag, pulling out strands of Jared's
dark hair that had gotten caught in the buckles.

Jared absorbed the new pain, idly wondering if a soul
could bleed to death, if that's why he felt so weak and
hollow.

He was dimly aware of the guards untying him, half dragging him into the next room, then cuffing him to another
set of iron posts. The steward appeared in front of him
and said something that sounded sharp, but the words were
murky smears, and he couldn't hold on to them long
enough to understand them.

Someone removed the wide leather collar.

His chin sank to his chest.

His mind drifted until fingers gently lifted his chin and

he found himself captured by hard gray eyes. They looked into him as if his inner barriers were completely crumbled, and there was nothing he could call his own—no thought, no feeling she couldn't examine and discard as a worthless trinket. He cringed as memories of his family kept trying to surface. He didn't want her to have his memories of his younger brothers, his aunts and uncles, his cousins, his father. His mother. No, he didn't want her to have his memories of Reyna, especially not the last memory of her standing there, bleeding from heart-wounds his brutal words had caused.

The gray eyes still held his, but the fingers drifted down his shivering body, brushed over the hair at his groin, gently circled him like a different kind of Ring, and finally circled the Ring of Obedience. He felt the tight band of gold expand until he felt nothing at all.

Turning slightly, she flicked her right hand toward the wooden table in the room. The guards' startled gasps didn't completely muffle the other sound—like a heavy coin spinning, like a child's hoop that finally loses speed and circles round and round, lower and lower until the ground claims it.

"Lady!"

The shocked exclamation meant something, but Jared felt too empty to react. His body hurt so much it didn't even register the usual discomfort that came from the Ring of Obedience—the discomfort that effectively kept a man's attention focused on the threat of pain.

"Hell's fire, Lady, Ring him!"

The psychic scents of the males in the room stank of fear.

Jared frowned and wished his thoughts weren't so fuzzy. Ring him?

He slowly realized it wasn't a heavy coin on the table, but the Ring of Obedience. The one he'd worn for the past nine years.

Before he could even try to shake off the emotional lethargy and physical weakness, to comprehend what it meant, Grizelle's fingers closed around him again and squeezed lightly. He gasped as pain shivered along his nerves.

Light flashed from her fingers, blinding him. A clap of

thunder shook the building. The unmistakable feel of power filled the room.

Grizelle stepped back and calmly stared at the nervous guards, the shocked escort, and the sweating, hand-wringing steward. "You have nothing to fear," she said. "He wears my Ring now."

The steward pointed a shaking finger at Jared's groin. "B-but, Lady, there's no Ring."

"Ah," Grizelle said. There were so many nuances in that small sound, so much ice in the calm smile. "But there is. He wears the Invisible Ring."

Jared's heart began to pound. The Invisible Ring?

The ghost of a memory drifted just out of reach.

The steward chewed his lip. "I've never heard of such a Ring."

Jared had. But how? Where?

"The witches in my family have been using it for generations," Grizelle said. She gestured toward the Ring of Obedience lying on the table. "It's ten times more powerful than that little toy." Then she paused. "Would you like a further demonstration?"

The men hastily assured her there was no need.

Jared closed his eyes. Hell's fire, Mother Night, and may the Darkness be merciful. Ten times more powerful. Ten times more painful. How was he supposed to survive that?

He wasn't.

No one survived being owned by Grizelle. And now he knew why.

He let his mind drift again, no longer interested in what was happening in the room. More senseless smears of words. Female anger boiling up like a violent storm on the horizon. Whimpers. Hands untying him, walking him to the final room. He stood where he was placed, passive.

Ten times more powerful, and he couldn't even feel it. Maybe he was numbed by too much pain. Maybe it was too subtle to feel after so much agony.

If only he could remember what he'd heard about how it worked, or why it was different from the Ring of Obedience.

Then again, maybe he should be grateful that he didn't remember.

The door opened behind him and the escort, who had stayed in the room to keep an eye on him, snapped to attention. "Lady?"

Damn. Something had happened while his mind had drifted. The escort's voice held cautious fear, a familiar tone that meant a dark-Jeweled witch's temper was one careless word away from exploding.

"The clothing you requested will be here any moment," the escort said. Jared heard the man swallow. "Is there something else, Lady?"

It took all of Jared's self-control not to turn around to see what she was doing. It took all of his concentration to identify the quiet sound of a lid being unscrewed from a jar.

"I want to look at those wounds," the Gray Lady said. "They need to be properly cleaned and this healing salve applied. I've plans for this one. I don't want him dying before I get any use out of him."

Her voice made Jared's skin crawl. Her psychic scent unnerved him. Even without the wild stranger's presence, it produced a kind of lust in him that went beyond the body's desires, the kind of lust a dark-Jeweled male felt in the presence of a dark-Jeweled witch. It made him crave her touch, made him want her hands on him.

He hated her for that most of all.

The escort hesitated, then said, "I can take care of it, Lady."

Relief flooded Jared when Grizelle left the small room. It would be better to feel another man's rough hands than have those gentle fingers touch him again.

When the guards delivered the clothes and the healing supplies a few minutes later, Jared's world narrowed to a fierce craving for water. He thought of asking the escort if he could drink from the basin—he would have drunk anything at that moment, no matter what had been added to the water to clean the wounds—but the man's angry growl killed the words before they could form. As he suffered the sting of warm water and cleansing herbs while the escort washed his back and belly, he wondered if Grizelle had known what kind of torment this would be or if she simply didn't care how long he'd been without water.

Jared endured the cleaning in silence, but he gasped when the escort smeared the healing salve into the lash wounds on his back. It felt icy after the warm water. It also quickly numbed his skin.

Released from a little more pain, he started remembering the advice Daemon Sadi had given him the year they had spent together.

Daemon had called it balls and sass. If a male went into a court cringing, for whatever reason, and regained a little strength or showed a little temper, it would be regarded as defiance by the Queen and the witches in her First Circle, and as a challenge by all the other males who feared losing their place in the court's pecking order. However, if a male went in with balls and sass, forcing the Queen and the other witches to remember that the danger of a dark Jewel couldn't be dismissed just because a man wore a Ring and was called a slave, he was treated more cautiously, faced fewer challengers among the males, and was thought of as a chained predator instead of as prey. In some courts, it meant the difference between surviving or not.

"I can do that," Jared croaked when the escort started smearing salve on the belly wounds. He wasn't sure about that, wasn't even sure he could stand up much longer since he was quickly reaching his threshold of physical endurance. Balls and sass were a fragile shield, but, right now, they were all he had. "I can do that," he said again.

"Shut up," the escort snarled as he hurriedly applied the salve.

Jared studied the grim face, the shadows in the eyes that avoided his. The escort was a Warlord who wore the Purple Dusk Jewel. How did he survive looking at the bruised, naked bodies of his Brothers? How did he survive looking at the ones who had been maimed or broken or shaved? Did he go home to a lover or a wife he felt some affection for? Did he have children he cuddled and played with and loved? Or had he picked up a witch at the auction one year, one already broken and barren, whom he mounted without considering her feelings or well-being? What did he think of the males bought and sold here? Had he ever looked up one day and seen a man he'd called a friend standing on the auction block?

Ah, the shadows in the eyes. The worry behind having to escort someone like the Gray Lady around the slave fair. *Look well,* Jared thought as the man finished applying the salve and stepped away. *Look at the price you may have to pay for one error in judgment.*

As if the thoughts had been sent on a psychic spear thread, the escort looked Jared in the eyes. Seconds passed in strained silence. "You're nothing but a pretty mouth, a dangle for the Ladies to play with," the escort snarled.

Jared smiled savagely. "I'm a Red-Jeweled Shalador Warlord. I'm stronger than you'll ever be, can unleash power you can only dream of. And I'm still here."

The escort's jaw tightened. His breathing became harsh. "Get dressed. Your dangle's for private viewing now."

The clothes had been dropped on a rough bench next to the small table that held the basin. Jared forced himself to look away from the basin full of dirty water, but not soon enough.

With a fiercely pleased look in his eyes, the escort used Craft to vanish the basin. "You may wear the Red, but you're still a slave, you're still Ringed. I might not know the power you wielded when it was yours to command, but I'll walk out of here a free man, have a cold dipper of water whenever I want it, have a tankard of ale once I've seen the Gray Lady safely onto a Coach, and tonight I'll mount a woman like a man's entitled to. And you? You would have gotten down on your belly and licked the bottom of my boots for a sip of fouled water."

"I won't deny it," Jared said. "But you, free? For now, maybe. The only difference between service and slavery is a circle of gold. If the Red can be chained, how long will the Purple Dusk stay free? If the right amount of gold marks changed hands tomorrow, how long do you think it would take to turn the handsome escort into a handsome slave?"

The escort's face flushed a dull, angry red. He raised a fist.

Jared didn't speak, didn't move. He just glanced at the door leading into the hallway and smiled knowingly. He watched the escort fight to hide the clashing emotions, saw the moment the man realized he wouldn't be able to justify the "discipline."

Lowering his fist, the escort spat out words like they were gristle. "In five minutes, I'm chaining you and taking you out of here." He flung open the hallway door but stopped in the doorway and stared at Jared with burning eyes. "I hope she cuts you apart a piece at a time."

"I imagine she will," Jared said, after the escort slammed out of the room. By force of will, he managed the couple of steps needed to reach the rough bench. Spreading the shirt, he sat on it carefully, grateful his shaking legs didn't have to support him for a minute.

Jared, if you're going skin-swimming at the pond, remember to spread the towel on the log before you sit on it or you'll have splinters where you least want them.

Where's that, Mother?

Ask your father.

So he had. Belarr had studied his son for a minute, muttering something about why couldn't they have had one girl so he could return the favor. Then Belarr had sighed and explained what he thought Reyna meant. That's the way Belarr always phrased it: *I think what your mother means is* . . . As if, despite being a strong Warlord, he felt the need to hedge when it came to explaining a woman's words, especially the words of the woman he'd married.

Sighing wearily, aching in ways that hurt deeper than physical wounds ever could, Jared pulled on the coarsely woven trousers and slipped his feet into the poorly made leather sandals. He picked up the scratchy shirt but couldn't bring himself to pull it over his head. Taking a careful breath, he turned toward the full-length mirror attached to the room's back wall. In the building where pleasure slaves changed hands, the entire back wall was a mirror. He understood the reason for that. He didn't want to think about why they'd put a mirror here, where it didn't matter if a slave looked well-groomed when he emerged.

His fingers shook as he lightly brushed the buttons on

the trousers' fly. Psychic sense, physical sense . . . he just couldn't feel the Invisible Ring. There was no way to tell how fine-tuned it might be, no way to know where the shifting boundary was between what was permissible basic Craft and what would bring agonizing punishment.

"Balls and sass," Jared muttered. Hard to judge the risks when there were no reference points. But he just couldn't pull that shirt over his head without doing something to protect the wounds. He'd listened to men scream when a shirt that had stuck to lash wounds was pulled off their backs, tearing off the fresh scabs with it. He'd seen what those men had looked like when the wounds finally healed.

Basic healing Craft. A thimbleful of power. That's all he needed to create a tight protective shield around his back and belly that would keep the shirt away from his skin.

Taking another careful breath, Jared created the shield and waited.

Nothing. No surge from the Ring, no angry footsteps in the hall.

Swallowing hard to push his heart back down his throat, Jared pulled on the shirt and studied the man in the mirror.

He wasn't dressed for an aristo outing, but even so he was a good-looking man, tall and well built, with that golden Shalador skin—not brown like the long-lived Hayllians or fair like other races, but sun-kissed, gold-dusted. A pleasing shade when combined with the dark-brown hair and brown eyes of the Shalador people.

Except his eyes were the rare Shalador green—eyes that could be traced back through the bloodlines to Shal, the great Queen who had united the tribes into one people.

Reyna's eyes.

He was the only one of the three boys who had her eyes.

He had been willing to destroy himself, but now that he was still alive, he wanted to survive. Sweet Darkness, he *had* to find some way to survive long enough to get home, long enough to talk to Reyna and take those words back.

Balls and sass. It was the only weapon he could safely use. He was wringing himself dry, squeezing what was left of his physical endurance, but he had to last until they reached the slave compartment in the Coach, had to make

Grizelle believe he was still a male to be reckoned with. For a little while longer, he had to hide the fact that he was nothing more than a hollow man.

Raising his trembling hands, Jared ran his fingers through his hair. It was a bit shaggy now, but with a little Craft, shaggy could be altered to bedroom disheveled. The Gray Lady was an old woman, but he was a bed-trained slave who had a few sweets he could offer that might entice her, might distract her, might help tip the scales to his advantage while he tried to figure out how much control this damned Invisible Ring had over him.

His stomach churned at the idea of encouraging the Gray Lady to enjoy him. But if it made her lower her guard, it might be possible to slip away and ride the Winds to Shalador.

Without warning, the escort opened the door and stopped short, unable to hide his surprise at the transformation of the naked slave he'd left into the Warlord who turned away from the mirror and smiled at him.

Pleased that he'd managed to unsettle the man, Jared walked toward him and held out his hands as if bestowing a favor. "If you're going to chain me, get on with it. The Gray Lady's waiting to dance." He hoped the escort would mistake the exhaustion in his voice for boredom.

"She didn't specify chains," the man said grudgingly.

"No, I didn't think she would. She strikes me as a discreet Lady, and chains tend to call attention to themselves, especially when the sound they're making becomes rhythmic. Don't you think?"

The escort's lip curled in a sneer. "I've never worn chains."

"I wasn't implying that *you* had worn them." Jared waited for the insult to sink in and then shrugged. "Or that you needed them. I just thought that since you earned a living restraining people, you might know a few interesting positions that aren't considered common in the courts. But perhaps not. Things like that are a bit like mounting a woman dog-style. It isn't to every man's taste."

Fury blazed in the escort's eyes. "You know what I can do to you?"

"Not a damn thing." Jared bared his teeth and added softly, "Come on. Try it. Let's see if this Ring really can hold the Red."

"Is there a problem?" Grizelle's voice settled over both men like a cold rain.

The escort reluctantly stepped into the hallway. "No, Lady."

"Then what's the delay?"

Jared gave the escort a smug smile, knowing it would infuriate the man because there wasn't any way he could respond to it.

Time to play the last act.

Mother Night, don't let my body fail yet.

Jared stepped forward, forcing the escort out of the way. He bowed to Grizelle, making sure the bow was exactly what Protocol dictated as proper for a Red-Jeweled Warlord to make to a Gray-Jeweled Queen.

If the Warlord wasn't a slave, that is.

The escort growled in anger.

Grizelle stared at him, but Jared thought he caught a flicker of amusement in the hard gray eyes.

So she liked balls and sass. Thank the Darkness.

Draining the little psychic strength he could summon in order to project the feel of a sensual man eager to please, Jared offered his right hand, palm down.

Grizelle hesitated a moment before lightly placing her left hand over his and allowing him to escort her out of the building.

Jared bit back a grin. The escort was now trailing behind them like a resentful, forgotten puppy.

It was full dark by the time they hired a pony cart and headed out of the auction grounds. Instead of going directly to the official landing place, they took a side road that circled around the low, flat-topped hill until they reached the ticket station, and the Coaches and drivers that could ride the Winds.

"Wait with the others," Grizelle said, as Jared helped her from the cart. She didn't bother to look at either of them as she walked toward the ticket station.

Jared held on to the cart, hoping the escort didn't notice

how much he needed to lean on that support to stay on his feet. He wasn't sure his legs would get him to the Coach before they buckled.

"I don't know where the others are," he finally pointed out.

"This way," the escort growled.

As they walked toward the man's partner, who had been guarding the other slaves, Jared glanced over his shoulder and saw a messenger boy hand a slip of paper to Grizelle just before she reached the ticket station. The boy ran off immediately, not even waiting for the usual coin.

Feeling a warning prickle between his shoulder blades, Jared stopped and watched her read the message.

So still. So silent. So gray. Nothing about her seemed different, so he didn't understand why he instinctively opened his first inner barrier and sent out a delicate Red psychic tendril. Even if her inner barriers hadn't been stronger than his, the tendril was too delicate to probe even surface thoughts, which meant there was less chance of it being noticed. But it would be able take a sip of her emotions and give him some warning about her temper.

He wasn't prepared for the blast of fear that raced back through the tendril and crashed into him.

Something had happened. Something had changed.

The fear hadn't been there during the ride here. He was sure of that. Hell's fire, he'd touched her, sat beside her. Even she couldn't have hidden feelings that strong while there had been physical contact between them.

The message, then. The mes . . .

As he watched Grizelle tuck her hands into the sleeves of her robe and walk into the ticket station, his waning endurance finally gave out. The world became fuzzy and slow.

So hard to walk, despite the hand on his arm leading him. Words began smearing again, mashing together and stretching out until they became a language of nightmarish shapes. Bodies appeared in front of him, out of nowhere. Someone tugged on his arm. He stopped walking. The smells of blood-bright fear and sickly brown sweat oozed around the word shapes.

Water.

Why did that have to be the one word that still made sense?

"She'll be taking . . . west-going Coaches?"

He thought that was one of the guards speaking, but couldn't be sure since the voice kept fading in and out.

"Bound to . . . Territory's west . . . Tamanara Mountains."

"That's what . . . figured . . . brought the rest . . . here."

Except they were walking again, endlessly walking, while the escorts swore under their breath and their blade-sharp anger cut into him.

Where were his inner barriers? Where . . .

Someone pulled at his arms.

"Ssiiitt."

His legs folded under him.

A gray voice. The word "water."

A cup at his mouth. Water trickling past his lips. He held it for a moment, savoring the wetness, before he swallowed. Then he tried to grab the cup and gulp, but hands pulled it away from him.

"Sslloowlly."

He obeyed. It was so important to obey, so important that this female voice that wasn't gray didn't take away the water.

Finally enough.

Ballsansass. That was important, too, although he couldn't remember why.

He slid sideways. The water had melted his bones. He hadn't known water could do that. Whiskey could, if you drank enough of it, but water? Who would have guessed?

Then he was melting and sliding, melting and sliding, sliding, sliding away into the safety of the night, into the sweet Darkness.

CHAPTER FOUR

"**S**he took the bait," the Fifth Circle guard reported with barely restrained eagerness.

Krelis leaned back in his chair, dropping his hands below the desk to hide the trembling he couldn't control. Dorothea's compulsion spell must have worked, which made him feel easier about the other spells she'd woven for him—not that he doubted the High Priestess's ability.

"While she was in Raej, did the bitch buy anyone who might be of value to us?" Krelis asked, watching the young man who reminded him of himself not that many centuries ago.

The blank look on the guard's face only lasted a moment. Then he stiffened and focused his eyes on the back wall of the Master's office. "My apologies, Lord Krelis. I didn't think to obtain a list of the slaves she bought."

"Nor did Lord Maryk think to include it in your instructions," Krelis said smoothly.

The guard squirmed a little, recognizing the trap within the words.

Krelis understood being torn between loyalty and survival. As a boy, he had loved Olvan, who had been a gentle but firm parent as well as a respected teacher and scholar. As a youth, he'd felt desperate to get away from the taint surrounding the frightened, withered man his father had become after that day at the tree. No one had needed to tell him that the longer a connection remained between father and son, the more distrustful the influential Queens would be when the time came to serve in their courts.

Forced to choose between loyalty and survival, he had

chosen survival. Loyalty, he discovered, could be bought easily enough.

So he waited to see which the guard would choose— loyalty to Maryk, who was not only an aristo but an experienced second-in-command, or survival by giving full allegiance to the new Master of the Guard.

Finally, the guard said in a low voice, "No, sir, Lord Maryk did not include obtaining the list in his instructions."

"No matter," Krelis said with a dismissive gesture. "Lord Maryk had more pressing duties to consider."

"Yes, sir. Shall I return to Raej and obtain the list?"

"Yes. By the time you return, Lord Maryk will be here with the slaves. We'll keep any that may be of interest to the High Priestess and send the others back to Raej to sell on the last auction day."

The guard saluted smartly and left.

Krelis rubbed his hands over his face. Maryk should be back by nightfall, the task completed. Then, perhaps, he could get some sleep.

CHAPTER FIVE

His stomach growled and threatened to chew his backbone.

Jared ignored it.

His muscles ached and begged to be stretched.

He ignored them, too.

The fierce need to piss had him swinging his legs over the side of the narrow bed. He pushed himself into a sitting position and fuzzily tried to remember what came next.

Rubbing sleep-crusted eyes, Jared looked blearily at the dark-eyed, dark-haired boy sitting cross-legged beside the bed.

"Davin?" Jared said hoarsely, knowing it *couldn't* be even before the boy's expression turned wary. His youngest brother would be nineteen now, not the ten-year-old he'd cheerfully said good-bye to before he'd torn his life apart.

"I'm Tomas," the boy said. "There's no Davin here."

Thank the Darkness for that.

There was something peculiar and faint about the boy's psychic scent, but Jared was too preoccupied to figure it out. "Where—"

"We're in the guest servants' quarters."

Jared shook his head and tried again. "Where—"

"Don't know what Territory—"

"Where's the damn chamber pot?"

"Oh." Tomas pointed at a door in the wall. "Over there."

Despite the urgency, Jared hesitated, finally awake enough to realize he was naked and only had a wadded sheet covering his groin.

Tomas grinned. "They're all outside, and Ladies don't

care if you show your dangle to other males." He scratched his head. "Other males don't care either."

"Sometimes they do," Jared muttered, remembering confrontations between pleasure slaves that had turned bloody because desperation had pushed someone over the edge. "Sometimes they care very much."

Tomas's grin faded. His face paled. He scrambled to his feet and bolted for the door. The jerky movement and the fear that now filled his dark eyes told Jared more than the fading bruises on the boy's bare arms, more than the old scars on the stick-thin legs that poked out of a pair of ragged short pants. And he realized what the boy's diminished psychic scent meant. Tomas was a half-Blood.

Having too much psychic strength to be landen but not enough to be Blood, half-Bloods were outcast bastards, wanted by neither society. If the Blood sire thought the unclaimed offspring showed potential, the child might be taken in and raised as a servant, maybe even trained to become an overseer for a landen village. Most of the time, half-Bloods became the slaves that looked after, and were used by, Blood slaves.

And sometimes there was no one crueler than someone who was, himself, enduring cruelty.

Cursing under his breath, Jared followed Tomas.

The bathroom had two toilets, three sinks, and two bathtubs. There were no partitions to give anyone the illusion of privacy, but at least the toilets were better than stinking privy holes.

Sighing with relief, Jared took care of business and tried to ignore the boy standing next to him. Tomas might have learned fear in the slave quarters, but the boy was just too brash to have learned caution.

"You ain't wearing a Ring," Tomas said in a hushed voice.

"It's invisible," Jared replied curtly, hoping that would end it.

"You sight shield a Ring so people don't know you're a slave, you'll get your back whipped off for good."

Jared clenched his teeth at the honest concern in the

boy's voice and pulled the chain to flush the toilet. "It's not sight shielded, it's invisible."

"Well, I can *see* that."

How could he explain something he didn't understand himself? "It's an Invisible Ring. It's like the Ring of Obedience, but stronger."

Tomas's eyes widened. "You have to wear something *stronger* than a Ring of Obedience? You that dangerous?"

"I guess so."

"As dangerous as the Sadist?"

Jared started to say something reassuring, but there was no fear in the boy's face, just a held-breath excitement. Aristos had good reason to fear Daemon Sadi, but not young half-Blood boys. So he said solemnly, "He taught me everything I know."

Tomas looked at him for a long minute, his mouth silently forming the word, "oh," and Jared realized he couldn't have presented better credentials to reassure the boy he was a "safe" male.

That grin that seemed to be Tomas's natural expression flashed again. "You'll be wanting a bath. We've got hot water and everything."

As Jared watched the boy dart around the room preparing a bath for him, the full import of their surroundings finally hit him. He wandered over to the tub that was already half-full of steaming water. "Why are we in the guest servants' quarters?"

" 'Cause the Lady took one look at the slave quarters and threw a polite icy fit."

Jared scratched the back of his head. Hell's fire, he was looking forward to getting clean. "How does one throw a polite icy fit?"

Tomas tugged on his earlobe and scrunched up his face. "Well, like the Lady did, I guess."

That told him a lot.

Tomas turned off the water. "In you go," he said, waving the wash sponge at Jared.

"Yes, Tomas," Jared said meekly.

Tomas hesitated, as if wanting to be sure that the adult

male he was ordering around really was teasing him. Then
he grinned and dropped the wash sponge into the water.

Jared settled into the tub, closed his eyes, and groaned
in pleasure. After soaking for a couple of minutes, he
opened one eye and looked at the boy kneeling beside the
tub. "So what did she do?"

"Well, the innkeeper was pleased enough at first to have
a Queen staying at his place, even if it *was* the Gray Lady.
He told her his servants would get her slaves settled into
quarters, but she insisted on seeing them before she'd go
to her own room. So he showed her the slave quarters and
she said, no, they wouldn't do."

"Were they that bad?" Jared asked. Pleasure slaves were
usually quartered together in a comfortable "stable" or in
tiny rooms adjoining the main bedchambers so they'd be
close by to indulge their Ladies' whims. Since they were
also kept fairly isolated from everyone except the court and
each other, he really didn't know what was considered normal slave quarters.

Tomas shrugged. "Looked like any other as far as I could
tell, although the privy holes did stink something fierce.
But the Lady said she wasn't going to have half of us coming down sick with a chill or worse by trying to sleep with
no blankets and nothing but bars and broken shutters over
the windows. Now, anybody could have told her you don't
seal up slave quarters tight 'cause breathing the stink would
make us sicker than fresh cold air, but the innkeeper just
eyed Thera and Polli and told the Lady if she just eased
the Rings a bit, the males would keep the females warm
enough, and with their blood heated like that, they
wouldn't even notice the cold.

"Well, the Lady just looked at the innkeeper until he
started to sweat, and she said, mild as if she was asking for
a cup of tea, 'Have you ever seen what happens to a man's
balls when you freeze them so deep they'll shatter if you
flick a finger against them?' You could tell he thought she
was bluffing, but he was sweating, too. Then one drop of
sweat rolled off his chin. It froze before it hit the ground
and bounced up like a little hailstone. And she just kept
looking at him. I thought he was going to mess his pants."

Having experienced that hard gray stare, Jared understood the man's discomfort all too well.

"So right away he offered these quarters," Tomas continued, handing Jared the soap. "Thera and Polli made up a bed for you, and Randolf and Brock carried you in. The Lady fussed over you for a bit and kept muttering to herself about whether the damage was permanent. After she approved the food the servants brought, she went back to the inn."

The Lady fussed over you. Jared soaped the sponge and started washing. In a way, it made sense. Badly scarred pleasure slaves weren't as valuable—except to witches who were aroused by the evidence of pain inflicted—and a healing man didn't perform at his best. But something in Tomas's voice told him that, even without knowing about the Invisible Ring, the others had realized that the Lady considered him different from the rest of them, and they weren't sure what to think about it . . . or about him.

He wasn't sure what to think about it either.

"Course, Blaed's going to be relieved to find out you're a pleasure slave," Tomas said. "The way Thera tore into him, I don't think he wants to stiffen anytime soon, and he's been worried that the Lady would want to be pleasured and he hasn't had much training. Not like you, being trained by the Sadist and all."

Jared bit his tongue and concentrated on washing his legs.

Tomas frowned. "Course, you don't need a stiff dangle, do you? They say the Sadist never gets stiff, and he's the best there is."

At a lot of things that were better left unmentioned.

Jared resoaped the sponge and started scrubbing his arms and chest. He didn't want to talk about Sadi, and he didn't want to think about pleasuring the Gray Lady. "Why did Thera tear into Blaed?"

Tomas shook his head. His voice filled with cautious admiration. "That Thera. When she gets pissy, she gets a look in her eyes that can singe your ball hairs."

The sponge stuttered to a halt. "That's a colorful way of putting it," Jared finally choked out.

Tomas tugged on the sponge. "I'll wash your back."

"No!" He didn't need this boy to act as his slave, and knowing too well how it felt to be at the mercy of someone's whims, he didn't want anyone else feeling like that because of him.

"I'll be careful," Tomas said quietly.

Thrown off stride by the boy's sympathy, Jared released the sponge. He'd forgotten about the lash wounds. Feeling no pain as Tomas washed his back, his hands gently explored his belly where the whips had cut him. It felt tender, but that was all.

"Don't know what the Lady did, but you've healed up just fine," Tomas said. "Didn't even scar."

Tomas's cheerful efficiency made his heart ache. Too knowing for someone so young, here was this boy reassuring a grown man that he hadn't scarred when his own small body looked like a battlefield.

Tomas deserved better than to be condemned to a life like this. Then again, they all deserved better.

Needing a distraction, Jared said, "Tell me about Thera and Blaed."

"Well, you see, none of the beds were made up, though there were clean sheets and blankets folded up on the mattresses. Thera started right in 'cause Cathryn—"

"Cathryn? I thought the other one's name is Polli."

"The Lady bought three females," Tomas explained patiently. "Thera, Polli, and Cathryn. Thera's a broken Black Widow. Breaking her might have taken her Jewels, but it sure didn't dull her temper. Polli's a broken witch. I think it made her soft-headed and skittish. Cathryn's just a Blood female, too young for breeding yet."

Jared ground his teeth. Just the thought of a Blood female being used as an aristo broodmare as soon as she became old enough to bear healthy offspring made him sick. Oh, they weren't broken like more and more strong witches were, but that was because they didn't have the inner power for more than basic Craft to begin with, and only unbroken females could produce more than one offspring. "How old is Cathryn?"

"She's little. Nine maybe. You want to hear about Blaed or not?"

His breath hissed between his teeth. "I want to hear."

"So Thera started making up beds. Polli was making up a bed, too, but she was moving slow, like something was paining her. Then Blaed walked over to Polli and said something to her, and the next thing you know, she had her back to the wall and she was screaming that she didn't have to spread her legs, it was her moontime, and she didn't have to spread her legs during her moontime.

"Before Blaed could say anything, Thera grabbed an apple from the bowl the servants had brought and threw it at him. Blaed's got good reflexes. He couldn't dodge it, but he managed to take it on the hip instead of in the balls.

"So there's Polli having hysterics, and Cathryn's crying 'cause she's scared, and Thera's screaming at Blaed, and Blaed's rushing toward Thera while she's reaching back for another apple, and Randolf and Brock are trying to jump in before it gets really nasty. And then the outside door burst open and the Gray Lady was standing there.

"The males all stopped cold, and I hushed Cathryn, but Polli was still wailing about her moontime—Hell's fire, even *I* could tell that whatever was paining her, it wasn't that— and Thera was still screaming about heartless pricks who couldn't keep their pants buttoned and holding that apple so hard she was squishing it to pulp."

Tomas jumped up. "You soap up your hair. I'll get a bucket of clean water to rinse with."

Jared soaped his hair, muttering all the while about the dire things that could happen to boys who got too bossy. The only response he got was a bucket of water poured over his head before he was ready.

Sputtering, he climbed out of the tub and grabbed a towel from Tomas. "If you don't finish the story, I'll throttle you."

Now certain that he could ignore remarks like that, Tomas just grinned, grabbed another towel, and gently patted Jared's back dry. "Turns out Blaed was just trying to be helpful. He noticed how Polli was moving and thought she shouldn't be lifting the mattress to tuck in the sheet.

After he explained that to the Lady, looking so scared I thought he was going to faint, she fixed a brew to settle down Polli. Then she looked straight at Thera, and said, 'Courtesy should be rewarded, not punished.' And then she looked at Blaed, and said, 'Remember that not all scars are visible.'

"After she left, we all ate and took baths. None of the males wanted to get near Polli, in case she had another fit. Didn't want to get too close to Thera, either. So all the females and you and me stayed on one side of the room and the rest of the males stayed on the other side." Tomas looked at Jared and shook his head. "And you slept through the whole thing. Matter of fact, you slept through all of yesterday, too. Come on, they left some food for you."

Disturbed, Jared silently followed Tomas back into the main room. Had the Gray Lady been talking about the lash wounds when she'd wondered about permanent damage? Or had she sensed the hollowness inside him? Now that he was no longer in pain or exhausted, he keenly felt the loss of whatever it was the wild stranger had taken with it. He knew, with absolute certainty, that he had no chance of getting free of the Invisible Ring without it.

"You still feeling bad?" Tomas asked.

Jared shook his head and sat down at the table that had one covered plate, a plate of toast, a cup, and a small pot of coffee.

Who had put a warming spell on the covered plate and pot of coffee? Polli, who sounded like she'd had her spirit as well as her inner web broken? The sharp-tempered Thera? Either of them would still have enough strength to do something as basic as this.

But when he touched the plate, he knew it had been neither one of them. Running his finger around the plate's rim, he found the spot where her finger had touched it, felt the ghost of the spark of power she'd used for the warming spell.

That she had done it at all spoke of concern and caring.

It made no sense.

"You'd best eat," Tomas said, pouring the coffee. "We'll be leaving here soon."

Jared picked up the fork and began to eat, reminding himself with each bite to eat slowly. He couldn't afford to have his stomach reject the meal in front of him just because he'd gulped it down, especially when he didn't know when he might get the next one.

While he ate, Tomas told him about the other slaves. Besides Thera, Polli, and little Cathryn, there were nine males, including Tomas and himself: Blaed, the pleasure slave; Thayne; Brock and Randolf, two former guards; a mind-broken male named Garth; and Eryk and Corry, two boys about Tomas's age.

Half-listening to Tomas's chatter, Jared reached for another slice of thick, buttered toast. What had the Gray Lady been thinking of to buy these particular slaves? He could understand buying the four healthy adult males, but what use could she have for a mind-broken male? Or broken witches who had probably been put on the block because they'd become emotionally unstable or were now barren and had no ability to produce an offspring? Or four children?

Or a Warlord who had killed the last Queen who had owned him?

"You ain't listening," Tomas said accusingly.

Remembering his younger brothers, Jared knew better than to bluff. So he waved his fork over the plate and changed the subject altogether. He hoped. "What is this?"

Tomas sulked for a moment, then shrugged. "Potatoes and eggs and pieces of beef. The Lady had bought a big skillet with the rest of the supplies, and this morning she taught Thera, Polli, and Cathryn how to make it."

The toasted bread caught in Jared's throat. He swallowed some coffee to force it down. "The Gray Lady was *cooking*?"

Tomas grinned. "I thought the innkeeper was going to die of shame, with her out there cooking in a skillet over an open fire as if what he served in the inn wasn't good enough. That's why we all got coffee and buttered toast this morning. The Lady told him she wanted the females

to learn how to make this while she could still have his
cook prepare *her* meal, but it would be best to give us the
coffee and bread, too, so we'd have something decent under
our belts."

"But this is good," Jared said, scooping up another
forkful.

Tomas's dark eyes sparkled. "Probably better than the
Lady got."

Jared frowned. "Why the supplies? Where are we going?"

Tomas rolled his eyes. "I was just telling you about her
buying an old pedlar's wagon and horses 'cause we're going
cross-country to her Territory, and we can't depend on
finding an inn when we need it."

"Why not go to the nearest village that has a Coach
station and buy passage?" Jared said, still frowning. "Why
take the chance of tangling with marauders or a pack of
rogues by going cross-country?"

Tomas jerked as if he'd been hit. He wouldn't look at
Jared.

Jared choked down the last mouthful. Was that why
slaves who went into Grizelle's Territory never returned?
Because they never got to the Territory in the first place?
Marauders and rogue packs were always male, but they
might have guarded home camps where they could keep
women. They'd have no use for male slaves, but what about
a broken witch who could cook a decent meal over an open
fire? Or a broken witch who could be given an aphrodisiac
that would make her so mad with need she could be
mounted all night and not care what they did to her until
the drug finally wore off? Or a young Blood female that
could become a breeder for the dominant male of the
group? What about an intelligent young half-Blood who
tried so hard to please?

Did Grizelle come to the auctions to act as a slave trader
for the marauders and rogue packs who hid in the Tamanara Mountains and wouldn't dare approach Raej because
they'd probably end up on the auction block themselves?

Jared's stomach churned. He closed his eyes, took a deep
breath, and willed himself to stay calm. What could he do?
Challenge a Gray-Jeweled Queen? If she unleashed the

Gray, she'd destroy him completely. Which might be preferable to finding out what would happen if she used the Invisible Ring. He understood the Jewels, but this thing he couldn't see, couldn't touch, couldn't sense in any way . . .

The outside door opened, and a female voice said, "Good, you're awake. At least we won't have to drag you to the wagon and dump you on top of the supplies."

Jared leaped up, knocking over the chair, his heart hammering in his chest. *It isn't her,* he thought as he looked at the startled dark-haired, green-eyed woman standing in the doorway. *It isn't her.*

"Maybe we would have been better off if we *had* had to dump you on top of the supplies," she muttered after a moment's silence. Then she gave him one sharp-eyed, head-to-toe look that plainly said there were already too many troublesome males around for her liking, and he was going to be another one. "Better prance on out there. She's ready to leave, and we wouldn't want the prize dangle to get dragged along like a reluctant puppy on a leash, would we?"

Anger flooded him, but it had no heat, no bite. It was like his blood was being clogged with ashes instead of flowing with fire.

And there was something very wrong with the way he *wasn't* responding to the presence of a witch, broken or not.

A sour taste filled the back of his mouth, and he started to shake.

The woman stepped forward, reaching out to him. "Are you still sick?"

Jared recoiled from her touch.

"He was doing fine until you came in," Tomas snapped.

Her eyes frosted over until they were green ice. "Be careful, little man," she said in an awful, quiet voice before she turned around and walked out.

"*Are* you still sick?" Tomas asked, looking anxious. "Should I tell the Lady you need to ride in the wagon?"

Jared continued to shake. When Tomas darted for the door, he managed to grab the boy's arm.

"No," Jared said, forcing the word out. "I'd—I'd rather

walk." He took a deep breath. Took another. "That was Thera?"

Tomas sighed. "That was Thera."

With one hand on Tomas's shoulder to steady himself, Jared left the guest servants' quarters and slowly followed the pedlar's wagon and the wary slaves who trailed behind it.

Thera had done him a favor without realizing it. At least he understood now.

He was still male. He still had the strength of the Red Jewels. He still had his skill in using Craft. What he had lost, what the wild stranger had taken away, was the fire and passion that made a Jeweled male a Warlord.

CHAPTER SIX

Krelis didn't stare at Dorothea SaDiablo, nor did he avert his eyes. One action would have been considered a challenge; the other, a lack of appreciation. Either error could cost a man freedom or flesh.

Instead, he looked at the disheveled young Warlord lying on the chaise lounge with Hayll's High Priestess.

Not a pleasure slave, Krelis decided as he studied the young Warlord's kiss-swollen, sulky mouth. Must be one of the toy-boys, maybe even an aristo youth from one of the Hundred Families who had been given the honor of serving in Dorothea's court. Didn't really matter, pleasure slave or toy-boy, except the toy-boys had social status so they couldn't be physically mistreated that much, and were still considered men. Pleasure slaves were considered geldings who still had their balls.

At least some of them did.

Dorothea gave the young Warlord one more throat-swabbing kiss before leisurely rising from the chaise lounge. "Did she take the bait?" she asked as she buttoned her gown, her hands smoothing the material over her firm, small breasts.

Krelis took a deep breath to steady himself. "Yes, Priestess—"

She cut him off with a sharp, restrained hand gesture.

Krelis's face tightened as the young Warlord smirked at him. He understood the youth's need to make some attempt at superiority, however temporary it might be, but a Master of the Guard was considered the dominant warrior in a court, and any undermining of his authority might lead to actions that could put his Lady at risk. The youth's Yel-

low Jewel was no match for his Sapphire, and the difference
in their Jewel rank was reason enough to give Dorothea's
new toy a disciplinary lesson. As for the difference in their
social rank . . . If the young Warlord *was* an aristo from
one of the Hundred Families and not from an offshoot,
Krelis could become embroiled in the kind of quarrel that
might lead to his dismissal—or worse.

He should have known Dorothea wouldn't miss, or ignore, silent challenges between two males who served her.

Looking over her shoulder, Dorothea gave the youth a
malevolent smile, and purred, "I won't be long, darling.
Why don't you amuse yourself? I want you hot when I
get back."

Krelis felt no pleasure at seeing the distress in the youth's
eyes. They both knew Dorothea's saying that in front of
another man was punishment, and more humiliating than
any physical discipline Krelis might have inflicted. They
both knew a warrior was more valuable to the court than
a handsome youth who could be replaced so easily. And
they both knew what could happen if the toy-boy wasn't
ready to please Dorothea by the time she returned.

Krelis started to turn away, but Dorothea didn't move.
She continued to stare at the young Warlord until his eyes
turned tear-bright and his muscles started to quiver. Swallowing hard, he opened his trousers all the way and slipped
his hand inside.

Satisfied, Dorothea led Krelis out of her sitting room and
began to stroll toward another wing of the SaDiablo
mansion.

"So the bitch took the bait," Dorothea said.

"Yes, Priestess."

"But?"

Krelis's mouth dried up. Sweat gathered in his armpits.
"She disappeared. She bought passage for the westernmost
station that could be reached by taking a Coach out of
Raej, but when the Coach finally reached the station, it was
several hours overdue and there was no one in it except
the drivers. Neither of them could explain the lost hours
nor what had happened to the Gray Lady and the slaves
she'd purchased at the auction."

"I see," Dorothea said. "Has she crossed the Tamanara Mountains?"

"No, Priestess."

"Are you sure?"

He wasn't sure, but he wasn't about to admit *that*. "We'll find her, Priestess. I swear it. I should have her location soon."

Dorothea said nothing for a moment. Then, with a hint of distaste, "From your pet?"

"Yes, Priestess."

Pet slaves had their uses, especially when it came to spying on other slaves. Using his status as Dorothea's Master of the Guard, he had gone to Raej early to inspect the available slaves, and found one who had been more than willing to be a pet in order to gain whatever favors Hayll might grant.

Dorothea hadn't been enthusiastic about his plan, but she had woven the spells he had requested, including the spells that would ensure that his pet was among those the Gray Lady purchased at Raej.

There was a lot of land between Hayll and the Tamanara Mountains, but those Territories now stood in Hayll's shadow and would offer no safety. There were also plenty of marauder bands who were more than willing to hunt down a Queen if they were offered enough gold marks and a promise not to be hunted in turn. All he needed was the signal from his pet and he'd have the Gray bitch.

Dorothea let a heavy silence build while she led him through the hallways. Finally, she said, "Do you still have my present?"

Remembering the white feather, Krelis shuddered. "Yes, Priestess."

"She always was a cunning bitch," Dorothea said softly. "She might have anticipated an ambush at a station since that's where the attack happened the last time. Did she have an escort waiting for her at any of those stations?"

"Yes. They were eliminated."

"Good. That means she *had* intended to go to that station and whatever had changed her plans was unexpected—

which means her court is probably just becoming aware that something went wrong."

"She could have sent the escort to the station as a decoy."

"She wouldn't have sent them there just to die. Grizelle isn't that practical."

Unlike you? Krelis thought—then hastily buried that thought. "If she buys passage on another Coach . . ."

"There aren't that many passes over the Tamanara Mountains. She'll have to reach a station located near one of them and travel overland for some of the journey, no matter what she does."

"She could ride the Winds."

Dorothea shook her head. "She's thwarted herself in that as much as she's thwarted me. There's some kind of spell that acts as a barrier across the Winds, preventing anyone from riding them into her Territory. Anyone trying to get into Dena Nehele from this side of the Tamanara Mountains *has* to use one of passes."

She smoothed her coiled black hair. "Find out where the slaves she purchased came from. If any of them were from prominent families, she might try bartering with their kin for assistance."

Krelis's shoulders sagged in relief. At least he'd done this right. "I've already sent someone to Raej for the list, Priestess."

Dorothea gave him a smile of approval. "I'm sure, once you have it, you'll be able to offset your miscalculations."

Krelis didn't acknowledge the threat beneath the words.

Dorothea's smile sharpened. He couldn't tell if it indicated approval or displeasure.

They finally stopped walking when they reached a Red-locked door.

"Since you have a little time while we're waiting for your pet to prove useful," Dorothea purred, "I'd like you to do a favor for me."

"Anything, Priestess," Krelis said quickly.

A pleased, vicious light filled Dorothea's gold eyes as she opened the door and gestured for him to enter the room ahead of her.

The darkened room stank of sweat and fear to the point where it almost overwhelmed the presence of a feminine psychic scent. Sufficient light came through the open door for him to recognize a bedchamber, but the bed was still too shadowed for him to see the occupant.

Dorothea raised her hand. The candle-lights on the bed tables brightened, softly lighting the room. Staying near the door, she gestured for Krelis to stand at the foot of the bed.

A young, naked Hayllian witch was tied spread-eagle in the center of the bed. As Krelis stared at her, she struggled against the leather straps around her ankles, trying to close her legs. Since she was also gagged, she could only make muffled sounds of distress.

It took Krelis a moment to get past the blatant, if involuntary, invitation to mount, and recognize her. He couldn't remember her name, just that he'd seen her a couple of times several years ago when a maternal second cousin of his had been courting her. That courtship had ended swiftly, and the only thing the cousin had said afterward publicly was that they weren't as well suited as he had thought.

But one night, over a couple of bottles of brandy, his cousin had muttered some other things about her. Since she no longer had anything to do with him or his family, Krelis had paid no attention.

Now he wished he had, just as he wished he could remember what it was about her that had made him keep his distance during his cousin's brief courtship.

"You know her?" Dorothea asked, a dangerous edge in her voice.

Sweat trickled down Krelis's sides. "I've seen her before, Priestess, but we were never formally introduced." That, thank the Darkness, was true.

Dorothea nodded as if satisfied. "She's a minor Queen from one of the Hundred Families. Her tendency to voice questionable opinions has caused great embarrassment and distress for her family. The latest unfortunate incident forced them to conclude that having her Virgin Night is the only thing that will settle her down."

Krelis's hands curled into fists. *Now* he remembered. A

mouthy little bitch who was always criticizing the High Priestess and talking about how a Territory shouldn't be ruled by a witch who was less than a Queen. Always talking as if she, who only wore a Rose Jewel, could gather enough Jeweled strength among the Hundred Families and the rest of Hayll to oppose Dorothea.

Not even the Hundred Families were invulnerable if Hayll's High Priestess decided to punish disloyalty. And since the Families had gained the most from Dorothea's rule, why would they oppose her anyway?

"I want you to take care of her Virgin Night," Dorothea said.

Panic knotted Krelis's guts. "Me?" His voice cracked. "But—"

"Yes, Lord Krelis?" Dorothea said with quiet malevolence.

Krelis licked his dry lips. "Priestess, I've never . . ."

Her amusement deepened his panic. "You regularly make use of the whores at one of the better Red Moon houses in Draega, so I doubt that you've *never* . . ." She let the words hang. He could almost see them becoming a noose around his neck. He should have realized Dorothea would make it her business to know about *that,* especially where it concerned the males who were the closest to her— and whose loyalty had to be watched the most carefully.

"Wouldn't a consort be better?" Krelis stammered. "They're trained for this kind of thing."

"I want you to do this, Krelis. As a favor to me." She studied him for a moment. "You needn't be concerned about filling her belly. This isn't her fertile time, so she'll still have that asset when her family contracts a marriage for her." When he didn't say anything, she turned to leave. "I think an hour should be more than sufficient, don't you?"

Krelis found his voice just as she was closing the door. "But . . . Priestess . . . what if I break her?"

Dorothea gave him a queer look before saying with deadly softness, "Lord Krelis, I think the question you should be asking is what will happen if you don't?" She closed the door.

Krelis heard the click of the physical lock. Then the Red lock snapped back into place, trapping him in the room. Using Craft, he could have destroyed the physical lock, could have destroyed the whole damn door for that matter. But his Sapphire Jewel, even though it was only one rank below the Red, wouldn't get him through a Red lock.

Not in one piece anyway.

His bowels loosened. Afraid of soiling himself, Krelis looked around frantically and spotted two doors in the wall opposite the bed. The first one was the dressing room. The second was a small bathroom.

Fumbling with his clothing and not caring if the bitch in the other room heard his own sounds of distress, he managed to sit on the toilet before the foul-smelling waste poured out of him. Each time he thought he was empty, his belly cramped again. When it finally stopped, he flushed the stink away and just sat there, his elbows on his knees, his head braced in his hands.

To break a witch. Oh, he knew it was done all the time now. It settled down the troublesome ones all right, and it didn't even take much effort. Make the sex rough, scare her while you're handling her, and then one hard thrust to tear through the physical barrier. Ride her hard, each thrust driving her closer and closer to her inner web until she plunged through it, out of control. Descend quickly into the abyss, catch her before she fell so far that her mind shattered, and bring her back up. What was left was a witch closed off from her own strength, from the Jewels she had worn, from everything but basic Craft.

Simple enough.

But to break a *Queen*. Blood males were supposed to protect them.

Then again, since it was his duty to destroy the Gray Lady, why should he flinch about breaking *this* little bitch-Queen?

With that question whirling through his head, Krelis cleaned himself and returned to the bedchamber.

From the first day he began his training as a guard, his ambition had been to serve in the High Priestess of Hayll's First Circle. Serving a strong Lady meant prestige and privi-

leges. Even more important, it meant safety. No one toyed
with Dorothea's males. Except Dorothea.

He'd planned to marry in a year or two. He was tired of
using the whores in the Red Moon house. He wanted a
woman of his own, one who wouldn't be spreading her legs
for anyone but him, one he could breed every few years to
give him the offspring he wanted. His family bloodlines
were good, his Sapphire Jewels were impressive enough,
and his promotion to Master of the Guard guaranteed he'd
be able to pick almost any witch he pleased.

Now all his plans, all his dreams might end in this stinking bedchamber because an aristo bitch couldn't keep her
mouth shut. Anger stirred in him as he stared at her pleading eyes, as he listened to the muffled sounds she kept
making.

Stupid bitch. It was her own fault she was here. It was
her fault *he* was here. Always mouthing off as if that would
change the reality of living in Hayll, as if anyone would
think *she* could rival Dorothea. Even if she actually had
the strength to rule, would she really be any different than
the others? No matter what she said, she'd soon be snapping her fingers and expecting the males to dance to her
tune.

That's the way it was among the Blood now—a game
of predator and prey, played out on a constantly shifting
landscape of power: who wore the darkest Jewels, who had
the most social prestige, who controlled the strongest males,
who was the most skilled in Craft, who was the most
dangerous.

Predator and prey.

Krelis stripped off his clothes and climbed onto the bed.
The weaker became prey. It was as simple as that.

His fear of failure churned inside him until it became a
hot, throbbing anger. Since he couldn't turn that anger on
the witch who frightened him, he unleashed it on the one
who feared him.

And discovered why men enjoyed breaking witches so
much.

CHAPTER SEVEN

"It's *my* turn to sit in the wagon," Tomas said angrily, refusing to yield when Eryk stepped in front of him.

"You're just a half-Blood," the older boy said, giving Tomas a shove. "You're just a stupid slave who has to do what he's told."

"So are you!" Tomas returned the shove with interest.

"Am not!" Another shove.

Swiping his rain-soaked hair out of his eyes, Jared swore under his breath as he turned around and slogged through the mud, hoping he'd reach the boys before they ended up bloodying each other's noses—or worse, since Eryk was strong enough to wear a Yellow Jewel and Tomas didn't have any way to protect himself. Hell's fire, didn't they have enough problems without having to deal with childish squabbles?

The savage muttering behind him told him that Brock and Randolf had also turned back. Good. There was nothing like annoyed adult males to shrivel a boy's temper.

Out of the corner of his eye, Jared noticed Blaed and Thayne scrambling to reach the horses pulling the pedlar's wagon before the shoving match spooked them.

"You don't have any rank," Eryk shouted. "You don't count for anything! My family's aristo. My family's important. You're just a bastard some landen bitch had because a Warlord's dangle got stiff. You don't deserve to sit in the wagon. You don't deserve to eat up our food. You don't deserve to *live.*"

Jared felt the emotional blows as if they had been directed at him. He was so intent on reaching the boys and letting that little prick-ass feel the lash of his temper, he didn't see the Gray Lady until her hand connected with the back of Eryk's head hard enough to make the boy stagger. The waves of fury coming from her hit the rest of them hard enough to make them freeze.

"How dare you?" she screamed at the cringing boy. "He has every right to his share of the supplies. He has every right to be treated with courtesy. He has every right to live, you selfish little prick!"

With a shriek of rage that had fear skittering up every male spine, she lunged at Eryk.

Jared lunged at her.

Their bodies hit with a thud. While he struggled to keep his footing in the slippery mud, she struggled to break free and reach the focus of her anger. They slid around in an ugly, fear-filled dance. Jared's hands tightened on her upper arms hard enough to bruise, but that didn't lessen her struggles or her venom-coated curses.

As she threw herself to the right, almost breaking his hold, her foot slipped and twisted. He saw pain beneath the fury in her eyes, felt the change in her body as she tried to ignore it.

Hell's fire, what was he thinking of to slide around on a muddy road in the pouring rain, challenging a Gray-Jeweled Queen? The boy had no claims on him. Why should he care if she tore the little prick into pieces? All she had to do was send one bolt of power through the controlling ring and she'd have all of them rolling in the mud begging for mercy.

Since it hadn't occurred to her yet, he wasn't going to give her the chance to think of it.

"Lady," he said through gritted teeth.

No response.

Fear shivered through him. Now that he'd committed himself to opposing her, he couldn't back down and hope to remain intact. All right then. Balls and sass.

He put all the arrogance and temper he could summon into his voice. "Lady! It's the males' right to discipline their own." That was true in a court. It was true in a Blood community. Slaves didn't have that privilege, but he was hoping she was too angry to remember that.

Apparently she was because she stopped struggling. As he loosened his grip on her arms, her hands tightened on his coat, and he realized she couldn't put her weight on her right leg.

Sliding one arm around her waist, he pulled her tight against him to support and distract her—and found himself distracted by the way his body responded to being so close to hers.

A hint of wildness floated up from somewhere deep inside him. Following that instinct, Jared wrapped a faint seduction spell around her as he lightly kissed her lips.

When he was done, she just stared at him. Well, good. Now he wasn't the only one feeling confused.

"Let us take care of the discipline," he coaxed as he stroked her wrinkled cheek with a finger and wondered why her skin felt so delightfully soft. "Believe me, having been boys ourselves, we're better at it."

He held his breath, waiting for her answer.

"All right," she finally said. "Just . . . keep him away from me."

"It will be our pleasure, Lady."

Her lips curved in a reluctant smile. "I think this is what my father calls 'things it's best a Queen pretend not to know.' "

Calls? Her father was still alive?

"I'd say that's just about right." Jared put some sass into his answering smile and watched, amazed, as color flooded her cheeks.

Looking around, she finally noticed Brock and Randolf holding Eryk and Tomas, and Blaed and Thayne watching everything while they soothed the nervous horses. Twisting her upper body in the other direction, she met Thera's frosted stare. The color in her cheeks deepened.

Feeling absurdly protective, Jared glared at Thera. She met him, look for look, and finally said in a voice so carefully neutral everyone knew she wanted to tear strips out of somebody, "Are you intending to help her into the wagon anytime soon, or are you waiting for that knee to swell up to the size of a melon?"

The Gray Lady let out a startled squawk when he swung

her up into his arms and carried her into the wagon. Settling her on a bench cushioned by a couple of blankets, he knelt in front of her. Thank the Darkness his mother had taught him a little healing Craft. He couldn't do anywhere near as much as a Healer could, but at least he could do something to help her.

Except he didn't have a chance. He'd just pulled off her boot and was debating how to broach the necessity of removing her trousers when Thera stormed into the wagon, followed by Polli, who stared at him as if removing a boot was a prelude to rape.

"We'll look after her," Thera said coolly. "You've other business to attend to."

Setting the boot on the floor, Jared rose slowly.

Polli pressed herself into a corner and started muttering about it being her moontime, her stock reaction to being within a male's reach.

Thera's answer to the unspoken challenge was to turn aside just enough for him to reach the door and leave.

He wasn't sure if it was seeing the Gray Lady in pain or Thera's dismissal that scraped at his temper, but by the time he reached the other men, he was looking for a fight.

And the best target was the sulky boy who had started all this.

Grabbing Eryk's coat, Jared hauled the boy up until he could look right into Eryk's startled blue eyes. Then he bared his teeth, and snarled, "Give me one reason why I shouldn't beat the shit out of you."

Eryk wailed, "I'm an aristo! My family's important!"

Pulling the boy so close their noses almost touched, Jared said with murderous calm, "Well, now you're an aristo slave, and your family's not here. But I am. You feeling cocky enough to take on a pissed-off Red-Jeweled Warlord? Because I won't hold back or pull back." As his anger swelled and became hot enough to burn away his control, Jared gave Eryk a fierce shake. "Don't you realize what could have happened? You put us all at risk! Didn't that aristo family of yours teach you anything about courtesy and honor? We could have all been hurt because of you!"

"I don't care!" Eryk weakly pounded Jared's arms and

shoulders. "I hate you! I hate you! I hope she does hurt you!"

Jared shoved him. Hard.

Eryk's feet shot out from under him. With his arms frantically windmilling, he landed on his back. Then he just lay there in the mud, looking up at the circle of grim-faced, hard-eyed men.

Jared wondered if, or when, Eryk would realize Brock had been standing close enough to catch him and didn't.

Brock opened his coat and hooked his thumbs into his wide leather belt. He stared at Eryk for a moment before meeting Jared's eyes. "Much as it shames me to admit it, he and I come from the same Territory. So if we decide it's a strapping, the duty falls to me."

Jared looked at the boy who, finally, began to realize the price of his behavior and then at the tall, solidly built Warlord who had trained as a guard. He didn't doubt Brock would apply his belt with the kind of force the boy wouldn't forget for a long time, but he couldn't stop thinking about the emotional blows that had been delivered in those boyish taunts—and he couldn't stop thinking about the Lady's comment about some scars not being visible.

"No," he said, knowing as he said it that he was declaring himself the dominant male. Knowing, too, that none of the other men wore Jewels that could challenge the Red, nor would they want to since having a dominant male meant the others didn't have to deal directly with the Queen. Taking a deep breath, he wondered if any of them could sense how much of a sham his claiming dominance really was. But they just watched him, waiting, so he crossed an invisible line he wouldn't be able to step back over unless a darker-Jeweled male joined their group. "Until I say otherwise, the little aristo Warlord is going to be Tomas's servant. He'll have to take orders, fetch and carry, do anything Tomas wants. If he causes any trouble, Brock will handle the discipline."

Eryk's face burned with humiliation. No one protested the judgment until Tomas stepped away from Randolf.

"I don't want him," Tomas said, pulling his shoulders back and holding his head up. It was hard to tell if there were tears mixed with the rain, but the clenched fists and quivering lips told them how hard he was struggling to keep his voice steady. "I don't want him. I know I'm just a half-Blood and not w-worth much, but there's plenty of things I can do. I know how to look after someone important, so I'm going to s-serve the Lady. Not like other slaves who do the mean work, but look after her personally, just like her First Circle does."

Holding himself with the same care a man did after a beating, Tomas walked toward the back of the wagon.

"Tomas," Jared called. "You'd better wait a bit."

The wounded look in the boy's eyes cut at him.

"But, Jared, it's my turn to sit inside."

Jared tried to smile. "Mine, too. But I got the impression Thera wasn't going to welcome any male, even a personal servant, until she got the Lady comfortably settled."

Tomas thought about that and nodded. "I'll wait 'til she's not feeling so pissy."

Jared didn't stop him when Tomas headed for the saddle horses that were tethered to the back of the wagon by long lead ropes. Since the Gray Lady and Thera had been riding the horses and were inside the wagon, the boy would have some privacy for his tears.

He studied the pedlar's wagon for a moment, then shook his head. The Gray Lady and Thera. What a strange pairing.

"Should we get moving, Lord Jared?" Blaed asked. "I'll lead the team for this turn."

Jared continued to look at the wagon. How much healing Craft would a broken Black Widow know, if she knew any at all? The Gray Lady must have some knowledge of it since she'd done a fair healing on him, but what if she was in too much pain to use that skill on herself? "Let's wait a few minutes. Then I'll see if it's all right."

"No reason why the rest of us can't start walking," Brock said, hauling Eryk to his feet. "Come on, prick-ass, let's get started."

"Where's Garth?" Jared asked, scanning the surrounding area. Not that he could see much in this rain.

"Still lumbering up ahead, I imagine," Randolf replied, not trying to hide his distaste.

It wasn't as easy to break a Blood-Jeweled male—not like the witches, who were vulnerable until their Virgin Night and were still vulnerable each month during the first three days of their moontime. But a darker Jewel could rip open the inner barriers and tear a man's mind apart, or unleash a tidal wave of power to shatter the inner web and cut a man off from his own strength in much the same way as a witch was broken. Since every slave knew it could happen to him for no better reason than the witch who owned him wanted it done, they didn't turn their backs on a man because of it.

But there was a *wrongness* about Garth, more than the confused, kicked-puppy look in the pale blue eyes that was so at odds with the tall, muscled, barrel-chested body. There was a sliminess to his psychic scent, as if he'd been touched by something tainted.

Maybe he had. Maybe that's what had broken him.

Pity for what had been done to him didn't make it any easier being around him, though.

"All right," Jared said. "What about Corry and Cathryn?"

"They were just ahead of Brock and me," Randolf said.

Brock took a firm hold of Eryk's arm. "We'll check on them."

After Brock and Randolf started up the road with the reluctant Eryk between them, Jared turned to Thayne. "It's your turn on one of the saddle horses, isn't it?"

Thayne glanced at the wagon and swallowed hard. "If it's all right with you, I'll keep Blaed company for a bit."

Meaning even the saddle horses were too close to Thera's temper.

Nodding his permission, Jared moved far enough away from them to discourage conversation. He took a moment to add a little more power to the Craft shields on his clothing. They did a fairly good job of waterproofing the fabric and keeping the mud and water from seeping into the boots. A little warming spell helped, too. But even with spells and shields, it was impossible not to feel the damp after a while, and if anyone knew a shield-spell that would have kept the rain off their heads, no one had mentioned it.

Jared took a deep breath, wishing it would settle his churning stomach. Sweet Darkness, don't let her be hurt badly. Pointless to hope that her arms wouldn't have bruises the shape of his hands.

Hurting her made him ache. It shouldn't have. Hadn't he crossed that line when he'd killed the last Queen who had owned him?

It shouldn't have made him ache. But it did.

When the rain started yesterday afternoon, the Lady was the one who had told them to use whatever Craft was necessary to stay as dry as possible. She was the one who had put the Craft shields on Tomas's clothes and had kept an eye on those among them who might not have the power to hold the shields. Even Garth. She was the one who had put some kind of shield-spell on the wagon's wheels and the horses' hooves so they wouldn't sink in the mud.

And she was the one who had come up with the rotation.

The rotation was fair. More than fair. Hell's fire, there were thirteen of them, including the Gray Lady, and four of them were children. She could have let the children ride on the outer seat or inside and let the adults stumble along. She could have let the other females stay in the wagon with her—and slave or not, no Blood male would have argued about it. But she'd worked out this rotation that included everyone so that they all alternated between walking and riding, and everyone had a chance to get out of the rain and eat and rest within the confines of the wagon.

Telling himself that he just wanted to check on Tomas and see if they could start moving again, Jared walked to the back of the wagon.

Tomas wasn't in sight. Jared sighed and raked his wet hair away from his face. He didn't relish stumbling around in the trees and bushes on either side of the road in order to find the boy. Well, the Lady's controlling ring would be able to locate Tomas quickly enough.

After giving the roan mare and bay gelding friendly pats, Jared stood on the bottom step and knocked once on the wagon's door.

Thera opened the door, shifting her body slightly to block his view of the inside. But he heard Tomas sternly tell someone to drink up the brew 'cause it wasn't doing any good while it was still in the cup.

Thera looked at Jared and shrugged.

Relieved to see humor instead of temper in her eyes, Jared shrugged in reply, as if to say, "He's male. What can you expect?"

"How is she?" Jared asked quietly.

"She wrenched her knee," Thera replied just as quietly. Then she added thoughtfully, as if she were trying to work out a puzzle that still had too many pieces missing, "I knew she had healing supplies in that private box of hers—I saw them when she took care of you. But when I suggested that she open it so that I could see if there was anything that might help her, she refused to let Polli or me touch it. Then Tomas stuck his head in to see what was going on and heard us . . . discussing things. He just stomped in and started scolding." Thera smiled. "He's a good scolder."

"I know," Jared said dryly. "So you got the healing supplies."

"I got the supplies," Thera replied.

But Jared was no longer listening to her. His thoughts were on the small chest the Gray Lady had brought with her. With the spell-lock on it, he'd assumed, along with everyone else, that it held gold and silver marks and other things she wouldn't want slaves to have access to.

Except he'd realized the first time he'd seen it that the chest had a Green-strength spell-lock. Which wouldn't have meant anything if there wasn't one slave who wore a Red Jewel and who could have easily broken that lock, if that same slave hadn't been singled out from the very beginning as being different from the others.

He wasn't sure if there was something Thera suspected about the chest that she wasn't going to mention.

Why hadn't the Gray Lady used a Gray lock on that chest?

"Anything else?" Thera said.

Did she sound a little defensive?

"Can we get moving?" Jared asked. "We should use what daylight is left and start looking for a place to camp."

"Sure. We'll keep her comfortable enough." Thera paused. "Are you coming in now? It's your rest period."

"In a few minutes." When Thera started to close the door, Jared put his hand against it and asked the question he really wanted to ask. "Is her knee the only place she's hurt?"

Thera didn't pretend not to understand. "There are a couple of bruises. Nothing that won't easily heal."

No anger. No criticism. Somehow that made it worse.

Thera opened the door a fraction wider, a silent invitation.

Jared stepped down and back.

"Shriveled balls won't be tolerated," Thera said tartly. "I may need you to sit on her if Tomas and I can't convince Lady Grumpy to stay put and let that knee heal."

"Not a good patient?" Jared asked blandly.

Thera snorted and shut the door.

Feeling a little better, Jared walked around the wagon and gave Blaed the nod to move out. It couldn't be a serious injury if she was already snarling and snipping. Painful, yes, but not something they'd need to find a Healer to deal with.

Brock was waiting for him. "How is she?"

Jared noted that the Purple Dusk-Jeweled Warlord automatically swung to Jared's left, an acknowledgment of subordinate rank.

"Already bored with the sickbed," Jared answered. He felt Brock relax. "Do you know any outrageous stories?"

Brock looked startled, then wary. "Depends on what you mean. Campfire talk? Things like that?"

Jared felt a shiver of apprehension. He knew the dangers of telling tales. In one of the courts he'd been in, a male guest, wanting to entertain one of the Ladies enough to receive an invitation to her bed, had repeated a funny but extremely unflattering story about an aristo witch. He'd named no names, recounting it as he'd heard it, but the story had been rich in detail—and the Lady, who was also a guest, recognized herself. He might have survived if several other guests hadn't also recognized her by those details.

Jared had wondered afterward if the man was the only one who didn't know why he'd had his tongue cut out before he was gutted.

"Well, spicy enough to distract an elderly Queen who's convalescing," Jared said, pushing aside the darker memories. Brock was about his age, old enough to understand walking the knife edge.

Brock understood very well, if his muttering was anything to go by.

"Look," Jared said testily, "Thera is as subtle as an avalanche and doesn't use a grain of caution about what she says or who she says it to. It hasn't been an hour yet and she's already calling the Gray Lady 'Lady Grumpy.' If we don't do something, those two are either going to end up in a spitting fight, which could end up with Thera being very dead, or she's going to try to brain the rest of us out of frustration."

Brock ran a hand over his short, light-brown hair. "For a broken witch, that one's scary. Hell's fire, there's not much to choose from, is there?" He gave Jared a quick, assessing, hopeful look. "You're trained for personal service. Couldn't you handle it?"

Jared clenched his teeth. He might not be able to stop himself from feeling ashamed because he was a pleasure slave, but he didn't have to let anyone see it.

Brock didn't miss much, though. "I meant no insult, Lord Jared," he said quietly. "Any man with working brains knows a consort—and a pleasure slave is nothing less than an unwilling consort—is trained to do more than warm a bed. He dances on temper's edge, and a good consort makes it easier for the rest of us. I just thought—well—" Brock sighed, resigned. "What kind of stories?"

A consort danced on temper's edge, but seldom felt the cut. Not like a pleasure slave did. And that tiny question that kept flickering on the edges of Jared's mind flashed to the front. How *would* the Gray Lady treat a consort . . . or a pleasure slave?

That thought stirred a memory.

"When I was fourteen," Jared said, "the Province Queen came to our village. Can't remember why now, or why she wasn't accompanied by the District Queen." He frowned, trying to remember. "Maybe that was the year the former Queen stepped down and the new one wanted to see everything in her territory. Anyway, all the boys old enough to have begun formal training but still too young to be allowed to stand with the men had decided to wait on the main street, just in case we could be of service."

Brock grinned at him in perfect understanding.

"My father is the Warlord of Ranon's Wood, so he was the Lady's escort while she was there. He had gone to the official landing place outside of Ranon's Wood to meet her Coach and wasn't home when I came downstairs, dressed in my best clothes. I casually told my mother I was going to meet a couple of friends—which was true since we were all going to be on the main street. She never said a word about my clothes, never asked where I was going. She just smoothed my collar and said, equally casual, that my younger brothers would be staying home with her that day.

"Ranon's Wood is a fair-sized village, but there weren't *that* many boys within that age group, so we all had a little piece of the walkway on either side of the street staked out as our territory. At the time, I thought we'd just been clever enough not to draw the notice of the older youths. I learned much later that they'd been asked to stay in the background unless specifically summoned."

"If your father wasn't there, who'd have that much influence?"

"My mother. She's a Healer." Warmed by the memory that was now as bittersweet as all of his memories of Reyna, Jared's voice swelled with unmistakable pride.

Brock nodded, silently respectful.

"My father's eyes glazed when the carriage reached the beginning of the main street and he saw all of us spread out like that. But the Queen ordered the carriage to stop and said she wanted to walk a bit. And walk she did. I was the first one on that side of the street, and my father, may the Darkness embrace him, never said a word. I don't know what the Queen was thinking, but I saw her glance at the street and immediately offered to escort her across so she wouldn't get run over by another carriage—not that there were any carriages moving on the street. She accepted my hand, and I led her across. Except then her official escort was on one side of the street and she was on the other. Naturally, the nearest boy offered to escort her back across.

"She never laughed at us, never gave us the slightest impression that there was something odd about being shepherded back and forth as she slowly made her way up the street. The last boy at the top of the street handed her back to my father, who had been keeping pace, and he took her into the coffeehouse.

"To this day, I have no idea where he was supposed to have taken her or if she got any refreshment before he slipped her out the back door to avoid more assistance." Jared smiled.

"Did he tell your mother?" Brock asked.

The mud and the rain—what did they matter compared to this?

"My mother and several other witches dined with the Queen that evening. Since it was Ladies only, my father stayed home with my brothers and me. For several days after that, every so often my mother would glance at him and giggle while his face turned red."

They walked for a minute in companionable silence.

Then Brock said, "Corry and Cathryn are walking up ahead. Randolf's keeping an eye on them, and keeping Eryk away from them." He paused. "They're holding hands."

Jared and Brock grinned at each other.

"Go on," Brock said, hitching a thumb toward the wagon. "Go warm up for a bit and make yourself useful. You might tell her that story. I think Thera would like it, too."

More than willing to get out of the rain and give his legs a rest, Jared waited until the wagon caught up to him. Then he let it pass. He stared at the back of it, turning the thought over and over in his mind, testing it against instincts sharpened by the cruelty he'd seen, and endured, over the past nine years.

Then he hurried to catch up, suddenly wanting the

warmth, wanting something to eat, wanting to see if he could read anything in those hard gray eyes when he told her the story.

He wasn't sure he trusted the Gray Lady. Yet he felt certain that in some other village on some other street, she, too, had allowed herself to be needlessly shepherded so that a few young boys could proudly say they had served.

CHAPTER EIGHT

Krelis stared at the spelled brass button in his hand and then at the uneasy guard. "Are you sure?"

The guard's face tightened. "I made no mistake, Lord Krelis."

Krelis waved his hand, an oblique apology for insulting the man's skill. His voice thickened with frustration. "What in the name of Hell is she *doing*?"

The guard shrugged. "There's a Coach station less than a mile from that inn—but there's a better inn right next to the station if she'd intended to buy passage and go on to the Tamanara Mountains."

Which is precisely what the bitch *should* have done.

"The innkeeper was sure it was the Gray Lady?"

"An old Queen dressed in gray with twelve slaves. I found that button in the guest servants' quarters because the slave quarters weren't 'comfortable' enough for her new toys. Maybe she's trying to tame the Queen killer with sugar instead of the lash."

Krelis felt his blood chill. "What Queen killer?"

"The Shalador pleasure slave who showed his temper a couple of weeks ago. He would have gone to the salt mines of Pruul, but she fancied him."

Krelis let his breath out slowly. Fool! He'd already seen the list of slaves, and the Sadist wasn't on it. Besides, the High Priestess only sold Daemon Sadi's services. She'd never sell him outright—and she'd never let a dangerous enemy have any kind of control over a male that deadly.

The name on the list had meant nothing to him, but he'd heard about that Shalador Warlord's butchery. Would that work in his favor? A dark-Jeweled male turned vicious wouldn't be tamed again easily. He might even hate the next witch holding the leash enough to strike a crippling blow with no provocation. Doubtful he'd survive if he tangled with the Gray—no loss if he didn't—but if he weakened her, it would make it that much easier to finish the kill once they found the Gray Lady.

"There's a Coach station in easy reach that would get her out of a Territory that stands in Hayll's shadow. Instead of going there, she buys an old pedlar's wagon, a team of horses, two saddle horses, and supplies." Krelis's voice rose. "To do what? What's the bitch's game?"

The guard shrugged again. "She set out on the road heading northeast, or so the innkeeper said. Lots of small roads branch off it, traveling west and northwest. She could have changed direction. Been lots of rain around there. She can't be traveling fast, and she's not traveling light. She packed that wagon with supplies."

Krelis's hand closed around the button. "Which still doesn't explain what she's doing!"

The guard shifted his weight from one foot to the other. "Maybe that attack in the spring was more successful than anybody thought. She's an old woman."

Krelis let the idea take root. "It *was* a vicious attack." The Gray Lady had escaped last spring, but the violent unleashing of power might have left her mentally unstable. Could she be wandering aimlessly, all the time thinking she was heading for the Tamanara Mountains and safety?

Krelis slipped the brass button into his pocket. At least he had something to report. "Let the marauder bands know where she was last seen. They'll know the land around there better than we do."

After dismissing the guard, Krelis slumped in his chair. So far his plan was working. If his pet hadn't left the spelled button, though, he would have had no idea where to start looking for her.

That Shalador Warlord troubled him a little. There had been no reason for her to go down to those slave pens and even less reason to buy him. She'd already bought a young pleasure slave. She didn't need another, especially one who had turned savage.

Or had she bought him with the intention of giving him to a Shalador Queen in exchange for help reaching the Tamanara Mountains?

Krelis smiled grimly.

If getting help from Shalador had been her plan, she was already too late.

Much too late.

CHAPTER NINE

An hour after sunrise, Jared gave a final pat to the bay gelding and roan mare that were already saddled and tethered to the back of the wagon, and approached the door. They'd broken last night's camp and were ready to move on, but courtesy and a healthy sense of self-preservation told him he should get the Gray Lady's permission first—especially since he'd never consulted her yesterday afternoon when he had decided they'd all had enough of slogging through rain and mud and had given the order to make camp.

He raised his hand, but it froze before he could knock on the door. No matter what Jewels he wore, no man would willingly step into that cramped space while two witches were arguing in sharp, low voices that would have been raised to full volume if they hadn't been trying to keep it private.

Jared stepped back, unsure what to do—and wished, again, that he hadn't begun the sham yesterday of being the dominant male. His *Jewels* might outrank everyone else's except the Gray Lady's, but what difference did that make? He was a *slave*. He was hollow inside. He didn't want to have authority over the other males. He didn't want the responsibilities that came with that authority. But he'd let a moment's temper make that choice for him, and now he was stuck with it.

But that didn't mean he couldn't back away now and just wait until *she* gave the order to move on.

Before he could retreat, Tomas opened the door, looking flushed and angry.

No longer muffled, Thera's voice had a dangerous edge.

"You *can't* walk. That knee healed better than I thought it would overnight, but it's not going to take that kind of exercise, and you know it."

"Then I can ride one of the saddle horses, or sit on the driving seat. That will give others the opportunity to be inside—"

"It isn't raining now," Thera interrupted. "If you're so concerned, let's stay in this camp for a day and give everyone a rest. The animals certainly could use it."

Jared winced. Thera sure knew how to twist a verbal knife. By the end of that first morning on the road, they'd all recognized the Gray Lady's love for animals. If she could have figured out a way to tuck the horses into the wagon to give them a rest, he was sure she would have done it.

"No." Was that physical or emotional pain in the Gray Lady's voice? "We have to keep going. I can—"

Tomas had been looking at Jared. Now he twisted around. "You can just sit and get better like you're supposed to," he shouted. "What if you slip in the mud and hurt yourself bad?"

"If I'm riding a horse—" The Gray Lady had to be gritting her teeth to make the words sound like that.

But Tomas wasn't going to be warned or silenced by mere words. "You've been walking in the rain for two days now, and you're a Queen."

"Queens don't melt in the rain."

"You could take sick or something. What if your throat gets sore and you can't talk? Then what are we going to do?"

An awful silence filled the wagon.

Jared held his breath, waiting.

Whatever was said next wasn't loud enough for Jared to hear, but Tomas grinned and scampered down the steps. His grin widened when the door closed behind him with a less-than-gentle slam.

"They're both feeling pissy this morning," Tomas said cheerfully.

Jared muttered, "Lucky us." He looked at the closed door, thought about the "discussion" that had just taken place, then shook his head. His mother had been right: When faced with staying in bed because of illness or injury, even the maturest adult turned into an obstinate child.

Giving in to the inevitable, Jared trudged to the front of the wagon and gave Thayne the signal to move out.

Everyone else was ahead of him, Garth so far ahead he'd be out of sight once he topped the small rise. Randolf was leading the rest of them, and Brock had taken a mid position so that he could keep an eye on the wagon and the walkers. Corry was walking between Polli and Cathryn. Blaed was paired with Eryk, who looked grateful to be included again after being shunned by everyone since yesterday's squabble with Tomas. Tomas walked alone, but there was no indication it wasn't by choice.

Jared turned up his coat collar and lengthened his stride enough to catch up to Tomas. The rain had stopped for the moment, but the morning air was cold—and those clouds piling up in the west were a sure sign that there would be another storm by afternoon.

Tomas gave him a quick glance that told him his presence was an intrusion that would be endured.

Jared smiled in reply. "If we walk together, we'll both have some time and privacy for thinking."

Tomas looked startled for a moment. Then he grinned and returned to his own thoughts.

Jared took a deep breath. As he released it, he felt some of the tension in his shoulders ease.

He hadn't thought about much in the past couple of days, if he didn't count the fierce daydreams about staying put in some kind of shelter where he'd be warm and dry, and eating something besides that traveler's fare the Gray Lady had taught Thera and Polli how to make. He'd learned nothing about the Invisible Ring. If it was shielded, he couldn't detect the use of Craft. There was no weight, no tightness, none of the things that made a man ever aware of a Ring of Obedience. Hell's fire, it might as well not be there at all!

Which wasn't helping him figure out a way to elude it. Except for the explosion Eryk had caused, they'd had no way to measure the Gray Lady's temper. A deliberately casual comment by Randolf, and Blaed's fumbling attempt to get information, indicated the Rings of Obedience weren't tightly held either. A test of obedience? A trap for the first man who tried to slip the leash? Was that why she didn't insist that they remain close to the wagon? Was she using the Rings to keep track of them? No way to tell. The Gray Lady kept shifting between acting cold and being concerned, which kept them all off-balance and wary of being near her—except Thera and Tomas. He could understand her putting up with Tomas's lack of subservience. He'd seen a number of Queens amuse themselves by indulging that kind of behavior in an otherwise powerless slave—and he'd seen what had happened to those slaves when the Queen no longer found it amusing. But he couldn't understand why the Gray Lady tolerated Thera's tongue and temper. And he still didn't understand what it was about this Gray-Jeweled Queen that made something inside him restless enough and hungry enough to keep forgetting why he should fear her.

All he knew for sure was that they were traveling through rough country, always heading west or northwest, and hadn't seen anyone since they'd left the inn. They were far enough north to feel the bite of autumn, especially at night, but he still didn't know what Territory they were in, and the Lady wasn't saying.

Or else the Lady didn't know.

Not a pleasant thought. Mother Night, *none* of his thoughts were pleasant! He understood why she wouldn't allow slaves to ride the Winds by themselves, but why hadn't she bought passage at the next Coach station if she was determined to bring them back to Dena Nehele?

And what was she afraid of? That the males would try to break the Rings of Obedience and then call in the Jewels and attack her? Doubtful. The stories whispered about her were sufficient reason for any sane man to think long and hard before challenging her. And in truth, there were only five out of the twelve of them who were whole enough and trained enough to be even a potential threat to her.

So there had to be some other reason for the flashes of anxiety he had picked up from her over the past couple of days, despite her effort to hide them. Did the message she'd received just before they'd left Raej have anything to do with this demand to keep moving?

Jared scowled. Whatever it was, it was her problem, not his.

He'd give it another day. Maybe two. He didn't know exactly where he was, but he did know he was still east of the Tamanara Mountains and south of Shalador. Another day or two, and then the hollow man masquerading as the dominant Warlord would test the leash attached to the Invisible Ring and see if it would reach as far as Ranon's Wood.

Just for a little while. Just long enough. After that, he would accept whatever happened to him.

To keep himself from traveling down that path, Jared broke the comfortable silence. "What difference does it make if the Lady's throat gets sore?"

Tomas shot him a nasty look.

"I wasn't implying that it wouldn't matter if she got sick," Jared said. Hell's fire, the boy was pricklier than a Warlord Prince.

"Well, if her throat gets sore and she can't talk, how's she going to tell us the next part of the story? She's the only one who knows."

Before Jared could say anything, Tomas launched into the story about a group of children who had been captured by a Queen who had become greedy and cruel. By banding together, they managed to escape and decided to travel to a protected Territory where the Blood still believed they were the caretakers of the land and Craft was a power used responsibly. They had a number of adventures, getting help from unlikely, and sometimes humorous, sources as they eluded troops of guards and marauder bands.

As Tomas retold the story, Jared wondered if any of the children had thought it strange that the children in the story had the same names as they did, or if that just added to the delight as they outwitted the forces the wicked Queen sent after them. He also couldn't quite dismiss the tiny spark of resentment that Thera and Polli had been transformed into children for the tale but none of the adult males had been included.

And the tale itself . . . A land and a people whose Queen still balanced power with honor standing against a land and a people corrupted by a twisted witch. Did the Gray Lady see herself as the last defense against Dorothea's influence and corruption of power?

What if she was?

The thought rocked him back on his heels, and a whisper of hope began to take root inside him.

What if she was? What did anyone really know about the Gray Lady? If she *wasn't* a deadly, ruthless Queen, why didn't traders from neighboring Territories correct anyone who spoke harshly about her? Or did no one disagree with the stories that were told because a fierce reputation kept her people and the bordering Territories better protected?

Tomas reached the point in the story where the children were standing on the edge of a cliff, with a fast-moving river far below them and a marauder band riding up to cut off any chance of escape.

"Then what happened?" Jared demanded, a little embarrassed that, despite his wandering thoughts, he'd still been listening to the story.

Tomas shrugged and wiped his nose on his sleeve. "Don't know. Maybe she'll tell us tonight—if her throat doesn't get sore."

"Ah." Was there a discreet way of telling the Lady that the adult males would enjoy the story, too?

"Jared!" Thera called from behind him.

Knowing it was childish but somehow blaming her because he'd been excluded from the entertainment, Jared hunched his shoulders and lengthened his stride. Maybe he could pretend he hadn't heard her.

Randolf, who was walking ahead of Jared, glanced over his shoulder and quickened his pace. Blaed, however, looked back and hesitated.

Jared glared at both of them.

"Lord Jared!"

Jared winced, swore softly, and turned around.

Thera stomped through the mud, her clenched hands

swinging from stiff arms, her color high, and her green eyes blazing with temper.

Jared glanced at Brock, who rolled his eyes but made no effort to get closer. Blaed, having turned back, swung to Jared's left, close enough to look supportive but still far enough away not to be included in the discussion. Even Tomas stepped away from him.

Were they giving him maneuvering room, or just trying to avoid getting hit by mistake if she tried to punch him?

"Lord Jared," Thera said again as she stomped up to him. "The Lady needs some entertainment."

Blood rushed into Jared's face and drained out again, leaving him shaken. Thera didn't have much tact, but even she should know better than to state it so baldly.

Thera hesitated for a moment, puzzled. Then her eyes blazed even brighter. "Not *that,* you fool. Although sitting on her may be the only way you're going to get her to be sensible and stay off that leg." She swiped at the hair that had escaped from the loose braid. "Hell's fire, you'd think the woman had never had to spend a day in bed in her entire life! She's so stubborn, so . . . so . . . ."

Jared bared his teeth in a smile. "So like in temperament?"

He braced for the punch. He wouldn't take it, but he'd dearly love an excuse to push her face into the mud.

She made a noise, like steam escaping a kettle. When she finally spoke, her voice was dangerously controlled. "You're the one who wears the Red, Warlord. So show some balls and *do* something."

She brushed past him and started walking, her dark braid bouncing against her back.

Brock raised his hands and shrugged, fighting hard not to laugh.

Blaed bit his lip, rolled his shoulders, and finally said hesitantly, "I have a chess set, if that would help."

Using Craft, the Blood had the ability to call in and vanish objects, allowing them to carry things without being physically burdened with them. Sadi had described it once as an invisible cupboard, its size dependent on a person's strength and how much power was siphoned off to maintain it.

Jared didn't ask what else Blaed—or any of the rest of them—might have that would be of interest to the group. When a man's body was someone else's property, material possessions could take on fierce importance and become emotional wounds if sharing them wasn't done by choice. All too often these small treasures were taken by a stronger slave or by someone in the court who wanted the object . . . or simply wanted the slave to feel the loss of it.

"It might," Jared said, letting nothing in his voice or expression make any demands. There had already been too many demands made on Blaed, who was barely twenty and the only other male who had been used as a pleasure slave. Jared remembered too well how he had felt at that age, and the harsh lessons he'd learned when sexual pleasure had been turned into a twisted game.

Blaed called in the chess set, protected by a cloth bag, and handed it to Jared.

"Thank you," Jared said. "I'll see that it's returned."

Relief visible in his eyes, Blaed smiled his acknowledgment and hurried to rejoin Eryk.

Jared trotted up to the wagon, which had passed him while he'd been "discussing things" with Thera. He wondered briefly why no one was riding the saddle horses, then shrugged off the thought. Either Thera and the Gray Lady were supposed to be riding this turn, or whoever was supposed to be had chosen to walk instead of being that close to two witches who were grating on each other's tempers.

He jumped to the bottom step, using a little Craft to keep his balance. Taking the muffled snarl that answered his knock as an invitation, he entered and closed the door quickly so he wouldn't tumble out. The wide shutters at the front of the wagon were opened enough to provide a little fresh air, but not much light.

A small ball of witchlight began to glow near the Lady's head.

Dressed in dark-gray trousers and a long, heavy gray sweater, she sat on one of the benches that acted as seats and beds, her back resting against the storage boxes stacked against the top side of the bench. A blanket was wrapped around her shoulders like a shawl. Her long gray hair, usually hidden by the hood of her coat, was pulled back in a loose braid. The dim light smoothed away the age lines in her face and made her look like the lovely young woman she once must have been.

Desire nipped at him unexpectedly, making his heart beat a little faster, making his blood heat.

He shouldn't be feeling like this, not for an old woman who had bought him in the same way she had bought the wagon and the horses. But . . .

Was there a man in Dena Nehele who found her touch exciting, who considered it a privilege and an honor to warm her bed? Did she have a consort or a lover, or did she use pleasure slaves? Would she enjoy having him caress her until his hands and mouth gave her release? What would she do if he kissed her until the desire humming through him consumed them both?

Dangerous thoughts—and foolish ones. He was thinking like a man who would be granted equal pleasure in the bed instead of a slave who might use his experience and training to his own advantage.

"What do you want?"

The surly tone, the wary look in her gray eyes, and the way her body stiffened slapped his thoughts back to something close to neutral. Had he slipped so much that his thoughts had shown on his face? Thank the Darkness his coat was long enough to hide his body's response. Or was it the Ring that had betrayed him?

Jared raised the cloth bag. "Would you like to play a game of chess to pass the time?"

"Chess?" Her eyes immediately brightened with interest. She swung her legs over the side of the bench, wincing when the right knee refused to bend.

The sharp look she gave him was sufficient warning not to say anything, so Jared settled on the other bench and pulled the box out of the cloth bag. Partly because it was practical and partly to test her, he didn't ask permission before using Craft to hold the box in the air.

There was nothing in her expression except eagerness.

Odd that she didn't ask where the chess set came from. Slaves were supposed to show any possessions they carried using Craft, including the Jewels which always traveled with them even if they were forbidden to wear them. But every slave he'd known tried to hide a few things—favorite books, a gaming set like this, personal mementos, pictures of loved ones. If Blaed had acknowledged having this, he wouldn't have been so fearful about admitting it.

But she didn't ask, and he found himself warming to her because of it.

Jared opened the box, which became the game board with its alternating black and light-gray squares.

"Red or black?" he asked, indicating the playing pieces.

"Black," she replied, pushing up the sweater's sleeves.

Even slogging through the mud, she moved with unstudied grace, and he'd been surprised when he'd carried her to the wagon yesterday to discover that the body hidden by trousers, layered tunics and a knee-length coat was shapelier than he'd expected. More solid, too. Now, seeing the strong wrists and forearms showing below the sweater, Jared readjusted his image of her a little more. She might be old in years, but she was still a vigorous woman who probably engaged in all kinds of physical activity. All kinds.

Keep your mind on the game, Jared warned himself as he began separating the game pieces. *Your body is getting far too interested in* that *kind of speculation.*

When all the pieces were separated and ready to be placed, he handed her the dice to roll for the Queen's rank.

She rolled a six, which gave her Queen the Purple Dusk Jewel and the ability to move six squares in any direction. He rolled a five, the Summer-sky. One rank difference, so she didn't have an overwhelming advantage.

After carefully slipping the dice into the cloth bag, Jared began setting up his pieces.

The board was thirteen squares by thirteen. The first five rows on either side were the player's territory. The middle three were the battlefield. After placing his two castles and the sanctuary, Jared quickly set up the rest in one of his favorite patterns, with his Queen safely tucked away behind one of the castles and enough of the stronger pieces nearby to provide protection.

Satisfied with his positioning, he glanced at her side of the board and clenched his teeth to stop the instinctive protest. Why was her Queen standing in the middle of her territory with other pieces in the way of her reaching the castles and sanctuary? What kind of strategy was that when the whole point of the game was to capture the Queen?

Unless the Blood in Dena Nehele played by a different set of rules.

Without warning, a shadow of anger slid through his veins, a feral anger that tasted of the wild stranger. He felt tempted by it, wanted to welcome it and fan it until it burned hot and bright.

Instead, he pushed it away. Anger was dangerous to a slave. And, Hell's fire, it was only a game. Why should he care how she set up her pieces?

He used Craft to create a larger, brighter ball of witchlight. With the witchlight floating over the game board, the rest of the cramped space disappeared until all that was left was the game and the old woman watching him, wearing a friendly but challenging smile.

Since he had the lighter-ranked Queen, the first move was his. Meeting her eyes for a moment, Jared smiled as he moved a Warlord Prince onto the battlefield and accepted the unspoken challenge.

She moved her Queen.

The game began.

His father had told him chess was a game of the heart as well as the mind, that it was a kind of training ground because it showed you your own weaknesses. Which was why you didn't play it with an enemy.

When he was young and first learning the game, that hadn't made much sense. But later, as he watched his father play with friends who dropped by for an evening game, he began to understand. Belarr always tried to protect the Healers on the board as well as the Queen, sacrificing any male piece if it could block the attack.

Reyna, on the other hand, tended to use the Healers as protection for other pieces, even the Blood males and witches who were the pawns in the game. Her Healers, Priestesses, and Black Widows were usually captured long before any of the stronger male pieces.

When he'd pointed this out to her one time, she had shrugged and told him to care for his own.

He'd told his father about this quirk in an otherwise intelligent woman, thinking Belarr would find it as amusing as he had.

Belarr, too, had shrugged, but it wasn't as lighthearted a movement as Reyna's had been. He'd carefully masked whatever he had been thinking and said, "Healers and Queens don't play the game well." Then he'd abruptly changed the subject.

At the time, Jared had thought Belarr's reaction was due to Reyna's returning home completely exhausted from a long and difficult healing. Now, watching the Gray Lady's Queen scamper around the board attacking, protecting, risking capture, the memory became shaded with a different meaning, a deeper understanding.

He passed up a couple of opportunities to capture, initiating attacks on the other side of the board where she had to use the stronger male pieces. Even then, she sacrificed a Priestess instead of a Prince.

He swallowed the anger that was building up inside him again. It was only a game, a way to relieve her boredom. But, Hell's fire, didn't the woman have any sense? You didn't sacrifice the distaff gender while there was still a strong male left standing unless there was no other move.

When she moved her Queen to protect a Blood male that couldn't escape capture, his temper finally snapped.

"Lady," he said through gritted teeth as he took the Blood male, "it's an insignificant piece. You shouldn't be risking your Queen for a pawn."

The air in the wagon chilled so much he could see his breath.

Startled, he looked at her.

The gray eyes that had been warm and friendly a moment ago were icy, hard, and reflected a fury that came from so deep within her they reflected nothing at all.

Never breaking eye contact, she reached out and deliberately knocked over her Queen. "There are no pawns."

Looking away, she began gathering up the captured pieces that were lying beside her on the bench, carefully setting each one into the box.

Watching the jerky movements of muscles clenched in anger was worse than feeling the lash.

"Thank you for the game," she said stiffly, feeling around for the last piece. "I'm tired now. I wish to rest."

As she picked up the last piece, a Blood male, her fingers closed protectively around it.

The cold dismissal stung, but he accepted it. After double-checking that all the pieces and the dice were back in the box, he slipped it into the cloth bag and left the wagon. He returned the game to Blaed with faint thanks and hurried away.

No one approached him. No one asked what had happened. Even Thera took a long look at his face and left him alone.

Not a game to be played with an enemy, because it exposed the heart's weaknesses.

All these long years later, he understood the quarrels between Belarr and Reyna as he never had before. Despite their Craft and their courage—or, perhaps, because of it—Healers didn't have a strong sense of self-preservation and would drain themselves to the breaking point before they'd back away from a healing. Which was why, by Blood Law, every Healer had to be served by at least one Jeweled male unless she had a Jeweled consort or husband who would assume the duty of protecting her from herself.

Was that why courts had originally formed around Queens? To protect them from giving too much of themselves?

Since he'd never served in a court before he was Ringed, he'd never been with a Queen he respected let alone wanted to protect, never experienced the fierce loyalty and pride that he'd heard filled men when they served a good Queen.

For the rest of the morning, his thoughts chased each other, swinging from the Gray Lady to Reyna and back again. Speculation and memories kept poking at him until he felt savage and frightened. He couldn't shake the idea that Reyna would like Lady Grizelle, and it troubled him. That Belarr would· probably consider her a good Queen troubled him even more, because Belarr would question the honor of a Red-Jeweled Warlord who would abandon a Queen during a difficult journey.

Hell's fire, he was a *slave*. He hadn't agreed to serve her. Why shouldn't he escape if he got the chance? He wanted to go home. He wanted to talk to Reyna. Wanted, *needed* to explain.

Belarr had never been a slave. There was no way he could fully appreciate the emotional difference. What would the Sadist do if he were here, wearing the Invisible Ring?

No answers. No answers. Just a churning uneasiness that came from knowing that he would have to make a choice soon.

Just when he thought the day couldn't get any worse, it started raining again.

"Hell's fire," Randolf snarled. "What's wrong with Garth now?"

"I don't know," Jared said as the big man ran awkwardly toward them, holding out his arms to help maintain his balance on the muddy road.

Garth tended to roam ahead of the rest of them and then shuffle back to keep them in sight, much as a pet dog would do. The fact that the Gray Lady didn't keep him on a tighter leash was another thing about her that baffled the other males. Granted, Garth couldn't ride the Winds by himself, if he had ever been able to, and it wasn't likely that he could get far enough away on foot to prevent the Gray Lady from incapacitating him with the agony that could be sent through the Ring of Obedience, but that leniency wasn't typical in a slave owner.

Jared shook his head. Right now, he wasn't interested in puzzling over the peculiarities of female behavior. He was cold, wet, and tired. The afternoon light—what little of it there had been that day—was waning, and the only thing he was interested in was finding a place to make camp and getting something hot to eat. So his voice had an edge to it when he said, "What is it, Garth?"

Garth gave no sign of having heard him. Instead of continuing toward Jared, he suddenly veered toward Corry and Cathryn, waving his arms as if he were trying to herd small farm animals into a pen.

"Shoo! Shoo!" Garth shouted, waving his arms.

There was something sadly amusing about watching Garth, but there was nothing amusing about the way the children froze, their eyes getting bigger and bigger, or the fear in Corry's face when he grabbed Cathryn's hand and ran back to the wagon.

"Garth," Jared yelled, starting toward him.

Garth changed directions and ran toward Eryk. "Shoo! Shoo!"

"Garth!" Jared put the crack of a lash into his voice. He held his ground when Garth turned again, and clenched his teeth when the big man grabbed his upper arms and lifted him off his feet.

" 'Rauders!" Garth shouted, shaking him. "Fight 'rauders!"

Jared felt Randolf's bristling temper and wondered if this was going to turn into a maiming fight. Then he felt Brock's battle calm and saw the other man silently come around behind Garth. Randolf might have been a well-trained guard before being made a slave, but in a fight, Jared would rather have Brock's steadiness at his back any day.

"Put me down, Garth," Jared said firmly.

"Fight 'rauders!" Garth insisted.

"When you put me down."

Garth dropped him.

Jared slipped on the mud and would have landed on his back if Garth hadn't grabbed him again, planting his feet so firmly on the road it made his bones rattle.

"Damn it, Garth!" Jared snapped as he stepped out of reach.

Garth just hopped from one foot to the other in an anxious, shuffling dance. " 'Rauders!" he said, growing more insistent and more frantic.

Jared eyed the big man, then took a deep breath and blew it out. Hell's fire. There weren't any marauders. No one but slaves owned by a stubborn idiot of a Queen would be traveling on a day like this. Most likely, Garth had spotted an animal moving through the brush and trees that bordered the road. Although . . . unless they had been startled for some reason, even animals would find a spot to shelter in, wouldn't they?

Made uneasy by that thought as well as Garth's continued distress, Jared sent out a wide psychic probe that spanned the narrow road and extended several yards on either side. A few seconds later, he choked back a shiver of fear.

Still out of sight but coming steadily toward them were thirteen Blood males—twelve Warlords . . . and a Sapphire-Jeweled Warlord Prince whose psychic scent had that distinctive blend of viciousness and passion that separated Warlord Princes from other males. They were a law unto themselves, no matter what Jewels they wore. And they were always dangerous.

Jared took a step back before he could stop himself. "Hell's fire, Mother Night, and may the Darkness be merciful." He whipped around to face Randolf and Brock. "Get everyone back to the wagon. Now!"

Brock narrowed his eyes as if that would let him see farther in the pouring rain. "Jared—"

"NOW!"

Brock and Randolf looked at Garth, who was now standing in the middle of the road with his legs far enough apart for good balance and his huge hands clenched. Nodding grimly, they wrapped their hands around his thick-muscled arms and dragged him toward the wagon, leaving Jared alone on the road.

Jared raked one hand through his dark hair and swore when the rain squeezed out by the motion trickled down his back.

Thirteen men, all of them wearing Jewels. He'd pulled back the moment his psychic probe had touched the Sapphire shield and he realized it belonged to a Warlord Prince, so there hadn't been time to discern how dark the other Jewels were. The Sapphire was probably the strongest among them, but that didn't help much. If he were free to use the Red Jewels, he could take a Warlord wearing the Sapphire. But the Red were only one Jewel rank darker than the Sapphire. That wasn't enough of an advantage against a man who was, by his very nature, a killer. A Warlord Prince wasn't going to stand back and let anyone strike at his lighter-Jeweled followers. And if he was rogue, he had nothing to lose and everything to gain from a fast, vicious strike that would leave most of them helpless.

Except the Gray. If that Gray strength was unleashed . . .

Jared shuddered, his mind suddenly filled with the image of a chess piece scampering around the board, attacking, defending.

You're a slave. Remember that! You're a slave.

It should have mattered. It didn't. He couldn't stand by and watch the Gray Lady risk herself in a battle while there was one man among them who was still standing.

The Warlord Prince and his men came into sight a couple of minutes later. In the waning light and the rain, they were nothing more than dark, moving shapes, but he felt the power that swirled around them.

And the anger.

For a moment he just stood there, torn between his instincts to protect and the reality of his position. As a slave, he was forbidden to wear the Jewels, and without that reservoir of power, all he had was the strength that was always within him. Granted, it was a deeper well than most of the Blood had, but not enough against a Sapphire who could draw on his reserves and sustain the attack.

Jared turned away and kept a measured stride as he walked back to where the wagon had stopped. He felt a swift, light probe brush against his inner barriers and pushed back instinctively, letting the Warlord Prince know for certain that he would face one man who was a Jewel rank darker.

As he approached the wagon, he smiled grimly. Interesting how easily all the males had responded to the protective instinct. Brock and Randolf had placed themselves so they effectively blocked the narrow road. Ludicrous since they weren't wearing Jewels and didn't have any weapons. Then he caught the look in Brock's blue eyes and wondered what hidden things the guard might be carrying.

Garth hovered near the wagon. The children and Polli were bunched next to the rear wheel. Thayne held the team of horses and anxiously watched Blaed, who was standing in the middle of the road, a peculiar, blank expression in his hazel eyes.

A jolt of realization swept through Jared, strong enough to take his breath away. Mother Night. Courteous, easygoing Blaed was a Warlord Prince.

As their eyes met, Jared felt some emotion—pain? regret?—flash through Blaed.

Knowing he'd have to talk to the younger man later—if there was a later—Jared nodded as he passed Blaed and continued to the wagon.

The shutters that gave access to the driving seat were wide-open. Shoulder to shoulder, Thera and the Gray Lady watched the road.

"Rogues or marauders?" Thera asked as Jared reached them.

Jared looked back. The thirteen men had stopped, barely visible in the rain.

He almost asked what difference it made, but his attention was caught by the quickly hidden look of relief in the Gray Lady's eyes.

"Rogues," she said quietly.

Thera narrowed her eyes and studied the Gray Lady. "They can be more vicious than marauders, and that's a Warlord Prince leading them."

Saying nothing, the Gray Lady backed away from the opening.

Thera gave Jared a puzzled look and followed.

A few seconds later, the shutters were slammed shut with enough force to startle the horses and the sharp, muffled voices told Jared a hot-tempered argument had started.

It ended just as abruptly.

Jared's body tightened as his anger warred with his fear: anger because the two of them were indulging in a temper tantrum while all of them were at risk from an outside danger; and fear because the continued silence might mean one of them, namely Thera, was badly injured—or dead.

The door opened a few minutes later. The Gray Lady emerged, followed by Thera, who was carrying one of the cloth bags they used to store spare clothes.

Jared breathed a sigh of relief when Thera appeared, only then aware of how badly his legs were shaking.

"Polli, come with me," the Gray Lady said quietly.

No one moved. No one made a sound.

"Polli, come with me," she said again, holding out her hand.

Polli looked at the Gray Lady, then looked at the rogues whose features were obscured by the rain. She backed away from the Gray Lady, shaking her head. "No. It's my moon-time. I don't have to spread my legs when it's my moon-time." She continued backing away as the Gray Lady slowly advanced. When she bumped the front wheel, her hands closed fiercely around the spokes. "It's my moon-time," she wailed, slowly folding up until she was sitting on the muddy road, her hands still clutching the spokes.

Because he wanted to argue and didn't dare, Jared stepped back until he bumped into Blaed. Betrayal burned his throat and stomach. Despite all of his experience during the past nine years, he'd begun to respect the Gray Lady. Now she was trading Polli—Polli!—to a pack of rogues so the rest of them could leave without a fight.

What made it even worse was that he understood her reasoning. Rogues tended to be more vicious because they had a price on their heads. They were either escaped slaves, or they'd broken their service contract with a Queen, or they'd refused to serve when a Queen had chosen them for her court. But they were still men, and any of them who hadn't been castrated would enjoy having a female to mount.

And who else could she give them? Sharp-tongued Thera, who was intelligent and useful? Little Cathryn?

Bracing one hand on the wheel, the Gray Lady leaned over and spoke to Polli, her voice too low for Jared to hear. As she spoke, she brushed a hand over Polli's head.

She must have used a calming spell, he concluded bitterly as the fear gradually left Polli's face.

The Gray Lady straightened up slowly. Polli scrambled to her feet. Looking thoughtful, Thera hugged Polli and handed her the cloth sack. The Gray Lady linked her arm with Polli's and, walking with care, led her toward the rogues.

Bitch, Jared thought as he watched the two women. *What lies did you tell her to make her so accepting?*

There was tightness in Brock's expression and anger in Randolf's eyes as the women passed them. Jared suspected that, if the trade didn't work, both men would be able to suppress their instincts sufficiently to let the Gray bitch fight her own battles.

"What's going on?" Blaed whispered.

Since the answer seemed obvious, Jared didn't bother to reply.

The Sapphire-Jeweled Warlord Prince urged his horse forward, meeting the two women halfway between his men and the wagon. He dismounted slowly, his eyes never leaving the Gray Lady. His lean, hard body moved with a warrior's grace as he cautiously approached, one hand resting easily on the hilt of the knife attached to his belt.

Too far away to hear, and not daring to probe in case it produced a violent reaction, Jared watched the negotiations. After one long, searching look, the Warlord Prince ignored Polli and seemed to listen courteously to the Gray Lady's offer.

Hell's fire, what if the man wanted to inspect Thera and Cathryn before accepting the woman offered?

A long few minutes later, the Warlord Prince raised his left hand. Two of his men immediately came forward and dismounted. One of them took Polli's bag and tied it to his saddle. The other led Polli to the Warlord Prince's horse and helped her mount.

Jared narrowed his eyes. All the stories he'd heard about rogues said they lived hard, desperate lives, so emotionally scarred by Queens and courts that they wouldn't yield to the distaff gender for any reason. Any female unfortunate enough to fall into their hands could only expect to be viciously used for the most basic and base needs.

So why did the Warlord who had helped Polli mount handle her so gently? Why was this Warlord Prince still listening courteously to the Gray Lady?

They talked for several more minutes. At one point, the Warlord Prince seemed aggravated enough that it took considerable effort to keep his temper leashed. At another point, he shook his head, his regret obvious. That's when the Gray Lady's shoulders sagged as if a great weight had settled on them.

When there didn't seem to be anything more to say, the Warlord Prince took her hand and raised it to his lips.

As he watched, Jared felt the emotional ground shift beneath him again. That gesture wasn't a meaningless salute as it would have been in a court. A rogue Warlord Prince who wore Jewels as dark as the Sapphire wouldn't bother with empty gestures. And it wasn't mockery.

Why would a rogue deliberately show his respect for a Queen?

Jared turned that thought over and over while the Gray Lady slowly limped back to the wagon. Her face looked pinched and pained, and she seemed more frail than she had a few minutes ago.

Brock and Randolf stepped aside as she reached them. If ordered to, they would have assisted her, but that subtle defiance—forcing a Queen to order every small thing she wanted from a slave—was the only safe way for a man to show disrespect. He couldn't be faulted because he did exactly what he'd been told to do. He just didn't do anything beyond that.

Jared watched her approach, knowing he'd have to make a decision within the next few seconds. He'd declared himself the dominant male. If he acted like a slave and stepped aside as Brock and Randolf had done, the others would accept that decision and act accordingly. If he responded as his instincts demanded and helped her, the others would, grudgingly, accept that, too.

The mental shove struck him without warning, the anger

behind it hitting his inner barriers like heavy surf. He turned his head and met the Warlord's Prince's stare.

She deserves the best you can give her, the man said, using a Sapphire spear thread.

She deserves whatever she can squeeze out of a slave, Jared snapped, unwilling to let this stranger sense how much her betrayal of trust hurt him.

They stared at each other, the other rogues and slaves forgotten.

It seems I misjudged you, the man sneered. *Despite your Jewels, you don't have balls enough and you aren't man enough to serve her.*

The Warlord Prince strode to his horse and mounted behind Polli, his contempt apparent in every line of his body. At his signal, his men turned their horses and rode back down the road.

Polli leaned to one side and looked back once.

The Warlord Prince didn't look back at all.

Jared shook with anger. How dare that son of a whoring bitch judge him? It was one thing not to do more than what was demanded in order to make it clear he wasn't there by his own choice. It was quite another to have a stranger, a man who hadn't had the balls to remain with the Queen who had chosen him, say he wasn't worthy of serving.

He turned on his heel. In three strides, he caught up to the Gray Lady at the same moment Thera reached her. Thera didn't look at him. She couldn't have picked up the argument since it had been conducted on a Sapphire spear thread, so the implied disapproval was her own judgment. Stung, he reacted by grabbing the Gray Lady's arm hard enough to make her gasp. He loosened his hold without apologizing for causing her pain and struggled to keep his temper leashed while he and Thera assisted the Gray Lady to the wagon's door.

She tried to raise her right leg to step up, but the knee wouldn't bend.

Thera swore under her breath.

Whatever the Gray Lady might have said in response remained unsaid because she noticed the children solemnly

watching her. Shadows filled her gray eyes as her gaze
moved from Eryk to Corry to Cathryn and, finally, lingered
on Tomas.

"At least one of them is safe now," she said so quietly
Jared almost missed the words. Then she looked back at
him. "A mile or so down the road, there's a lane on the
right-hand side. Follow the lane for another mile. On the
left-hand side, there'll be an entrance to a clearing that has
some kind of a shelter. We'll camp there tonight."

A lot of orders were implied in those words, the main
one being that he would lead them to the shelter. If he was
going to force her to acknowledge the enslavement instead
of pretending he was serving her as if he were a free man,
now was the time to make it clear she was going to have
to give specific orders for each action.

The pain and weariness in her face, the shadows in her
eyes, and the anxiety he could sense in her stopped him as
much as the Warlord Prince's condemnation.

"I'll take care of it," Jared said quietly, making sure his
voice remained neutral and in no way implied loyalty. He
wasn't certain she deserved loyalty, no matter what that
rogue bastard thought, but he was cold, wet, and hungry,
and no defiance right now was worth delaying the moment
when they could eat and rest. But, Hell's fire, seeing her
in pain chewed at him until he wanted to lash out at something, anything, until her pain went away.

Leading with her left leg, the Gray Lady climbed the
steps into the wagon. Thera glanced sharply at Jared and
said nothing as she followed the Gray Lady inside.

If the other men noticed an edge in his voice when he
gave the order to move on, no one mentioned it. They
didn't question his insistence that Cathryn and Corry sit on
the driving seat and Eryk and Tomas ride the saddle horses
tied to the back of the wagon since it was the most sensible
way of keeping an eye on the children. Nor did they question his order that Brock and Randolf take up a rearguard
position. And one look at his face made them swallow any
comments they might have made about the oddly protective
way Garth walked beside the wagon instead of rambling
ahead as usual. He had made the decision that, at least for

the time being, they weren't going to act like slaves, and no one was going to challenge that decision.

Taking point, Jared walked ahead of the wagon, trying to sort through his conflicting emotions. He'd *seen* the Gray Lady hand a slave over to a pack of rogues, and he couldn't ignore the bitterness it produced in him any more than he could ignore the way his protective instincts kept pushing at him. But that Warlord Prince kissing her hand, making that deliberate gesture of respect. Was there a hidden reason for handing Polli over to that rogue bastard? Maybe not hidden, just not obvious. There were things about the Gray Lady that he didn't understand—yet. That made him uneasy.

And where were the rest of them going if a pack of rogues was considered the safer choice?

Blaed had been walking a couple of steps behind him for several minutes. Jared waved him forward, no longer able to ignore the younger man's unhappiness or his own curiosity.

"Thayne knew about you," Jared said, keeping his voice conversational.

Blaed shrugged, an action that seemed more resigned than unconcerned. "We've been friends since we were boys, even though he's a couple of years older than me, so he would have known."

And had been enough of a friend to say nothing. "How did you do it?"

"I didn't," Blaed said quickly, his hazel eyes holding a plea for acceptance—and a hint of defiance that was more in keeping with his true nature.

You can't help being what you are, Jared thought as he looked at the young Warlord Prince, *any more than men like Brock and Randolf can help being wary of what you are.* "Someone else put a spell on you to hide your . . . ?" His voice trailed off as he tried to think of some way to phrase it that wouldn't sound insulting.

Blaed bit his lip and nodded. "He said a Warlord Prince my age, being used as a pleasure slave, would be twisted out of all recognition or have the heart torn out of him.

He said I hadn't come into my strength yet and had too much potential to be wasted that way." Blaed gulped. "So he put this spell around me. He said it would mask what I was as long as I was around Warlords, but another Warlord Prince's presence could break it."

He. A male who could create a spell so subtle no one had realized it existed. No blurring of Blaed's psychic scent, no sense of Craft. Just a masking of an essential difference between Blaed and the rest of them.

Jared felt a chill run up his spine that had nothing to do with the falling temperature or the rain. He studied Blaed as if he'd never seen him before. A good-looking face that would mature into a handsome one. A well-toned body that needed to fill out a little more. Medium-brown hair that was long enough for a woman to run her hands through it. Hazel eyes that reflected a temperament that hadn't sharpened yet.

Looks meant nothing. It was the potential within the flesh that had to be considered carefully—and, also, who would recognize that potential and want to shape and hone it into a fine, sharp weapon.

"You know the Sadist." Jared didn't make it a question.

Blaed paled a little. "I think he's the reason I ended up at Raej so quickly. My training was . . . accelerated."

Jared snorted. "I'll bet the part of the training you were supposed to be learning got accelerated, too."

Blaed's eyes widened.

Jared's lips curled up in a twisted smile. "He trained me, too."

There was no need to put into words that uneasy mixture of revulsion and excitement, the embarrassment of feeling like a voyeur when the young men who were being trained watched an experienced pleasure slave play a woman's body until mild arousal became blinding heat and she screamed throughout a prolonged climax. No need to talk about the shame they'd felt because they had stiffened and ached for release while Sadi rose from the bed as flaccid as he'd been before the first kiss. No need to talk about the private lessons, those times when that bored, cold expression that so effectively masked the Sadist's thoughts and feelings was set aside and they'd seen enough of the man beneath to feel trust and terror.

"I take it there wasn't a Warlord Prince serving your previous Queen," Jared said.

"Only him." Blaed shrugged. "Minor Queens usually can't lure a Warlord Prince to serve in their courts. And Territory Queens usually won't let a minor Queen keep an enslaved Warlord Prince because he's too hard to control."

Minor Queens usually didn't get a chance to hold the Sadist's leash, either—unless the High Priestess of Hayll was rewarding them for some reason.

"How long were you in that court?"

"Six months altogether. He was there for the first four, then the contract that that Queen had with Dorothea SaDiablo ended and he was 'loaned' to another Queen."

"Queens don't usually give up a freshly trained pleasure slave," Jared said thoughtfully. "Even if he is a Warlord Prince. She *did* know you were a Warlord Prince when she acquired you?"

Blaed nodded. "Although once he put the spell around me, everyone seemed to forget that. After he was gone, she became uneasy about using me, for no reason I could figure out, and sent me to Raej."

There could have been other spells Sadi had wrapped around Blaed to cause that uneasiness and ensure that the young man would end up at Raej quickly—spells the Sadist wouldn't have mentioned.

"Why?" Jared said quietly, thinking out loud. "Why would he go through the effort of making sure you ended up at Raej, where you'd just be sold to another witch?"

Blaed hesitated. "He was there when I was being sold. When it got down to his Lady and the Gray Lady being the only ones still bidding on me, his Lady stopped bidding all of a sudden. I think he . . . arranged . . . that so that I would end up with the Gray Lady."

Jared swore under his breath. The Sadist and the Gray Lady. What in the name of Hell was he supposed to think about *that?*

Nothing, for the moment. Finding that clearing before they lost the light was the first priority.

They reached the lane. Hoping it was wide enough to accommodate the wagon, Jared waved at Thayne, who was leading the horses, and then pointed to the lane.

Thayne waved back.

As Jared and Blaed walked down the lane, looking for the entrance to the clearing, Jared thought of one thing that would change now that everyone knew Blaed was a Warlord Prince. "Since a Warlord Prince is a higher caste than a Warlord, that makes you the domin—"

"Forget it," Blaed said sharply. "I wear the Opal; you wear the Red. That still makes you dominant as far as Jewel rank is concerned. And you're older than I am."

"Not by that much," Jared muttered.

"By enough. And you made the Offering to the Darkness before you were made a slave, didn't you?"

"Yes." *But you didn't,* Jared added silently. Which might explain why Blaed was willing to follow rather than lead. Maybe, despite Warlord Princes being *born* Warlord Princes, they had to mature into that temperament in the same way they matured into their full psychic strength. If Blaed had been a few years older or had made the Offering before he'd been enslaved, he probably wouldn't have yielded so easily to another male regardless of which one of them wore the darker Jewel.

"Besides," Blaed said, confirming Jared's speculations, "you haven't done anything I would have done differently."

"I'm so pleased you approve," Jared said sourly.

Blaed kept his eyes on the trees and thick clumps of bushes on the left-hand side of the lane. "Maybe I don't want to become a battleground the way you are. Maybe I'm just trying to avoid that day for as long as possible."

Jared stopped walking. Blaed stopped and turned to face him.

"You know," Jared said, choking on the words. "You all know, and yet—"

"No," Blaed said. "The rest of them don't know. They see what you've chosen to let them see—a dominant male."

"Then why do you know?"

"Because I'm standing on the edge of the same battle-ground." Blaed smiled bitterly. "If I wasn't a slave, I would've made the Offering a couple of months ago and settled into what I am instead of trying to keep it leashed. I'm guessing it's the same with you. My father would say you haven't grown into your skin yet."

Instead of responding to that remark, Jared started walking. He wouldn't think of it now. *Couldn't* think of it now—especially because he felt the wild stranger stirring deep inside him.

But he was so shaken by Blaed's words, he didn't notice the Sapphire psychic wire strung across the lane until he tripped over it and landed hard in the mud.

A moment later, Blaed let out a shout that had Jared scrambling to his feet, expecting an ambush of some kind. When nothing happened, he swore with all the creative violence he could muster.

"Do that again without a good reason and I'll break your neck," Jared snarled.

Blaed ignored that remark and pointed to thickly entwined bushes that didn't look any different than the others. "There's a gate there. Or something. Some of the bushes shimmered when you tripped."

They tried every opening or unlocking spell they could think of. Nothing.

"Why would a Warlord Prince put a Sapphire trip wire across the lane?" Jared asked Blaed.

"Wasn't meant as a trip wire," Blaed replied absently as he continued to study the bushes. "You were supposed to sense it and stop. Since he went through the effort of making sure we stopped here, that means the entrance to the clearing is here. Somewhere."

Jared looked around. If Blaed was right, the key to getting into the clearing had to be nearby.

Walking back to the place where he'd tripped, Jared studied both sides of the lane. Opposite the bushes Blaed said had shimmered was a tumble of boulders as tall as an average man, and furry with moss.

Something about their shape tugged at him, disappearing when he took a couple of steps closer. He stepped back, and kept stepping back, until he was on the other side of the lane. He looked at the stones again and swore silently.

He was either losing his mind or his self-control, because the way the boulders had tumbled together, they looked like a woman clothed in moss rising up from among the other stones.

Smiling bitterly, Jared crossed the lane, then reached out and cupped a stone breast.

Polli's face flashed through his mind.

His fingers bit into the moss as another face filled his mind. It wavered between young and old, but there was no mistaking those hard gray eyes. If any woman had stone breasts to match a stone heart, it was the Gray Lady.

He felt the slight tingle of a spell being keyed. A moment later, Blaed let out a yip of surprise.

Jared twisted around, his eyes widening as a section of the bushes changed into a simple wood pole strung with vines.

He hurried away from the boulders before Blaed turned to look at him, not really sure why he felt the need to keep access to this place a secret from the rest of them.

"How'd you unkey the illusion spell?" Blaed asked.

The wagon came around a curve in the lane, saving Jared from having to think of a lie.

"I'll check things out," Jared told Blaed as they lifted the wooden pole off its supporting posts and laid it aside. "You bring the others in."

Jared took a deep breath and cautiously followed the straight path that led to the clearing. It was barely wide enough for the pedlar's wagon and longer than he expected. His careful psychic probes didn't tell him anything. That didn't make him feel easier. If that rogue had been able to persuade a Black Widow to make the illusion spell to hide the entrance to the clearing, were there other illusions he wasn't able to detect?

Passing between the two stone posts that marked the end of the path, Jared stepped into the clearing. He waited a moment, straining all of his senses to detect anything that might be a danger to them, then sighed with relief when nothing happened.

The clearing itself was fairly large—a couple of acres surrounded by trees and thick undergrowth on three sides, backed by a steep, rocky hill. On the left side of the clearing was a corral and a small stone building built into the hill. It was large enough to shelter half a dozen animals in bad weather, or at least keep feed and gear dry. Also built into the hill was a one-story stone building. Between the building and the corral was a small wooden structure that probably contained the privy hole.

Jared couldn't summon up enough interest for whatever else the clearing might contain. As soon as he figured out how to rekey the illusion spell on the gate, he was going to spend his thoughts and energy on nothing but getting dry, getting fed, and going to sleep.

The wagon passed him, its wheels almost scraping the stone posts that marked the clearing boundary. The other slaves followed behind the saddle horses.

As he passed Jared, Blaed said, "I put the pole back in place," then pointed a thumb over his shoulder.

Jared's breath huffed out in an impatient sigh as he waited for Garth who was, for the first time, trailing behind everyone instead of roaming ahead.

"Come on, Garth," Jared said, waving the big man forward.

Garth stopped two yards away from the stone posts, and shifted his weight from one foot to the other. His head swiveled in the opposite rhythm as he kept eyeing the posts.

"Come on," Jared snapped.

Garth raised his hands, then let them slap against his thighs. He seemed to want to say something, but he made no sound. Finally, he let out a low, distressed cry and bolted past the posts.

"Hell's fire," Jared muttered, watching Garth trot toward the others. The big man stumbled a little every time he looked anxiously over his shoulder at Jared.

Jared turned his back on the group and stared uneasily at the stone posts with their rounded tops. Were they supposed to be a rogue's idea of a bitter joke or a blatant symbol of male strength?

He didn't have time to decide because, seconds later, he realized Garth must have understood something about the posts that he hadn't.

A psychic storm swiftly began to surround the clearing. Jared felt it hum along his nerves and scratch at his bones, felt the pressure of power that would build and build until its destructive release tore through anyone who wasn't strong enough to withstand the onslaught.

Hell's fire. There must be a spell set in the posts to trigger all the defensive spells around the clearing if some key wasn't used within a certain amount of time. But *what* key? *Where?* That rogue bastard hadn't mentioned this. Had the omission been deliberate?

With his heart beating so hard it pounded in his temples, Jared looked at the wagon pulled up close to the stone building and the people standing near it. There wasn't time for them to run across the clearing and down the path before the defensive spells triggered and the psychic storm hit.

He hadn't realized he'd been descending instinctively to the level of the Red until he felt the wild stranger's presence as keenly as if he'd stepped into its lair. And, in a sense, he had. Here he could tap his full strength. Here his power was raw, primal—and savage. Here it belonged to the part of himself he had tried to push away and deny.

Now he reached for the strength of the Red, regardless of the cost, using it to quickly probe the gathering storm.

Layer upon layer upon layer of protection spells, defensive spells, spells honed to destroy flesh but not hurt the land. White, Tiger Eye, Rose, Purple Dusk, Opal, Sapphire. Strength woven into strength.

Jared probed further, fully aware of how their time was running out. He almost withdrew, but decided to check the last couple of layers of spells just to be certain his idea would work.

It *should* work. If he formed a Red shield around everyone, and if the Gray Lady formed a Gray shield just behind it, they *should* be able to withstand the storm. They might lose the horses, but even all the spells combined shouldn't be able to completely destroy a Gr—

As his Red probe touched the last layer, his heart stuttered. He forgot how to breathe.

They weren't going to survive.

Forming a tight net above all the other layers of strength was the Ebon-gray, the second-darkest Jewel.

The only Ebon-gray in the Realm of Terreille was Lucivar Yaslana, a half-breed Eyrien Warlord Prince who was Daemon Sadi's half brother.

He'd only heard stories about Yaslana. They made the Sadist sound like an amiable man. He didn't want to imagine what had been added to that Ebon-gray spell, but he was certain it would be able to smash through Red and Gray shields—and smash through their minds as well.

A shriek of terror and an anguished cry made him focus on the physical world.

Little Cathryn was doubled over, clutching her head. So was Tomas. Thera and the Gray Lady were reaching for the children.

Savage rage flooded through him, cooled by a growing fear as all the power around the clearing began to constrict and press down on their minds. He didn't feel anything yet except a pressure coming from beyond himself, but the weakest of them would be the first to be destroyed. And the weakest were the children and the two adults who were broken—Garth and Thera.

Hell's fire, the rain had drowned his wits. The Warlord Prince would have told the Gray Lady! Not enough time to reach her physically, and no time to worry about breaking rules. He directed a Red communication thread at her. *Lady . . . *

Nothing.

She was holding on to Tomas, probably shielding the boy's mind with her strength.

Which was no reason not to answer him!

Jared tried again. Hell's fire, Mother Night, and may the Darkness be merciful! She wore the Gray. Of course she could hear the Red!

Painfully aware he was losing precious seconds, he tried a Sapphire thread. When he got no answer, he used a Green communication thread, putting a bit of temper in the sending. *Lady.*

The Gray Lady whipped around to face him.

How do we quiet the protection spells? Jared demanded.

Her fear pounded against him. *He said you'd know the key. I thought he told *you*.*

Jared's mind blanked for a second. *Why in the name of Hell would he think *I'd* know?*

I don't know.

With the words, Jared caught a whiff of memory from her. *Your Warlord will know the key.*

Your Warlord. The words assumed a bond a slave would never dream of, an honorable bond of service between a male and his Queen.

Damn that rogue bastard to the bowels of Hell, was this some kind of *test*?

It didn't matter. If they were going to survive, he had to stop thinking like a slave and start thinking like a Warlord.

Jared turned back to the posts. Garth had sensed—or understood—something about them, and it made sense that the key wouldn't be hard to reach if the rogues weren't going to put themselves at risk every time they entered the clearing. Which meant it *had* to be here!

Damn you, he thought as he felt the wild stranger pushing at him. *Damn you. Help me!*

It exploded from its hiding place. He wanted to howl as its savagery filled him, flooded him, as razor-edged instincts blinded his ability to think. A moment later, it retreated, leaving him feeling raw and viciously clear-minded.

Sweating heavily despite the cold and the rain, Jared created a large ball of witchlight.

On the facing sides of the posts, someone had carved the thirteen ancient symbols of power deep into the stone—six on the left post, seven on the right.

How was he supposed to choose the right three?

Jared paused, then shook his head. Of course it was three.

He found the symbol for male on the left stone. His finger hesitated over it before moving to the triangle beneath it. Using Craft, he traced the triangle's deep lines with one finger, filling them with witchlight.

In a court, the male triangle of Consort, Steward, and

Master of the Guard formed the tightest bond with the
Queen. They were companions, advisors, protectors.

None of the other symbols on the left post pulled him,
so he turned to the right. His finger traced the outline of
the symbol for female.

The male triangle was the core of a court, but the Queen,
the female, was always its heart.

He sank to his knees and traced the last symbol carved
into the post, the Blood's most revered symbol—the symbol
for the Darkness.

The Blood honored the Darkness because it meant end-
ings and beginnings; it was the fertile dark of land and
womb that nurtured the seeds of life; it was the psychic
river the Blood came from and returned to; it was the abyss
the Self descended into to reach its own strength; it was
the vastness that contained the spiderweb-shaped psychic
roadways called the Winds. It was all those things, and
more.

As the last line filled with witchlight, Jared felt the jolt
of power funneling into the stone posts. The witchlight in
the symbols became so bright he had to squint. It flashed
once and then faded, the little bit of power he'd used to
create it already expended.

In that moment after the flash, Jared saw a pale triangle
form between the three symbols before it, too, faded.

The protection spells quieted. The psychic storm quickly
dissipated. Rekeyed, the illusion spell turned a wood pole
strung with vines into thick, unpassable undergrowth.

Jared stayed on his knees, too tired and shaken to stand
up. He sank back on his heels, his head bent, his hands
resting loosely on his thighs. This exhaustion wasn't caused
by draining too much of his power. He used more than that
for everyday living. It wasn't even caused by the sharp fear
he'd felt.

For a few moments when the wild stranger had filled
him, he had felt so alive and whole. Now he felt empty and
hollowed out again, and it cut at him. But he wasn't sure
he was ready to fully embrace that part of himself, to bind
himself to that kind of responsibility, and until he was . . .

Strong hands gripped his arms and pulled him up. Blaed smiled solemnly. Brock looked respectful.

"Let's get you inside," Brock said.

"The horses." Jared's voice sounded thick.

"I'll help Thayne and Randolf with the horses."

"I can—"

"You've done enough," Brock said sharply.

"You've done enough," Blaed agreed quietly.

Jared gave in, needing their support more than he wanted to admit.

As they walked toward the one-story stone building, Garth hurried up to them, stopping just short of barreling into Jared. The big man studied Jared's face for a moment, then made a sound like a grunt of satisfaction, and hurried away.

Thayne smiled shyly and raised his hand in a casual salute.

Randolf stood by the corral, watching Garth, his expression unreadable.

Jared was too tired for Randolf's moods, but he couldn't quite dismiss the man's animosity for the broken Warlord.

"We should pay more attention to Garth," Jared said quietly as they neared the building.

Brock made an exasperated sound. "Garth's not that bad. It could've happened to any of us."

"He knew about those protection spells before the rest of us did."

A brittle silence followed Jared's words.

"He was the last one," Jared insisted. "Nothing started to happen while he was still on the path, so I'd guess there's something built into those spells to make sure all the rogues have time to get into the clearing. It's the last person in who has to rekey the illusion spell in order to stop the defensive spells from triggering. If I'd paid attention to his distress, we would have had more time to figure out the key before the storm came down on us."

"You don't know that," Blaed protested, keeping his voice low.

"All I'm saying is Garth seems to understand some things. Maybe it's a holdover from his training. Hell's fire,

I don't know. But we'd be fools not to pay more attention to what sets him off."

"All right," Brock said. "I'll—"

The door opened.

Brock and Blaed released their supportive hold on Jared's arms.

Jared walked toward the Gray Lady, alone.

In the light coming through the open door, her gray eyes looked almost black from exhaustion. Her voice quavered when she quietly asked him if he was all right. She looked frail, and he suspected her pride was the only thing keeping her on her feet.

Her frailty made him want to push her until she struck out and proved she was still strong and powerful.

"Thank you, Warlord," she said solemnly.

"I live to serve, Lady," he replied, his voice lightly laced with bitterness to hide another emotion he didn't want to acknowledge.

Tears filled her eyes. She turned and retreated into the room as quickly as she could manage with her injured knee.

Jared rocked back as if she'd slapped him. Shame filled him until he wasn't sure he could stand beneath the weight of it. He tried to dredge up enough anger to burn away the shame, but it wouldn't come.

Swallowing hard, Jared looked behind him. Brock and Blaed had discreetly disappeared to finish the chores.

"Jared?" Tomas stood in the doorway. "You coming in or you going to stand there letting the rain in until Thera gets mad enough to hit you with a skillet?"

"Maybe it would help," Jared muttered as he followed the boy inside and firmly closed the door.

Silence strained tempers already frayed by fear and exhaustion, broken only by the scrape of utensils against plates and murmured requests to pass something that couldn't easily be reached. They choked on the food that had been bought with a young witch's life, but they ate it. Their bodies needed fuel. Landens might envy the Blood's magical powers, but they didn't understand the price that went with it; didn't understand how fiercely that inner fire could burn, especially in those who wore the darker Jewels; didn't understand how quickly it could consume the body that housed it if no other fuel was available.

So they ate in silence, never meeting each other's eyes, each one wondering whose life might pay for the next meal, the next shelter.

Jared sighed with relief when the meal finally ended.

Thera picked up her plate and walked over to the kitchen area of the large single room to begin cleaning up. Within moments, the only ones left sitting on the benches on either side of the long wooden table were Jared and the Gray Lady.

He'd deliberately sat at the opposite end on the opposite side, as far away from her as he could get. Now, with the others dallying with the last chores in order to stay away from her and nothing but the long table separating them, he looked at her for the first time since she'd met him at the doorway and thanked him.

After a minute, she raised her head and met his cold stare.

There was nothing in her gray eyes. Nothing at all. As if all the fire in her had been doused.

Then she flinched and fixed her eyes on the chipped blue jug filled with autumn wildflowers that sat on the table.

Why? Jared wanted to ask her. He could understand that Sapphire-Jeweled bastard riding back here ahead of them to create the psychic wire in order to make sure they found the clearing. But why had the man taken the time to fill a jug with flowers? Because he was certain the Warlord Prince had done just that.

He understood the rogues giving up the shelter and providing supplies in exchange for Polli, even if that son of a whoring bitch *hadn't* given them the key for the protection spells. But the flowers gnawed at him. They were a sign of affection, something a man gave a woman to lift her spirits. Was the Warlord Prince *that* grateful to get a female? Or was there another reason for the gesture?

Jared watched her reach out and delicately touch the petals of a dark-orange flower. He didn't ask.

His bitter reply when she had thanked him had wounded

her deeply. It shouldn't have mattered, but it did—because a rogue who should have hated her for owning slaves had given her flowers.

She rose slowly, her hands braced on the table to support her.

Jared clenched his fists and forced himself to stay seated as she slowly, painfully, limped toward the door.

The other men glanced at her, glanced at him, and quickly looked away. He was the dominant male. His refusal to help her amounted to an order for the rest of them, and only a direct order from her would countermand it.

She had reached the door before Tomas spoke up. "Lady? Aren't you going to tell us the next part of the story?"

Jared turned to look at her. Her eyes were closed. Pain deepened the lines in her face.

"Not tonight," she said in a husky voice. She stepped out into the rain, hobbling over slippery ground to the wagon.

Guilt stabbed at Jared. As glad as they were to get away from her, she was even more relieved to get away from them. A Queen should never feel that way about the males who served her.

Jared shook his head. He *didn't* serve her. She had bought him. He owed her no loyalty. No matter how many back roads they traveled, they'd have to come close to the Winds sooner or later. That's when he'd try to slip the leash. To go home long enough to see his family, and talk to Reyna.

The dishes were washed and put away about the same time the thin mattresses, blankets, and pillows that they'd found in the cupboards that filled the left side wall were spread out over the floor.

As Jared started pulling off his boots, he noticed Thera's longing glance at the hipbath and folded screen that stood in one corner of the room. He understood the longing. He'd been wet for three days, but that didn't mean he felt clean.

Shaking her head, Thera picked up the kettle heating on the stove, dropped a gauze herb bag into two mugs, and filled them with hot water.

Jared shoved his foot back into the boot and went over to her. "We could move the hipbath over near the stove for warmth," he said quietly. "It wouldn't take much Craft to heat the water, and the screen would give you privacy."

Thera didn't look at him. Picking up a spoon, she poked at the herb bags. "Is that how it works among your people? Giving one woman an extra dollop of courtesy evens out giving another one none at all?"

Jared's temper flared, but he kept his voice even. "You approve of what she did today?"

"Even good Queens sometimes have to make bitter choices." Thera lifted the herb bags out of the mugs, set them in a small bowl, and picked up the mugs. "Step aside, Lord Jared. I want to turn in now."

"You're going out to the wagon," he said accusingly.

Her green eyes became shadowed with something that sent a shiver up his spine, reminding him that, even when she was broken, it was wiser not to tangle with a Black Widow.

"Are you going to try and stop me?" she asked too gently.

Jared stepped aside. When she closed the door behind her, he let out the breath he hadn't realized he'd been holding.

A few minutes later, little Cathryn realized she was the only female in a room full of men.

"Where's Thera?" she asked, her eyes darting around the room as if looking for a way to escape.

"Thera's staying in the wagon," Jared said soothingly. "She and the Gray Lady need to be alone tonight."

The men stirred, instinctively wanting to ease Cathryn's fear while bitterly knowing there was nothing they could do without escalating that fear into full-scale panic.

Corry worried his lower lip while he watched Cathryn. Then he pushed his mattress over until it touched hers. "It'll be all right, Cathryn. I'll sleep right beside you."

"You can't," Cathryn said shrilly. "You're a boy."

Blaed cleared his throat. "Since Corry's taken on the duties of an escort, it seems to me he's entitled to claim Escort's Privilege."

Cathryn looked uncertain.

Corry looked hopeful.

Eryk and Tomas looked envious.

Jared closed his eyes. Sweet Darkness, please don't let them start squabbling. Cathryn couldn't handle it, and the rest of them wouldn't tolerate it.

"What's that mean?" Cathryn finally asked.

Blaed tugged at his collar as if it had suddenly become too tight. "Well, it means that, when a Lady is feeling a bit nervous for any reason, it's an escort's duty and privilege to stay nearby, especially when she's sleeping."

"Really?" Cathryn said doubtfully.

Blaed put one hand over his heart. "Really. My cousin served as an escort, and he explained it to me."

No one spoke. No one dared move until Cathryn lay down on the mattress and shyly smiled while Corry tucked the blanket around her.

His eyes shining with pride and pleasure, Corry got settled on his own mattress, as close to the edge as possible.

Jared looked away to hide his smile. He'd bet his boots that, by morning, those two would be curled up together like two puppies.

The rest of them settled down. The candlelights that sat on a couple of small tables tucked against the walls were extinguished, but the fire in the hearth still provided enough light to see by.

Jared pulled off his boots and set them beside his mattress. Tucking the blanket around him, he vanished the rest of his clothes and sighed with pleasure. With luck, he'd be up early enough to wash before Cathryn woke up, before Thera and the Gray Lady stirred.

Despite his fatigue, sleep was a long time coming. The events of the day kept chasing each other, refusing to be stilled. He thought about the pride and pleasure in Corry's eyes, thought about Thera's remark about courtesy. No matter how he justified it, he couldn't dismiss the knowledge that he, not Thera, should have been sleeping in the wagon tonight. He was the experienced pleasure slave. This would have been a perfect opportunity for the Gray Lady to use him without calling attention to it. And he could have used those private hours to learn more about her, which was essential if he wanted to find a way around the Invisible Ring, to ease his way home.

Too late now.

Jared looked at the jug of flowers sitting on the wooden table and couldn't shake the feeling that, somehow, he'd made a mistake.

CHAPTER TEN

Krelis settled into a corner of the small carriage, soothed by the driver's murmurs and the horse's clip-clop rhythm. He could have hired one of the horseless coaches that were starting to fill up Draega's wide streets and replace this quainter way of traveling, but they never felt quite right. Besides, there was something a little distasteful about using Craft to perform a task previously done by an animal. Oh, he'd heard the arguments in favor of the new coaches—no dependence on an animal's well-being, cleaner streets, work for the coach drivers who had gotten tired of draining so much of their strength so that their inferiors could ride the Winds—but seeing another connection lost between the Blood and the land sometimes made him feel like he was standing in front of a closed window, trying to feel the wind.

Krelis shut his eyes. He was just tired and impatient for news—and troubled by the High Priestess's coy remarks about giving him a little more help. He understood her wanting to eliminate an enemy whose existence continuously undermined her plans for Terreille, but to sidestep explaining the arrangements she had made . . .

He understood that, too. She was probably still feeling raw about the last Master's betrayal. It would take some time to earn her trust.

Besides, the first rule of the court was, Dorothea was never wrong.

Even with that interference, it shouldn't take the tame marauder bands long to find the Gray-Jeweled bitch. The spelled brass buttons he'd given his pet would lead them right to her. And they, in turn, would send him the buttons they found so that he could extract any messages his pet might have added.

No, it wouldn't take much longer.

Then, maybe, he could get some sleep.

CHAPTER ELEVEN

Refreshed by a quick morning bath and a change of clothes, and fortified with strong, heavily sugared coffee, Jared stepped outside and wondered which would be more dangerous: asking Thera if she intended to make breakfast or having the men combine their limited cooking skills and risk her sharp-tongued wrath if the food was only marginally edible. Although, with Polli gone, Thera would need more help than Cathryn could give her, and no one expected a Queen to do chores, even though the Gray Lady had surprised them all by doing her share before she injured her knee. So Thera's new helper would have to be male, and she'd just have to choke on it.

Jared smiled. Maybe they could draw straws every morning. Short straw got to help Thera for the day. That would certainly start the mornings off with a kick. And since everyone would have an equal chance, no one could resent him for getting stuck with the duty.

Still smiling, he started walking toward the pedlar's wagon. The air had a crisp, clean bite to it, and the sky, for the first time in days, held no threat of rain.

Out of the corner of his eye, Jared noticed Tomas trotting toward him from the direction of the privy hole. He raised his hand in greeting, but his smile faded when he saw the boy's worried expression.

Spiders and other insects were to be expected in a little wooden structure that enclosed a hole in the ground, although the herb bags that were hung in the corners not only freshened the air but seemed to discourage crawling company. Even though he hadn't seen them, there were probably mice around—maybe even rats.

Jared stiffened. Ordinary rats could be enough of a nuisance, but disturbing a nest of viper rats could be deadly. And young boys weren't always sensible.

He could still feel the sharp fear that had jabbed at him the summer his brother Davin had been bitten by a viper rat; could still remember how the venom had caused the six-year-old boy's forearm to swell grotesquely. Even with Reyna's healing skill, Davin had been ill for several days.

"Tomas?" Jared searched the boy's face for any sign of illness or injury. "What's wrong?"

Tomas didn't look back at the privy hole. His worried brown eyes fastened on the wagon. "They're both feeling pissy this morning."

Jared sighed, both annoyed and relieved. "So what else is new?"

"I—I think Thera's sick. She acted real funny when I asked them if they wanted some coffee. And the Gray Lady didn't say nothing either, and you *know* she likes coffee."

Yes, he did. Jared had never thought of coffee as a sensual experience until he'd watched the Gray Lady drink her morning cup.

Jared drained his cup and handed it to Tomas. "Tell Blaed and Thayne to do what they can with breakfast. I'll see what I can do for the Ladies."

Glad to hand the worry over to someone else, Tomas dashed for the stone building.

Jared squared his shoulders and forced his legs to move toward the wagon. Prudently standing to one side, he knocked on the door.

No answer.

He knocked harder.

Still no answer.

Were they too weak or too sick to call out?

His heart climbed into his throat as he pushed the door open.

"Get out!" Thera's voice was full of temper edged with fear.

Jared stood on the top step and swore silently. Thera and the Gray Lady sat on the benches, two lumpy shapes hunched under a mound of blankets. Tomas was right; neither of them looked well.

And, Hell's fire, it was *cold* in there! Were they both masochists or was this a subtle punishment for the males, a way to strip the pleasure out of having slept in a warm room? Maybe Thera couldn't have sustained a warming spell all night, but the Gray Lady certainly could have with a minimal amount of her Gray strength.

Jared opened his mouth to make a stinging comment . . . and tasted the difference in the air. Thera was in her moontime.

It was one of those things that remained unspoken between the genders. Once a Blood male passed puberty, he became sensitive to the smell of moon's blood and could recognize it no matter how carefully a woman tried to mask it. Jared wasn't sure if it was a subtle change in a woman's psychic scent or a slight difference in her physical scent or a combination of both that alerted the males, but they could taste it in the air, smell it when they passed her on the street.

It was the time when every sexually mature witch became vulnerable. For the first two or three days, doing more than basic Craft was physically painful for her, and the stronger the witch, the more of her psychic strength had to be drained into the Jewels during those days because her body couldn't tolerate it.

During that time, unless she had the protection of other witches, she was at the mercy of the males around her.

Within a family, that sharpened the males' territorial and protective instincts. Within a court, it sharpened the tempers of all the males in the First Circle. Within a village, men learned to ride the ebb and flow of women's moods, concentrating their attention on the women in their families, their lovers, and particular friends who had to tolerate affectionate bullying and overprotectiveness.

"Would you like some coffee?" Jared asked, glancing at the Gray Lady. Hell's fire, she really didn't look well either. Maybe she had caught a chill. The Darkness only knew why the rest of them hadn't gotten sick after walking in cold rain for the past few days and sleeping outside on wet ground. Maybe that's why she hadn't answered him yesterday until he'd contacted her with a Green communication thread. Maybe she'd already started to become ill and didn't feel physically strong enough to wear the Gray. The Green could be her Birthright Jewel. It would make sense that she'd ease back to her Birthright Jewel if she wasn't feeling well. Damn. How sick was she? A chill could turn into something serious if it wasn't taken care of. But it could just be a griping belly. That could make a person feel miserable without being serious. If he asked, would she tell him what was wrong? Doubtful, unless she became very sick. And if she did . . . What in the name of Hell was he supposed to do if she did?

And why did it matter so much if she was sick or not?

He didn't want to think about that. So he focused his attention on the fact that neither of them had answered his first question and tried again. "How about some hot water for a brew?"

"Thank you," the Gray Lady said dully. "That would be welcome."

Jared closed the door and blew out a breath. After breakfast, he would clear everyone out of the building and give the two women some privacy if they wanted a hot bath. And he'd have to remember to give Thera discreet opportunities to take care of her private needs.

There wasn't anything he could do for the Gray Lady without knowing what was wrong with her, but if she allowed him to look through her healing herbs, he knew several brews that would help ease Thera's discomfort.

The Sadist had taught him every one of them.

At the time, it had amazed him that a man who was a master at emotional cruelty was so well versed at easing a woman's physical discomfort. On the other hand, he never saw Daemon give one of those brews to the Queen who controlled them or the aristo witches in her First Circle. Those brews found their way to the female servants' living quarters and the women who would get no other pampering.

Brock met him at the door when he returned to the stone building.

"Problem?" Brock asked quietly.

"Thera's feeling a little bitchy," Jared replied, wondering if men from other Territories used that phrase in the same way.

Brock's shoulders relaxed. "Ah. Well, we can give her breathing room and keep the pups from pestering her. What about the Gray Lady?"

Jared shrugged and lied to himself that he didn't feel concerned. "She might have a stomach chill or something."

Blaed and Thayne both had more skill at a stove than he'd suspected, and a few minutes later he and Tomas were carrying full plates and cups of hot water to the wagon. Keeping his distance so that he wouldn't upset Thera, he set a plate and cup next to each of them and retreated after mentioning the availability of the hipbath.

After breakfast, while the Gray Lady and Thera took the opportunity to bathe, Jared opened the wagon's door and shutters to freshen the air inside. Tomas swept the narrow bit of floor with a broom he'd found in a cupboard in the stone building. Jared shook out the blankets. Together, they made a cozy nest on each of the benches. Jared put a warming spell on the blankets, which would keep the women comfortable but wouldn't be as noticeable as warming the inside of the wagon.

"There," Tomas said, smoothing out a wrinkle in a blanket. "They'll be feeling better in next to no time."

Jared just smiled and said nothing. Tomas was a clever boy, and since he obviously knew what a woman's moontime was—who wouldn't after a few days in Polli's company?—he'd figure it out fast enough.

By the time the Gray Lady and Thera were tucked into the wagon as comfortably as possible, the sun had been up a couple of hours—not that anyone complained about getting a later start than usual.

After giving the order for them to move on, Jared waited until everyone else had reached the lane before stepping between the stone posts. He and Brock had already double-checked the buildings to be sure everything was just as they'd found it. The rest of the fresh food that had been left for them was now in a cool-spelled box in the wagon. There was nothing . . .

The chipped blue jug had been empty when he'd gone back to make the last check. Rinsed out and empty.

When he'd checked outside the buildings, there had been no sign of a bouquet of flowers tossed aside.

It didn't bother him that she'd taken that Sapphire-Jeweled bastard's flowers with her. Not at all. It was simply annoyance with himself that he hadn't thought of that ploy to gain favor with her. It was a natural response, an instinctive rivalry. A favored male was always granted special privileges. He needed that leniency more than a stranger who wasn't even around. It wasn't like the rogue would have any sexual interest in a woman old enough to be his mother—Hell's fire, his *grandmother. He* certainly didn't have any interest. Not really. After all those years as a pleasure slave, his body was confused and just reacted to anything female. The fact that he didn't respond that way to Thera and sometimes wanted to kiss the Gray Lady until her bones melted didn't mean anything.

So it didn't mean a thing to him that she had taken that bastard's flowers with her because he was *not* jealous.

Damn.

Jared closed his eyes and shook his head. He'd gone about dealing with the Gray Lady all wrong. He should have remembered that she liked balls and sass, would probably have been more responsive to a male companion who made an effort to be charming. So from now on, he'd be charming even if it choked him. He used to be able to charm women. How many times had he coaxed Reyna into letting him have an extra nutcake? A boy who could charm his mother into spoiling his appetite for dinner should be able to grow up into a man who could wrap an elderly Queen around his little finger—especially when that man had received a year of intense, private training in how to do just that. He should be able to charm a Queen.

Even a Gray-Jeweled Queen.

Maybe even charm her enough to coax her into making a detour to Ranon's Wood, if he couldn't find a way to slip the control of the Invisible Ring.

Taking a deep breath, Jared opened his eyes and studied the posts. Today it seemed so obvious, so easy. He traced the symbols for wind, water, and fire, then walked down the path until he reached the lane. After putting the wooden pole back on its posts to hide the way into the clearing, he walked across the lane and stood in front of the moss-covered boulders.

Wind, water, fire . . .

He caressed the face of the woman rising from the stones—and through the stone, felt the protection spells around the clearing rekey.

. . . and earth.

Because a Queen wasn't just the heart of a court, she was the heart of the land.

Slipping his hands into his coat pockets, Jared hurried to catch up with the others.

"Hand it over, you stupid turd!"

Jared broke into a run. Randolf never had that edge in his voice with anyone except Garth.

Rounding a curve where the lane fed into another road, Jared slowed to a cautious walk.

Garth held one hand behind his back, dodging and circling while Randolf tried to grab that arm.

Jared wouldn't have been amused if he'd found Eryk and Corry playing "gimme." And he was less than amused to find Randolf baiting Garth, and not just because Garth was broken. Every man had his flash point, that inner line he wouldn't be pushed beyond without striking back. Garth stood a head taller than most of them, even topping Brock by a few inches, and outweighed all of them—and all that weight was bone and hard muscle. It was easy to forget what a man his size could do because he always had that confused, kicked-puppy look on his face.

That look wasn't on Garth's face now. He moved with a warrior's assurance, and his pale blue eyes glittered with malevolence.

"Randolf!" Jared shouted.

Randolf lunged at Garth.

Garth dodged and gave Randolf a shove that sent the man flying.

"Jared!" Garth bellowed, striding toward him.

"Pull him down!" Randolf yelled as he got to his feet.

Jared backed away. Shields weren't considered permissible Craft for slaves, so a smart man tried to frighten his victim into shielding without using Craft himself. That way, the witch who owned them, alerted by her controlling ring to a forbidden use of power, punished the offender—the victim—with pain sent through the Ring of Obedience.

A man made helpless by a Ring was an easy man to kill.

Jared didn't think Garth had that much cunning left, which really didn't matter since Garth wouldn't need Craft to snap him in half, and he wouldn't stand a chance in a fight without it.

Jared dodged, slipped, tried to scramble out of reach.

Garth grabbed the back of Jared's coat and set him on his feet hard enough to make his teeth rattle.

"Jared," Garth said, holding out his huge, clenched hand.

Swallowing hard, Jared held out his hand. He shuddered with revulsion as the brass button Garth had been holding dropped into his palm. The button had the same slimy feel as Garth's psychic scent.

Anger washed through Jared. All this over a *button*?

He looked up just in time to see the knife leave Randolf's hand, aimed straight for Garth's back. "NO!"

Garth spun around, knocking the knife away with his forearm.

Randolf looked shocked.

Jared stared at Garth and wondered what the man had been before he'd ended up on the auction block at Raej.

Cold fury filled Garth's face as he walked over to where the knife lay in the road. He stepped on the blade, grabbed the hilt, and snapped the knife in half. Returning to Jared, he pointed at Jared's hand. Sweat ran down his face and his hand shook as if he were fiercely struggling against something.

"Jared," Garth said. The glitter faded from his eyes, replaced by the confused, imploring, familiar look.

"It's a button, Garth."

Garth made a frustrated sound.

Jared waited, but he could see Garth was losing the inner battle.

Garth raised his arms and let them fall, his big hands slapping his thighs in a gesture of defeat. Shaking his head, he walked away.

Randolf didn't move until Garth was well past him. Then he turned on Jared. "Now do you understand why I don't like him?"

Jared looked at the brass button. Holding a handful of phlegm wouldn't make his stomach any queasier.

His face twisting with disgust, Randolf walked over to Jared, plucked the button out of his hand, and tossed it into the bushes beside the road.

Jared rubbed his hand on his trousers.

Randolf bared his teeth. "What's it going to take to convince you that he's a danger to us?"

"Leave him alone," Jared snapped. "He's not dangerous unless he's pushed. He can't help being broken."

"He's not just broken, he's *tainted.*"

Jared's body tightened until it shook. To call one of the Blood tainted was a vicious insult, because blood was the connection between the body and the psychic strength. Someone who was condemned as being tainted was considered so fouled that his blood would contaminate whatever it was used for. That person's blood couldn't be given for an offering, couldn't be used for any Blood ceremony, couldn't be used for a healing.

"You don't know that," Jared said, forcing the words out.

"And you don't know he's not. He's out of sight half of the time, and whenever he's around the rest of us, he's always watching."

"He's mind-damaged, Randolf."

"Oh, I won't argue that someone tampered with him, but after seeing him just now, do you still believe he's as mind-damaged as he seems?"

Jared said nothing.

The anger gradually drained out of Randolf. "It's your

decision, Lord Jared. You do what you think is best." He turned and walked away.

Jared waited until Randolf was out of sight before he walked over to the knife lying in the road.

The blade was broken into small pieces. A man's foot couldn't break tempered steel like that. Craft could.

Hell's fire, Mother Night, and may the Darkness be merciful.

If Garth wasn't as damaged as he seemed to be . . .

Jared raised his hand but stopped before he raked his fingers through his hair. His hand still felt slimy, fouled.

If someone had created a spell around Garth so that he would *appear* to be mind-damaged, in the same way Sadi had created a spell to hide Blaed's true nature . . . But *why?*

His snarl echoed the wild stranger's fiercer one.

"Pet." A word slaves despised even more than "tainted." The wild stranger circled the thought and snarled again. Pet.

Why *had* the Gray Lady excluded the adult males from the story time? Because she thought they wouldn't be interested, or because she didn't want them to hear a tale about an escape to a land where the Blood still lived with honor?

Pet.

Jared started up the road at a fast walk.

Could a man be a pet without being aware of it?

Thera would know. Being broken didn't erase her knowledge or training, merely kept her from using it.

Jared looked around.

He couldn't see the wagon.

He couldn't see any sign of Randolf or Garth.

He started running.

Thera was the only person in their group who might have the answers he needed; was the only one who understood the Black Widows' Craft.

The Gray Lady was the only person in the entire Realm of Terreille who wore the Gray Jewels; was the only Queen and the only *free* person who outranked Dorothea SaDiablo.

Both of them were lying in the wagon, feeling unwell enough to be vulnerable to an unexpected attack.

And until he had some answers, there was no one he could trust to help keep them safe.

Jared stared at the swift-moving, mud-colored water. On either side of the swollen creek were the remains of the bridge they needed to cross. As he watched, the water seduced another plank of the bridge and took it for a wild ride downstream, abandoning it at the tangle of branches and debris that had piled up at the curve.

Brock hooked his thumbs into his leather belt, took a deep breath, and blew it out. "Well, that's inconvenient."

"For us," Jared agreed.

Brock narrowed his eyes. "I wondered if it could be a marauder ambush, so I took a chance and probed the area. There's no Blood around here but us. We've been visible long enough to have company if it was coming." He shook his head. "I think one of the trees that had been uprooted in the flood smashed into the bridge and pulled it down."

"Maybe." Jared wished he had insisted on talking to Thera. But when he caught up with the others, Blaed had curtly informed him that both women were sleeping, and there had been an edge to the young Warlord Prince's voice that had warned him not to push. Since his own anxiety had diminished once he could keep an eye on the women, and he didn't see any reason to aggravate the aggressive, protective instincts Blaed was fighting to keep leashed, he'd decided to wait until he could talk to Thera without drawing the other men's attention. Now, looking at the remains of the bridge and wondering if it had been the flood or Craft that had destroyed it, he regretted that decision.

"Maybe," Jared said again. "Or maybe the company just hasn't gotten here yet. Or maybe there's Blood out there who outrank you and are shielded so you're not aware of them."

He tensed when Brock's hand closed on his arm, forcing him to turn and face the other man.

"I was a First Circle guard, Warlord," Brock said, anger simmering in his voice. "The Purple Dusk may not be one of the darker Jewels, but I've got the training, and I know what to look for. When I probe to find something, I find it, if it's there at all."

Jared wasn't sure of that, but he didn't know that much about a guard's training, so he didn't disagree.

"What's happened, Jared?" Brock said, releasing Jared's arm. "You've been straight with me since we started out, and now all of a sudden you're talking smoke."

Jared turned to face the water, not so much to turn away from Brock but to keep his back to the others. He and Brock worked well together, and he liked the man. But liking and trusting weren't the same thing, and trust was what Brock was asking for now.

Keeping his voice neutral, Jared said, "If you could kill the Gray Lady, would you do it?" He flicked a glance at Brock, whose face and eyes were carefully blank.

"If she died out here, we'd be free," Brock answered, his voice giving nothing away.

"Would you kill her?" Jared pressed.

Brock seemed reluctant to answer, but finally said, "No."

Brock's answer should have made Jared feel easier. It didn't. He watched the water steal another plank from the bridge. "It could have been marauders."

Brock huffed.

"It could have," Jared insisted. "What if they destroyed the bridge to force us to take another road, find another bridge where they'll be waiting for us?"

"You mean waiting for her," Brock said slowly, rubbing his chin. "They'd have no reason to think we'd fight. Slaves, if they're smart, don't take sides. If their owner wins, they wouldn't survive the punishment if they'd helped her enemy, and they wouldn't survive what the others would do to them if they fought for her and the enemy won. By doing nothing, a slave wouldn't be any worse off and might even be granted the freedom to serve without a Ring."

"The only thing he'd be granted is the chance to whore his honor for the illusion of freedom," Jared snapped. "He'd never really be trusted, never really be free. He wouldn't be wearing a Ring he could feel or see, but—" The words suddenly stuck in Jared's throat. "But he'd be trapped by it all the same," he finished softly.

Freedom from pain. Freedom from the constant physical reminder that your body belonged to someone else who could use you, hurt you, sell you, maim you simply because she wanted to. Freedom to have a lover, maybe even children. Freedom, for the price of giving up honor.

And all a man would have to do was blindly obey.

Like he'd been doing since they'd started this fool's journey.

Rage boiled up in Jared.

"Jared?"

As Jared shook off Brock's restraining hand, he noticed the three boys scrambling among the boulders a little ways upstream, jostling each other as they threw sticks into the creek.

Jared roared to vent some of his temper. "Tomas! Eryk! Corry! Get away from there!"

Tomas grinned and waved. "We'll be careful," he shouted.

"Keep an eye on them," Jared snapped, pushing past Brock.

Ignoring the worried looks of the others waiting by the wagon, Jared headed for the Gray Lady, who'd been wandering around in the field next to the creek since they'd had to stop. She limped toward him, her arms wrapped around her belly, too focused on the ground just ahead of her to notice his approach until he was almost on top of her.

Jared grabbed her arm, too angry to be careful. "Make the Ring visible. Prove it's there. *Prove it.*"

Her eyes widened. She opened her mouth, but no sound came out.

His hand tightened. "Or add the Ring of Obedience to it. I'm not going to play your games. I'm not going to fall for your tricks. You may own my body, but you're never going to own my soul."

She stared at him as if he'd lost his mind.

Right now, he wasn't so sure he hadn't.

"The Ring of Obedience," Jared snarled.

"No." She tried to pull away from him. "You wear the Invisible Ring. That's sufficient."

"It's not going to be sufficient for long. I'll fight you with everything I am. You're not going to own me. Not that way." She had to strike back now. She *had* to. No witch would allow a slave to state bluntly that he was going to fight without punishing him for it. And once that pain blazed along his nerves, he would know for certain the Invisible Ring existed and she hadn't played him for a fool.

She didn't strike back. Instead, she snapped, "You presume a great deal, Warlord. What makes you think I want to own you in any way?"

"A bill of sale, Lady."

For some reason, his response upset her. She yanked her arm out of his grasp, stumbling back a couple of steps. "Is wearing the Invisible Ring making you suffer?"

"Yes!"

"Good!"

He opened his mouth to blast her with the foulest language he knew . . . and tasted something in the air that shouldn't have been there.

Wariness and fear shadowed her eyes as he stared at her. She slowly backed away from him.

Jared shook his head. "You can't—"

The scream came a second after he felt a surge of power.

Whipping around, Jared saw Eryk standing on top of the boulders, his arms windmilling frantically to keep from falling backward into the creek. Tomas held on to the front of Eryk's coat, leaning back and pulling hard, trying to keep the older, heavier boy from falling.

There was no sign of Corry.

Before Jared could move, another surge of power hit the boulders, shattering the rock and tossing both boys into the air. They screamed as they fell into the rushing water.

Garth burst out of the bushes at the same moment, holding up his trousers as he raced downstream and leaped into the water.

"CORRY!"

Jared whipped around again, responding to the Gray Lady's voice.

She was running—*running!*—toward a break in the trees a little ways downstream from the bridge.

Jared watched her for a moment in frozen disbelief. Then, swearing viciously as he gave in to instinct, he took off after her, counting on his longer legs, the difference in their ages, and her inexplicable moontime to stop her from doing something courageously foolish.

She must have used Craft somehow to make her knee work as if it were fully healed. And, Mother Night, she had speed!

In that moment, when he knew he wouldn't catch her in time, he would have admired her if he hadn't been so furious with her.

Instead of scrambling down the slope to the water's edge, she lengthened her stride for the last few paces and made a Craft-enhanced leap, flying over the sloping dry land and new shallows. As she neared the middle of the creek, a blast of power struck her, spinning her round and round, smashing through the Craft she'd used.

She hit the water on her back and disappeared.

Thera's voice, shrill and furious, filled Jared's mind in the same instant the Gray Lady hit the water. *Don't use Craft! *Don't use Craft!* There's a spell here that twists it and turns it back on you!*

Jared veered to the right, downstream, pushing himself harder. Using Craft, he could have lifted her out of the water as soon as he caught sight of her and floated her to dry ground. Instead all he could do was try to get ahead of her and think of something then.

He plunged down the slope, grabbing at trees to stay on his feet. As soon as he had a clear view of the creek, he stopped and scanned the water, looking for some sign of them. He spotted Corry thrashing helplessly, slowly drifting toward the tangle of branches and debris.

Slowly. As if something was holding the boy back. As if someone's feet were digging into the creek bottom.

Damn that woman. This wasn't a chess game!

Muttering vile promises of what he was going to do when he finally got his hands on her, Jared looked around for something, anything he could use to reach them. Then he bared his teeth in a feral smile.

Like to like.

If he couldn't use Craft to help, he would play the game by the enemy's rules and use it to destroy.

Raising his right hand, he aimed for the ground in front of a slim, tall tree that stood at the water's edge several yards downstream and unleashed the Red.

The ground around the tree exploded, tearing out part of its roots before his Red strength rebounded, heading straight for him.

Jared dove, rolling the rest of the way down the slope.

The blast of power sizzled over his head, tearing up the ground where he'd been standing.

Cautiously raising his head, Jared watched the tree topple into the creek. Still tethered to the land by what was left of its roots, it bounced on top of the water.

Scrambling to his feet, Jared plunged into the water, cursing as his feet tangled in submerged undergrowth. Once he pulled free, he swam across the current, fighting to reach Corry.

It took seconds, seemingly centuries for him to reach the middle of the creek. He pulled his legs under him and planted his feet to test the water's depth. It broke against his shoulders.

Too long, Jared thought as he ducked under the water, clamped his hands around the Gray Lady's waist, and yanked her to the surface. *She's been under too long.*

She gasped for air, swallowed water, and choked. Jared swore as he wormed one arm between her belly and Corry's back to hold her up. At least he didn't have to worry about losing Corry. She could barely breathe, and her arms were still wrapped so tightly around the boy it was going to take a couple of strong men to pry him away from her.

She coughed up water, and Jared swore again.

"Breathe, damn you, breathe!" Jared shouted at her. "You are *not* going to die just to get out of a fight!"

"Sounds fair," she gasped.

Relieved that she could breathe enough to talk, Jared's arm tightened around her until she squeaked.

"We're going to play hop frog," Jared said, working to keep his voice calm while his instincts shivered a warning that some terrible danger was coming closer.

"I am *not* going to jump over your shoulders," she growled.

"Not leap frog. *Hop* frog. Didn't you play any games when you were a girl?"

"You can't hop if you can't touch the ground."

"The tallest one hops. The shorter ones just hang on for the ride. I used to do this all the time with my little brothers when the creeks were running high. It's fun." And thank the Darkness Reyna had never found out about it.

"Only a boy would think a stupid, dangerous game was fun."

"Lady, you've got a lot of brass to call anything anyone else does stupid or dangerous."

He made the first hop before she could sputter a reply, letting the current push them a ways before planting his feet again. On the second hop, his foot slipped and they all went under. Since the Lady was too busy coughing and cursing him to say anything useful, he hopped again.

They reached the toppled tree on the fourth hop.

Jared grabbed the tree to keep his balance while he started to walk them toward the bank.

"Jared!" Blaed rushed down the slope to the water's edge. Bracing himself against the tree, he waded in far enough to yank Corry out of the Gray Lady's arms. "We've got to get out of here. Thera says a spell's been triggered and the power feeding it is going to hit this place anytime now."

Hell's fire, Mother Night, and may the Darkness be merciful.

They scrambled for the bank.

"I brought the saddle horses," Blaed said. "The others took the wagon and will get as far away as they can before it hits."

"Go," Jared said as soon as Blaed reached dry ground.

Blaed didn't bother to answer. Carrying Corry, he climbed the slope as fast as he could.

Jared half carried the Gray Lady the last few steps to the bank and didn't think it strange that she was struggling so hard until she tried to take a step up the slope and almost fell.

"Go," she said, trying to push him away while balancing on her left leg. "Go."

"Feather-brained, mule-headed woman," Jared growled as he ducked under her batting hands and hoisted her over his shoulder. "Stop squirming, or you'll get us both killed."

"I can—"

"Shut up," Jared said in a deceptively mild tone that no one but a blithering idiot—or a Queen—could have failed to understand.

Her breath came out in an angry hiss.

Choosing to interpret that as agreement, he scrambled up the slope.

"I told you to go," Jared said when he reached the top and saw Blaed holding both horses, waiting for them.

"Why should he take orders any better than you do?" the Gray Lady muttered against his back.

Jared set her down too hard next to the bay gelding. Her gasp of pain hurt him, but he didn't allow himself to think about it as he tossed her into the saddle and swung up behind her.

There wasn't time to think about anything.

As soon as Blaed swung up behind Corry, they kicked the horses into a gallop and raced across the field, angling toward the road.

How much time did they have? And how would the spell unleash? Would it radiate from a central point or just fan out on this side of the creek? The damage a psychic unleashing could do would depend on the strength of the person who had fed the spell. His and the Gray Lady's inner barriers should be able to hold against that kind of unleashing, but the others might not survive it. If the spell manifested in some physical way . . .

Wind? Water?

They reached the road at the same moment the spell unleashed.

Jared glanced over his shoulder and saw a mature tree explode skyward like a burning arrow released from a bow.

The muscles in his chest locked. He couldn't breathe.

Behind them, a huge ball of witchfire consumed the trees around the creek and expanded outward at a fierce speed.

Jared urged the gelding on, trying to wring a little more speed out of the animal.

Witchfire had a radius. It had a limit that depended on the amount of power that had been used to create it. It could heat and it could burn—sweet Darkness, how it could burn!—but it couldn't continue expanding after the power was exhausted. With all the rain they'd had over the past few days, it wasn't likely that the witchfire would spark a natural fire. They should be safe enough . . . if they could outrun it.

He saw the wagon rattling down the road ahead of them.

He heard the witchfire roaring behind him.

Too slow. Too slow!

Jared pressed against the Gray Lady. If the witchfire caught up to them, he'd risk the working distance of that twisting spell and throw a Red shield behind them. Even if that spell turned his own strength against him, the shield might buy her enough time to escape the witchfire.

They were gaining on the wagon.

The witchfire was gaining on them.

The roan mare Blaed was riding squealed and shot ahead of them.

Jared felt the heat on his back.

He raised his hand at the same moment the Gray Lady raised hers.

Swearing when he saw the Green Jewel in her ring, he grabbed her wrist and pulled her hand down before she could throw up a shield. He'd risk the range of the twisting spell and having his own power turned against him, but he'd be damned if he'd let *her* risk it.

Fire roared behind them.

The wagon was too close now. Too close.

The gelding raced past a tree a second before the fire consumed it.

"We made it!" Blaed shouted. "Mother Night, we made it!"

Jared glanced back.

A wall of witchfire filled the road behind them, but it wasn't moving forward anymore.

"Thank the Darkness." Jared pressed his cheek against

the Gray Lady's head as he reined in the laboring horse. When the gelding slowed to a stumbling walk, he slid off its back. He wasn't sure his legs would hold him, but they couldn't afford to ruin the horses. "Come on, boy," he soothed, sliding the reins over the gelding's lowered head so he could lead it. "A little farther and you can rest."

He looked at the Gray Lady slumped in the saddle, her face hidden by her wet, tangled hair. His eyes narrowed.

Funny. He wouldn't have thought gray hair would look that dark when it was wet.

"Jared!" Brock shouted.

The wagon had slowed to a walk, too. Brock swung off the driving seat and jumped to the ground.

Jared waved at him. "Keep them walking."

Brock started toward him, looked behind Jared at the Gray Lady, and hesitated. Then he waved an acknowledgment and turned around.

The wagon door opened. Looking pale, Thera braced herself in the opening. Her green eyes swept over Blaed, who was leading the mare, and Corry, who was still in the saddle, pale and shaking. They lingered for a moment on the Gray Lady, and finally settled on him.

Jared had the uneasy feeling she was looking for some kind of answer. Problem was, he didn't know the question.

Before he could say anything, she stepped back and closed the door.

Jared looked at Blaed and frowned. "I told you to go."

Blaed shrugged. "Thera told me to bring you back. If I had to fight with someone about it, better you than her."

Jared grunted. Then he slanted another look at the young Warlord Prince. "You like her."

"She's got a Harpy's temper," Blaed snapped as his face colored.

Jared grinned. "You like her." The grin faded. Slaves couldn't afford those kinds of feelings.

They walked for several minutes before Jared whistled sharply and raised his hand, calling a halt. The horses were cool enough to stand for a few minutes while they changed into dry clothes and got the Gray Lady settled into the wagon. She hadn't said anything since he'd tossed her onto the gelding's back. She had to be in pain. Her enduring it in silence reminded him why he was so furious with her.

The moment the wagon stopped, Thera threw the door open and scrambled down the steps, almost falling in her haste.

Wondering why she seemed so tense now that the danger was over—it *was* over, wasn't it?—Jared reached up to help the Gray Lady dismount.

And found himself reaching for a gray-eyed, dark-haired, *young* witch dressed in the Gray Lady's clothes.

She frowned at him, and said, "What's wrong?" at the same moment Thera said, "I'm sorry."

Fury blinded him. Hell's fire, he had *hated* witches who hadn't made him this furious.

Snarling, he clamped his hands around her waist and hauled her out of the saddle. As she fell forward, the Green Jewel hanging from a gold chain around her neck slipped out of the torn coat and tunic. Her gasp of pain and surprise—and the bruises already darkening on her shoulders and chest where she must have struck submerged rocks—stopped him from letting go of her until she had time to grab the gelding's saddle to keep her balance. Then he stepped back, not trusting himself not to strike out.

"Who are you?" he said roughly.

"I'm sorry," Thera said again.

Looking puzzled, the witch's gray eyes flicked to the men Jared could feel gathering behind him, to the children who had emerged from the wagon, to Thera, and, finally, to him.

She started to raise her hand to brush back her tangled hair, but didn't complete the gesture. Pulling what was left of her braid over her shoulder, she studied the dark hair, and then muttered, "Hell's fire."

"Who are you?" Jared roared. He didn't know which made him more furious: that his mind had been tricked into believing this was the Gray Lady or that his body hadn't been fooled.

She wobbled a little when the gelding shifted nervously, but she squared her shoulders and raised her chin.

The admiration he felt for the strength and pride he saw in her eyes only fueled his temper, and the wild stranger inside him started howling at him to protect, protect, protect. He tried to push it away by reminding himself that he was a Ringed slave, but instincts that had been bred into Blood males over dozens of generations weren't easily banished by a Ring or a word.

In a commanding voice, she said, "I am Lady Arabella Ardelia. On the Gray Lady's behalf, I'm taking you to Dena Nehele."

Behind him, Brock and Randolf swore quietly.

Jared ground his teeth. Arrogant, stubborn, courageous, feather-brained little fool! Did she really think men like Brock and Randolf would just shrug and continue to obey her unless she used the Ring of Obedience and brutally revived their fear of the kind of pain it inflicted? Especially once they realized she was handicapped right now by more than physical injuries?

He took a step toward her.

"Stay back," she said, her body tensing.

Jared bared his teeth in a savage smile. "You want me to stay back? *Use the Ring.*"

Her eyes widened.

Jared held his breath, waiting. She *had* to use the Invisible Ring now. She had to. She'd been able to avoid using it when he'd challenged her a short while ago, but she couldn't now that he'd challenged her in front of the others. His Jewels outranked hers. He was a danger to her. If she didn't use the Ring to pull him down, he could smash through her inner barriers and tear her mind apart. Damn her, she *had* to use it to protect herself, to reassert her control over all of them. She *had* to hurt him to prove that she could still brutally control the strongest male among them—and would inflict the same kind of pain on the others if the males didn't continue to obey her.

Instead, she let go of the saddle and tried to brace herself for a fight.

Swearing, Jared closed the distance between them and scooped her up in his arms. "You don't need a pleasure slave," he snarled as he stomped to the wagon, "you need a keeper."

"I do not—"

"Shut up."

"Jared," Thera warned as he brushed past her and the children. "She needs attention and—"

"In a minute." He shouldered the door open and kicked it closed in Thera's face. After setting his bundle of wet, bedraggled witch on the bench, he stepped back and leaned against the door, preventing anyone from interrupting them.

One of the shutters behind the driving seat had fallen open during the wild ride. Using Craft, he closed it and created a ball of witchlight, floating it near the bench so he could take a good look at her.

She wasn't pretty—he'd always associated pretty with delicate—but there was a kind of strength in her face that would ripen into beauty in a few more years—a beauty that was a reflection of the deep inner strength strong Blood males found more arousing than a lush body.

Sadi had once said strength attracted strength, that a strong witch's psychic scent acted like a catnip on strong Blood males. Even if the attraction wasn't sexual, they'd still want to touch her, smell her, cuddle up next to her. It was part of a witch's power over the males, something that soothed her chosen as well as filling them with possessive savagery.

Standing there, Jared felt the pull of her psychic scent—the same pull that had been luring and confusing him since she'd bought him. Knowing she wasn't the old woman he'd thought she was, he felt his blood start to simmer with a dangerous hunger.

And flavoring all of it was fury fueled by relief.

Since fighting would help him keep his distance until he had time to think, he lashed out. "You mule-headed little idiot! You had no business jumping into that creek. You could have been killed—or didn't you think about that?"

"If I hadn't jumped in, Corry—"

Jared rode right over her. "Corry's male. Males are expendable."

Her gray eyes turned almost black with temper.

Remembering how their chess game had ended, he abandoned that line of attack and chose another. "Was this some kind of game?" he demanded. "The little witch decided to masquerade as a grown-up, go to Raej, and buy a few slaves for fun?"

"Not for fun," she snapped. "For the Gray Lady."

"For the Gray Lady. Of course. How could I forget? Do you even know her? Or was that the best disguise you could think of?"

"Of course I know her." She raised her chin and glared at him. "I'm in her First Circle."

Jared narrowed his green eyes. A young, talented witch *might* serve in a Territory Queen's First Circle in order to receive special training before ruling a Province or District on that Queen's behalf. "How old are you?"

"Thirty-seven."

He laughed, but there was no humor in the sound. If the little witch wanted to play games, he'd play games.

He raked his eyes over her in a way that couldn't be interpreted as anything but an insult. "I'd guess fifteen. Maybe sixteen."

"I'm twenty-one!"

She sounded too outraged to be lying.

"And with the Gray Lady's consent, you went trotting off to Raej, pretending to be a Gray-Jeweled Queen." He shook his head and tsked. "Not a very sporting thing for a Queen to ask of a young protégée . . . unless, of course, she was trying to eliminate a rival."

Her eyes glittered with suppressed fury, but her voice became dismissively chilly. "I told you everything you need to know."

He studied her for a moment. That she'd taken an insult to the Gray Lady personally was a strong indication that she *was* a member of the First Circle—or at least a member of the court. And, perhaps, telling the truth.

He saw her shiver and leashed his temper. What was wrong with him that he was fighting with her when she needed attention? His father would have skinned him for neglecting his duties for such an indulgence.

Stepping away from the door, Jared reached for her coat. "I'll help you get out of those wet clothes."

"No," she said quickly, her hands clutching the front of

the coat and tunic, holding them closed. She pressed her back against the storage boxes, her body tensing as he bent over her. "I can manage."

Jared closed his hand over one of her ice-cold fists and tugged gently. "You're cold, exhausted, bruised, and can't even stand up without falling over. According to all the rules my father thumped into my stubborn head, this is exactly the sort of circumstance when a Queen should put aside her pride and let someone help her."

He tugged again. Her fist tightened.

He tried dredging up the smile that used to charm Reyna into giving him an extra nutcake.

She stared at him as if he'd grown fangs.

"Hell's fire, Lady," Jared growled as he tried to loosen her hands. "This can't be the first time a man has offered to undress you."

She said nothing.

All right, he understood her being nervous. They'd been arguing. It was her moontime, and she was vulnerable. Her disguise had failed for some reason, and she didn't have the Gray Lady's reputation to hide behind anymore. But, Hell's fire, you'd think she'd never—

Jared took a good look at her pale, tight face and backed away so fast he yelped when he hit the door. His hand shook as he pointed a finger at her, and said accusingly, "You're a virgin. Hell's fire, Mother Night, and may the Darkness be merciful, *you're a virgin.*"

Still clutching the coat, she eyed him warily. "There's no reason to get hysterical. It's not contagious."

Jared raked his fingers through his hair, dizzied by the conflicting emotions spinning through him. "What's wrong with your people? What's wrong with your *family?* How could they let a virgin Queen out of her home village without an escort, let alone out of the Territory?" His temper roared to life with a vengeance. "What kind of man is your father to let you go to a place like Raej?"

"What do *you* know about my people or my family?" She swung her legs off the bench and sucked air through her teeth. "And don't you dare insult my father!"

Jared took a step forward. "If you stand on that leg, I'll

do what your father should have done. I'll put you over
my knee and wallop some sense into you! I swear it!"

"Unlike some people, I don't sit on my brains, Warlord!"

"That's highly debatable, Lady!"

Someone tried to open the door and smacked his arm
since he was still blocking it.

Jared cursed, thought about throwing his weight against
the door to give whoever was on the other side a taste of
wood, heard the feminine snarl, and thought again. Rubbing his arm, he stepped farther into the wagon to let
Thera enter.

"That's enough," Thera said, her eyes chips of green ice.
"The Lady needs care, which even a male should be able
to figure out."

Jared bared his teeth at her, at the same time wondering
if a man could be castrated by a look.

Thera tossed a blanket at him. "Hang that up and get
out of those wet clothes before you get sick and become
completely useless. I'll help the Lady."

He'd just bet she'd help the Lady, Jared thought as he
used Craft to hang the blanket. He called in the cloth traveling bag he'd been given to store his extra clothes and dug
through it, looking for something to wear that didn't smell
too ripe.

Of course Thera would help the Lady. Why wouldn't
she? Two of a kind, that's what they were. Stubborn, tem-
peramental, always sure they knew better than a man even
if he had more experience, always so damn sure they could
do just fine on their own, thank you very much.

Not finding anything clean to wear except the thin tunic
and trousers he'd been given at Raej didn't help his temper.
He tossed them back into the bag and stripped. Smelling
ripe would keep everyone away from him, which suited him
just fine. Besides, after what they'd just been through, they
needed time to recover, time to think, time to plan. And
while they were doing that, he was damn well going to find
a way to wash these clothes.

"I'm sorry," Thera said, her voice a little muffled by the
blanket. "When Garth got Eryk and Tomas out of the
creek, I pulled out the chest with your healing supplies.

Foolish. My wits must have been scattered . . . or else those damn spells were muddling my head. There was no reason to try to drag it outside since they were bringing the boys to the wagon. It was heavier than I thought."

"It would have gotten heavier," the Lady said quietly. "Several spells had been put on it to prevent anyone but me from moving it."

Thera sighed. "I should have realized that. *I should have realized that.*" She sounded fierce and upset. Then she sighed again. "Anyway, when I pulled it out the door, I dropped it on the steps. The back of it got punctured and must have torn the tangled web that created the illusion."

Jared kept still, hardly daring to breathe. He had the feeling whatever they might say to each other now might not be said at all if they remembered he was there.

"It doesn't matter," the Lady said. After a moment, she added, "Besides, you knew anyway."

Jared could almost feel Thera's shrug. "I guessed. Since I was trained in it, it's easy enough for me to recognize the Hourglass's Craft." Another bit of silence. "I guessed," Thera said, sounding careful, "just like you guessed I wasn't broken."

What?

Jared stared at the blanket. Then he closed his eyes and swallowed hard. Hell's fire, Mother Night, and may the Darkness be merciful. Thera. Unbroken. They'd all been fencing with a Black Widow who still wore the Jewels and had the full use of her particular Craft.

"Come on," Thera said. "Let's get you out of those wet clothes."

Hearing the familiar sounds of someone getting undressed, Jared hurriedly pulled on layers of clothes. If he added warming spells to them, they should keep him comfortable enough for the next few hours since his coat was soaked. Even Craft couldn't instantly dry material. At least he didn't think it could. The next time he met a hearth-witch, he'd ask her.

The rustling on the other side of the blanket stopped.

"Mother Night," Thera said. "You're a mess. Didn't you miss *any* of the rocks?"

Jared clenched his hands to keep from tearing down the blanket. He gritted his teeth to keep silent.

She was hurt. She was hurt. She was hurt.

All the training that had lain dormant for the past nine years came rushing back, overwhelming him with its fierceness. He wanted to lift his head and howl out his frustration. He wanted to hold her, yell at her, examine every bruise, and then kiss her to soothe the hurt.

How dare she be so careless, jumping into the creek like that? She was lucky she only had bruises instead of broken bones. How dare she, a *virgin* who was so terrifyingly vulnerable to a male attack, make a journey like this without even *one* loyal male to look after her? Didn't she realize how precious Queens were, how vital to the Blood's survival? And how dare she create this frenzied need in him to protect without giving him the outlet of honorable service?

Well, he'd be damned if he'd let her get away with it.

Fuming, Jared vanished the traveling bag and called in his Jewels. Two thin, wooden, rectangular boxes floated in front of him. He opened the first one and stared at his Birthright Opal, the gold jewelry gleaming against the box's black-velvet lining. He brushed his finger over the ring and pendant. He'd worn the pendant since the Birthright Ceremony he'd had when he was seven, but the Opal ring had been made just before he'd made the Offering to the Darkness and came away with the Red. It had been a gift from his parents for his eighteenth birthday.

That was the only day he'd ever worn it.

He closed that box and vanished it, then opened the box that held the Red. Except for a few desperate moments over the years when he'd slipped on the ring, craving the feel of it on his finger, he hadn't worn the Red Jewels—hadn't worn *any* Jewels—since the night he was Ringed. Slaves weren't allowed to acknowledge their strength openly, not even the strength that was their birthright.

He slipped the Red-Jeweled ring onto the third finger of his right hand. His left hand covered it protectively as he savored the bond that had been denied for nine years.

Taking a steadying breath, he licked his lips and picked up the pendant. No clasp to break or open. Just a chain of carefully formed gold links, long enough to let the power in that reservoir rest beside his heart.

He used Craft to put on the pendant. The cool gold settled around his neck, then warmed against his skin.

As he vanished the wooden box, Jared realized it was very quiet on the other side of the blanket.

Quiet and tense.

They knew he'd called in the Jewels. Even during her moontime, the one thing a witch continued to channel power through was the controlling ring linked to the Rings of Obedience. The controlling ring—and the males in the court who served her—were her only defense against slaves who would have taken advantage of her vulnerability to break free or destroy her.

Right now it didn't matter if the Invisible Ring was linked to the controlling ring. The Queen who wore that ring was in no condition to fight him.

Which made him angry all over again.

He pushed the blanket aside.

Thera rose from the other bench, defiant.

Ignoring her, he looked at the young Queen now dressed in a long gray skirt and gray sweater.

"Even if we don't push the horses, we'll be able to get back to the clearing before dark," he said.

"No." The Lady chewed her lower lip. "We have to go on."

"There's nowhere else to go," Jared said, biting back his temper. "Short of dragging them, you're not going to get anyone to go back to that creek. This road didn't branch off anywhere between here and the clearing. We won't make it any farther before nightfall anyway. We're going back."

"We have to go on," she said stubbornly.

Jared ground his teeth and tried to find something to say that he wouldn't have to apologize for later.

"Jared's right," Thera said after a moment. "We need time to rest—and to prepare. The clearing is the best place to do both."

"That attack might not have been meant for us," the Lady said quietly.

"Doesn't really matter, does it?" Thera said just as quietly. "We were lucky this time. If we're not up to strength and able to think clearly, we might not be as lucky next time."

The Lady sighed. "All right. We'll go back to the clearing."

"Thank you, Lady," Jared said testily. It galled him that she had argued with him but had yielded to Thera.

Squeezing past them, he reached the door.

"One thing," he said, looking over his shoulder at Thera. "Since you're not broken, what Jewels do you wear?"

Thera looked amused. "I wear the Green, Lord Jared."

Mother Night.

Two of a kind, Jared thought, flinging open the door. He strode to the bay gelding and mounted. "We're going back to the clearing," he told Brock. "I'll take point. You and Randolf take the rear guard. Thayne, you lead the team. Blaed, you're with me." He looked at Eryk and Tomas, who were huddled in blankets, and little Cathryn, who was clinging to Corry. "You children ride inside the wagon."

Brock gave one pointed look at the Red-Jeweled ring on Jared's right hand and nodded.

As Jared nudged the gelding forward, he heard Tomas say, "You know, I thought she was kind of frisky for an old lady."

Great. Wonderful.

Was he the only one who hadn't figured it out?

As soon as he passed the wagon, he urged the gelding into a trot, not waiting for Blaed.

A minute later, he caught up to Garth. The big man hadn't changed his wet clothes before heading back down the road. Jared slowed the gelding to a walk and waited for Garth to look at him.

He studied the man's face. What lay behind those pale blue eyes? "Thank you for saving Eryk and Tomas."

Garth just looked at him. Then his lips curved in a slow smile. He raised one huge hand in a casual salute and turned his attention back to the road.

Too many things hidden, Jared thought, as Blaed joined him. A Green-Jeweled Queen pretending to be a Gray. A broken Black Widow who wasn't broken. A mind-damaged man who kept showing flashes of training and intelligence.

And, possibly, an enemy who might wear the face of a friend.

Too many questions.

Jared put those thoughts aside. There wasn't time for questions. But later, when they were all safely tucked away in the clearing, he intended to get some answers.

Using Craft to balance the two steaming mugs, Jared rapped once on the wagon's door and went in without waiting for a response.

The witchlight he'd created earlier had grown small and dim, the power that had sustained it almost exhausted. He couldn't see her face in the gloom, but opening his first inner barrier a crack was enough to sense her pain—and her fear of the male strength that might descend on her now that her ability to protect herself was so impaired. Wasn't that why she'd chosen the cold solitude of the wagon to the warmth and company in the stone building?

After feeding the witchlight a few drops of his Red strength so that they'd be able to see each other, he thought about using a warming spell to make the wagon more comfortable.

And decided against it.

"Here," Jared said, handing her one of the mugs. "This brew won't help your bruises or your knee, but it should ease the other discomfort a little."

She cradled the mug for its warmth. "Thank you," she said quietly.

Jared sat on the opposite bench and sipped his coffee. He understood the hesitation. One of the first things the Blood learned when they began their formal training was how to probe food and drink for substances that shouldn't be there. It didn't always work. There were subtle poisons, substances that were harmless until they were added to something else, sedatives that could react fast enough to leave a person at the mercy of an unsuspected enemy. She'd be a fool not to test it.

Watching her rub her finger around the mug's rim, he wondered if she could do even that much Craft right now.

"I made a cup for Thera, too," Jared said.

She took a tiny sip, then stared at the mug in surprise. "It tastes good." She studied him without quite looking at him. "Where did you learn to make a healing brew?"

"My mother is a Healer. I picked up a few things." Which wasn't quite a lie. He *had* picked up some basic healing Craft from Reyna. The moontime brews just didn't happen to be part of it.

But the words did what he'd expected them to do. A Healer was a respected woman, and there was the implicit faith that a Healer wouldn't create a brew that would harm.

He knew better. In places that stood in Hayll's shadow, Healers weren't always well trained or respected, and some had made the choice to harm others in order to save themselves.

Watching her shoulders relax as she took another sip, he felt relieved that the healing Craft was still strong in Dena Nehele.

He didn't want to hurt her. She was hurting so much already. But her self-imposed exile had made it possible for him to talk with her privately without calling attention to it, and there were questions he had put aside while they returned to the clearing, ate, and settled in for the evening, too weary to do anything more.

So he tried to keep his voice gentle and soothing, and sent out psychic tendrils of reassurance so that his strength and maleness wouldn't intimidate her so much she wouldn't talk to him.

"Lady . . ." Jared paused. Frowning, he sipped his coffee. What was he supposed to call her? Did the people in the court address her as Lady Arabella Ardelia? Formally perhaps, but surely not in a normal conversation. Lady Arabella? That made him think of a fair, dainty woman who wore ruffles and lace, not this tall, strong-boned, solid-muscled young woman with generous curves. Lady Ardelia?

Yes.

A woman as strong as the land, with a heart of fire.

The Lady, on the other hand, might have a different opinion.

"What do your people call you?" he asked, surprised at how much her answer might disappoint him.

For the first time since he'd entered the wagon, she looked directly at him. Her lips twitched. "My father calls me Bella. My mother calls me Belle." Her expression darkened, and her lips curled in a silent snarl. "My cousin calls me belly button." She sipped the brew and muttered under her breath, "I never liked my cousin."

Jared wisely raised his mug to his lips, covering the smile. "Which do you prefer?"

"Lia," she said. "When I was seven, I decided I wanted to be called Lia. So that's what everyone calls me now—except my parents."

"And your cousin," Jared added, not bothering to hide the grin.

She muttered something extremely uncomplimentary.

Lia. The name flowed over him like a warm summer wind. Lady Lia. He could imagine the village children calling to her to see the new puppy, the new kitten, the new bit of Craft that had been learned. He could hear the affectionate way the men and older women talked about her. Have you heard what Lady Lia's been up to lately?

And in the court, now and when she established her own . . . Lady Ardelia. The strong young Queen with too much courage.

Which brought him back to the beginning.

"Why?" he asked quietly.

For a while Lia just sipped the brew and didn't answer. Then she sighed. "It's the last time, you see. The Gray Lady was attacked after the spring auction, and her escorts were killed. Dorothea SaDiablo was behind that attack. The Gray Lady insisted that she had to go to Raej one more time so that our enemies would know that the strength of a Gray-Jeweled Queen still protected Dena Nehele. The males in the First Circle felt that the risks far outweighed whatever might be gained. They politely requested that she remain within the borders of Dena Nehele—and then they pulled out every scrap of Blood Law and Protocol they could find about the rights and privileges of males in the First Circle. By the time they were done, she realized their request really amounted to a command—which they vehemently denied, of course."

"Of course," Jared said politely.

She looked at him with keen suspicion.

"That doesn't explain why you're here," Jared pointed out.

She fiddled with her mug. "She couldn't go to Raej again. Even if the First Circle hadn't found a way to stop her, she couldn't go. We almost lost her the last time, and if we'd lost her before—" Lia quickly sipped her brew.

"Before?" Jared's green eyes narrowed as he watched her.

"Before the new Queen was fully trained to take her place."

Which meant that the majority of the Warlord Princes and other Queens in Dena Nehele had already agreed to accept the Gray Lady's chosen successor.

"Why did they send you? Why not a more experienced Queen?"

She worried the ragged edge of the blanket beneath her. "Well, I look a lot like Gran, and I'm the only other Queen in the family."

For a moment, Jared couldn't think of anything to say. Couldn't think at all. "Gran?" His voice cracked and rose to a squeak. "*Gran?* The Gray Lady is your *grandmother?* How?*"

Lia blinked. "The usual way. Her daughter had a daughter."

Jared drained his mug. All right. An illusion web spun by a gifted Black Widow had been able to fool the eye, had been able to somehow mask the fact that Lia wore a Green Jewel so that strangers wouldn't be able to tell it wasn't the Gray Lady. But there was nothing that could fool a male into believing any other kind of witch was a Queen—especially if he focused his attention on her.

So it made sense that they would need a Queen to impersonate a Queen. And maybe the family bond made it easier to create the illusion web, especially if Lia resembled her grandmother. Maybe there hadn't been another Queen willing to take the risk. Or maybe the Gray Lady hadn't felt she could ask someone outside of her family. Or . . .

Jared's shoulder blades twitched. He kept hoping there was another answer because, if there wasn't, he was going to be furious all over again, and he couldn't afford the luxury of telling her what he thought of the males in her Territory.

"So," he said pleasantly while the anger started simmering his blood, "since you were the only other Queen in the family, and the Gray Lady's successor, you decided to do this yourself."

She eyed him warily. "Yes." When he started swearing again, the kind of inventive curses that were designed to make another man flinch, she snarled at him. "Why are you so snappish about my father?"

"What kind of man would stand back and let you do this?"

"What would you have done if your Queen ordered you to let your daughter go?"

"I would have fought it!"

"He did! He lost." She winced and wrapped her left arm around her belly. "And now he's going to yell at me when I get home. He'll hug me and get teary about the bruises, and then he'll yell at me."

Since he wanted to do a bit of yelling himself, Jared leaned forward and patted her shoulder gently. And found he now understood his father's outbursts while still able to remember how it felt to be on the receiving end. "Doesn't seem fair, does it? Getting yelled at when you've already been through a hard time and survived it."

She shook her head and sniffed.

The pats changed to soothing circles.

Jared hesitated. "There had to be other ways of letting Dorothea know the Gray Lady is still a formidable adversary. Was going to Raej to get a few more slaves really worth this risk?"

Her eyes became brutally hard. "There are no slaves in Dena Nehele," she said coldly, and shifted just enough to let him know his touch was no longer welcome.

Hurt by the withdrawal, he matched her coldness. "Well,

if you keep your precious Territory clean of the stink of slavery, what *do* you do with the slaves you buy?"

"Send them home, of course. That is, if they want to go home."

That stopped him.

Stopped his brain, stopped his heart, and withered his anger.

"Home?" Jared's voice broke. His heart started again with a leap. "You send them home?"

Cupping both hands around her mug, Lia finished the brew. "Yes, we send them home—or invite them to stay if 'home' is no longer a safe place for them." She closed her eyes for a moment and took a couple of deep breaths. "Dorothea SaDiablo wants nothing less than to control the entire Realm of Terreille. That's been her goal since she became the High Priestess of Hayll centuries ago. Since outright war would have devastated the Realm, she had to find a different way of waging war on the rest of the Blood."

"Fear," Jared said softly. "Over time, fear between the genders would undermine a Territory."

Lia nodded. "And she *has* time since Hayllians are a long-lived race. The seeds of distrust are sown village by village while she nurtures the lighter-Jeweled witches who have the same twisted nature that she does. Strong males who might not submit to one of her pet Queens are usually Ringed young, before they become 'dangerous.' Mature males who challenge the new rule are declared rogues and are either hunted down and killed or go into hiding. All of the dark-Jeweled witches and most of the Queens are broken young so there's no one left for the males to bond to except Dorothea's chosen."

Jared set his mug on the floor and clasped his hands tightly, unable to say anything. Would slavery have been his fate even without that youthful mistake? Would the Shalador Queens have demanded he submit to a Ring of Obedience in order to control his Red strength?

No. Not in Shalador.

"It happens slowly," Lia continued. "Over several generations. On the surface, nothing seems to change because it's so subtle at first. A new interpretation of Protocol. A wariness when dealing with the stronger witches. Rumors. Stories of mistreatment. The alliance with, and dependence upon, Hayll grows and grows until the day comes when one of Dorothea's pet Queens rules the Territory. By breaking or enslaving the strongest and the best, they keep the rest of the people submissive, too afraid to fight or speak against them.

"For a long time, Gran couldn't see any way to fight Dorothea except to form strong alliances with the Queens in the neighboring Territories. Then, a few years ago, a Queen's nephew was taken from the court where he was in training, along with three other young Warlords. She searched for weeks, trying to find some trace of him. She'd almost given up when she received an unsigned note that said the young Warlord was unharmed and continuing his training—in the High Priestess of Hayll's court. If the Queen welcomed Hayll's next gesture of friendship by agreeing to meet with the Hayllian ambassadors to discuss some 'concessions,' her nephew would continue his training, unharmed. If she refused, as she'd been doing for several years, her nephew would be sold as a slave at the Raej auction."

Feeling chilled, Jared wrapped a blanket around his shoulders. "She refused."

Lia nodded. "One of the witches in her First Circle volunteered to go to Raej to buy the Queen's nephew. She took two guards with her. None of them came back."

"So the Gray Lady went the next time."

"Yes. Besides wearing the Gray Jewels, Gran can be very intimidating when she wants to be. Her friendships with Queens outside of Dena Nehele have always been discreet, so there was no reason to believe anyone at Raej would connect her with the young Warlord."

Jared's heart thudded against his chest. "She bought him?"

Lia shook her head. "He wasn't there. Not that time. To justify her presence, she bought a couple of other males, choosing by instinct. Once she got them to Dena Nehele, she offered to help them return home. At first, they didn't

believe her and kept looking for a trap. When they finally
did believe her, they didn't want to go home because, at
best, it would put their families at risk and, at worst, they'd
end up dead or enslaved again. So they stayed."

"And the Gray Lady continued to buy slaves."

"It became a subtle way to fight Dorothea. Some of the
males went home, fiercely determined to keep Hayll's taint
from spreading. Others settled in Dena Nehele or one of
the surrounding Territories."

Jared cleared his throat. "Did she ever find her friend's
nephew?"

Lia shuddered. "Yes. The fourth time she went to the
auction."

Someone hesitantly knocked on the wagon's door. Grateful for the interruption, Jared answered swiftly.

"Here," Blaed grumbled, thrusting a plate of sandwiches
and apple slices at Jared. "Thera got hungry. She also
wanted another mug of that brew you made."

"I prepared two more gauze bags before I came out
here," Jared said as he took the plate and the two filled
mugs.

"I know. The brew's in one of those mugs, too." Blaed
scowled at the mugs and then shrugged. "You'll know
which one when you taste it."

Jared thanked him and hoped Blaed made it back to the
stone building before he fell asleep.

They ate in companionable silence. Jared didn't want to
break the easiness between them, but Lia had only told
him the first half—the half, he noticed, that didn't have
much to do with her.

Jared rubbed his face, willing himself to stay awake a
little longer. "All right. The Gray Lady needed to make
one more appearance at Raej. I understand that. Sort of.
But, Lia, once you'd purchased the slaves, why didn't you
buy passage to a Coach station closer to Dena Nehele's
borders?"

"I was going to but . . ." Lia bit her lip. "The message
came, and I got scared."

He remembered the note she'd been given just before

she went into the ticket station. And the fear in her after she'd read it. "What did it say?"

" 'They're waiting for you in the west.' "

"Do you know who sent it?"

Lia shook her head. "A masculine hand, but I didn't recognize the writing. I thought it might be a trick, too. That's why . . ." She waved a hand to indicate the wagon, supplies, everything. "I didn't know what else to do."

"You did well, Lady," Jared said with warm approval. "But wasn't there a Coach station near the inn where you got the wagon and supplies? Why didn't we take another Coach from there to Dena Nehele instead of making this journey?"

Lia turned her face away from him. Her fingers worried the blanket. She nibbled her lower lip.

Jared felt the warning prickle between his shoulder blades. His heart began to pound painfully against his chest. "Why didn't we take another Coach, Lady Ardelia?" he asked softly.

"Everything cost more," she said hurriedly, defensively. "You have to hire two guard escorts if you're going to buy slaves so that one can stay with the slaves while the other accompanies the buyer, and they charged me a third more than the witch ahead of me. I couldn't go into the auction grounds without the escorts, and when I argued about it, that bastard in charge just smiled and said, 'That is the fee, Lady.' And the bidding went higher than we'd anticipated, always more than the person's 'working value.' "

She was no longer talking to him, explaining to him. He wondered how many times over the past few days she'd argued this with herself.

And what, exactly, was she trying to justify?

"I think some of the other buyers were just bidding against me to force the price up," Lia continued, sounding more and more desperate. "But it was the last time, don't you see? I couldn't walk away from the ones we'd been asked to look for. I couldn't. I tried to fool them by bidding on a few slaves and stopping when the price started to climb, but it didn't work, and after buying passage for the first Coach, there weren't enough marks left to buy passage again so I had to do something else, didn't I?"

Jared considered the expense of purchasing the horses, wagon, clothing, and supplies for this desperate gamble. Outfitting them for this journey probably cost her half the fare for herself and twelve slaves.

But that still wasn't an answer. In his youth, he'd given enough explanations at breakneck speed to know when someone else was trying to provide a smoky truth to hide the real reason for something.

He leaned over and covered her hands with his. The moment he touched her, he knew.

"How many were you supposed to bring back, Lia?" he asked softly, baiting her. His anger was rising again. And beneath the anger was grief.

So close, he thought. *So close.*

"We didn't set an exact number," Lia mumbled.

"How many?"

She trembled beneath his hands and wouldn't look at him.

"Who were you asked to look for?" Jared asked, struggling to keep his voice gentle.

She swallowed hard. "Eryk and Corry. Blaed and Thayne. Polli."

Jared's hands tightened until she made a small, hurt sound. Not trusting himself, he released her and shoved his fists into his pockets. "If you were supposed to bring Polli back, how could you give her to that rogue bastard?"

Lia's head snapped up. "Prince Talon is *not* a bastard—of any kind," she said hotly. "He's a good, honorable man. Besides, he's Polli's uncle. Since he was the one who asked us to look for her, why shouldn't I send her with him when there was the chance?"

Jared stared at Lia and then shook his head to clear it. That hard-eyed Warlord Prince was Polli's uncle? Well, that explained why she'd been willing to go with him.

"That's how I know the message wasn't a trick," Lia said, bristling. "The escorts who were waiting for us at the western Coach station were attacked. When we didn't meet Talon as planned, he and some of his men started looking for us." Tears filled her eyes. She slumped, as if her body couldn't stay upright once anger no longer supported her. "My uncle was leading the escorts who were supposed to bring us home."

Jared moved to her bench and put his arms around her. He stroked her hair and rocked her, murmuring soothing noises while she cried out the fear and grief she'd had to hide.

When she finally quieted, he called in a handkerchief and let her sniffle into it for another minute before slipping a finger under her chin, forcing her head up.

"Want to tell me the real reason you didn't buy passage?" he asked gently. Before she could say anything, he pressed a finger against her lips. "Let me tell you what I think happened. You arrived at the auction ground as soon as it opened and spent the day going from auction block to auction block until you found all of the people you'd come for. Probably took you the best part of the day, too. I imagine you bought a couple of the others while you were searching so that it wouldn't be obvious you were waiting for particular slaves to come to the block, but you would have been careful not to overspend at that point. Then, once you had the five you came for, you still had enough marks to buy three or four more slaves. But you wouldn't have settled for the first ones who came on the block after that. You would have looked for people who could still appreciate the gift of freedom. Since there were so many and you could take so few, making those hard choices took some time. Right?"

Reluctantly, she nodded.

"Now, by the time you'd made your next-to-last purchase, there were still plenty of gold marks left to buy the double passage that would get you to a Coach station close to the Tamanara Mountains. And don't give me any nonsense about the escorts bringing the marks with them for the next step of the journey. I had originally trained as an escort, Lady, and no man who serves in that capacity would have let you leave without making sure you had the means to get home on your own." He raised his voice to drown out her indignant sputters. "So there must have been a secondary plan if you couldn't meet them as agreed. Which meant you had the funds for that second passage."

"I told you—"

Jared pressed his finger against her lips again. "You came to buy five, and they were expensive purchases. Brock and Randolf would have been expensive, too. But Garth? You might have paid more than a simple, expendable laborer was worth, but it wouldn't have lightened your purse by much." When she started to protest, he held his hand firmly over her mouth. "Raej might be the prime slave fair and slave-owning might be an aristo indulgence, but even there a young, half-Blood male like Tomas wouldn't go for much. With the way aristo Blood males have been mounting landen females, you can go into just about any village and buy a starving little bastard of either sex. And little Cathryn— a pretty Blood female that an aristo male would use as a breeder after his broken wife produced the one child she'd be capable of bearing. But Cathryn's only nine, and if healthy offspring are the intention, she isn't going to be useful for several more years. So she wasn't going to go for much either. Thera? I can't imagine you had much competition bidding for a broken Black Widow with a vicious temper. Which leaves me."

She stared at him, wide-eyed.

Jared took his hand away from her mouth and found he needed a moment to steady himself. "It was me, wasn't it? Until you bought me, you still had the funds to buy passage on another Coach."

Lia shook her head, but he saw the truth in the shadows that darkened her gray eyes.

"I know where the bidding starts for a fully trained plea-sure slave—even a vicious one. And even though you weren't bidding against anyone, the auction steward wouldn't have accepted a price that was much less than the starting bid would have been. So I was the purchase that emptied your purse a little too much."

She wouldn't look at him.

"You can't tell me I have things in the wrong order, Lia. It was almost closing when you came down to those pens. So I was the last one." Taking the handkerchief, Jared wiped the fresh tears from her face. "Why, Lia? Why were you even down there?"

"I don't know," Lia said, her voice catching. "I just needed to go down there. I knew there was something I needed to see." She gave him a defiant look through eyelashes that were spiky from the tears.

Jared frowned. "A compulsion spell?"

Lia jerked. Her eyes widened, then narrowed thoughtfully. After a moment, she shook her head. "I would have sensed it."

"Would you? If a darker Jewel—"

"You wouldn't believe the drills I was put through," Lia replied sourly. "No. I know what compulsion spells feel like. And I was drilled in how to look for all kinds of illusion webs, which is why I sensed something odd about Thera." She shook her head again. "If it *was* a compulsion spell, it was awfully subtle."

He wouldn't have expected any other kind if it came from Hayll. Subtle and twisted. Now was probably not a good time to remind her that being able to recognize a *kind* of spell didn't guarantee being able to recognize a *particular* spell.

Had he been the bait for a trap? Had Dorothea deliberately warned Lia away from that Coach station so that she'd be stranded still within Hayll's reach, forced to travel overland instead of riding the Winds?

"Wait," Jared said. "If you were planning to let us go, why didn't you tell us at the inn? Why did you buy the wagon at all? No, look." He gripped her shoulders. Remembering her bruises, he lightened his hold. "If you'd told us then, there were five of us who could have ridden the Winds and you would have had plenty of marks to buy passage for the others."

She searched his face and, after a moment, reached a decision. "There's a . . . wrongness . . . here. I can't explain it better than that. I didn't sense it until we were all together. In a way, I *still* can't sense it, but . . ."

"Go on."

"At first I thought it was the illusion webs Thera and I were using, but it's more, Jared, and I can't pinpoint the

source. It's like catching something out of the corner of
your eye but not being able to see it when you try to look
directly at it. I couldn't risk bringing that wrongness into
Dena Nehele. I couldn't risk having someone who might
be full of Hayll's kind of poison living freely among my
people. So I decided to keep everyone together and let
them think they were still slaves until I could find the
source."

Jared leaned back. "You let Polli go."

Lia took a deep breath, let it out slowly. "I told Talon
about the wrongness. He'll take . . . precautions." She
smiled bleakly, her eyes so full of shadows. "Besides, the
wrongness is still here."

He didn't say anything for a couple of minutes. Then he
stood up. "Come on," he said. "You'll sleep better on a
mattress in front of the fire than on a hard bench out here
in the cold."

"No." Lia hunched her shoulders. "I'll stay here."

"No, you won't."

There was more snap than shadow in her eyes now. "You
can't—"

"I'm claiming Escort's Privilege." *Checkmate, little witch,*
Jared thought as he smiled at her. When a Queen's escorts
weren't available, another male could take on the duties of
looking after the Lady. Since it was a temporary arrangement, Queens rarely refused a male's claim—especially if
his Jewels happened to outrank hers.

She muttered and sputtered while he bundled her up and
carried her out of the wagon. Her comments about escorts
poking their noses into personal concerns became more
pungent after he asked her if she needed to use the privy
hole.

"There were extra mattresses, so I put down a double
thickness for you," Jared said as he carried her to the
building.

"I don't need—"

"Thera got a double mattress, too."

That shut her up so he didn't mention Thera's reaction
to Blaed's proprietary courtesy, or that Thera had tried to

bite Blaed when the young Warlord Prince tucked the covers around her. No point giving the little witch ideas.

The men were all awake when he brought Lia into the building, but no one spoke, no one stirred. Subdued by their presence, she let him settle her on the mattresses and fuss with the blankets. Her only response when he snugged his mattress up to hers was to turn her face away from him.

The rejection stung a little, but he stretched out beside her and tried to ignore it.

A few minutes later, the slow, steady breathing told him everyone else was asleep.

Jared propped himself up on one elbow and watched Lia.

Knowing he would be free once they reached Dena Nehele felt like a different kind of slavery. He couldn't run now, couldn't escape, couldn't go home. Her explanation had been fine as far as it went, but she hadn't known about the wrongness when she bought him—which meant she had risked herself and the others to keep him from going to the salt mines of Pruul. How could he walk away when she needed his strength?

He couldn't. As much as he wanted to go home, he couldn't leave her now.

As he blinked back tears, he slipped his hand under Lia's blanket, searching for her hand. She might have turned her face away from him, but her fingers curled trustingly around his.

Lying there, watching her sleep, he was torn between what he wanted to do and what he had to do. He no longer needed any tangible proof that the Invisible Ring existed, because the Ring no longer mattered. There was only one choice he could make now and live with. Until this journey ended and Lia was safely home, his strength, his maleness, belonged to her.

Sighing, Jared settled down and closed his eyes.

My father would say you haven't grown into your skin yet.
He'd barely had time to get used to the feel of his Red strength when he'd been tricked into slavery. So maybe Blaed's father was right about that. And if that *was* true . . .

Had being enslaved somehow frozen him in that transition between youth and man? If he'd remained in Ranon's

Wood, would he have eased into the more aggressive nature of an adult Red-Jeweled male, the change happening slowly so that what he felt inside was just *more* instead of *other*?

Jared opened his eyes and stared at the dark ceiling above him.

Other. Like the wild stranger. The part of himself that had been suppressed for nine years, until rage had let it burst free. The *adult* Warlord who kept pushing at him to embrace it, accept it.

He would have to embrace it, would have to accept it, no matter how much he feared it. He needed that strength and aggression if he was going to keep Lia safe.

Two nights from now, the full moon after the autumn equinox would rise. For a Shalador male, it was the night of the dance.

And the dance would be the right time to call the Warlord back to himself.

CHAPTER TWELVE

Settled into one of the dainty chairs that were scattered around her sitting room, Dorothea SaDiablo sipped her morning coffee while she studied her Master of the Guard. She had one leg tucked under her, which made her red-silk dressing gown split enticingly high. Her hair flowed over her shoulders, creating a sleek, black frame for her half-bared breasts. She looked more like a whore in the most expensive Red Moon house than a High Priestess.

Then again, Krelis thought, all women were whores. Some were just honest about it.

"Have you any news?" Dorothea asked, setting her cup on the low table in front of her. She picked up a warm breakfast pastry shaped like a crescent, broke it in half, then delicately licked the torn edge. And all the time, she watched him.

It took effort not to shift his weight from foot to foot, but he reminded himself that he was no longer a Third Circle guard who didn't understand the dangers of accepting an aristo witch's sexual lures.

"Well?" Dorothea put the half crescent in her mouth, closed her lips around it, pulled it out again. Slowly. While she watched him.

Krelis had to clear his throat before he found his voice. "No, Priestess, I have no news. But even riding the Winds, it takes time to reach Hayll," he added quickly.

"Of course," Dorothea purred. "I'm simply concerned that the more time it takes to complete this little task, the more chances she'll have to slip away."

He understood the threat beneath the pleasantly spoken words. "She won't escape, Priestess. I swear it on my life."

Dorothea smiled brilliantly. "I'm sure you do."

Krelis's legs turned to jelly. Before he could think of some way to respond, the door between the bedroom and sitting room opened.

The Warlord toy-boy didn't look sulky or defiant this morning. And he didn't have the sated look of a man who had spent a hot night in bed. He looked haunted, numb, as if he'd passed beyond fear sometime in the early hours and was only beginning to feel the tingle of reawakened emotions. The hunger in his eyes was focused on the coffeepot and basket of pastries, not on the barely dressed woman.

Krelis watched Dorothea's expression change. She reminded him of a satisfied cat who had just remembered the mouse beneath her paw.

"It's still early, darling," Dorothea purred. "Go back to bed."

Flinching, the Warlord obeyed.

After tossing the half crescent back into the basket, Dorothea raised her arms and stretched luxuriously. "There's nothing quite like staying in bed on a rainy morning, don't you think?"

For a moment, just a moment, Krelis pictured the three of them tangled in satin sheets and wasn't sure if he felt revolted or aroused. Then common sense—and a healthy dose of fear—grounded him. Hoping she'd overlook his hesitation, he tried to smile. "It's a necessary indulgence for Ladies. Unfortunately, the mundane tasks we males perform don't disappear in rainy weather."

"And I've kept you from your tasks long enough," Dorothea said with a knowing smile. "I imagine your mother enjoys rainy mornings."

The verbal knife slipped past all his defenses and left him bleeding. "I imagine so, Priestess," he said weakly.

A muffled, pitiful weeping came from behind the bedroom door.

Turning toward the sound, Dorothea stroked her breasts.

Krelis fled.

He walked back to the guards' quarters, completely unaware that he was getting soaked to the skin.

Aristo word games. Sentences with layers of meaning.

He remembered the mother of his childhood as a lovely woman content with her life; a woman who filled the house with her laughter and singing; a woman whose eyes lit up when his father was in the room.

He remembered the woman who fought with a witch's passion when the Healer tried to refuse to help Olvan; the woman whose pride and courage had shamed the merchants when they tried to insist that she pay immediately instead of sending her a monthly account as was customary; the woman who looked her neighbors in the eye until they avoided her.

He remembered the woman whose courage finally crumbled after so many years of isolation; the woman who became emotionally bitter and brittle; the woman whose eyes were full of contempt for the man she'd loved; the woman who kept her distance from her son, as if he, too, would place a burden on her that was past bearing.

He remembered the woman who crept back to her family, leaving him to deal with the merchants and face the neighbors, leaving him with that soul-withered husk of a man who spent his days rereading beloved books and never going beyond the garden gate, leaving him to share in his father's shame for no other reason than because he was male.

And he remembered the woman who brought him back into her family once he'd severed all ties with Olvan; the woman who had looked at him out of dead eyes; the woman who flaunted a string of lovers, who spread her legs for any male who had some position and power.

Oh, yes, he imagined his mother stayed in bed on rainy mornings.

Krelis reached his rooms and stripped out of his wet clothes.

Aristo games. Witches' games. He still didn't really know the rules. Despite having ties with the Hundred Families, his people had been countryfolk. He hadn't been raised to play these games. Dorothea must have known that.

Which made him wonder, for the first time, why she had chosen him to be her Master of the Guard.

CHAPTER THIRTEEN

Jared slipped out of the stone building, pausing to take a deep breath of crisp night air. No one would follow him. He'd made it clear since the evening meal that he wanted to be alone. Lia was settled for the night and wouldn't need him for a little while.

Jared smiled. Lady Ardelia had spent the past two days resenting needing him at all, giving him dark looks and muttering under her breath every time he'd carried her from the table to her mattress. Every time he'd carried her to the privy hole, it had taken her resentment half an hour to thaw enough for her to speak to him again. And every time she'd tried to get around him, he'd remind her of Escort's Privilege and wisely stay out of reach for a few minutes while she muttered and snarled.

But his "unreasonable" attitude and stubbornness about not letting her walk on her injured leg had produced swift results. By combining his basic healing skills with Thera's and Lia's knowledge of healing, they had almost fully healed her knee, enough so that this afternoon she'd been able to hobble around as long as she held on to something—usually Tomas's shoulder.

Her efforts to resist help from him had irritated and amused him in equal measure. At least she'd had sense enough to restrict her helpers to Thera and the children. It would be ludicrous to feel jealous about them, and he could tolerate Blaed's courtesies to Lia because Blaed was interested in Thera. But the other adult males . . .

It wasn't so much jealousy, he decided as he studied the full moon and clear sky. It was the possessiveness and territoriality that was a male's response to a witch's moontime.

Especially a witch who was also a virgin. It was the sexual potential of the other males that put him on edge, made him watch them with suspicious eyes whenever they got too close to Lia. After all, they hadn't known each other when Lia bought them a few days ago—and a few days didn't buy a lot of trust when balanced against instincts bred into males for generations—and those instincts had been riding him hard since they got back to the clearing.

Or, perhaps, it was the way his own blood heated every time he touched her that was making him edgy.

Fortunately, the other males had decided not to test his self-control.

Shaking his head, Jared walked to the north end of the clearing.

He would have thought a Queen would enjoy a little pampering. The witches who had controlled his life for the past nine years certainly had. Hell's fire, a pleasure slave who didn't jump to satisfy the slightest whim could lose what few privileges he had—or worse, find himself tied between the whipping posts.

Then again, Reyna had never been gracious about Belarr's pampering during the first three days of her moontime either. The first day she'd snap and snarl at him about his constant fussing, even though it hadn't been constant. Belarr had the administrative duties as the District Queen's agent for Ranon's Wood to handle, as well as three young sons to keep occupied so they would give Reyna some peace. It was like a moon's blood ritual between them. Reyna would snap and snarl until Belarr would respond with, "When you married me, you granted me the right to fuss." That would usually silence her. Perhaps it was being so vulnerable that made it hard for her to yield, because on the fourth day, when she *could* wear the Jewels again and use Craft, she enjoyed Belarr's pampering.

Once, after Reyna's temper had been especially harsh, Jared had asked his father why he tolerated being treated that way. Belarr had said, "Even a man who is loved and trusted is feared a little during these days. If showing a bit of temper makes her feel safer, that's fine with me since there's no cruelty in it. Besides, this is a small price to pay for the rest of the days . . . and the nights," Belarr had added quietly, smiling.

Jared smiled at the memory. He didn't think Belarr had meant for his son to hear that last bit. Or maybe he had. The sons had understood early on that, when it came to Reyna, their father had the dominant claim.

Tomorrow would be the fourth day of Lia's moontime. Maybe she would let him fuss without snarling at him.

When he reached the edge of the clearing, his smile faded. He looked back at the stone building. Nothing stirred.

Good. This night, which was usually a public celebration, wasn't something he wanted to share. Not this time.

Jared stepped into the woods beyond the clearing, following the winding footpath through the trees until he reached the narrow creek. Part of it had been diverted to spill over carefully arranged stones into a small, man-made stone pool, then spill over again to flow into a stone-supported channel for a few yards until it rejoined the rest of the water.

Jared closed his eyes. It had been so long, but if he *really* listened, he could hear the drums in the wind gently stirring the trees, and the water dancing over the stones.

He opened his eyes and called in the crystal goblet. His uncles had given it to him, along with the small silver chalice, after he'd made the Offering to the Darkness. Like the Jewels, he had carried the goblet and chalice with him, hidden from the witches who had owned him because he hadn't wanted to risk having them taken away from him.

Holding the goblet under the falling water, he filled it and drank, pouring out the last swallow to share it with the dark land.

Filling the goblet again, Jared stepped over the narrow creek and followed the path to the second clearing.

He'd found it the first day they'd returned to the main clearing. While Brock and Randolf had gone out to hunt fresh meat, he'd cautiously probed the clearing's defensive shields and discovered they extended beyond the cleared land. So he'd followed the path to this small, second clearing, also strongly shielded but for different reasons.

It was a perfect circle that had been seeded with grass. A few feet in from the perimeter, two large stones had been carefully placed to support a slab of granite, forming a small altar. In the center of the circle was a shallow fire pit surrounded by stones.

The land had absorbed the giving done here, becoming a sacred place. Unlike the Sanctuaries that had a formal altar and a Priestess to tend them, these small places were found throughout the Realm of Terreille. Private places, where the Blood came to reaffirm their bond to the land and the life that sprang from it; where they quietly made the descent into the abyss until they reached their cores and opened their inner barriers; where the power flowed through them and they became a channel between the night sky and the dark land, giving one kind of strength and taking back another. It was in places like this that the Blood came to honor the Darkness.

Placing the crystal goblet on one side of the altar, Jared called in the small silver chalice and set it on the other side. Moving with the measured step of ritual, he walked to the fire pit, created a tongue of witchfire, and lit the pile of kindling and wood he'd gathered earlier to create a small bonfire.

Almost ready.

He undressed, leaving his clothes on the path just beyond the circle. Shivering, he returned to the altar and called in the folding knife he'd honed that afternoon. He knelt before the altar, carefully opened his wrist, and let the blood, hot from the vein, flow into the small silver chalice. Once the chalice was filled, he put a warming spell on it to keep the blood heated. Then he vanished the knife, pressed his thumb over the wound, and walked back to the edge of the clearing.

On the edge of Ranon's Wood was a natural bowl. Surrounded by the grassy slopes was the large dance circle, its dirt carefully sifted and raked. At the new and full moons, the witches gathered there to dance privately with their Sisters. But the full moons after the spring and autumn equinox were the public celebration of the male.

As the sky darkened and the moon began to shine, the

males would gather in the streets, quietly talking, watching the women drift casually toward the circle.

As they followed the women, they would hear the drums, the Craft-enhanced sound rising out of the bowl and filling the countryside. Then the Priestess's voice would rise above the drums in wordless song, calling them to the dance. Another witch's voice would be added to hers, and another's, and another's.

Slowly the males would flow up the slope and down the other side, filling in the spaces that had been left between the women as the Priestess lit the bonfire. One by one, the women's voices would quiet. The Priestess would tip the large silver chalice and cast the circle with Craft and the blood the witches had offered for the dance. By the time the circle was completed, it was only her voice and the drums, calling.

The Wisdom Dance, the elders' dance, came first. Standing at the edge of the circle, the Priestess would extend her hand and bring the first man across. She continued bringing men across the circle, finally stepping out as the last man who chose to dance stepped in.

The drums would change the beat. The fiddle and flutes would take the place of the women's voices. And the men would dance the steps that had been danced since the time of the great Queen Shal.

After the Wisdom Dance, the Priestess's voice would rise again with the drums. The elder males would come to the edge of the circle and bring across the young males who had gone through the Birthright Ceremony for the Boys' Dance.

The Wisdom Dance expressed experience and dignity; the Boys' Dance celebrated high spirits and energy.

Then came the Youths' Dance for the males who had gone through puberty but had not yet made the Offering to the Darkness.

After the Youths' Dance came the dance celebrating male power in all its primal glory. The Fire Dance. The dance of sex.

Consorts, husbands, and males who were handfasted could wear short loincloths if they wanted to. The other males, those who had made the Offering but were not yet formally bound to a woman, indicated their willingness to become lovers by wearing nothing but their Jewels and their pride.

A hot dance. A grinding dance whose steps were as formal as all the others and yet blatant and arousing, promising pleasure.

You're not old enough for the Fire Dance, Jared.

But I've made the Offering!

Yes, you have. But in most other ways, you're still a youth.

I'm ready for the Fire Dance, Father.

Jewels or no, being a man is more than having a hard cock.

But—

We'll talk again before the spring dance. Everything has a price, Jared. You can't take a man's pleasure without taking a man's responsibilities, too. You may be ready for the one, but you aren't ready for the other.

Jared watched the fire rise toward the sky.

Had that been part of it? Still sulking like the youth he truly was, had he ignored the warnings and accepted that witch's invitation in order to defy his father's judgment and prove he was a man?

Except Belarr had been right. He *hadn't* been ready for the Fire Dance. He had briefly enjoyed a man's pleasure and then paid a brutal price.

Stepping forward, Jared inspected the wound on his wrist. It had already begun to clot.

He called in the knife again, reopened the wound, then vanished the knife. Using Craft and the blood dripping from his wrist, he cast a circle big enough to contain the altar and enough space around the bonfire for a single dancer.

As soon as the circle was cast, he used healing Craft to seal the wound.

He closed his eyes, swaying slightly. He could hear the drums and the women's voices calling the Shalador males to the dance.

His heart began to beat in time with the drums.

His blood heated.

He opened his eyes.

On the other side of the bonfire was another male, a phantom shape with blazing green eyes and golden skin.

Jared's breath caught as the wild stranger bared its teeth in a smile that challenged him to embrace—to *accept*—what it meant to be an adult Red-Jeweled male.

Primal and savage, the Warlord had come to the dance.

The drums got louder.

Returning the smile, Jared began the Fire Dance.

Round and round they went as the music became more urgent, more demanding. Round and round. Skin glistened with sweat from the heat of the bonfire and the heat of the dance.

Emotional chains that he hadn't known were there broke and melted away. Social restraints burned in the fire.

Faster and faster. Heart pounding. Feet pounding.

Side by side now, they danced, drawing the male fire closer and closer to the surface until it consumed everything else.

The drums became more insistent as the music built to the climax.

Jared kept dancing, dancing, dancing.

His body throbbed as the Warlord, with a savage smile, slowly faded as it filled him, flooding him with a fierce, triumphant hunger.

The drums faded, and the Fire Dance came to the end.

Jared stumbled away from the fire and sank to the ground, exhausted and painfully aroused. His body quivered and burned as he stretched out full length on the cold ground.

Too sensitive to bear the prick of grass, he rolled onto his back and stared at the moon.

He needed. Mother Night, how he needed!

His rational mind supplied a terrifying word for the intensity of his condition.

Rut.

Except for Warlord Princes, Blood males rarely experienced the rut, that savage, almost uncontrollable need for sex. That Warlord Princes went through the rut once or twice a year was one of things that made them what they were—and one of the reasons they were considered so dangerous. During the rut, their tempers rode the killing edge for so long almost anything could provoke them into violent destruction. Other males weren't safe around a male in rut. Even women weren't safe from the cold rage that was entwined with hot desire.

What made it so hard to control was that simple release brought no relief from the sexual madness. A male's need could easily outstrip a woman's endurance, but a male in rut focused all his energy on one woman and couldn't tolerate being handled by anyone except her, could barely tolerate other women's presence since they both excited and enraged him.

Jared started to shake. The rut shouldn't have happened. He was certain other males didn't experience this after the Fire Dance. There would have been whispers, warnings. And not every male who danced the Fire Dance had a lover waiting for him when it was done. Hell's fire, he'd never sensed anything like this in his father. There had always been a light in Belarr's eyes after the dance, and he'd been impatient for his sons to settle down and get to sleep once they got home, but there had *never* been any hint of *this*.

Could it be . . .

Jared swallowed hard, dug his fingers into the earth.

Could this have happened because all the years when he should have done the Fire Dance and hadn't been able to had funneled into this time, his first time? That all the sexuality he should have celebrated and had to suppress during the nine years of slavery was the reason the hunger was so potent now?

His rational mind would be overwhelmed soon. If he didn't act in the next few minutes . . .

There was no one in their group who could contain him unless Lia used the Invisible Ring against him. Even if she did, would she use it forcefully enough to contain a male in rut?

Lia.

Involuntarily his hunger sharpened, found a focus.

Getting to his feet, he released the power in the circle he'd created, retrieved his clothes, and dressed.

The fabric pressing against his throbbing cock maddened him, and he bared his teeth in a savage smile. His green eyes narrowed as he picked up the small silver chalice and took a sip of his own blood, pleased by the zing of power and strength it gave him.

"Mother Night," he whispered, raising the chalice to the sky for a moment. Lowering it, he slowly poured the blood onto the ground before the altar. "Sweet Darkness, accept this offering from one of your sons."

He drank half the water in the crystal goblet, then poured the rest into the chalice to clean it. He gave the blood-tinted water to the land, dried the goblet and chalice with his shirt, and vanished them. After placing a shield around the fire pit so that the bonfire could safely burn itself out, he left the small clearing.

As soon as he entered the main clearing, he saw her standing in the doorway, wrapped in a blanket. She was staring at the path that led to the lane and didn't notice his slow, predatory approach until he was close enough to see the sadness in her eyes change to surprise.

"What are you doing out here, Lia?"

"I—I woke up and saw you were gone. I thought—"

She didn't have time to tell him what she'd thought before he pulled her into his arms and kissed her with rough desperation. He ran his hands over her body, frustrated by the blanket and the layers of clothes that separated skin from skin. He wanted to tear away those barriers so that he could kiss her, lick her, caress her until she was as frantic as he. When she tried to pull back, he tightened his hold and pressed her hips against his so that, even with all the layers between them, there was no way she could miss that he was fully aroused.

He kissed her again, tasted fear—and realized her heart wasn't pounding with excitement and her body wasn't trembling because of building passion.

Let her go, a voice inside him warned. *Let her go. No woman, especially a virgin Queen, should experience this kind of fear.*

The warning disturbed him, but he couldn't let her go. He had no control over the hands exploring her body. He couldn't give up the maddening pleasure of rubbing against her.

He felt rage building in response to her fear. For one moment, his mind cleared and horror washed through him as he realized how easily he could destroy her right now.

"Lia," he said urgently. "Lia, I'm in rut. Your fear is making it worse." Pressing his lips against her temple, he licked the frantic pulse. "Please don't be afraid of me, Lia. I won't hurt you. I swear by the Jewels I won't hurt you."

"Jared." She sounded breathless. "Jared, I can't—"

"I know. I know. Could you . . ." He took a deep breath to steady himself. "Could you hold me? Please?"

The shaking hands that had been pushing at his chest stilled.

Jared waited, hardly daring to breathe.

He stifled a groan as Lia's hands slowly, hesitantly, slid down his chest and settled at his waist. He forced his hips to stay still. After a minute, she gained enough courage to slide her arms around him and stroke his back.

It wasn't enough, but as she relaxed against him, it soothed the hunger sufficiently that he didn't feel so wildly out of control.

After a while, she leaned back and looked at him.

His hands slid up her back and over her shoulders, finally cupping her face. He traced her lips with the tip of his tongue. Since she didn't protest that action, he kissed her again, this time letting his mouth softly melt into hers.

When he raised his head, he saw confusion in her eyes—and maybe a little hunger.

Looking flustered, Lia turned her head slightly, then frowned at his wrist. "You're bleeding."

A different kind of tremor went through him. He wanted her to turn her head a little more, close her mouth over the wound, and lap the drops of blood welling up from his wrist. He wanted to make a small nick in the hollow of her throat and drink from it.

Jared dropped his hands, shaken.

A Queen didn't accept blood from any but her First Circle.

A male didn't accept a Queen's blood unless he was offering to surrender his life to her will. A court contract was a formal, written agreement weighted by honor and Protocol. A blood bond was a lifetime commitment.

"Come inside," Lia said. "Your wrist needs care and you need something to eat."

"Lia . . ."

"Come inside."

She led him inside, walking slowly but more easily. When they reached the kitchen area, she created a small ball of witchlight, enough to see by but not enough to disturb the others.

He stood passively while she used healing Craft on his wrist. He watched her dab an herb paste over the wound. All he could think of as she wrapped some gauze around his wrist to protect it was how good her hands felt and how much he wanted her to stroke him.

"You're using too much Craft," he said as she warmed some of the meat left over from dinner and sliced the bread without using a knife.

"Don't fuss now, Jared," Lia replied, keeping her voice low. "You can fuss tomorrow."

"Promise?"

She looked startled for a moment and then sighed. "Promise."

Pleased by that, he managed to bite back another comment when she used Craft to heat a mug of water for an herbal brew.

A soft stirring. A change in the feel of the room as someone rose and approached them.

Snarling, Jared whirled around.

Thera gasped and took a step back.

The hunger inside him grew knife-edged teeth that savaged his self-control as he caught the slight muskiness in her psychic scent that signaled a sexually mature witch. Lia's scent was a blend of muskiness and innocence that helped sedate the hunger. Thera's scent enraged it.

After glancing at Lia, Thera licked her lips. "Lord Jared, if you require—"

"Go away," Jared snarled. He felt insulted by the offer. Insulted and a little humiliated that she had so little respect for him that she would offer to take him in front of Lia.

Which made him want to hurt her. Badly.

"Go back to bed, Thera," Lia said softly.

Thera glanced at Lia again and nodded.

Jared stood there, saying nothing, not even daring to look at Lia until Thera was once more tucked in on the mattress next to Blaed's.

Lia touched his arm. "You need to eat and get some sleep."

"Do you think I'm such a whore that I'll willingly go with any woman who snaps her fingers?" he asked harshly.

Her eyes widened. "You're not a whore, Jared."

"That's exactly what a pleasure slave *is*, Lady."

She rubbed his arm to comfort him. "Well, you're not a pleasure slave anymore." She hesitated. "Thera made the offer out of friendship for you and concern for me. I don't think it was an easy thing for her to do. Let it go now. You're not thinking clearly."

Rage and hurt swirled through him, confusing him. Submitting to her gentle coaxing, he felt a little steadier when she placed the food on the table and then sat next to him, even allowing him to feed her small bites of bread and meat. By the time he finished the meal, he was shivering from fatigue.

"Come to bed now," Lia said, guiding him to the mattresses. "Can you put a warming spell on the blankets?"

Stretching out on his mattress, Jared nodded.

Her fingers lightly brushed his dark hair. "Sleep, Jared."

He tried because she'd asked him to. But the spell-warmed blankets didn't stop the shivering, and the presence of the other males made him tense and angry. He also knew they were all awake now and aware of the reason for his tension . . . and feared it.

Half an hour later, he gave up and crept under Lia's blankets.

"What—"

"Let me hold you, Lia," he whispered against her ear. "I need to hold you."

"You're freezing," she hissed, tucking the blankets around them.

He settled her comfortably against his side, offering his shoulder for a pillow. Now that he had his arms around her, the other males didn't bother him as much. The tension eased. Warmed by the blankets and even more by Lia's presence, his body relaxed.

Resting his cheek against her soft hair, Jared slept.

CHAPTER FOURTEEN

"WHAT?" Dorothea SaDiablo shrieked.

Krelis's fury overwhelmed his usual fear of Dorothea's temper. "It's not the Gray Lady. It's some little Green-Jeweled bitch-Queen who used an illusion web to trick herself out so she could prance into Raej *pretending* to be the Gray Lady."

Dorothea's gown swished like an angry cat's tail as she paced her private receiving room. Her eyes narrowed to slits. Every breath came out as a hiss.

Krelis watched her, saying nothing, unwilling to pull her attention back to him. While he waited, his left thumb rubbed the palm of his right hand. He'd clenched the two brass buttons so hard while he'd unraveled the spells on them and extracted the message that they'd left a sharp impression in his flesh.

Those impressions would fade. The kind of impression Dorothea would make on his flesh if she decided this was somehow his fault . . .

"Why?" Dorothea finally said, slowing to a more thoughtful pace.

"We know the Gray Lady was hurt in the attack last spring," Krelis said cautiously. "Perhaps more than we'd realized."

"But not enough. The Gray is still strong in Dena Nehele." Dorothea tapped a long, red-tinted nail against her lips. "But if the body had been maimed . . ." She waved a hand at Krelis, as if he had dared to interrupt her. "An illusion web would be able to hide any disfigurement, but a crippled limb wouldn't function properly and would be quite noticeable, especially since Grizelle's stride is as well-known as her power. What did your pet have to say about the little bitch?"

Watching Dorothea's hand stroke her rich red gown from breast to thigh, it took a moment for the words to sink in.

"She's a young Green-Jeweled Queen. Her name's Arabella Ardelia. She *says* she's taking them to Dena Nehele on the Gray Lady's behalf." He almost told her the rest and decided against it. Those kinds of details were *his* problem.

"Grizelle's daughter is a Black Widow," Dorothea said, more thinking out loud than talking to him. "A well-trained one. She'd certainly be capable of creating an illusion web like that. But to trust a *young* witch with the task . . ."

Krelis shrugged. "Maybe she resembles the Gray Lady more than other witches in the court."

Dorothea stopped pacing, an arrested look in her eyes. Then her lips curled in a malicious smile. "Of course." She swayed toward him, lightly stroked his face, and drifted away. "You have a delightful mind, Lord Krelis."

Krelis wasn't sure if his knees had jellied from the hot little sexual jolt she'd given him or from his fear of what her nails might have done to his face.

Then he remembered all the plans that were being threatened by that little bitch-witch, and his fury drove out everything else.

"I swear to you, Priestess, this Arabella Ardelia will never reach Dena Nehele." Krelis laughed nastily. "Well, she may reach it, but what's left of her won't be any good to anyone."

Dorothea gave him a sharp, assessing look. "No," she said slowly. "She is not to be harmed."

Krelis stared at her.

"She is not to be harmed," Dorothea repeated. "Bring her here."

"Why would you want that filth in Hayll?" Krelis's voice quivered with outrage.

Dorothea smiled as if he'd done something pleasing. "A young witch who would be trusted with such a task must be highly valued by the Queen and her First Circle, but she's still just a pawn we might be able to use against the Gray Jewels—especially if Grizelle feels some emotional attachment to the girl. Here the little bitch can be taught to be of service." Dorothea's gold eyes glittered. "And if her own stubbornness or Grizelle's unwillingness to extend some courtesies to Hayll results in the girl being disciplined, it's something the Master of the Guard should see to personally. Don't you think?"

Krelis bowed. "I would be pleased to teach the little witch how to serve." More than pleased.

Dorothea studied him for a moment, then smiled. "I thought so."

With a measured stride, Krelis walked across the large courtyard that formed the center of the guards' quarters. Discreetly hidden from the SaDiablo mansion by a stand of trees, the quarters were close enough for the guards to answer a summons quickly and yet still far enough away not to intrude on aristo pleasures.

It also meant that the screams that accompanied punishment were distant enough not to arouse the Black Widows in Dorothea's coven or the other witches in her First Circle. Or the High Priestess herself.

And it meant that the female slaves who took care of the guards' needs weren't blatantly in evidence. Not that the witches didn't know about them. They knew, just as they knew that the common female servants were used by the court males in the same way.

Krelis walked toward the end of the courtyard, his eyes fixed on the naked man tied between the whipping posts. Using a hard cock was one way to get rid of anger.

This was another.

Krelis stopped a few yards away from the whipping post and waited for Lord Maryk to join him. "Everything ready?" he asked calmly, pleased that his voice betrayed none of his doubts or fears.

Lord Maryk looked at him for a moment, then nodded.

Moving slowly, as if he were stalking prey, Krelis circled the whipping posts until he stood in front of the marauder leader.

"I helped you," the man spat as he struggled against the

leather straps holding him taut. "Is this how you honor your agreements?"

Krelis slapped the marauder, just hard enough to sting. "You're a fool," Krelis replied, filling his voice with contempt.

"We were ready for them. A perfect ambush about a mile from that bridge. I told you that. I brought you the buttons. How were we supposed to know the bitch would unleash witchfire like that?"

Krelis cocked his head. "You didn't try very hard to find out what happened to the wagon, did you? Didn't try very hard to catch up with the bitch when you could have taken her by surprise."

The man looked at him defiantly. "We found the clearing. Found that rogues' nest for you."

"Found it empty," Krelis snapped. "If it hadn't taken you *three days* to pick up the trail, it would have been stuffed with prey."

"Wouldn't have mattered if they were there or not," the man argued. "I *told* you what those protection spells were like."

"Yes, you told me," Krelis replied, making sure the man understood he hadn't believed half of what he'd been told. "But you didn't have to take the risk. You didn't have to flush them out. All you had to do was keep them in and send a message to me. I would have been there with enough trained guards to take care of them."

"I don't see you sending any of your trained guards to do the hunting," the marauder sneered. "I don't see any Hayllians risking themselves against the Gray Lady."

Rage burned Krelis.

Doubts and fear froze him for a moment, then, circling the whipping posts, he snatched the knotted, triple-tailed whip from a guard's hand.

The whip whistled through the air. Struck. Cut deep.

"Beg for mercy," Krelis snarled as he applied the lash over and over again. "Beg for Hayll's mercy, and maybe I'll let you go."

The man screamed, begged, pleaded.

Deaf to all of it, Krelis let his anger sing through the whip.

Long after the marauder stopped screaming, Krelis finally dropped the whip and turned away.

Eyeing him warily, Lord Maryk stepped forward. "What should we do with that?"

Krelis didn't look back at the mess that had once been a man. "Castrate him and break him," he said harshly. "Then let the slave Healer see what she can do. If he lives, work him."

Krelis walked away, fighting the need to run.

Once he was safely inside his office, he closed the shutters on the windows that overlooked the courtyard and pulled a bottle and glass from a corner cabinet. His hands shook as he poured a large brandy, downed it, and poured another. By the third glass, he felt like he could take a steady breath.

Turning, he stared at the two brass buttons that sat in the center of his desk.

Deceitful, Gray-Jeweled bitch. Deceitful, cowardly bitch to hide within the borders of her Territory. It was one thing to be up against the Gray Lady's cunning; it was quite another to have some Green-Jeweled chit running around making a fool of him. He should have had her by now. It would have been *finished* by now if the little bitch had shown some sense or leadership ability. About the only rational thing she'd done was continue to head northwest toward the Tamanara Mountains, and even then her choices had no rhyme or reason. She was either very smart or very stupid. Either way, it shamed him that she'd eluded him so far.

Unless someone else was behind this.

Like that Shalador Warlord.

No. The man had spent the past nine years as a pleasure slave. *He* wouldn't have many useful skills outside the bedroom, while he, Krelis, had spent centuries training to be a warrior, a guard.

He would show everyone, including the older guards who still had doubts about his ability to command, that he was

worthy of being Master of the Guard by bringing the Gray
Lady to her knees.

Except Dorothea wasn't helping, which was something
he hadn't calculated on and didn't dare point out. Perhaps
it was better to say she was helping too much. That trap
she'd convinced another Black Widow to set at the creek
hadn't done anything except spoil a good ambush. And no
amount of gold marks and promised favors would keep
marauder bands on the hunt if they became worried about
getting caught in someone else's trap.

There was nothing he could do about Dorothea, but that
little bitch-witch . . .

She was threatening all his plans, all his dreams. What
made these puny, flash-in-the-pan races think they could
be anything but Hayll's servants? The Green-Jeweled bitch
might see a hundred years. He could reach five thousand.
Who was she to snuff out his ambitions? She would be gone
in a finger-snap of time while he would reap the rewards or
suffer the disappointments for centuries to come.

While he might fear being so close to her, Dorothea had
the power and the vision to rule the entire Realm of Terreille. Hell's fire, almost half the Realm already stood in
Hayll's shadow. And all those Territories would eventually
need overseers to remind them of Hayll's greatness and
ensure that they remained loyal.

When the time came, why shouldn't he be one of them?
Why shouldn't he receive the wealth of a Territory's tithes
and the power that was the right of those who ruled?

And with that influence, why shouldn't he have a light-
Jeweled witch for a wife, one who would be so grateful for
the safety he offered that she'd submit to his wishes, in bed
and out? Why shouldn't his children serve in important
positions in a court?

Lady Arabella Ardelia threatened all of it. *All* of it.

Krelis carefully set the glass on the desk.

He would find her. He would bring her back to Hayll.
He would teach her how to serve like a good little witch.

Just like he'd taught that other little bitch-Queen.

CHAPTER FIFTEEN

"So what's wrong with the horses?" Jared asked.

Blaed and Thayne exchanged looks, each one waiting for the other to say something.

Watching them, Jared tried to still a growing uneasiness. He'd pushed the group hard yesterday, partly to put as much distance between them and the clearing as possible and partly because pushing himself physically was the only way he knew to stay sane and not hurt anyone. Thank the Darkness, the rut had only lasted one day, but it had been a long, miserable day. If his pushing had injured the horses . . .

Jared eyed the team hitched to the wagon. "Is one of them lame?"

"No, no, nothing serious like that," Blaed said hastily.

Jared ground his teeth. The rut might be over, but his temper was still frayed. "Then why aren't we moving?"

Thayne gave Blaed a "go on, tell him" look.

Blaed glared at his friend and then turned back to Jared. He looked like a man who had just bared his throat after handing a witch a well-honed knife. "It's just—" Sighing, he raised his hands in a helpless gesture. "We think they're sulking."

Jared stared at the two younger men long enough to make them squirm. *"Sulking?"*

Thayne flinched.

Blaed huffed, then gingerly put his hand on Jared's shoulder, leading him a little ways from the wagon.

Confused, Jared let himself be led. Brock and Randolf were on the saddle horses, scouting ahead. The others had stopped walking once they realized the wagon had fallen so far behind and were just starting to drift back to find out why. Lia was safely tucked in the wagon. And Thayne already knew what the problem was.

So who wasn't supposed to overhear this conversation? The horses?

"I know you've been feeling a little . . . overprotective . . . lately," Blaed began cautiously.

"*You've* got balls to say that to me," Jared snapped.

"The point is," Blaed hurried on, "does Lady Lia *have* to stay in the wagon? And there's no point snarling about it not being the proper form of address. Tomas started calling her that and, since she didn't mind, the rest of us just followed his lead."

But not in front of him, Jared thought. They'd called her Lady Ardelia when he'd been within earshot. He understood why, but it still made him snappish. "The Lady has healed remarkably well, but she's in no condition to be walking for hours over rough ground."

"She doesn't have to walk," Blaed soothed. "If we used some blankets for padding and she bundled up well so she wouldn't get chilled, couldn't she sit on the driving seat for a while?"

Jared's teeth hurt. He tried to relax his jaw. "What's that got to do with the horses?"

Blaed sighed. "Thayne's real good with animals. Better than anyone else I know." He sighed again. "He thinks they miss her. You didn't spend much time leading them, so you probably didn't have the chance to notice the difference in how they responded whenever she took a turn at walking. Didn't you wonder why she always stayed near the wagon? It's because whenever she moved too far away, they tried to follow her. One time when she went into the bushes to answer a call of nature, the only thing that stopped them from going with her was Garth grabbing the harness and digging his heels in. And she sings to them."

Jared rubbed his hands over his face. Great. Wonderful. "Didn't you explain to them that Lia's in the wagon?"

"She's downwind, Jared."

"Fine. All right. I'll ask her."

Giving Jared's shoulder a cautious pat, Blaed stepped out of reach.

Jared marched to the back of the wagon and spent a minute glaring at the door. The horses weren't the only ones sulking today. She'd let him fuss yesterday. It was the only thing that had gotten him through the rut. Sex might have helped, but he wasn't sure. The kind of sexual fury that had roared through him wouldn't have been easy to control, and there had been times yesterday when he'd been clearheaded enough to imagine what he'd be like in bed.

It had terrified him, and he'd clung to the knowledge of Lia's virginity like an emotional lifeline. Even the rut was daunted by the risks and responsibilities of the Virgin Night.

So he'd fussed. He'd pampered and petted. He'd kissed and cuddled. She'd asked him to brush her hair. She'd let him feed her. She'd rubbed his back, making him ache for release and yet soothing him until it was almost enough.

Between the times when he'd gone to the wagon for the relief her presence gave him, he'd tried to work off the energy, tried not to see the other males as rivals.

It had been a physical and emotional strain for everyone, and he'd blinked back tears when, halfway through the restless night, he'd felt the rut waning.

He hadn't realized something else would wane, too.

He'd said good night to Lady Cuddles, and woke up to Lady Grumpy.

"Jared?" Tomas peeked around the side of the wagon.

"You don't want to be around here during the next few minutes," Jared growled.

Owl-eyed, Tomas darted back to the others.

Taking a deep breath, Jared rapped on the wagon door—more a warning than a request to enter—opened the door, and ducked the boot that went whizzing over his head. He got the door closed before the second boot, aimed lower, could join its partner.

Retrieving the boot, he rushed into the wagon, tripped over the other boot, and swore.

She was sitting in the dark. Naturally. What good was sulking if you made yourself comfortable?

He made a ball of witchlight, then leaned against the door.

After one good glare at him, Lia stared at her feet.

Jared waggled the boot. "Didn't your grandmother ever tell you it isn't courteous to throw a boot at your escort?"

"Go sit on a pricker bush."

So much for courtesy.

On the other hand, since she wouldn't let him fuss, annoying her was almost as pleasing.

Settling back to enjoy himself, Jared shook his head and tsked sadly. "It wounds my tender sensibilities to hear you say that."

"If you sat on a pricker bush, your sensibilities aren't the only tender things that would be wounded."

Jared narrowed his eyes and tried to remember he was enjoying himself. "You let me fuss yesterday."

"That was yesterday. I'm mad at you today."

"Why?"

"Why?" Lia's voice rose to an outraged screech. "Why? Because I let you fuss yesterday. I let you treat me like some oversize baby bird whose mama keeps stuffing it with food—"

"I didn't stuff you," Jared grumbled.

"—I didn't argue with you when you snarled everyone out of the wagon or when you got nasty with Tomas—"

"I didn't get nasty."

"—I didn't say a word when you bundled me up in so many blankets I couldn't move at all. All right. Fine. You needed to fuss. But that's no excuse for today."

"Today?" Jared raised his hand to rake his fingers through his hair and almost clobbered himself with the boot. Tossing it aside, he rubbed his hands over his face. Was aggravation supposed to be one of the privileges of serving? "What did I do today?"

His ignorance seemed to outrage her even more.

"Thera's moontime isn't any further along than mine, but do you fuss about her? No."

Jared bristled. "Blaed doesn't need any help fussing about Thera."

"Doesn't matter. The point is, you insisted that we stay in the wagon yesterday, and we did. But this morning, when Thera decided to walk, you didn't say a thing. Not the littlest yip or snarl. Then when *I* said I wanted to walk, you bundled me up and chucked me in here. *That's* why I'm mad at you." Lia sat back, crossed her arms, and pouted.

"That has nothing to do with your moontime," Jared shouted. "It has everything to do with the fact that Thera has two legs that work and you don't."

Her lower lip quivered.

Jared took a deep breath and released it slowly. He'd seen too many sulks and pouts used as manipulative games. Most of the time it had brought an edge to his temper and a stubborn refusal to respond. But he suspected this wasn't Lia's usual way of dealing with opposition of any kind. She had the safety of eleven other people weighing on her young shoulders, and she was feeling the strain.

"Look," Jared said, trying to bring his voice back to soothing, "when we stop to rest for the midday meal, you can walk around a bit."

"We're not moving now," Lia pointed out.

Which reminded him of why he was there in the first place. "That's because I wanted to see if you were willing to compromise."

Amazing how fast a pouting witch could change into an alert Queen.

"What compromise?" Lia asked, watching him a little too sharply.

"Well, I thought you might like to sit on the driving seat for a while. But you have to promise not to throw your boots at me, and you have to promise to keep the blankets tucked around you so that you don't get chilled."

"There's not much difference sitting on the driving seat and sitting in here," Lia said calmly. "So I'll stay here."

Jared rubbed the back of his neck. "Sure there is. You can get some fresh air, see some of the countryside . . . hum to the horses."

Lia's smile was far too knowing and smug for his liking. "Having trouble with Boots and Button?" she asked sweetly.

Jared raised his eyebrows. "What kind of names are those?"

Lia shrugged. "They answer to them."

"What did you name the saddle horses?"

"Flirt and Handsome. If the bay had been a stallion, I would have named him Stubborn, after you."

Jared smiled wickedly. "That's not the only thing a stallion and I have in common."

Her mouth opened, but no sound came out.

He liked the way she blushed, the way she suddenly turned shy.

"So do you want to go out and hum to the horses or stay in here with me?" he asked.

If he hadn't found it so amusing, he would have been insulted by the speedy way she burst out of the nest of blankets.

He carried her outside, ignoring her mutters about walking, and presented her to the horses—and tried not to resent the cooing and petting they received. Then he settled his bundle of witch on the driving seat, tucking the blankets around her to his satisfaction.

"Well, that was simple enough," Blaed said as he and Jared watched the happy horses and Thayne set off at a brisk walk.

"Simple as could be," Jared replied, dropping a hand on Blaed's shoulder. "Especially since you're going to keep her company."

"But—" Blaed looked wistfully up the road.

Jared followed the direction of Blaed's attention. "It *was* your idea to have Lady Lia sit out here, Blaed. Not that I told her that. So there's no reason for her to feel annoyed with *you*." He gave Blaed a friendly punch in the arm and smiled too innocently. "Tell you what. You look after my Lady, and I'll look after yours."

Knowing there was nothing Blaed could say to that, Jared jogged up the road to join Thera, leaving Blaed to entertain Lia.

Frustration felt so much better when shared.

*   *   *

"Want some company?" Jared asked when he caught up to Thera.

"No."

"Too bad." Knowing Blaed was watching, Jared threw one arm around Thera's shoulders.

Thera turned her head and stared at the hand so close to her teeth.

Resisting the instinct to jerk his hand away, Jared hoped she'd let him keep all of his fingers.

"I have an idea," Jared said cheerfully. "Why don't you just think of me as another older brother?"

"I don't have a brother, older or otherwise."

"I don't have a sister. Let's pretend."

Her huff turned into laughter.

It jabbed his heart.

He'd thought she was in her late twenties, about his own age. Now, with her face softened by humor, he wondered if she was even close.

"Where are you from, Thera?" Jared asked, curious about her.

The laughter died. The softness disappeared from her face, making it look older again.

"Nowhere," she said tightly.

He heard the pain in her voice and wanted to ease it without betraying Lia's confidence about their being set free. "Perhaps, when we reach Dena Nehele, you can persuade the Gray Lady to let you return to your family."

Because he was touching her, he felt the fierce grief that flashed through her before she was able to lock it away again.

"I have no family," Thera said coldly.

Sorry for having brushed against a heart-wound, Jared tried to find something else to talk about. "Blaed likes you."

"Blaed's a fool," she snapped.

Thinking of how Blaed looked at her, with too much of his heart in his eyes, Jared's sympathy for Thera rapidly faded.

"Tell me," he said politely, "does being a bitch come naturally to you, or do you have to work at it?"

He'd expected her to lash out at him. It unnerved him to see tears fill her eyes and spill over.

"Thera," he said softly, trying to hold her close to comfort her while she struggled to break away from him.

She stopped fighting and rested her head against his chest. "It's safer to be a bitch. Can you understand that?"

"Yes, I can understand that," Jared said, gently wiping the tears away with his hand.

"It's hard to let go of a useful weapon. Hard to trust."

"I know." He hugged her once, then eased back, pleased when she didn't shake off the arm draped companionably around her shoulders.

After they'd been walking for several minutes, he broached the question that had nagged at him for the past few days. "What were you doing at Raej, Thera? Why was a Green-Jeweled, unbroken Black Widow submitting to the humiliation of the auction block?"

"To escape. Why else?"

Dry, sharp amusement lit her green eyes for a moment. When it faded, Jared looked into a spiritual desert.

Thera took a deep breath, let it out slowly. "My mother wasn't very bright." Her laugh was tinged with bitterness. "The landens always think being Blood and using Craft has to mean we're all very powerful, very wealthy, very intelligent. It doesn't necessarily mean we're any of those things. We're just Blood.

"She was pretty and gentle and had an innate sweetness that made her shine. Or it would have if she'd stayed in her home village living a life that suited her. But one day, a Warlord from the Province Queen's court rode through the village and saw her. Courteous and admiring, he spent the afternoon with her, carrying her market basket and acting as if he'd never seen anyone quite so wonderful. Then he rode back to the court, and she was pleased to have been admired.

"A few weeks later, the Province Queen summoned her to the court and offered her a place in the Fifth Circle. She was awed, flattered, and overwhelmed by the way the aristo members of the court acted.

"He was there, a favored Second Circle male. He gallantly offered to escort my mother through the intricacies of court life. Since he was the only person she knew there, she accepted his company with open arms. He couldn't bear to be away from her. He begged her to marry him. And he begged to see her through her Virgin Night.

"He broke her. An accident, they said. It happens sometimes. Even with all the care that's taken, it happens sometimes. So sorry.

"Of course, he couldn't marry her after that. Neither his family nor his Queen would grant permission for an Opal-Jeweled Warlord to marry a broken witch who wasn't aristo. But she could be his lover, and in his heart she would always be his wife. It didn't take her long to discover there wasn't much difference between being a lover and a slave. At least, not in a court that had spread its legs for Hayll.

"He liked to hit. He enjoyed hurting anything or anyone who was weaker. He used to slap her to excite himself before he mounted her."

"Why didn't she leave him?" Jared asked.

"She had signed a contract to serve in the court. The Queen wouldn't release her. Staying with him protected her from the other males." Something fierce began to glow at the back of Thera's eyes. "He didn't think she'd challenge him about anything. But when I had the Birthright Ceremony and it was time for her to formally grant him paternal rights, to give him a claim to me, she denied paternity. Said it wasn't his bloodline that ran in me. What could he do? Granting paternity is a public ceremony, and there are no second chances, no retractions.

"She sent me to her sister. My aunt had left the home village a few years before—I never found out why." Thera paused for a moment. "Auntie had a lover, a Purple Dusk Warlord. They'd never formalized their union in any way. There were no records to link one to the other. He was a good man, solid and strong, easy-tempered. He worked hard for the first hug I freely gave him."

Jared smiled sadly. He could imagine the pleasure and

relief the man had felt when he finally overcame her sire's viciousness. "What was his name?"

Thera shook her head. "He had a sister, a Sapphire-Jeweled Black Widow who lived in another village. She was a force to be reckoned with, and males who tried to force themselves on women, Blood or landen, usually found themselves impotent for weeks afterward. She spent a few days each month with her brother and Auntie. She had friends in her own village; she also had enemies. So she spent those first days of her moontime where she had the protection of the one male she could trust.

"She was born to the Hourglass, like me. Like calls to like. I'd barely settled in with Auntie when I met her. The next day, she began my training."

"You were very young to begin training in the Hourglass's ways," Jared murmured.

Thera nodded. "Yes. Because of that, there was a lot she couldn't teach me. I wasn't mature enough mentally or emotionally to endure it. It wasn't formal training. More like I'd show her how much I could do of what she'd shown me the last time. Sometimes we took the next step in that lesson; sometimes she began something new.

"She never actually said anything, but we all understood that her training me had to be a secret, that my being a Black Widow had to be a secret. By the time I reached puberty and would have been recognized for a child of the Hourglass, I'd learned how to mask my psychic scent well enough to fool even a darker Jewel.

"The ugliness had started by then—Queens and darker-Jeweled males muttering about Black Widows being dangerous, how they were emotionally unstable because of their journeys into the Twisted Kingdom, how only Hayllian witches had the lifespan and the maturity needed to handle the Black Widows' Craft. The males began to break young Black Widows—for their own good, of course."

"Bastards," Jared snarled softly.

"The month before I turned eighteen, the Black Widow showed up unexpectedly. She said she'd been thinking about me while she was weaving a tangled web of dreams and visions. She said if I didn't make the Offering to the

Darkness before the next moon, I never would. And if I didn't have my Virgin Night before the Offering, I would never reach my nineteenth year."

Thera leaned against Jared. Surprised by her sudden weariness, he slipped his arm from her shoulder to her waist to support her.

"Auntie's lover saw me through my Virgin Night," Thera said quietly. "He wasn't happy about it, but there was no one else we could trust, so he accepted his duty. He was generous and kind. When it was over and we were sure my inner web was intact and I still had my Jewels and my Craft . . . I think he was more relieved than I.

"A week later, we went to a Sanctuary a couple of days' ride from Auntie's village. The Priestess there and the Black Widow were friends. I made the Offering and came away with the Green Jewels.

"The day after I turned eighteen, my sire sent a message. My mother was dying and asked to see me."

"You went back to the court," Jared said, his temper simmering.

"I went back."

"It was a trick."

"It was a trick," Thera agreed

"Your mother wasn't dying, was she?"

"Oh, yes, she was," Thera replied too calmly. "He'd tortured her. After what he'd done to her, there was nothing she *could* do but die.

"She hadn't asked for me. She hadn't wanted to see me. The anguish in her eyes was all the warning I needed. I was the last cruelty, you see. She'd thwarted his having any control over me, so now he'd take me. He wanted her to know that all the sacrifices she'd made, all the pain she'd suffered was for nothing.

"He dragged me into the next room. There was a grille in the wall beside the door. There was no way she couldn't hear what was happening in that room.

"He raped me."

"Wait a minute!" Jared protested. "You said he wore the Opal. You outranked him. You were stronger."

"She dragged herself to the grille and pleaded with him

to stop. She couldn't really talk, couldn't really form words. Not that it would have made any difference."

"Thera!" Red mist coated the road and land around them. Jared shook his head to clear the rage from his vision.

Thera stared at nothing. "When he found out he was too late to break me, he beat me." Her eyes frosted. She looked fiercely triumphant. "And I let him."

"Why?" Jared's voice broke.

"To buy time. I'd slipped under his inner barriers just enough to find out why he'd done this. Revenge, Jared. He knew where Auntie lived. He'd learned enough to know about her lover and the Black Widow sister. He planned to have them all killed because my mother had defied him. He intended to make sure I had no one to run to if I managed to get away from him again. But he'd wanted me under his control before he ordered the executions. That was his first mistake.

"So I fought hard enough to enrage him, to excite him with the spilled blood. And while he raped me again, I sent a message to Auntie on a distaff thread and told her to leave, to vanish and never look back. The Green was strong enough to reach that far. I knew they'd warn the Black Widow.

"Even Auntie wouldn't have recognized me when he was done. My mother died the next day. The day after that, he sold me to an acquaintance. He never told the man who I was. Since I couldn't speak clearly, my owner gave me a name. By the time the bruises and swelling went down, I'd woven illusion spells around myself. I didn't look like a fresh, young eighteen-year-old." Thera laughed harshly. "I drooled a lot. Staggered around glassy-eyed. Anytime a male sat down, I'd climb into his lap and ask him if he'd like to be castrated because I was sure it would make him feel better not to have those nasty urges.

"The son of a whoring bitch couldn't sell me fast enough.

"I've had nine owners in the past year. Sometimes the old one remembered to tell the new one my name. When he didn't, I took another name, confusing the trail even more. My sire tried to keep track of me, you see. He never found my aunt or her lover or the Black Widow. Different names, a different place. They vanished like dreams."

Jared didn't know what to say. His grief for her made him ache. "You'll never look for them, will you?"

"No. My sire lost me two owners ago. The name doesn't match. The description doesn't match. And by manipulating the last bastard into putting me on the auction block . . . no name, no land, no people. I became no one and anyone. I'd intended to snare some weak-willed fool who wouldn't even be able to remember buying a female on the auction block. Once he got me out of Raej, I, too, would vanish."

Thera bit her lip and shook her head. "But Lia bought me, so I guess I fouled that spell." Pulling away from Jared, she started walking quickly.

Staggered by what she'd told him, Jared stood in the road for a full minute before he hurried to catch up to her. When he was an arm's length behind her, he said, "Then your name isn't Thera?"

She looked over her shoulder. What he saw in her eyes chilled him. "It is now."

"Landens." Randolf made the word for the non-Blood of each race sound like an obscenity.

Ignoring Randolf's surliness, Jared rubbed his chin. The village nestled in the lowland a mile from the hilltop he'd chosen as their midday resting place looked fairly prosperous. From a distance, anyway. His father had always been fair about the tithes required from the landen villages that were bound to Ranon's Wood, but he'd seen ragged, half-starved people in other Territories who were stripped of so much of their goods and harvests there wasn't enough left for the whole village to get through the winter months.

"We might be able to get supplies there," Jared said slowly, turning to look at Lia.

She stared at something in the distance and didn't answer.

Jared waited, knowing her answer wouldn't really have anything to do with supplies—because the Winds ran over that landen village, and anyone she sent was going to be tempted to catch one of those psychic roadways for a fast ride home.

Hell's fire, *he* was certainly tempted, and he *knew* free-dom waited at the end of this journey. Would men like Brock and Randolf, who still believed they were slaves, be able to resist a chance to escape?

"You'll need marks to pay for the supplies," Lia said abruptly.

Jared narrowed his eyes and studied her stiff back as she slowly walked to the wagon and went inside. He felt the absence of something—as if she'd closed some inner door he hadn't been aware of, leaving him on the outside. He couldn't define it, couldn't even say what was suddenly missing except that, without warning, she'd taken some-thing away that she'd shared with him until now.

And he resented the loss because he'd done nothing to deserve it.

Fine, he thought as he brushed past the others and strode toward the wagon. If she wanted to give him the cold shoul-der all of a sudden, that was just fine with him. He'd be a good boy and run her errands for her. Just see if he didn't.

Why in the name of Hell had she shut him out?

He pulled up short to keep from knocking her down when she came around the corner of the wagon.

"Here," Lia said, holding out a thick bundle of folded marks.

Jared stared at her. There was no color in her voice, nothing he could read in her gray eyes.

She was hiding something from him.

Resentment simmered, deepened into hurt.

He took the marks and riffled through the various de-nominations of gold and silver. She could have bought pas-sage on a Coach for herself, Thera, and the children with what he held in his hand.

Which made him wonder just how much of her remaining funds she'd given him . . . and why.

Working to make his voice as colorless as hers, he said, "Am I supposed to buy supplies or the village with this?"

"You should have enough with you to buy what's needed," Lia replied carefully.

"If I needed more, I could contact you?" Jared watched her, not sure what he was looking for. "You could use

Craft to send it to me." Damn her, why was she doing this to him? Why was she holding herself as if he'd just beaten her?

"Take it with you, Jared." She took a deep breath.

Jared held his breath and waited. There was something else she wanted to say, something she wanted to tell him. He could feel it. Had she discovered something about the danger that traveled with them?

She let her breath out and said nothing.

Vanishing the marks, Jared mounted the bay gelding. "Anything in particular you want me to look for? Any—" No, he wouldn't ask her about personal needs. She didn't want him to meet any personal needs.

She was a good Queen. He'd give her that. It was his error that he hadn't realized it was a Queen acting responsibly toward a strong, distressed male and not a woman responding as a woman when she'd let him hold her, kiss her, caress her.

His mistake. One that wouldn't be repeated.

Thera approached them, followed by Blaed.

"Take Blaed with you," Thera said.

Jared knew the words were meant for him, but Thera kept looking at Lia, who hissed in anger.

"Lord Jared's perfectly capable of obtaining supplies," Lia said.

"Of course," Thera agreed calmly. "But two of them will get it done faster. There's not enough food left to put together a midday meal. How much daylight do you want to waste?"

The gelding snorted and backed away from the female tempers that gave the air a stormy tang as a silent, vicious argument took place.

"Fine," Lia finally said through clenched teeth. "Blaed will accompany Jared to the village."

Circling wide around the two women, Blaed mounted the roan mare.

"Ladies," Jared said coldly.

Receiving no response, Jared shortened the gelding's reins and turned the eager horse toward the village. He couldn't blame it for wanting to get as far away from that anger as possible.

Blaed didn't break the silence until they reached the bottom of the hill. "You and Lady Lia have a fight?"

"If we did, I wasn't invited to participate," Jared snarled, urging the gelding into an easy canter.

"Lia trusts you," Blaed said, raising his voice above the rhythmic sound of pounding hooves. "You know that, don't you?"

Jared reined the gelding in and slowed to a walk. He glared at the younger man, who met his temper with a steadying calm. "Did Thera shove you into coming with me because you were fussing her too much or because she thought I needed a keeper?"

"Maybe she thought you needed a friend," Blaed replied quietly. "Lia's upset. It has something to do with you. Stands to reason you might need to do a bit of snarling yourself."

"Well, your reasoning's faulty," Jared snapped. And then swore.

Blaed made no comment, which was all the comment he needed to make.

"It has nothing to do with trust," Jared said after a minute. He wouldn't let it hurt him. He wouldn't. "Who else could she have sent? Randolf with his surly contempt? The children? Garth?"

"Brock," Blaed countered. "Thera."

"Thera would have needed an escort."

"Thera doesn't need anyone to watch her back."

Hearing the tightness in Blaed's voice, Jared studied the Warlord Prince thoughtfully. "No, she doesn't," he agreed slowly. "What she needs—although she'd deny it with her last breath—is a patient man who could coax her into letting him warm her feet at night."

Blaed smiled. "I could say the same about a certain Queen."

"I suppose you could."

They sighed in unison.

"Come on," Jared said. "My mother always said a full belly dulls a sharp temper."

"Did your mother have a sharp temper?"

"Occasionally, when we'd annoyed her past her formidable endurance. But she was referring to my father, my brothers, and me. Not that any of us could compete with her temper when she was really fired up." Jared shifted in the saddle to get more comfortable. He smiled wryly. "It wasn't always easy for her, living with four males. After all, when a boy's first learning to serve, who better to practice on than his own mother? Shalador boys are given strict boundaries, but an intelligent boy can get into a fair amount of trouble without ever stepping over those lines. And my brothers and I were intelligent boys. Every so often, when all of us had frayed her temper, she'd throw up her hands and shout at the top of her voice, 'I'm an intelligent woman, a skilled Healer. Why am I living in a house with four males?' My father would answer meekly, 'Because you love us?' And she'd look at him and start to laugh. We always got sent to bed early on those nights. Took me years to figure out it wasn't just so we wouldn't annoy her further."

Blaed's laughter faded as they approached the village.

Not a good time to stir up memories and unspoken longings, Jared thought. Not when the Winds were within reach.

"Do you ever think about going home?" Blaed asked quietly.

Jared fixed his gaze between the gelding's ears. "I think about it." What would he do if Blaed tried to bolt? The Gray Lady was going to send the young Warlord Prince home anyway. Since he was one of the five Lia had been looking for, his family must know the Gray Lady intended to set him free. But what if his family *didn't* know? What if the request to find him hadn't come from them? They, and Blaed, would believe he was rogue. His family might hide him for a few days, but after that? No chance to dream. No chance to love. "You're not going to do anything foolish, are you?"

Blaed stared straight ahead. He swallowed hard. "No, I'm not going to do anything foolish."

Thank the Darkness.

They rode into the village.

It looked too well kept to be deserted, but the streets were empty.

"Looks like someone spotted us," Blaed said, watching the buildings on their right.

Jared nodded, keeping an eye on the buildings on their left. The lightest possible psychic probe had confirmed how many people were hiding within those buildings. Most of the time, landens realized it was suicide to attack one of the Blood, especially the Jeweled Blood, but sometimes desperation and sheer numbers could balance out power at a horrific cost.

"Call in your Jewels," Jared said softly. He reached into his shirt and pulled out the Red Jewel so that it was visible. "Let them see they're dealing with the Opal and the Red. If anyone has any ideas about tangling with the Blood, that should be enough to discourage them."

Nodding, Blaed quickly used Craft to settle his Opal pendant around his neck, then slipped the Opal ring on his finger.

As they rode slowly down the empty main street, Jared added, "And stay shielded."

As if realizing a deserted street would cause suspicion, a door opened a few yards ahead of them. An old man stepped out, leaning on a cane for support.

The young bucks won't face us, so they shove an old man into the street to do what they don't have the balls to do, Blaed said on a spear thread.

Worried by the bitterness in Blaed's voice, Jared reined in the gelding and nodded to the old man. "Good day to you."

"And you, Lords." The old man clutched the cane with both hands.

Jared scanned the street. "I see we haven't arrived on market day. Is there a place we can get supplies?"

The old man hesitated. "Don't have a market day as such, Lord. But the old woman across the street keeps a store. Food and such. Likely you'll find what pleases you there."

The Blood couldn't read landens' thoughts without linking with them, which usually tore apart minds that had no inner barriers, but landen emotions were on the surface and easily read.

The old man's sorrow speared Jared. "Thank you," he said, struggling to keep his voice neutral.

The old man raised a gnarled hand. One finger brushed the brim of his hat. "The Blood are good and kind."

Blaed turned the mare sharply. *He might as well have cursed us.*

Leash it, Jared snarled. *They're frightened people.*

Blaed took a deep breath. *My apologies, Warlord. I'll brush off my good manners.*

Jared nodded, not trusting himself to reply. He understood the sting of the old man's words. He'd never heard that phrase until he became a pleasure slave. Not a compliment and, in the Territories that stood in Hayll's shadow, far from a truth. Landens said it the same way a person said "good dog" to a snarling, vicious animal—as if saying it might make it true, might allow them to escape the encounter intact.

Tying the horses to a post outside the store, they stood in the doorway, giving their eyes time to adjust to the dim interior.

An old woman stood behind a counter at the back of the store. Her shaking hands were pressed flat on the wood so they could see she held no weapons, would pose no threat.

Jared stepped inside, moving slowly.

"A good day to you, Lords," the woman said. Her voice shook, but it wasn't because of age. "May the Darkness shine upon you."

Jared smiled. "Thank you, Lady. We're in need of supplies."

She gestured toward the neat shelves, the small, high-sided tables piled with vegetables and fruits. "What I have is yours, Lords."

Wondering at the regret he heard in her voice, Jared nodded to Blaed, who began to explore one half of the store while Jared looked over the other half. Since she was obviously a shopkeeper, why would she regret selling her wares?

The woman's behavior was forgotten as soon as Jared rounded a table and saw the fruit hidden behind the apples.

"Honey pears!" he exclaimed, delighted with the find. Grinning, he cradled one arm and began a careful selection. They'd always been his favorite fruit, all the more special because they ripened after the first harvest celebrations. Small, sweet, and juicy, they didn't keep well unless they were preserved—Reyna always put up jars of brandied honey pears for the Winsol feast—but he'd always thought the fresh fruit tasted better. And had always thought Reyna's grandmother extraordinarily farsighted to have planted two honey pear trees on the family land for the gluttonous pleasure of her great-grandsons.

Two apiece, he decided as he gathered the pears and wondered if Lia had ever tasted one. They'd be expensive. Always were since . . .

Jared's mind stuttered to a halt.

. . . since the trees only thrived in the soil of southwestern Shalador . . . and the land that bordered it.

Jared walked to the counter and carefully set down his armful of pears at the same time Blaed set down a large bag of potatoes.

"These are practical," Blaed said, smiling indulgently at the pears. When Jared didn't respond, he shrugged and went back to gathering supplies.

It was the hardest thing he'd done in a long, long time, but Jared kept his voice casual as he asked, "How far is it to Shalador?"

"Two full days' ride north, Lord," the old woman replied.

Nodding, Jared turned away to select some apples.

Two days to the border. Three days to Ranon's Wood.

If he rode the Red Wind, he could be home in less than an hour.

He could send Blaed back to the wagon with the supplies and stable the gelding here. By the time they cooked and ate the midday meal, he'd be home. Rested, the gelding could catch up to them easily before they stopped for the night.

An hour. All he needed was an hour to see his family,

to talk to Reyna. He'd be gone three hours altogether, four at the most.

He . . . couldn't go.

The pain almost doubled him over.

He couldn't go. Three hours, three days, it made no difference. If it wasn't for Lia's compassion, he'd be in the salt mines of Pruul right now. And she'd be home. Oh, the unknown enemy Dorothea SaDiablo had set among them still would have been there, the danger still would have walked beside her, but surely the Gray Lady's warriors would have been waiting for her at the mountain pass and would have protected their young Queen at any cost.

But out here? Brock and Randolf still believed they were slaves, and both were bitter enough to step aside rather than risk themselves for their owner. Eryk and Corry wore Birthright Jewels, but they were too young and had too little training. Whatever useful knowledge Garth had was locked inside him. Little Cathryn had few defenses; Tomas, none. Thayne was a light-Jeweled Warlord but not a fighter. Blaed would fight, if for no other reason than to protect Thera.

And Thera would fight for reasons of her own.

Jared straightened up. A shiver ran down his spine.

Unless she really served elsewhere.

Unless her past was just a story shrouded in a Black Widow's Craft.

Unless there was another reason why she'd changed her name.

She wasn't among the ones Lia had been sent to bring back. She'd admitted she'd used a spell to draw the right kind of owner.

Or just a particular one?

She and Lia spent a lot of time in the wagon. Alone.

Green against Green. But if one of those Greens was somehow backed by a Red-Jeweled Black Widow High Priestess?

Hastily gathering the apples, Jared set them on the counter, noticing that Blaed had added a bag of flour, a small block of salt, and two bags of sugar.

"I think that will do it," Jared said, fighting the urge to abandon the supplies and race back to the wagon.

Fool! Thrice-times fool for leaving her. She was too trusting, too gentle. She'd see the enemy's smile but not the knife until it was too late. She didn't have any experience with this kind of treachery.

"I think we should add a few vegetables to this," Blaed said. "Onions, at least. And we need meat."

Why was Blaed watching him like that? Why was Blaed *really* here? To help? Or to warn Thera if he returned sooner than expected?

What's wrong, Jared? Blaed asked. *All of a sudden, you're jumping at shadows.*

Jared added a braid of onions to the supplies. *Am I?*

A flash of Opal-strength anger touched him.

I'm worried about them, too. Lia's upset, Thera's edgy. Neither of them will say why. Blaed's temper flared. *You're not the only one who believes in honor, Warlord.*

They turned away from each other and began selecting vegetables at random, ignoring the old woman who watched them anxiously.

Jared took a deep breath. Returning to the full counter, he used Craft to float the vegetables so they wouldn't bruise the fruit and offered the wide-eyed woman a shrug and a smile.

Deciding that he, at least, was finished, he watched Blaed pick up winter squashes and put them down without choosing any of them. And remembered something about the Warlord Prince's training that he shouldn't have discounted.

What do you think Sadi would do if he were here? Jared asked.

I wish he was, Blaed replied, facing Jared. *Then whatever was troubling Thera and Lia wouldn't trouble them for long.*

Their eyes met and held.

Yes, if the Sadist had been with them, at least one of their group would have quietly disappeared by now.

Jared turned to the old woman. "Meat?"

"No, Lord," she said. "There is a butcher just down the street."

"Fine. What do we owe you?"

"What I have is yours, good Lords," she whispered. Blaed's snarl had her backing away from the counter, her hands protecting her throat.

"We came here to buy supplies, not steal them," Blaed said.

The woman looked pleadingly at Jared. "I meant no insult, Lord."

"I know," Jared soothed. "I know." Worried that she might collapse, he waited until she seemed a little calmer. "How much?"

Her eyes darting from him to Blaed and back again, she pulled a piece of coarse paper and a slim stick of charcoal from beneath the counter and began writing figures. She totaled them, then licked her lips and said nothing.

Jared tugged the paper out from under her hand, read the total, called in the wad of silver marks, and paid her.

"If you're thinking of telling me it's fair that we carry what we each selected, think again," Blaed said dryly.

Relieved that Blaed had shaken off his anger so quickly, Jared gave him a wicked grin and obligingly vanished half the supplies, including the bag of potatoes. The Warlord Prince could have taken all the supplies without thinking twice. It was just the principle of sharing the work. "Happy?"

"Ecstatic." Blaed vanished his half. Facing the old woman, he gave her the slight bow that denoted courtesy to a woman of less rank.

Flustered, she smiled shyly.

"A moment, Lord," she said when Jared started to leave.

Nodding to Blaed, who went out, he turned back to the old woman.

She went to a small shelf behind the counter and took down a sealed glass jar. "Fruit preserves," she said, handing the jar to Jared. "I make it myself. It's good on morning biscuits."

"Thank you. How—"

"A gift, Lord. Please take it."

Touched, Jared kissed her hand. He vanished the jar and gave her the same slight bow. "Lady."

When he turned again to leave, she placed a hand on his arm. "Don't go back to Shalador, Lord," she said hurriedly. "There's nothing for you there. Shalador lies in ruins. They say all the good Queens are dead, and those who are left have sold themselves for Hayll's pleasure."

"Why?" Jared said sharply. "How?"

"War." She shook her head. "Terrible war."

Jared braced his hands on the counter and closed his eyes.

Belarr was a Red-Jeweled Warlord. He'd know how to protect Ranon's Wood. He'd keep Reyna and the boys safe.

Except they weren't boys anymore. His brothers were old enough to fight. Old enough to die.

He swallowed hard, afraid he was going to be sick.

"Lord?" The old woman patted his arm.

Jared opened his eyes His vision blurred when he saw her concern.

"I . . . I do not understand this Darkness that the Blood honor," she said hesitantly. "It is not . . . evil?"

"No," he replied wearily. "It's not evil."

"Then may it watch over you, Lord, and protect you."

Jared tried to smile. "Thank you."

She walked around the counter and took his arm. "Come. I'll walk you to the butcher's."

"I can find it."

She led him out of the store. "I'll walk you."

Blaed took one look at him and stiffened. "What's wrong?"

Jared shook his head. He called in the silver marks and handed them to Blaed. "Go to the tavern and see if you can buy a few bottles of brandy and whiskey. That should be enough. I'll get the meat."

Is it a good idea to dull our wits? Blaed asked.

It's always a good idea to dull pain.

Jared followed the old woman to the butcher's. There were a few men on the street now. Silent. Watching. Including a man in a bloodstained apron.

The old woman raised a hand in greeting. "This Lord would like to buy some meat."

The butcher eyed Jared warily. "The Blood are good and kind."

Smiling, the old woman reached up and patted Jared's cheek. "Some of them truly are."

Jared turned back to the man in time to see his startled expression shift to a more businesslike one.

"You're traveling, Lord?" the butcher asked once they'd entered the shop and the small glass-enclosed counter was between them.

"Yes."

"Got some beef that would cook up just fine over a fire."

"That's fine."

"Got some fresh sausages, too. Quick and easy in a skillet."

"Fine." Jared watched the butcher efficiently select and wrap up the meat.

The butcher glanced at Jared, then at the packages. When Jared said nothing, he cut and wrapped more meat.

"I don't think you want more than this, Lord. It would only go bad before you could eat it, even with magic."

Jared called in the gold marks and handed two of them to the butcher.

"That's too much, Lord."

"It doesn't matter."

Jared vanished the rest of the gold marks and the packages of meat.

The butcher fingered the gold marks thoughtfully. "A gang of men—Blood—came through here two days ago. They were looking for a pedlar's wagon and a group of travelers. A vicious witch, they said. Dangerous. Thought she might be running to Shalador for some reason. Asked about a Shalador Warlord who might be with her."

Jared finally focused his attention. "And what did you tell them?"

"What could I tell them? No one like that had come through here, had they?"

His attention sharpened. "And now?"

"Now?" The butcher shrugged. "What could I tell them now that's any different? Haven't seen a wagon or a witch. Two Lords rode in to buy supplies. Who can tell what Territory they came from? Was busy with my shop, wasn't I? Didn't see what direction they came from . . . or what direction they took when they rode out."

"Thank you," Jared said quietly.

The butcher hesitated, scratched his jaw. "Even in a tucked-away village like this, we hear things. You know?"

Jared nodded.

"If you aren't heading someplace in particular, I've heard some talk that going west is the best choice. The Tamanara Mountains are still some distance away, and they're full of rogues—vicious bastards who'll gut you faster than you can spit—but if you can slip past them . . ."

"I've heard that, too. About the rogues," Jared said, opening the shop door. "Might be better to head south."

"It might at that," the butcher said, smiling.

Outside, Blaed was mounted and waiting for him.

They rode out of the village at a walk.

Blaed caressed the Opal-Jeweled ring on his right hand. "I know I should put it away, but, Hell's fire, it feels good to wear it again."

Jared twisted in his saddle. "If you put those Jewels aside before we get to Dena Nehele, I'll cut your balls off. I swear it."

Blaed stared at him. Then he lowered his head and pursed his lips. "Since she treats us like a court circle and not bought flesh, we should act like a court circle. Is that what you're saying?"

"That's what I'm saying."

Blaed studied the glowing Red Jewel hanging from the chain around Jared's neck. "Suits me." He paused, and added, "You going to insist on the Jewels all around?"

"Everyone who can wear them."

Blaed nodded thoughtfully. "Shouldn't be a problem. At least, it shouldn't add to the ones we already have."

Jared felt a prickle between his shoulder blades. "What problems are those?"

Blaed snorted. He sounded amused.

Warlord Princes were a law unto themselves, Jared thought as he watched something shift in Blaed's hazel eyes. A different breed of men, no matter what Jewels they wore. Men who rose to the killing edge as easily as other men slipped on a comfortable coat. Men who spent their lives dancing on the knife edge. Violently passionate—and passionately violent.

"Yes, I'm dangerous," Blaed said softly, as if he'd heard Jared's thoughts. "I'm younger than you and less experienced, but you can't dismiss what I am. You came close to what it's like to be a Warlord Prince that night when you were in rut. Do you know why you didn't kill the rest of us? She balanced you, grounded you. If Lia wasn't the kind of Queen she is, you would have come out of it surrounded by corpses. That's what's inside me, all the time. Banked, that's true, except for those times when it becomes too fierce to control and I have to surrender to the bed and give in to the rut. The only hope I have of not becoming a vicious killer, of not being a butcher when I'm sheathed between a woman's thighs is serving a Queen who can balance me, ground me. It's not so fierce then. In fact, as long as there's no provocation, it's fairly easy to control when you're grounded by a strong Queen. Or so my father told me."

Jared licked his dry lips. "What if you couldn't . . . what if there's no relief, no release?"

Blaed didn't have to ask who Jared was talking about. "He never gets aroused. Never. But the rut has to be siphoned off somehow." Blaed shuddered. "I think it's best not to think about how he does it."

"We're running," Jared said. "You know that."

Blaed nodded. "We're being hunted. I know that, too."

"One of us serves Dorothea SaDiablo."

Blaed digested this and nodded again. "At least one of us."

Jared narrowed his eyes. "You're thinking of Garth?"

"Hard not to."

Jared scanned the countryside. Then he opened his inner barriers enough to make a strong psychic probe.

Nothing. Not even a pocket of emptiness that might have

indicated a psychic shield. A lighter-Jeweled psychic shield, he amended. If there was a Red Jewel out there, he might not be able to sense it. But a Red wouldn't go up against another Red. Not alone.

"Whom do you trust among us?" Jared asked suddenly.

"Besides Lia? Thera. Thayne because we grew up together. You."

Jared hesitated but had to ask. "Do you trust Thera because you're attracted to her or because you truly believe she's not a danger?"

"Oh, she's a danger," Blaed replied, "but not to Lia." He paused, then chose his words as if he were picking his way over rough ground. "Even when they were both trying to deceive everyone with those illusion spells, I think they recognized something in each other, something that made them friends despite the deception. Hell's fire, Jared. Right from the start, they quarreled like friends who just couldn't see eye to eye. So, yes, I trust Thera. Besides, I think she's the kind of witch Dorothea would see as a rival, not a tool."

Jared thought that over and, reluctantly, had to agree. "What about the children? Do you trust them?"

Blaed shook his head. "Too vulnerable. Useful as a weapon against us, though, unless you can hold Lia down during an attack."

"Damn."

"What's in our favor is that Dorothea's pet has to be in a constant cold sweat by now."

"Why?" Jared asked, curious.

Blaed made that amused snort. "Jared, do you know where we're making camp tonight?"

Jared thought about it for a moment and huffed. "No." Then he started to sweat. He *didn't* know. Lia wandered off the main roads for no reason he could figure out, sometimes wandered off the roads altogether for a little while whenever the terrain permitted. Always heading north or northwest, true, but this was rolling countryside, sufficiently wooded to provide plenty of hiding places for a pedlar's wagon and a small group of people. If a man didn't know where to look for her . . .

He'd assumed he'd be able to catch up to them if he left for a few hours. He'd assumed he'd be able to *find* them.

"Have we got any spare rope?" Jared asked.

"We've got the leads we were using for the saddle horses. Why?"

"I'm thinking of tying one end around Lia's waist and the other end around mine."

Blaed chuckled. "Better make sure it's long enough for her to go into the bushes by herself."

"Maybe," Jared growled.

Blaed's laughter stopped almost before it began. The roan mare snorted and danced as his hands tightened on the reins. Something predatory flickered in his eyes.

Jared started probing, searching. "What's wrong?"

"Thayne," Blaed said through gritted teeth. "He says Thera and Lia are snapping at each other. Everyone's uneasy."

"Damn!" Jared dug his heels into the gelding's sides a second after Blaed kicked the mare into a full gallop.

Blaed, Jared said a minute later as they charged up the hill and swept past an anxious-looking Thayne. *We've got two lead ropes.*

Blaed bared his teeth. *That suits me just fine.*

Yes, Jared thought as he and Blaed dismounted and strode toward the quarreling women. That would suit both of them just fine.

Jared picked up a fist-sized rock and threw it as hard as he could. The midday meal he'd eaten an hour ago felt as hard as that rock in his stomach. Even the honey pear, ripened to perfection, had tasted bitter.

Fool. Thrice-times fool!

What was he doing here? He could have been with his family now. He could have talked to Reyna. He could have been *home* instead of walking along another of these excuses for a road.

He could have been in his mother's house again and, if she'd been willing to forgive him, could have felt her arms around him, easing the hurts and worries like she used to do when he was a boy. Mother Night, how he'd missed being held by Reyna.

He threw another rock.

Lia hadn't expected him to come back. He'd seen it in her eyes before she could hide it. She'd expected him to grab the chance of a little distance, catch the Winds, and disappear.

That's why she had given him all those marks. *That's* why she had intended to send him alone.

What would she have done when he didn't return? Ride into the village herself to buy whatever she could with the remaining marks?

Had Thera guessed? Was that why she'd insisted on Blaed going with him? So that Blaed could return with the gelding and supplies?

Well, if Lia was going to let one male slip the leash, why not all of them? They wouldn't assume it was because he outranked her. Any man who had worn a Ring of Obedience knew how well it could control a darker-Jeweled male. Or would they assume he'd been able to slip the leash because he wore the Invisible Ring?

Which was the point, damn it! *He wore a Ring.* So it wasn't the Ring of Obedience. She'd placed a Ring on him, and even if his body couldn't feel it, his heart did—and that Ring got heavier with every step he took away from a fast journey to Ranon's Wood.

But it wasn't the Invisible Ring that held him back. The fact that she had expected him to escape was proof enough that she didn't intend to use it to control him. What really kept him here was the debt he owed Lia—his strength on the journey in exchange for the freedom she'd purchased.

And, damn her, she had hurt him. The witches who had owned and used his body had never been able to hurt him as deeply as she had.

He watched Blaed canter toward him. He must have fallen so far behind someone had started to worry. Not Lady Ardelia, of course.

He liked Blaed, but he wished it had been Brock who had come looking, a man closer to his own age. Then again, despite pleasure slaves being at the top of the slave hierarchy, most other slaves seemed to think that once a man was used in bed he couldn't remember what the word "honor" meant, let alone live by it.

Maybe Lia thought the same thing.

Well, he'd take whatever company he could get. He was tired of sulking by himself.

Thera swung down from behind Blaed.

Jared swore under his breath.

Blaed wheeled the roan mare and cantered back to the wagon.

Thera fell in step beside Jared. "Want some company?"

"No." He lengthened his stride.

"Too bad." Since she wasn't tall enough to throw her arm over his shoulders, she settled for wrapping both arms around one of his, forcing him either to slow down or drag her.

He slowed down. Reluctantly. "Let go."

She ignored the snarled order. "Being an only child, I don't have any firsthand experience, but it's been my observation that one of the duties and privileges of a younger sister is to be a ripe boil on her older brother's backside."

"Well, you certainly qualify for that," Jared growled. "Though you should keep in mind that the way to get rid of a boil is to lance it."

They walked in silence for a few minutes.

"What went wrong in the village, Jared?"

Jared looked at the cool eyes watching him so intently. Then he looked away. "Nothing went wrong in the village. We left to get some supplies. We came back."

Thera tucked some stray hairs back into her braid. "Lia was glad to see you."

"Of course she was."

Thera nodded as if something finally made sense. "I don't think Brock or Randolf would have come back."

Which had nothing to do with anything. Lia should have known *he* would come back. Damn her.

Thera waited a minute; then, when he didn't say anything, asked, "What do you think will happen once we get to Dena Nehele?"

Jared clenched his teeth. Damn damn damn.

"Lia's asked me several times, privately, if I had finished my formal training. Each time, when I told her that I hadn't, she mentioned that her mother was a Sapphire-Jeweled Black Widow who would be very pleased to have a Green-Jeweled apprentice or journeymaid."

"Mother Night," Jared muttered.

"Only a cruel person would say that to a slave—unless the slave was never intended to be a slave. Don't you think?"

Jared bit his tongue.

Thera nodded as if he'd answered. "That's what I thought, too. You know what else I think? I think she had a reason for the choices she made in Raej, that she chose each of us because she felt she had something to offer us. Except you."

Stung, Jared stopped walking. "She has something to offer anyone with the sense to see it."

"That's what Blaed said."

"Blaed's a fool."

Thera bristled. "He is not!"

"You said he was. This morning."

"That was this morn—"

Jared sucked air when Thera's hands clamped on his arm. "Listen," she said, cocking her head.

A rhythmic pounding. Off to their right. Out of sight.

He probed cautiously, recoiling when he brushed against a slimy psychic scent. "It's Garth."

Thera released him and started walking toward the sound.

Swearing, Jared grabbed the back of her coat. "Stay here."

She turned icy green eyes on him. "You can come with me."

Keeping a firm grip on her coat, Jared muttered, "Blaed and I are going to have a little talk about tethers."

Thera made a sound a feral dog would envy.

They found Garth, his large hand filled with a stone that he was using to pound something he'd placed on a flat rock. His teeth were bared. His face was contorted. He grunted with each impact as he pounded, pounded, pounded.

"Garth," Jared called, approaching warily. "Garth!"

Garth stared at Jared with blue eyes filled with a killing rage.

Jared hesitated, then stepped closer because he'd caught a glimpse of something shiny. "What are you doing?"

Garth's mouth kept working, but no words came out. With an anguished bellow, he threw down the stone and ran away from them.

Jared took another step toward the rock.

"Jared, be careful," Thera said.

Shiny brass buttons, mashed and useless, with pieces broken off.

Buttons.

And something else. Something in the buttons he could almost sense.

"Jared . . ."

He heard the sharpness, the intensity in Thera's voice.

Careful. Careful.

With a delicate psychic tendril, he probed one of the buttons.

It happened too fast. One moment there was only that psychic sliminess. Then a psychic fog shot out of the buttons and rapidly changed into thick, sticky strands full of tiny hooks.

It looked like a badly woven net, Jared thought as it came down over his mind. The tiny hooks dug into his inner barriers, securing the strand. Another strand touched. More hooks dug in.

More strands. More hooks.

It surrounded him in seconds and immediately started to constrict. If it sealed his inner barriers, it would lock him inside himself.

Like Garth.

And then he knew what it was.

He poured the strength of the Red into his inner barriers, poured everything he had into his inner defenses.

It was a tangled web. The kind of web Black Widows used for their dreams and visions. The kind they used to entangle a mind and draw it into a living nightmare.

He struck out desperately, but the power only got

through the shrinking spaces between the strands. Fed by his own strength, the strands in the tangled web swelled like fat slugs.

Panicked, he tried again and again.

No, Jared! Don't attack it! Don't feed it! Thera's voice sounded like ice-coated fire.

Trembling, he obeyed.

Was this how Garth had felt? Had he done the same thing, unwittingly aiding in his own destruction?

Hold your inner barriers, Jared, Thera said. *I know how to get rid of this.*

She didn't sound as confident as her words, but since he didn't see another choice, he again obeyed. His body was shaking, but he felt distanced from it, unconnected. If he tried to raise his arm, how long would it take his body to receive the message—if it received it at all?

Without warning, a psychic knife came whistling down—a long, sleek blade, its edge glowing with icy Green fire.

It hit his inner barriers with enough force to make him gasp. It struck again and again, slicing through the sticky strands, charring the severed ends.

As sections of the tangled web fell away from him, little balls of psychic fire struck them, burning them to ash.

He endured the blows as Thera's Green knife continued to hack at the tangled web.

Finally, enough had been cut away for him to be aware of something outside himself. Something that sounded like a roll of thunder, like the roar of a waterfall.

Like the sound of power gathering before it was unleashed.

Leave it, Thera! Jared shouted. *Get away from here!*

The Green knife paused.

Mother Night, Thera whispered, swiftly breaking contact with him.

Jared shook his head to clear it. His connection to his body still felt sluggish. Strands of the tangled web were clinging to his inner barriers, making him feel tainted, but he was no longer imprisoned.

Hands grabbed him. He stumbled.

"Jared!" Thera shouted. "There must have been another

spell in those buttons. I can't tell how strong it is. I don't know if we can shield against it. We have to run."

His legs just wouldn't obey him. "Go," he said. "I can't run."

Swearing, Thera tugged him away from the rock, toward the road. "Damn you to the bowels of Hell, you stupid man. RUN!"

She gave him a vicious clout. He couldn't tell if it was physical or psychic, but it got his legs moving until he was running away from the rock, running up the road.

Feet pounded behind him. Two horses galloped toward him.

Seeing them burned away the last of the sluggishness.

He ran faster.

How dare she ride toward danger? How dare she risk herself? When they got out of here, he'd show her the sharp edge of his temper. Just see if he didn't.

Blaed! Jared roared. *Protect Lia! Shield Lia!*

Get down! Thera yelled. *GET DOWN!*

He saw Blaed sweep Lia out of the gelding's saddle, pull her to the ground, and cover her.

He tasted bitter jealousy that he was still too scrambled to use Craft, that he wasn't the one shielding her, protecting her.

Thera knocked his legs out from under him. He went down hard, then tried to shake her off when she landed on his back. Wrapping her arms around his head, she buried her face against his neck, and enclosed them both in a Green shield.

The ground shook under him as the area around the flat rock exploded. Small stones and dirt rained down on them.

Thera pressed against him harder and kept muttering, "Mother Night, Mother Night, Mother Night."

Moments later, years later, there was silence.

Thera rolled off him, quickly stood up, and moved a few feet away.

Shaken by everything that had happened, Jared moved more slowly. He noticed that Blaed, too, was slow getting to his feet.

Lia, on the other hand, strode toward Thera, her face tightened by anger. Her gray eyes looked stone hard.

"You stupid bitch," Lia shouted. "I've been lenient about allowing you to use more than basic Craft, but I *did not* give you leave to play around with spells you have no training to handle."

"Nothing would have happened, *Lady,* if you hadn't tried to block it," Thera shouted back. "If anyone's to blame for this, it's *you.*"

Jared shook his head, as if that would clear away the confusion. What were they talking about?

"Who do you think you're talking to?" Lia shrieked.

"A sexless bitch, that's who! If you had any heat between your legs, you wouldn't be wasting a male like him." Thera jabbed a finger in Jared's direction. "You would have ridden him for all he was worth long before now."

Lia hissed. "How would you know what a normal woman feels? You'd sheath anything that was willing to get between your thighs!"

Letting out an outraged howl, Thera threw herself on Lia.

Jared watched them go down in a tangle of limbs just as he got to his feet. He watched them roll on the ground, hitting, shrieking, scratching, tearing at each other's clothes and hair.

Shock locked him in place.

Witches didn't fight. At least, not physically. Never physically. Witches fought with words, fought with Craft. But not physically.

Because something happened to witches when they crossed that line.

Blood males were fiercely aggressive and might engage in quarrels that ended in blows, but they never completely lost themselves in that kind of fight. Witches did. They became feral, cold-blooded, deadly. They became something even strong males feared because their savagery surpassed anything a male was capable of, and they had no mercy.

Thera and Lia rolled toward him. The shock cracked,

shattered. A leg kicked out and hit him hard, knocking his feet out from under him.

He fell on top of them. His fear turned into white-hot anger.

He was only going to separate them, he assured himself as he tried to ram an arm between them. He wasn't going to attack them, wasn't going to hurt either one of them—especially because he wasn't quite sure which body parts went with which woman.

One of them threw a punch that skimmed the side of his head.

Snarling, Jared tried to plant his palm on the bottom witch's chin and give her head a good thump—and then yelled when two sets of teeth clamped down on his hand.

Hearing another male's angry roar, Jared rolled, dragging Thera and Lia with him. He realized his mistake a moment later when he opened his mouth to try to draw a breath and inhaled a mouthful of long hair.

Another roar. A shriek as the weight on top of him suddenly lightened. Blaed yelling, "No, Garth! NO! That's Lia! THAT'S LIA!"

One shove got Thera off him. Jared scrambled to his feet.

Garth held Lia over his head. Blaed stood in front of Garth, but not close enough to help if the big man flung Lia to the ground. Brock and Randolf were a careful distance up the road, breathing hard as if they'd come running to help but now were no longer sure of what to do.

"Put her down, Garth," Jared said firmly.

Garth turned to face him. "P-p-protect!"

"You did protect Lia. You got her out of the fight."

The angry flush that colored Garth's face slowly changed to bewilderment.

Jared noticed the fresh blood darkening Garth's left sleeve.

Probably something had cut him during the explosion—a sharp stone or even a small branch with enough force behind it to act like an arrow.

"You did well, Garth," Jared said, walking toward the big man and hoping he looked far more sure of himself than he felt. "Stopping the fight was good. Prince Blaed and I will handle the rest."

He held out his arms.

Garth hesitated, finally gave a grunt that could have meant anything, then carefully lowered Lia into Jared's waiting arms. After giving Lia's shoulder a thumping pat, he started walking up the road toward the wagon.

"Put me down," Lia said, squirming.

Jared tightened his hold on her and bared his teeth. "When the sun shines in Hell." Hearing a vicious curse, he looked over his shoulder in time to see Blaed haul Thera to her feet. Apparently Blaed's temper was as sharp and hot as his own, and that pleased him.

Lia squirmed again, then yipped when his fingers clamped down harder. "I can—"

"Shut up." Jared's temper soared a little higher when he saw Thayne jogging toward them with the saddle horses. With Thayne there, that meant there wasn't an adult looking after the wagon or the children.

It's all right, Blaed said on an Opal spear thread. *Eryk and Tomas are holding the team, and Thayne put a shield around everything. He'll know if anything touches it before we get there.*

Get her to the wagon, Blaed. He couldn't even say Thera's name. She'd saved him, but she also had attacked Lia, and he couldn't untangle the feelings.

Blaed had Thera up on the roan mare and was galloping toward the wagon between one curse and the next.

Jared found his way to the gelding blocked by Brock and Randolf. Randolf was sweating and thoroughly shaken. Brock looked grim.

"What happened?" Brock asked.

"Later," Jared snapped, shoving between them to reach the gelding.

The trip back to the wagon was too swift to cool his temper or soothe the fear that still jangled his nerves.

Handing the gelding's reins to Tomas, Jared pulled Lia out of the saddle. The other three children clustered around the roan mare, watching him. "Stay here," Jared told them. Not that he thought any of them would be anxious to be in a small, enclosed space with two snarling witches who had just torn into each other. Hell's fire, *he* didn't want to be inside the wagon with them either.

Ignoring Lia's muttered protests when he picked her up, Jared marched into the wagon and dumped her on the bench opposite Thera. Blaed stood nearby, blocking any escape through the shutters that opened onto the driving seat, his muscles quivering with the effort of keeping his own anger in check.

Rubbing his teeth-marked hand, Jared leaned against the door and started putting shields around the wagon—physical shield, psychic shield, aural shield. No one was going to interrupt or overhear this little discussion.

Blaed gave him a look that said, *what do we do now?*

The women weren't paying any attention to him or Blaed. A good thing, too, since he had no idea what to do next.

Still breathing hard, Thera dabbed at her lip, then stared at the fresh blood on the back of her hand. "Hell's fire, Lia, you split my lip."

Lia pushed her hair away from her face, and said contritely, "I'm sorry." She studied all the strands of hair now tangled around her fingers. Her eyes narrowed. "Then again, maybe I'm not. Did you have to rip so much hair out?"

"Wasn't deliberate. My arm jerked when *someone* who didn't have enough sense to get out of the way fell on us."

"Oh."

They looked at him.

Jared gave them a cold, hard stare.

Their eyes dropped to the hand he was still rubbing. Both of them shifted on the benches, putting them a little closer to Blaed.

"We're sorry we bit you, Jared," Lia said meekly, glancing at him through her lashes.

"You're not the only one who got hurt," Thera complained, rubbing her shin. "I slammed my leg into something miserably hard."

"Yes," Jared said coldly. "Mine."

"Oh." After an awkward silence, Thera huffed and

pushed her hair back. "Well, I doubt anyone's going to have the balls to ask questions about what happened."

Blaed growled.

"Except you two," Thera added, regarding Blaed with respectful wariness. "Which was the point."

Blaed's muscles seemed to swell with the anger he was holding in.

Jared's eyes narrowed. Where was the fury that had made Thera and Lia tear into each other? Their tempers couldn't have cooled *that* fast. But they were sitting there like friends who had had a minor spat instead of . . .

"You did this deliberately," Jared said slowly. "You scared the shit out of all of us deliberately."

"Of course," Lia replied, looking surprised. "Thera and I realized we had to shift everyone's attention away from the explosion so that no one would ask about it until we had time to figure out what happened."

"You *lied* to us."

"We didn't *lie*," Lia said indignantly. "We were *pretending* to have a fight in order to create a distraction."

His mind understood the distinction between "lie" and "pretend," but his emotions weren't interested in being that picky.

"The fight *did* provide a reason for the explosion," Thera said.

"And we used Craft to make sure our voices carried far enough so that everyone in the group would know," Lia added.

Jared forced his teeth apart before he cracked some of them. A few seconds. That's all it had taken for one of them to send a thought to the other. Something like, *We have to do something to keep the males from asking questions.* "You planned this in the time it took for you to get to your feet, but you couldn't take a few more seconds to send a communication thread to Blaed and me to tell *us*?" He smacked a fist against the door, causing both women to jump. "You just started flinging out insults and tearing into each other without a thought about how we'd feel. You used Craft so that everyone could hear—"

The air in the wagon chilled. He saw the shift in their

eyes. They'd been willing to placate him up to a point, and he'd reached it.

"You forget yourself, Warlord," Lia said coldly. "A Queen doesn't have to explain herself to any man."

True, Jared thought, but hadn't he earned a little consideration?

Lia's expression softened. "If we'd told both of you it was an act, you wouldn't have responded the same way. Not emotionally. And the other males would have wondered why."

Jared couldn't say anything. *Wouldn't* say anything.

"Besides," Thera added with deadly calm, "you responded to it even though you *knew* what had happened back there. In fact, you know better than the rest of us. What exactly was Garth trying to destroy, Jared?"

Jared shuddered as it came rushing back, making him realize how right they'd been about a witch fight shifting the focus of the males' attention. "Buttons," he said hoarsely. "Three brass buttons. He was smashing them with a stone."

Thera nodded. "Metal holds a spell fairly well."

"What's the point of having exploding buttons?" Blaed asked.

"A weapon," Lia said.

Thera shook her head. "The explosion happened because Jared tried to probe them—or maybe because I cut through the tangled web closing around Jared's inner barriers."

Lia paled, and Jared felt a swift, light brush against his inner barriers—a feminine touch seeking reassurance that he was all right.

"The buttons must have had another use," Thera said. "The explosion and the tangled web were there to prevent anyone who didn't have the key from finding out *what* they were being used for. I wish we had one of them intact to study."

A chill went through Jared. "Could they be used to track us?"

Thera shrugged. "Sure. A drawing spell, a summoning spell. Either of those can be fine-tuned so that anyone who wasn't looking for a specific signal wouldn't notice it."

Lia nodded thoughtfully. "And using a button is very clever. Even if someone noticed it, who would think twice about a brass button lying beside the road? You'd just think it fell off someone's coat. You might pick it up—"

"No." Jared realized he'd been rubbing his hand against his thigh. "They feel slimy. No one would keep it after touching it."

"Garth did," Lia pointed out.

Jared took a deep breath, then let it out slowly. "Garth had one the day we left the clearing. The day we reached the creek. Randolf had been trying to get it away from him. Garth had his hand closed, behind his back. I don't know if Randolf knew what Garth was holding or simply wanted to be difficult because he hates Garth."

"What happened to the button?" Thera asked, watching him sharply.

"Garth gave it to me. Then Randolf took it out of my hand and threw it into the bushes. He said Garth was tainted. He said maybe Garth wasn't as mind-damaged as he seems." Jared swallowed hard. "I began to wonder about one of us being a pet even before—" He stopped, remembering in time that Lia hadn't told anyone else about the wrongness she felt.

"I think it's time I had a little talk with Garth," Thera said grimly. "But I'll need an excuse to be alone with him, something that won't make anyone wonder why I want to see him right after the explosion."

"He was bleeding," Blaed said quietly.

"That would do it. The bad-tempered Queen making me patch up the male hurt by my careless spell."

"A tangled web like the one that almost entangled Jared means a fully trained Black Widow," Lia said softly.

"I know," Thera replied.

The two women stared at each other.

"I didn't mean what I said about your not having skill," Lia said. Then she glanced at Blaed. "I didn't mean any of what I said."

A wicked twinkle lit Thera's eyes. She slanted a look at Jared. "And I didn't mean what I said about your interfering with the spell—or being a sexless bitch."

When Thera didn't add anything, Lia blushed.

Jared decided that Thera had being a younger sister down pat. "I'd feel better if we could put some distance between us and anyone who might become curious about an unleashing. Can we move the wagon while you're doing this?"

Thera nodded. "Keep the others away from it though. In case I trigger something."

Blaed jerked. "What do you mean—" He snarled at Lia when she started pulling him toward the door.

Jared snarled at him.

"Well," Thera said dryly, "a pissing contest between you two ought to keep everyone occupied."

As soon as Lia was clear of the steps, Jared pushed Blaed out the door. Then he looked at Thera, said, "He gets to fuss tonight," and closed the door before she could throw something at him.

Thayne had joined the children and the saddle horses, trying to soothe all of them—not an easy task since Randolf kept pacing and throwing dark looks at the wagon and Garth. Blaed stood an arm's length from Lia, looking sulky. Still and silent, Brock kept his distance from everyone.

Jared met Brock's eyes for a moment, then turned his attention to Lia, who was staring at Garth as if she'd like to gut him.

"Garth!" Lia's voice had a whiplash sharpness that made every man flinch. "Into the wagon. That arm needs tending."

Garth shifted his feet but didn't come forward.

"Garth!"

Garth's pale blue eyes focused on Jared.

"Go on, Garth," Jared said, keeping his voice firm but kind. "The arm needs tending."

Cautiously circling around Lia, Garth entered the wagon.

"Let's move out," Lia said. "Thayne, you lead the team. Corry and Cathryn, you ride the mare. Tomas, you and Eryk take turns leading her. When you get tired, switch."

"Yes, Lady," Tomas said solemnly.

"I may not like him," Randolf said, "but if you let that

Black Widow bitch tend Garth, he's liable to walk out of that wagon with one arm instead of two."

Lia took a swing at Randolf, only missing because he jerked his chin back at the same time Jared grabbed her.

"Whatever problem I have with her is my business, but you'd damn well better remember that she outranks you, Warlord."

Swearing under his breath, Jared dragged Lia over to the bay gelding. "That's enough," he growled. "Don't confuse them to the point of panic."

"I wasn't trying to confuse him," Lia said through gritted teeth. "I was trying to hit him."

Jared boosted her into the saddle, then handed the reins to Blaed before he stormed back to Randolf. The only thing that kept him from throwing a punch of his own was Brock joining them. He settled for a searing look that made Randolf shift uneasily.

"Tempers are running hot right now," Jared said. "If they get any hotter, it's going to be real uncomfortable for us. So keep your tongue and your temper leashed."

"This really started over some messed-up spell?" Brock asked.

Jared caught a flicker of worry underneath Brock's bland tone. Understandable, certainly. If he hadn't seen the two of them in the wagon, hadn't been told straight out the fight had been staged, he'd be more than a little worried, too, about having two Green-Jeweled witches going for each other's throats.

"Guess so," Jared said, shrugging. "I was just tucking myself back into my pants when Thera came rushing toward me, yelling at me to run. It didn't seem like a good time to start asking questions. And after . . ." Jared rubbed the back of his neck and looked away.

Brock snorted. "The whole damn Territory probably heard *that.*" He paused, snorted again, then gave Randolf a friendly slap on the shoulder. "Come on. We'll take point. No sense riling things up more than they are."

Jared waited until the two guards were moving up the road before returning to Lia.

Everything all right? Blaed asked, handing the reins to Jared.

For now, Jared replied.

I'll stay behind the wagon and keep on eye on things.

*Thera wants . . . * Seeing the look in Blaed's eyes, Jared let it go. Blaed the man might care a great deal about what Thera wanted, but Blaed the Warlord Prince would do whatever he felt was necessary—regardless of what Thera wanted.

Nodding to acknowledge Blaed's choice, Jared mounted behind Lia and gave Thayne the signal to move on.

They were right, he thought as he wrapped one arm protectively around Lia's waist. He'd never admit it to either of them, but, damn them, they were right. He wouldn't have responded the same way if they'd told him the fight was an act. They shouldn't have *needed* to tell him. If he hadn't been so mentally scrambled, he should have realized it after the first shouted exchange.

And a Queen *didn't* have to explain herself to any man, even the ones who served in her First Circle. Lia was right about that, too. A Queen might talk to all of her First Circle about the day-to-day concerns of the court, but there were also circumstances when only her Steward and Master of the Guard were told *why* something was required. Sometimes she didn't even tell *them*.

Blind trust was part of the price of service, and the day a male couldn't give that kind of trust to his Queen was the day when, in his heart, he no longer served.

Jared understood that, had been raised to accept it.

But he didn't have to like it.

An hour later, Garth left the wagon, looking dazed.

Half an hour after that, there was still no sign of Thera.

Jared handed the gelding over to Tomas, then hurried to the back of the wagon to join Lia and Blaed.

They found Thera curled up on one of the benches, shaking.

"Cold," she said as Blaed raised her to a sitting position and Lia wrapped her in spell-warmed blankets. "So cold."

"Whiskey would help," Jared said, settling on the other bench to get out of the way.

Blaed called in two bottles of whiskey. He handed one to Jared, opened the other, and helped Thera take a couple of swallows since she was shaking too hard to hold the bottle.

Jared offered the other bottle to Lia. After shuddering through a couple of sips, she handed the bottle back and settled next to him on the bench. He took a healthy swallow, hoping it would soothe nerves frayed from waiting.

Thera pressed her face against Blaed's shoulder and continued to shake. Blaed held her tightly, murmuring reassurances while he coaxed more whiskey into her.

"I need to wash," Thera said plaintively. "I need to wash."

"Soon," Blaed promised. "I'll heat some water and help you."

When Thera didn't protest, Blaed raised worried eyes to Jared.

Jared shared the worry, and not just because he liked Thera and was concerned about her. She was a strong witch, and something that could shake her this badly was a danger to all of them.

Lia held out her hand. Thera grabbed it.

In the confined space, Jared felt power flow between them—not just the power of the Jewels and Craft, but the power of the feminine, strength anchoring strength.

Thera's shallow breathing eased, became deeper. She took another sip of whiskey. "Garth knows."

"Do you?" Lia asked quietly.

Thera started shaking again. Her hand clamped on Lia's.

"Tell us what you can," Lia urged. "We'll deal with the rest."

Thera took a deep breath. "Garth knows." Pressing closer to Blaed, she stared at Jared as if each kind of contact was a thread that helped anchor her.

Slipping off the bench, Jared knelt beside her, keeping his eyes locked to hers.

"It's not like the tangled web that almost trapped you," Thera told him. "It's less and more and worse."

Jared nodded.

"It's like someone rooted a psychic weed inside Garth's inner barriers that produced runners that could cover an area with voracious speed. Some of the runners went down below his inner web and then turned upward outside his barriers, forming a tangled net to keep him locked in. Other runners spread out inside his barriers, so he's doubly caught."

"What did you do?" Lia asked, watching Thera intently.

Thera licked her lips. "I—Mother Night, Lia, the mind that created that is so vile, so obscene." It took her a minute before she could continue. "There's great anger inside him. He must have tried to rip the runners away from the root because I noticed that he could open his first inner barrier a little. So I cut away the tangle surrounding his inner barriers and then . . ."

"You squeezed through that little opening, not knowing how fast that 'weed' might reclaim its ground, to clear a path to wherever Garth had retreated within himself," Lia said, her voice flattened by anger.

"You would have done the same thing," Thera said defensively.

She would have, Jared thought, and couldn't choke back the snarl.

"I don't think what I cut will grow back. I think that's why something was added to make his psychic scent so repulsive—so no one would push past it. It felt like . . . like . . ."

"Falling headfirst into a giant spittoon," Jared said.

Blaed shuddered. Thera and Lia turned a little green.

"If I throw up on you, it's your own fault," Thera said. She took a quick sip of whiskey.

Lia pressed a hand to her stomach and swallowed. "Don't talk about throwing up." Releasing Thera's hand, she sat back. "Is he broken?"

Thera's eyes narrowed thoughtfully. "I'm not sure. I had the impression this was done hurriedly."

Lia nodded. "Because it was meant to be temporary. He could have been broken back to his Birthright Jewel."

"What's the point of all this?" Blaed asked.

Jared eased back onto the bench. "Destroying the one Queen capable of opposing Dorothea SaDiablo."

"But Lia isn't the Gray—" Blaed stopped.

Jared knew the moment Blaed put some of the pieces together and realized Lia must be more than just a young Queen serving in the Gray Lady's court.

The young Warlord Prince swore quietly, passionately.

Lia squirmed.

"So Garth's the only one who knows who the enemy is," Blaed said through clenched teeth, "but there's no way to find out."

"Not for a few more days," Thera said. "By then, all the runners I cut will have withered enough for him to break through."

Lia closed her eyes. "A few more days," she said wearily.

Jared slipped an arm around her shoulders to support her. "We've got a few advantages now. First, there were three buttons. That means three attempts to signal someone or leave an indication of our direction have been fouled. Second, whoever's following us isn't going to expect slaves to be wearing their Jewels."

"Unless the bastard somehow reported that you're wearing the Red," Blaed pointed out. "But you're right that they'll have more opposition than they're expecting."

"And third," Jared continued, "we're less than three days away from my home village. If we push, we might be able to make it in two."

"No," Lia said, trying to pull away from him. "We knew bringing people out of Raej would be risky, and it was a risk they'd have to share for the chance of freedom. But I'm not going to let a village of people who have nothing at stake take the risk of having Dorothea's wrath descend on them."

Jared looked at Blaed and Thera. "My father is the Warlord of Ranon's Wood." If the war in Shalador had reached a small village like Ranon's Wood . . . No. He wasn't going to think about that. *Couldn't* think about that. "We can get shelter and help there. And we can get a Coach to take us to the mountain pass." He squeezed Lia's shoulder. "The

Gray Lady's warriors would be waiting at the pass for you, wouldn't they?"

Lia nodded reluctantly.

"What about all the rogues?" Blaed asked.

Lia rubbed her hands on her trousers. "Gran has an arrangement with all of the rogues in the Tamanara Mountains."

"Gran?" Blaed and Thera said in unison.

"The Gray Lady is Lia's grandmother," Jared said, watching them. "Lia is her successor."

Thera started sputtering. "You fool. You idiot." She stopped because Blaed's response was much pithier and far more creative. She nodded approvingly. "What he said."

Blaed's hazel eyes blazed with anger. "Are you sure about getting a Coach that will get us safely to the pass?" he asked Jared.

Jared nodded. "If, for whatever reason, my father turns down the request, I'll steal the damn thing. We'll get to Dena Nehele."

"Do I get any say in this?" Lia muttered.

"No," Jared and Blaed said.

She gave Thera a dark look. "You're not being helpful."

Thera responded with a cool, measuring stare. "You've risked yourself and your land's future to bring some people out of Raej—which really means out of Dorothea's control. One of those people has been trying to betray you during every step of this journey. The enemy's remained undetected because he's linked somehow with Garth. I got that much. It's ingenious, actually. That link produces a sense of—"

"Wrongness," Lia whispered.

"Wrongness," Thera agreed. "Nothing to trace, nothing to detect, no stray thoughts or emotions that might alert someone. All of that is channeled to the one person whose psychic scent is already fouled." She paused. "I'm with Jared on this. Once the enemy realizes the protection he's been hiding behind has fallen, he'll have to bolt or strike. You need a stronger escort than we can give you to get back to Dena Nehele."

"Wait a minute," Lia said, sitting up straight.

"No, *you* wait, Lady." Thera's green eyes flashed. "You've been the target all along. Not us, Lia. *You.* Don't try to deny it. You'll only sound like a fool."

Gray eyes clashed with green.

Jared braced himself, not sure what to expect.

Lia lowered her eyes first. Leaning forward, she rammed her fingers into her hair. "How did it go so wrong?" she asked no one.

"Dorothea's probably asking the same thing," Thera said dryly.

Lia looked up. "You could go. There's nothing to hold you. No one will stop you, any of you, from catching the Winds and going home."

Thera took a deep breath and let it out slowly. "If you make that same offer to everyone here, some, like Tomas and Cathryn, will stay with you because there's nowhere they'd rather be; some will stay to safeguard Dena Nehele's future; and one will stay to destroy it."

Thera took a last sip of whiskey and handed the bottle to Blaed. "I've decided I'd like to settle in Dena Nehele and take you up on your offer to finish my training with your mother, if she'll have me. So I have a strong interest in the land's future and the Queen who will rule there. Besides, I'm not going to raise my children in a Territory that stands in Hayll's shadow."

Blaed paled, then gulped some whiskey. "W-whose children?"

"Probably yours," Thera snapped. "Unless you annoy me too much."

Blaed took another gulp of whiskey. As he linked his fingers with Thera's, he gave them all a silly grin. "We're really not slaves?"

Lia wrapped her arms around her stomach, bit her lower lip, and shook her head.

Blaed's grin got sillier when he looked at Jared. "Is there a Priestess in this village of yours?"

"What?" Thera yelped.

Jared coughed politely. "There used to be. I'm sure she'd be pleased to officiate over a handfast."

"Wait a minute!" Thera growled, tugging futilely to free her hand. "I haven't agreed to—"

"Excuse me," Lia said in a strangled voice. "I have to find a bush." She flung the door open and tumbled out of the wagon.

"I'd better—" Jared began.

"Stay," Thera said.

Tomas was right. She *did* get a look in her eyes that could singe a man's ball hairs.

"Sorry," Jared muttered as he bolted out the door.

Thera's shout was muffled by the wagon door banging shut.

Ignoring a stab of envy, Jared corked the whiskey bottle and vanished it.

And realized he was missing a witch.

A quick probe of the surrounding area was rewarded by an annoyed mental jab.

A minute later, Lia emerged from behind the bushes, less than pleased to see him.

He matched her stride and waited.

"We'll go to Ranon's Wood," Lia said quietly.

"Fine," Jared replied politely.

He knew that would be her decision—not because of the help they'd find there, but because it was his home. If she'd realized it was that close, she probably would have headed there a lot sooner.

Getting her charges home. Getting one more to safety before her luck ran out. She'd focus on that until they reached Ranon's Wood.

Too late, she'd realize her error.

Jared smiled in anticipation. It was going to be such fun watching Lia try to dodge around his father's code of honor.

CHAPTER SIXTEEN

B arely dawn. Barely light enough to see.
   Didn't matter.

Krelis drove his knife into the straw man that hung from the whipping posts. He didn't strike between the ribs and into the heart for a fast kill, but in the belly, in the guts. Over and over again.

The straw man swung back and forth with each blow. Back and forth.

Over and over and over.

There was nothing wrong with his plan. *Nothing.*

Except that bitch-Queen had tricked him from the very beginning.

Except the High Priestess was becoming impatient.

That wasn't good. It wasn't *safe.*

But it wasn't his fault that Gray-Jeweled bitch had tricked him. It wasn't his fault that the side scheme Dorothea had arranged with another Black Widow had ruined a good ambush. It wasn't his fault that his relatives regarded his mother as the family whore, an accommodation when a more socially powerful male deigned to visit them. It wasn't his fault that the damn man who had sired him couldn't keep his mouth shut, couldn't accept that all of *Terreille* was slowly changing, not just the lousy little Province he lived in.

It wasn't his fault.

Stab stab stab.

"Lord Krelis."

And now he had to deal with that aristo bastard Maryk who must resent every breath he took because Maryk now had to yield to him when, just six months ago, Maryk had been giving him orders.

"Lord Krelis."

Breathing hard, Krelis stepped away from the straw man and stared at his second-in-command.

Something slithered in the depths of Maryk's eyes as he regarded the figure tied to the whipping posts.

"He was a difficult slave," Maryk said carefully, lifting his voice at the end to make it almost a question.

Puzzled, Krelis looked at the straw man.

He saw the blood. Smelled the bowel. And couldn't remember the exact moment he'd exchanged the straw practice figure for a living man.

"I'll take care of it," Maryk said quietly. "Get cleaned up."

Krelis dropped the knife and walked away, stumbling a little now that the fury was gone. Stumbling a little, and feeling more than a little sick, because the something in Maryk's eyes was pity.

CHAPTER SEVENTEEN

"Well?" Jared asked when Blaed met him where the main road forked with a stony track.

Blaed patted the sweating mare's neck, then lengthened the reins to give her a chance to stretch her back.

"I didn't see any sign of riders passing down that track," Blaed said cautiously, "but it's stony ground." Then he took a deep breath and huffed it out. "Hell's fire, Jared, I'm not a trained guard. I can handle a knife, and I know how to fight with Craft, but I could have looked at something obvious and not known it. The track does seem to run straight north. It's wide enough to accommodate the wagon, although there's a stretch that looks like it was cut out of the rock. No maneuvering room there."

"So once we're in that stretch, we're committed to going forward."

Blaed nodded.

Jared rubbed his thumb over the saddle horn. "Anything else?"

"There's a large nest of viper rats among the boulders. I didn't see them, but I heard them."

Jared smiled grimly. "If we lock the boys in the wagon, we just might avoid having one of them get bit."

Blaed waited. "Well?"

Jared looked back up the road he'd spent the past hour scouting, probing. "I found signs of a large group of riders having come this way recently. A day ago. Maybe two. But I didn't find them."

Blaed rubbed his neck. "A Red probe can cover a lot of ground."

"And a Black Widow can spin a web that would defeat that probe."

An uncomfortable silence settled between them.

The four of them had gathered inside the wagon late last night. During the talking and planning, a lot of things had been revealed.

Lia had told Thera and Blaed the reasons the "Gray Lady" had gone to Raej one last time. She'd told them about the wrongness she had felt and about the warning note that had sent them fleeing cross-country.

But she didn't tell them why she hadn't been able to buy passage on a second Coach.

Then Thera had told the three of them about the tangled webs she'd created for the wagon.

Jared still wasn't sure if he'd have felt easier if he'd known about Thera's precaution earlier, but that kind of skill in a witch not fully trained had served as a sharp reminder of why Black Widows, with their ability to ensnare or deceive a person's mind, were so dangerous.

She'd called it a mirroring web. A fairly simple tangled web. When triggered by a psychic probe, the web returned a message more subtle than a thought or a feeling. The probe would touch the web and deliver a simple message: *Nothing there.*

While they were still at the inn Lia had brought them to after leaving Raej, Thera had embedded four of those tangled webs into the wood of the wagon—one on each side. She couldn't—or wouldn't—say why she'd done it. But Jared suspected she'd been covering her own tracks, just in case her sire had somehow been able to trace her to the slave auction. It didn't really matter who she'd originally created those webs to hide, the result was the same: How many times during their journey had someone probed for them after finding one of those brass buttons and found "nothing there"?

And had he really seen evidence of an abandoned camp when he'd scouted the road an hour ago, or could those men have been hiding nearby in the land's many dips and hollows, shielded by a similar kind of tangled web?

Jared broke the silence first. "The road loops, then heads north."

Blaed nodded slowly, looking at the track that forked with the road. "The track's a shortcut then. If marauders blocked both ends, we'd be trapped on it." He closed his eyes. "Jared, the Winds cross that track right near the stretch of boulders."

Jared swore fiercely. While it was customary to use the official landing places—and it was certainly safer since there wasn't the risk of dropping from the Webs onto precarious ground—the Blood could catch the Winds or drop from them anywhere along the way. Which meant they could have unwelcome company without any warning.

If they abandoned the wagon and horses, he could put a Red shield around all of them and they could ride the Winds the rest of the way to Ranon's Wood. Even shielded, riding that dark a Web would be an uncomfortable ride for the lighter-Jeweled among them—and a desperate one for Cathryn, Tomas, and Garth, who couldn't ride *any* of the Winds without the protection of a Coach.

If they did it, it would have to be the Red Wind. A lighter Web would be easier on the others. It would also increase the risk of having enemies riding the Wind with them.

But all it would take was one Red-Jeweled marauder unleashing enough power to break his shield and the others would have no time to drop from the Wind before their minds were torn apart by the power in the Red Web.

"I know," Blaed said quietly. "I did think of it. I also considered letting everyone capable of it ride the Wind of their Jewels."

"You'd let Thera ride alone?"

"No. Even if I *was* willing, she wouldn't ride the Winds alone. Between them, she and Lia would gather up the children and Garth."

"Taking all the same risks with none of the strength to back them."

"So we stay and take the risks overland."

Jared rubbed his forehead, trying to quiet the headache that was starting to bloom. "So we stay."

"Serving in a First Circle's not easy, is it?" Blaed said dryly. He shifted in the saddle. "A trained guard would know how to defend against an ambush."

"A trained guard would know how to create one, too," Jared countered. The headache was pounding in time with his heart. "You're sure about Thayne?"

"I'm sure about Thayne. And we all agreed that, while a child could be misled enough to drop the buttons for someone to find, none of them is old enough or strong enough to handle a connection with the spells tangling up Garth."

"That narrows our choices, doesn't it?" Jared sighed. "Does taking an innocent life get balanced somehow by destroying an enemy? I couldn't sleep last night, so I kept asking myself what my father would do if he were here."

"Did you get an answer?"

Jared snorted. "No. Not from him anyway. But I know what my mother's answer would be. Then again, she's a Healer, and Healers feel quite strongly about life."

"So do some Queens," Blaed replied.

Jared shortened the gelding's reins. "Yes, may the Darkness help us, so do some Queens."

Jared climbed among the tumbled boulders, looking for a place that would give him a little privacy. After a minute, he found a spot cupped by surrounding boulders that rose a little higher than a man's waist. Anyone who noticed him would think he'd just climbed up to take a look around. In fact—he unfastened his trousers and grinned at the wet rock in front of him—someone had already found this place.

The grin faded. As he took care of business, he studied the people gathered around the wagon.

Hell's fire, why had the back axle broken now? Was it an accident caused by the stress of traveling over rough ground or a deliberate act to delay them in the worst possible section of this track?

As Jared straightened his clothes and turned to climb down, he caught a glint of metal among the rocks.

His heart slammed into his throat as he stared at the brass button.

Then a prickle between his shoulder blades made him look up.

The dust cloud coming down the road made no sense— until he realized a sight shield hiding horses and riders hadn't been extended far enough to cover the sign of their passing.

Looking in the other direction, he saw another dust cloud rapidly approaching the wagon.

Blaed! Jared roared. *It's a trap!*

Blaed didn't turn, didn't answer. For a moment, Jared wondered if he'd been wrong to trust the Warlord Prince. Then Blaed ran to the front of the wagon while the others scattered among the boulders.

Taking one deep breath to steady his hard-pounding heart, Jared turned south again, raised his hand, and created a Red shield that spanned the road, extending it upward until a rider wouldn't be able to unleash his power without hitting the shield.

The sound of boots scrambling on stone came from behind him.

Whirling, Jared saw the three marauders just before one of them unleashed a bolt of Purple Dusk power directly at him.

Throwing a Red shield around himself, he flung himself to one side, gritting his teeth as the boulder that had been behind him exploded. Chunks of rock hit his shield hard enough to make him feel the blow.

Before the marauders could strike again, he unleashed the Red in two short bursts. The first blast shattered the marauders' shields. The second tore through their bodies.

Jared scrambled through the boulders, reaching the road at the same time the marauders reached the Red shield. It sizzled as they unleashed their Jewels against it.

They'd come on foot. A good move, Jared realized as he extended the shield so that it formed a barrier along the top of the boulders on either side of the road. A few dead horses would have made an effective barricade.

Jared started backing away, extending the Red shields as he moved toward the wagon.

Strikes against the side shield pulled his attention away from the men in the road. As he turned to strengthen that side, he saw a dozen more marauders suddenly appear.

Not only had they come down the road from both directions, the bastards were dropping down from the Winds!

The next few minutes passed in lightning-fast images. The wagon exploded when blasts of power struck it from two sides. A ball of witchfire set what was left on fire. A horse screamed. A man roared. More and more marauders gathered a few feet behind the Red shields, unleashing their Jewels against it, forcing him to draw more and more of his own strength into maintaining and extending the shields as he continued to creep back toward the wagon.

Suddenly, the Green Jewels unleashed farther up the road, one on each side.

Jared heard men scream, felt something in the land die as it exploded and burned. He couldn't extend his shields to surround their little group because he didn't know where the others were, didn't know where Lia was among all the shattering boulders. There was so much power sizzling around them, his efforts to contact the others through a psychic link yielded nothing.

A blast of power coming from behind him hit the boulders above his head, knocking him down. Momentarily stunned, Jared felt the Red shield across the track break.

He created another a few yards in front of him.

"Give it up," one of the marauders yelled when he reached the new shield. "You can't win against us, slave. Give it up!"

"When the sun shines in Hell," Jared muttered, strengthening the shields. He darted among the boulders that had fallen into the track, constantly extending the shields as he continued to work his way to the burning wagon and the section of the road where he'd seen the others run for cover.

Blast after blast rocked the shields. Jared continued to unleash short bursts of power to break through personal shields and inner barriers, but for every marauder who fell, two more took his place.

Two bursts of power were unleashed on the road directly in front of him, and a thick cloud of dirt rose up, blinding him while he tried to regain his footing on the edge of the newly made pit. Choking, he rubbed his eyes to clear away the tears and dirt and didn't see the man rushing out of the cloud.

Strong hands grabbed him and hauled him behind some boulders.

A Purple Dusk shield formed a dome around them and the boulders in front of them.

"Hell's fire, even the Black Widow knows how to fight better than you do," Randolf growled, crouching beside Jared.

Resisting the urge to ram a fist into Randolf's face, Jared snapped, "I was never trained for this."

"Neither was she, but she knows enough not to be polite or dainty about it," Randolf snapped back. "You're wasting our best weapon."

Refusing to respond, Jared started to extend the shield on his side of the road and hit a Green shield that returned the contact with enough punch to make him feel like a baby bolt of lightning had run up his spine and scorched his lungs.

Jared shook his head to clear it and tried to convince his chest to expand enough so that he could try to breathe.

"Told you she fights better than you," Randolf said.

Marauders dashed among the boulders on the other side of the track. Collisions of psychic power caused the energy to veer off in all directions, striking wildly.

A woman screamed in rage.

A man roared a fierce battle cry.

Somewhere among the boulders, a child screamed in terror.

That scream chilled Jared. He turned to Randolf. "What's our best weapon?"

"Your Red Jewels," Randolf said abruptly. Shoving Jared closer to the ground, he raised his right hand, which now wore a Purple Dusk ring, and unleashed fast arrow bolts of power.

Pushing against Randolf's restraining left hand, Jared raised his head high enough to see a marauder trying to crawl back between the shattered boulders and the bottom of the Red shield. Blood gushed from the man's severed leg.

Randolf waited until the man's body filled the gap. He unleashed the Purple Dusk again, severing the other leg just above the knee.

Jared stared at the Warlord guard. Crouching comfortably, Randolf returned the stare with a steady gaze.

"You did exactly what they counted on you doing," Randolf said quietly. "You threw your strength into defending instead of fighting. If I were up there, I would have gambled that way."

"Why?"

Randolf ignored the question. "They've thrown twice as many men against you as they've got pinning down the rest of us because they want to eliminate the Red." He snorted. "I doubt they were expecting our Ladies to show so much teeth and temper. Once you're gone, though, they've got the numbers to pull the rest of us down and take whatever they've come to take."

Randolf didn't need to say the obvious. There was only one person—now, maybe two—who was worth this much effort and this kind of cost.

"You defend well, Warlord," Randolf said. "Now it's time to kill."

"The bodies lying among the boulders aren't resting, *Warlord*," Jared replied, feeling foolishly like an adolescent who'd just had an older male dismiss his efforts as barely adequate.

"You're wasting your strength that way. The way you've been doing it, you need two strikes—one for a man's shield and one for the inner barriers. Plus you're feeding the shields."

Jared ground his teeth. "I know that."

"Stop feeding the shields."

"If I do that, they'll fall in a minute," Jared protested.

Randolf eyed him grimly. "Then a minute's all you have. A fast descent to your core, come up under their inner barriers and unleash. Hold your strength in a half circle." He drew a small figure in the air with his finger. "Keep the baseline directly in front of you. Then fan out the Red in front of that line. If you unleash in a circle, you'll take out all of us as well as them."

Jared swallowed hard. "I've never tried anything like that. What if I can't control it that way?"

"Then, if we're lucky, we'll all be destroyed completely," Randolf replied harshly. "If we're not lucky, you'll be looking at a lot of empty but still-living husks." His hand clamped down on Jared's arm. "No mistakes. No second chances. And no time to get squeamish. It's a fast kill. We need to cut the odds." The hand on Jared's arm gentled. "And I won't tell anyone if you puke your guts out afterward."

Not understanding that last comment, Jared swallowed again, took a deep breath, turned inward, and dove into the abyss.

Except during his training when he'd been mentally tethered to an instructor, he'd never made a fast dive down to his core, his inner web. The speed and the panicky feeling that he was falling and out of control terrified him. If he plunged through his inner web, at best he'd cut himself off from his own power and destroy his ability to wear the Jewels; at worst, he'd shatter his own mind.

He flashed past the level of the lighter Jewels, gaining speed.

White, Yellow.

He was falling too fast. But there was no time to slow down the descent.

Tiger Eye, Rose.

If he failed, Lia . . .

Summer-sky, Purple Dusk.

A woman had screamed.

Opal, Green.

A woman had screamed.

He stopped thinking, let the Warlord in him reign. The dive changed instantly from a frantic, barely controlled plunge into a graceful, savage dive. His heartbeat drum kept the slow, steady rhythm as he flashed past the depth of the Sapphire and gathered his strength, preparing to make the turn just above his inner web.

This is what Blood males meant when they talked of rising to the killing edge. The mind cleared of all distractions. A lifetime was contained between heartbeats. He had all the time he needed to think, to act.

Jared made the turn and began his ascent. Above him, he saw those other minds as flickering, Jewel-colored stars, as candle flames that were about to be snuffed out by a wild Red wind. He drew a mental line, creating the half circle the way Randolf had told him.

As he continued to rise, he waited, waited.

A few Opals, but nothing stronger.

As he rose to the level of the Green, he unleashed the Red, flooding those smaller containers until they burst from within.

Up, up, up. Jewel stars exploded. Above the White were the colorless candles of the non-Jeweled Blood. He snuffed them out, too.

A hand clamped on his shoulder. Fingers dug into his arm.

Ignoring the hand, he turned and made another leisurely descent. Not so deep this time. He didn't need to go deep. The Red still throbbed in his blood.

"Enough, Jared," a harsh voice yelled in his ear.

He understood it now. Create a frame around the Jewel stars. Hold the power within that frame.

He turned slightly, his eyes seeing and yet not seeing the boulders on the other side of the road.

A box. A neat box to hold those little candles. His mental frame brushed against a Summer-sky star. Recognizing the psychic scent, he pulled the frame away from Corry's terrified mind.

And unleashed again.

More Jewel stars burst. Died.

A fist clipped his chin, snapping his head back.

Snarling, Jared twisted to face whoever dared interfere with him.

Fear filled Randolf's brown eyes—fear and grim acceptance.
Jared blinked.

The heartbeat drum sped up.

Before he was aware of it, he slid away from the killing edge.

He blinked again and looked around.

Randolf hadn't told him the psychic explosion might also
manifest as physical destruction.

Jared stared at the shattered faces, the exploded heads.

Breaking away from Randolf's restraining hands, Jared
leaned over the boulder that had been giving them a little
cover and heaved.

A strong, callused hand covered his forehead. Another
hand soothingly rubbed his back.

"You could have told me," Jared gasped. He heaved
again.

"Would have made it harder for you," Randolf said
roughly.

Panting, Jared tried to spit out the sick taste. He straightened up slowly.

Randolf took a step back.

"Have you ever done that?" Jared asked, wiping his
mouth with the back of his hand.

Randolf nodded. "Yeah. I've done it. There are good
reasons why the dark-Jeweled Blood are feared, Jared."

A blast of power striking a nearby boulder reminded
them that the battle wasn't over.

Jared threw a Red shield around both of them. They
sprinted across the road, choosing a place that would hide
them from anyone above them.

"Hell's fire," Randolf said with grudging admiration.
"Despite all the power they're throwing against her, the
Black Widow is still managing to hold that Green shield."

On the other side of that shield, dozens of marauders
continued to unleash the strength of their Jewels, trying to
break through.

The blasts of power coming from their side of the road
were mostly focused on the remains of the wagon. Thera
was probably using it for cover. Was Lia with her?

Jared pushed away from the boulders, feeling a little light-headed. "Shall we give the Ladies a hand?"

Randolf grabbed his arm and yanked him down.

"There's something odd about that shield," Randolf said, narrowing his eyes. "Never seen anything like that. Didn't even know you could *do* that."

Jared didn't see anything at first. Then he noticed the weird flickering inside the shield—flashes of Purple Dusk inside the Green. He could almost feel the elation of the men who were sending bolt after bolt of power against the shield.

"The Purple Dusk is probably her Birthright Jewel," Jared said. "If the reservoir of power in her Green Jewel is almost gone, she'd switch to her Birthright."

"If that was the case, there would be a Purple Dusk shield *behind* the Green one. But it looks like she's blending the strength of her Birthright Jewel with the strength of her Green. Damned if I know how."

One of the marauders shouted something. The blasts stopped. A few seconds later, *all* of them unleashed at the same time.

Once.

Twice.

On the third collective strike, the Green shield broke and the Purple Dusk power inside it turned into a roaring wall of witchfire that swept across the boulders.

Men screamed in agony, caught in that flood of fire.

The witchfire burned out in a few seconds.

It was more than enough.

Jared closed his eyes, unable to watch as the bodies ravaged by the fire began to fall.

"Mother Night," Randolf whispered sickly. "Mother Night."

Shuddering, Jared pressed his forehead against his knees.

He heard horrified shouts coming from the boulders above him.

He couldn't move. He *had* to move. Had to find the others. Had to find Lia.

In the tense seconds that followed, there were no more blasts of unleashed power. No more shouts.

Silence, except for a rhythmic pounding somewhere close by.

"The bastards who were left caught the Winds and fled," Randolf said, cautiously getting to his feet. "I don't think there were many of them."

Jared slowly raised his head, but couldn't bring himself to look across the road. Even using the boulders for support, it took a couple of tries to get to his feet.

"I've never—" Jared stumbled over the words.

Randolf wiped a sleeve across his clammy face. "Nor I. Not like that. Never like that."

Jared raked a dirty hand through his hair. He took a deep breath and willed his quivering legs to move. "Let's find the others."

They found Corry and Cathryn a few feet up the road, half-hidden by piles of stones that had been large boulders a short time ago.

"You can drop the shield now, Corry," Jared said, noting that the Summer-sky Jewel the boy wore around his neck didn't have even a flicker of reserve power left.

"I-is it done?" Corry whispered. The faint freckles on his nose and cheeks stood out lividly against the pasty skin.

"It's done," Jared said.

Corry slowly uncurled. Cathryn remained in a tight ball.

Corry patted Cathryn's shoulder. "It's all right now. It's all right."

Cathryn's eyes remained terrifyingly blank.

Corry shook her gently. "Cathryn? It's all right now."

Jared crouched down, wondering if he dared to touch her.

A minute passed before Cathryn took a shuddering breath and blinked. She looked at Jared and burst into tears.

Corry put his arms around her and rocked her. Then he pressed his face against her shoulder and started crying.

Jared rested a hand on Corry's bright red hair. Recognizing there was nothing he could do for either of them, he left them.

A few moments later, Eryk stumbled into the road. He

would have fallen if Randolf hadn't caught him. He looked at Jared, and his eyes filled with tears.

"I tried," Eryk sobbed. "I tried."

Randolf pulled the boy into a fierce embrace. "You're safe. That's what matters."

"T-Tomas," Eryk said. "Tomas . . . I tried!"

Leaving Randolf to deal with Eryk, Jared hurried toward the wagon. Thayne was nearby, swaying on his feet as he soothed the gelding, mare, and one of the wagon horses. When he turned, Jared saw the burns that covered the left side of his face and his left arm.

"You shielded the horses," Jared said. Seeing the sorrow and pain in Thayne's eyes, Jared glanced at the wagon. He quickly looked away from the remains of the other horse. "How badly are you hurt?"

Thayne tried to smile. "I'll live."

Blaed walked down the road toward them, moving so carefully Jared's body ached in sympathy.

Do my eyes look that haunted? Jared wondered.

"I killed them," Blaed said, his voice trailing away.

Jared understood what wasn't being said. To protect Thera and Lia, Blaed had made the choice to step onto that private battlefield inside himself and wholly embrace the violent nature of a Warlord Prince. What Jared had needed Randolf's instruction to do, Blaed had done instinctively—and had been no more prepared for the results of that kind of killing than Jared had been.

Before Jared could think of something to say to Blaed, Thera suddenly appeared, staggering from exhaustion and sobbing uncontrollably. Thin to begin with, she now had the gaunt, dried-husk look of a witch who had channeled too much power through her body.

"Lia?" she said plaintively, a desperate look in her eyes. No answer.

When Blaed moved toward her, she stumbled away from him, holding her arms out for balance.

"Lia!" Thera looked around frantically.

Ice coated Jared's spine. Where *was* Lia? Was she too hurt to answer?

"LIA!" Staggering over to the boulders, Thera tried to

climb. Her body shook with the effort. Sobbing hysterically, she sank to the ground. "LIIIAA!"

Jared turned toward the boulders, opening his inner barriers as he searched for Lia's psychic scent, probed for some trace of a Green Jewel.

He found nothing.

"LIA!" Jared shouted.

He scrambled through the boulders, slipped on torn-apart bodies, barely aware of them except to feel relief that they were male.

A groan to his left made him tense, crouch.

A male hand wearing a Purple Dusk ring appeared above a boulder, found a handhold.

Jared pointed his Red-Jeweled ring toward the man rising behind the boulder and waited.

Brock stared at Jared, blood streaming down his face.

"Did they take her?" Brock asked hoarsely.

Jared didn't answer.

"Is the Lady safe? Is the boy all right?" Brock's blue eyes begged for an answer.

"What happened?" Jared asked. Somewhere in the rocks behind him, he heard Thera calling for Lia.

Brock licked his lips. He coughed and spat out blood. "Too many of the bastards. One group came at me. While I was trying to hold them, a couple of them circled around. Eryk was trying to shield Tomas, but he only wears the Yellow. They broke through his shield. Tossed him aside and grabbed Tomas. Next thing I know, they're standing up on that rock over there"—Brock jerked his chin toward a flat boulder a few yards away—"yelling if she didn't give herself to them, they'd throw the boy to his death. I told her—I *told* her to stay down, stay hidden. Told her I'd get Tomas. Made it this far when my shields broke and they were on me. Last thing I saw before I went down was Lady Lia running toward that boulder and Garth swinging that damn broken axle like a club."

Brock spat again and then said in a bewildered voice, "She was shielding that broken bastard. And there was some kind of Craft wrapped around that axle. They couldn't touch him, and he was smashing through skulls like they were ripe tomatoes. Why did she do it, Jared? Why did she shield a male who's already half-dead? Why did she risk herself for a half-Blood?"

There are no pawns.

Jared didn't answer. There was something he'd forgotten. Something important. But how, in the name of Hell, was a man supposed to think with that damn pounding?

A woman screaming in rage.

A man roaring a battle cry.

A child screaming in terror.

Then he remembered the other danger that lived among the boulders.

Jared ran to the flat-topped boulder and climbed up it as fast as he could.

He saw Garth first.

The big man stood at the edge of the large nest of viper rats, pounding, pounding, pounding the faintly squeaking bodies into pulp. Tears ran down his face, and each breath came out as a sob.

Jared looked to the right and saw Lia crawling away from the nest, dragging Tomas with her.

Jared slid down the boulder, landing hard on his hands and knees. "Lia!" When she didn't respond, he crawled after her and grabbed her foot. "Lia!"

She didn't answer him, didn't notice him. With one arm wrapped around Tomas's chest, she kept trying to crawl away from the nest.

Jared leaned forward to grab the back of her coat, lost his balance, and fell on top of her.

She still tried to crawl.

"Lia!" Thera cried.

Jared rolled off Lia and looked up.

Blaed and Thera stumbled toward him.

"Let go, Lia," Thera gasped, dropping to her knees beside the now-still body. When she couldn't pry Lia's fingers open, she used Craft to rip Tomas's tunic around the clenched hand.

Blaed dragged the boy a few feet. Thera went with him.

Breathing hard, Jared turned Lia onto her back.

Her tunic was so torn, she was almost bare to the waist.

He looked into glazed gray eyes that stared back at him, unseeing.

Numb, Jared saw the smears of blood, the grotesque swelling of the viper rat bites on her jaw and neck, the swelling above her left breast. Aching, he listened as Lia struggled to breathe. Desperate, he tried to remember something, *anything*, about healing Craft that would save her.

Thera knelt beside him. Tears ran down her face.

"Tomas?" Jared asked.

"We'll honor him as Blood," Thera replied.

Jared waited for Thera to do something.

She simply knelt beside him, her hands pressed against her thighs.

"Help her," Jared said, frightened by Thera's calm shell.

Thera licked the tears from the corners of her mouth. "I only know a little basic healing, Jared. My knowledge of poisons is limited to what a Black Widow needs to know for herself. There's too much venom in her. I'm s-sorry. I don't h-have the s-skill."

Watching Thera curl in on herself, Jared didn't realize the pounding had stopped until the broken axle, now slimed with gore, thumped down beside him and a heavy hand squeezed his shoulder hard enough to crack bone.

He looked up at Garth's tear-stained face.

"Yyyou fffind help," Garth said, fighting for each word. "Yyyou go. Yyyou take—" He pointed at Lia. "Fffind help. Fffind sssafe place."

Help. Safe place.

Hope shot through Jared.

Closing his eyes to concentrate, he sent out a summons on a Red spear thread. North, toward Ranon's Wood. *Belarr!*

He waited a moment, then tried again. *Belarr! I need help!*

No answer.

Even if Belarr was still angry with him, he wouldn't ignore a call for help.

Father!

No answer.

He tried an Opal thread. *Mother! We need a Healer!*
Silence.

Lia's breathing sounded harsher.

Jared sent out a broad summons at the depth of the Red, letting it spread in an ever-widening circle as far as he could push it. There was the risk that an enemy might answer, but he felt desperate enough to believe any answer was better than none. *Please! I need help!*

Not knowing what else to do, he tried again and again.

Here.

At first, he wasn't sure he'd been answered.

Here.

Not a communication thread. This was far more subtle. He couldn't tell whether it was a male or female who had answered him. Couldn't even tell what direction it had come from.

Here.

It would guide him. He couldn't have explained why he believed that, but as he felt that coaxing tug, he was sure of it.

Jared opened his eyes and got to his feet.

"Something?" Thera whispered.

The painful hope in Thera's voice decided him. "A chance," he said as he picked up Lia.

"She can't go like that," Thera said, calling in her dark-green, hooded cloak. "She'll get cold."

Jared wasn't sure Lia could feel anything at this point, but he didn't argue. He and Blaed held her upright while Thera draped the cloak around her and pulled up the hood.

Jared wrapped his arms around Lia, resting her head against his shoulder. He looked at Blaed. "Get to Ranon's Wood as fast as you can, any way you can." He hesitated, hoping it would be true. "We'll join you there."

Blaed slipped an arm around Thera's waist. "May the Darkness embrace you, Jared."

"And you."

Here.

Putting a Red shield around Lia, Jared caught the Red Wind and followed the promise of help.

*   *   *

Had it been a trick after all?

Jared stared at the large, rough-looking traveler's inn. Somehow, the clean windows and the small flower beds on either side of the brightly painted door made the rambling stone building look rougher, like a sweaty laborer standing next to a woman dressed for an afternoon tea.

Not a sleek or refined place, Jared decided. Definitely not to aristo tastes, but definitely Blood. There was an unmistakable feel to a place where the Blood resided, a psychic residue that was absorbed by wood and stone.

Turning away from the inn, Jared focused his attention on the nearby road that led to a Blood village a couple of miles away. Was that his destination?

Sighing, he reluctantly turned back to the inn. The coaxing tug that had guided him had stopped here. If whoever had answered him was in the village, wouldn't the tugging have continued? Here, then.

A cautious probe had told him there were twenty people in the inn, three of them women. Maybe one was a Healer.

Jared looked over his shoulder at the faint outline of a cloaked body. He'd taken the precaution of wrapping a Red sight shield around Lia before they'd dropped from the Winds to this landing place, and he'd used Craft to float her so that it wouldn't be obvious to anyone who might look out a window that he wasn't alone. For a moment, he listened to her labored breathing, both pained and relieved by the sound.

He hadn't found the Red-Jeweled person who had guided him there when he'd probed the inn on his arrival. That's why he was still standing on the landing place, even though he knew Lia's life was trickling away with every minute he hesitated.

Decide, he thought. *Decide before she takes a breath and then doesn't take another.*

Jared raked his hands through his hair and brushed at his clothes. He smiled grimly. He doubted the owner or the customers were dressed much better, so at least he wasn't going to look out of place.

All right. He'd rent a room where he could safely tuck

Lia while he tried to find someone with the healing skills to help her. Failing that, he'd use the healing skills he had. Failing that . . .

Jared straightened his shoulders. He wouldn't fail. No matter what he had to do, he was *not* going to just sit back and watch her die.

He added an aural shield and a psychic shield to the sight and protective shields already around Lia so that the others wouldn't detect her psychic scent or hear any sounds she might make. The shields would make her completely invisible to anyone who wore less than the Red. Even another Red would only pick up a faint outline.

Jared took a deep breath. As he breathed out, he wrapped psychic threads around himself and Lia that sent out a feeling of danger and violence. With his Red Jewel hanging in plain sight, those projected feelings should be enough to keep everyone at a distance. All his efforts to prevent anyone from knowing she was there wouldn't be worth anything if someone bumped into her.

With Lia floating upright behind him, Jared strode to the inn.

Balls and sass, he repeated under his breath. *Balls and sass.*

The door opened onto the common drinking room. To the left was a partially open door that led into a small, private room.

A heavy silence descended as every man in the room turned toward the door, including the bushy-bearded, Green-Jeweled Warlord standing behind the bar—a man who looked big enough and strong enough to wrestle with Garth and come out the winner.

Standing in the doorway, Jared looked at every face. No one but the innkeeper met his eyes for more than a second. Except for the innkeeper, the men were either lighter-Jeweled Warlords or Blood males who wore no Jewels at all.

Jared slowly walked to the bar, relieved that the men, picking up the scent of danger and violence that swirled around him, carefully moved out of his way. Calling in the gold marks he hadn't returned to Lia after his trip to the village, Jared placed one on the bar and looked the Green-Jeweled Warlord in the eyes.

The innkeeper calmly returned the look, but Jared noticed a flicker of something else in the depths of the man's eyes. Relief?

"What's your pleasure, Warlord?" the innkeeper rumbled.

Jared let the silence spin out a little before he answered. "A room with a bath, if you have it. Dinner. A bottle of good whiskey."

"Have a room that shares a bath with one other. All the others use the common bathing rooms."

"Is the other room occupied?"

That flicker again in the innkeeper's eyes. "It is."

Damn.

Jared turned slightly away from the bar and scanned the room. No one admitted being the other room's occupant. However, tucked between the staircase leading to the upstairs rooms and the inner wall of the small, private room was a round table that held an open bottle and a half-full glass of red wine.

The prickling started between Jared's shoulder blades as two things struck him: Wine wasn't usually served in a place like this, and all the men were standing or sitting on this side of the room, as if no one wanted to get too close to that table.

He had to get Lia out of this room before whoever was sitting at that table returned.

"I'll take the room," he said to the innkeeper.

The man took the gold mark. He set a bottle of whiskey and a key on the bar. "There are glasses and a jug of water in the room."

Noting the number, Jared slipped the key into his pocket and picked up the whiskey.

He took a couple of steps toward the stairs and stopped, clutching the bottle with suddenly numb fingers.

The table was no longer unoccupied.

Daemon Sadi raised the wineglass in a mocking salute.

Balls and sass, Jared muttered silently as he walked over to the table, careful to keep Lia hidden behind him. Balls and sass.

"Prince Sadi," Jared said politely.

"Lord Jared," Daemon murmured.

The golden eyes watching him looked deceptively sleepy. That deep voice flowed over him like warm water over bare skin. That beautiful face might have been carved from ice for all the feeling it revealed.

"What brings you here?" Jared asked, feeling sweat trickle down his sides. He didn't have time for this. *Lia* didn't have time for this. "It's not the sort of place I'd expect to find you or your Lady."

"You're right about my current Lady. This wouldn't be to her taste." Daemon sipped his wine. "But I sometimes find places like this a refreshing change from a court."

"Then you're alone?" Jared couldn't mask his surprise fast enough.

"My Lady and I have reached an agreement. I spend a few days away from the court each month."

"What does she get in return?"

The Sadist smiled.

Jared shuddered.

"I don't hurt her as much as I want to," Daemon said too softly. Another wineglass appeared on the table. "Join me, Lord Jared."

It wasn't an invitation or a request.

Feeling sick, Jared tried to smile. "It would be a pleasure, but let me wash the travel dirt off first." He didn't wait for Daemon's consent, but turned toward the stairs, using Craft to float Lia in a counterturn so that she ended up in front of him.

Sweet Darkness, please don't let the Sadist notice her, Jared silently prayed as he climbed the stairs, painfully aware of those golden eyes watching every move.

As soon as he was out of Daemon's line of sight, Jared grabbed Lia and hurried down the corridor. The inn was larger than he'd thought, and it took him a couple of minutes to find the side corridor that held his room.

He put a Red shield around the room, a Red lock on the door. He pulled back the bedcovers, dropped all the shields around Lia, and laid her carefully on the bed.

When he vanished her clothes and looked at her, the

strength went out of his legs. He sat on the edge of the bed and stared at the viper rat bites.

They had swollen to twice the size they'd been when he'd taken Lia away from the wagon a short time ago. In the center, where the rats' teeth had broken the skin, the bites looked pus-filled and yellow. The rest of the swollen skin was an angry, red-streaked purple that darkened to black.

The only viper rat bite he'd ever seen was the one his little brother Davin had gotten. Granted, that was years ago, but he didn't remember it looking so dark and malignant.

Jared tucked the bedcovers around Lia's still body. "I'll find someone to help," he whispered, gently brushing her dark hair away from her pale face. "I swear it."

There had to be a back staircase, a servants' staircase, *some* other way to reach the ground floor without using the stairs where Sadi waited for him. Hell's fire, he'd climb out a window if he had to. One way or another, he was going to find a Healer and drag her back here. And no one, not even the Sadist, was going to stop him.

After probing the corridor to be sure it was empty, Jared slipped out of the room and Red-locked the door.

He'd taken one step when a phantom hand clamped around his throat and slammed him against the wall next to the door. Strong, slender fingers squeezed, cutting off his air. Long nails pricked his skin.

Jared tried using Craft to pry that crushing hand away from his throat, but it just absorbed the strength of the Red and squeezed harder. Knowing it was useless, he raised his hands as if he could physically pull the hand away. His own nails scratched his neck as his efforts became more desperate, but there was nothing to fight, nothing to grab. He could do nothing, while it could kill him.

Finally, too breathless to fight, he dropped his hands to his sides and leaned against the wall.

A sight shield slowly faded.

Daemon leaned against the opposite wall, his hands in his trouser pockets, his golden eyes still sleepy.

"Give me one reason why I shouldn't tear your throat out," Daemon said too quietly.

"You've no reason to," Jared gasped. "Isn't that reason enough?"

Daemon made a sound that might have been laughter. "You really shouldn't play games with anyone from such a perverted race as Hayll, little Warlord. You say I have no reason. I say I do. Where do you think that leaves you?"

"Dead."

Daemon smiled. "Exactly."

Hell's fire, it hurt to swallow.

"What are you doing here, Jared?" Daemon asked.

Working to breathe, Jared studied Daemon. The man looked as if he was just making small talk with an acquaintance instead of choking someone to death. Then again, unlike his half brother, who was known to be a walking explosion, Daemon seldom gave any indication of his mood.

"What are you doing here?" Daemon repeated.

This time Jared heard the snarl of temper under the calmly spoken words.

Struggling to sound calm despite the phantom fingers pressing into his neck, Jared replied, "The witch who owns me is ill. I was ordered to find a place where she can rest."

"And you couldn't find a closer Blood community between where you were and here?" Daemon shook his head. "Try again."

Jared didn't dare blink let alone breathe. How did Daemon know where they'd been?

"I told you—"

Daemon cut him off. "When the Gray Lady left Raej, you were with her. Why aren't you still with her, Jared?"

Jared swallowed carefully and wondered how to answer. If he could trust Daemon, there was no one better to help him. If he couldn't . . . "Ownership changed hands a few days after we left." That was true in a way. Once Lia's illusion web had broken, the Gray Lady was no longer part of their little group.

"What happened to the Gray Lady?"

Jared tried to shrug. "She's probably back in Dena Neh-ele by now."

The phantom hand pulled him away from the wall and slammed him back into it.

Something malevolent flickered in Daemon's eyes. "Dor-othea's Master of the Guard is hunting for the Gray Lady. Every band of marauders who preys in this part of the Realm has been sniffing around for a particular quarry. Does that sound like Grizelle's safely returned to Dena Nehele?" Daemon sighed and looked at the ceiling. "This is becoming tedious, so I'll make it easy for you. You have three chances to give me a believable answer. After that, I'll take the information I want. But I'll make sure I leave enough of your mind intact so that you're able to fully understand what I'm doing when I tear your little witch apart." He paused. "What are you doing here, Jared?"

For a moment, Jared felt too stunned to even try to an-swer. Even the agony of the Ring of Obedience was a mild threat compared to this. He'd have no chance against Dae-mon. His inner barriers would be forced open, his thoughts, feelings, memories picked over like tawdry goods at a mar-ket stall. At best, it would be a mental rape. At worst, he wouldn't necessarily be broken, but he could still be sav-aged so badly he'd never fully recover.

And what would happen to Lia? Daemon made no secret of his revulsion for the distaff gender.

Jared licked his dry lips. "It's none of your business, Daemon."

Daemon smiled, a sweetly murderous smile. "Puppy, when you wailed for help, and I answered, you made it my business."

Hell's fire, Mother Night, and may the Darkness be merci-ful. Why hadn't he thought of that sooner?

"Although," Daemon added, "I hadn't expected you to show up shielding some battered slut."

"She's not a slut," Jared said hotly, pushing away from the wall.

The phantom hand slammed him back again, hard enough to make him wonder if he'd have cracked ribs as well as a crushed throat.

Daemon said nothing.

"I told you," Jared said through gritted teeth. "The witch who owns me ordered me to bring her—"

The phantom nails stabbed him, breaking the skin. Blood trickled down his neck.

"Liar," Daemon snarled quietly.

Jared shivered as he watched the gold eyes glaze with cold fury. He bit his tongue to keep from whimpering.

"She owns me," he said weakly as the fingers tightened a bit more.

Contempt joined the fury in Daemon's eyes. He looked pointedly at Jared's groin. "You wear no Ring, Warlord. And you're down to your last chance."

"I do wear a Ring," Jared said, gasping for breath. "I wear the Invisible Ring."

Unexpectedly, the phantom hand eased its vicious grip.

Daemon studied Jared. Then one finely shaped black eyebrow rose, and he asked mildly, "Which one? The Silver or the Gold?"

Which one? Jared thought desperately. *Which one?* How in the name of Hell was he supposed to know which one? It was *invisible!*

"I—"

A loud thump came from his room.

Jared turned toward the door without thinking. Releasing the Red lock, he rushed inside.

Lia was crawling toward the door, her eyes glazed and unseeing. Her right arm was curled, as if she were still dragging Tomas's body away from the viper rats' nest.

"Lia," Jared murmured, hurrying to reach her.

As he crouched in front of her, he heard the door quietly close. Heard the snick of a lock.

He slowly straightened and turned.

Daemon leaned against the closed door, his hands still tucked in his trouser pockets. In silence, he watched Lia's efforts.

"Who is she?" Daemon asked quietly.

Jared took a deep breath and let it out slowly. "Lady Arabella Ardelia. The Gray Lady's granddaughter."

Daemon didn't move, but Jared sensed a change. Not exactly surprise, but a swift reassessment.

"Viper rats?" Daemon said, his eyes narrowing as he studied Lia.

Jared nodded. He had no chance against the Sadist, but he'd make Daemon go through him in order to get to Lia.

Daemon shrugged out of his tailored black jacket, tossed it on a chair, and began rolling up the sleeves of his white-silk shirt. "Get her on the bed. We'll finish this discussion later." He stepped through the bathroom door.

Daemon returned before Jared had a chance to settle Lia.

"Wait," Daemon said. He unfolded two sheets, then re-folded them to make a pad. Placing them on the left side of the double bed, he smoothed the sheets.

What kind of spells was Daemon putting on the sheets? Jared wondered, holding Lia a little tighter to his chest.

Satisfied, Daemon said, "Put her on those. It'll be easier than stripping the bed later and disturbing her."

Jared did as he was told. He bit back a snarl when Daemon knelt on the bed beside Lia. "Is there a Healer in the village?"

Daemon's hands glided over Lia's head, slid down her swollen neck. "Even if there is, I doubt she'd be much help. You need someone who has some skill in healing Craft and a knowledge of poisons." His hands glided over her shoulders, over her breasts.

Thera had said the same thing, Jared reminded himself as he watched Daemon's hands move over Lia's body. There was nothing personal or sexual about the way Daemon explored her, but Jared couldn't push aside the memory of watching those hands with their long, black-tinted nails roam over other female bodies for a very different purpose.

Especially when those strong, slender fingers drifted through the triangle of hair between Lia's legs and curved to cup her.

Jared snarled at the intimacy.

"If you don't know how to behave in a sickroom, get

out," Daemon said mildly, giving Jared one piercing look before he turned his attention back to Lia.

Stung, Jared clenched his teeth. Of course he knew how to behave in a sickroom. His mother was a Healer. He closed his eyes and took a deep breath to steady himself.

The first rule of a sickroom was that no anger, no fear, no violent emotions were permitted because they could be absorbed into a healing, neutralizing or even destroying a Healer's efforts.

He opened his eyes when Daemon sat back.

"If someone hadn't taught her how to contain an injected poison, she'd be dead by now," Daemon said.

"Her mother is a Black Widow." The bites looked bigger, darker. "Isn't there anyone . . ." Jared's voice faded.

Daemon got off the bed. He called in two leather carrying boxes, opened them, and started looking through the various jars. "I know enough healing Craft." Amusement and something else Jared couldn't identify flickered in Daemon's eyes. "And poisons are an interest of mine. Those bites have to be opened and the venom drawn out. If you don't have a strong stomach, you've got five minutes to acquire one."

Jared swallowed hard. Frowning, he gingerly touched his throat.

Daemon gave him a knowing look before calling in a mortar and pestle. "There's no physical damage. Well, not much. I didn't think I'd actually have to crush your throat to convince you to be reasonable. There are many kinds of illusions, Jared."

Jared winced when his fingers brushed against one of the cuts made by the phantom nails. "But you would have."

Daemon poured a jar of dried herbs into the mortar. "If you'd done something to harm the Gray Lady, yes, I would have."

"Why are you so interested in the Gray Lady?"

Daemon's golden eyes turned to hard, yellow stones. "Because she stands against Dorothea."

"There's nothing more we can do," Daemon said wearily, wiping his hands on a soiled towel.

Jared braced his forearms on the bed, too tired to sit up straight.

They had done all they could, but had they done enough?

They'd worked for hours, applying herb poultices to draw the venom, draining the pus and fluid that Daemon had explained were the result of the healing Craft Lia had used. They'd gone through the cycle three times. In between those cycles, Daemon stroked Lia's body, soothing her while she burned with fever. Sure that Reyna had never used her hands quite that way, Jared had clenched his teeth and leashed his emotions while he assisted by doing all the mundane tasks required.

At the end of it, though, the swelling had gone down and the ugly, malignant look of the bites had faded to the color of pale bruises. Lia was breathing easily and no longer feverish.

Jared smoothed the already smooth covers and stood up. He swayed from fatigue.

"Here," Daemon said, calling in a long dressing robe. "Get cleaned up. I'll see about getting something to eat."

Jared took the robe. Maybe a hot bath would ease his aching muscles enough to convince his body to keep going. "I'm not hungry."

"Being tired is no excuse for being an idiot." Daemon finished putting the empty jars back into the leather carrying cases. He vanished them, along with the mortar and pestle. "If you expect to be of any use to her tomorrow when she needs you, you'll eat and get some rest tonight."

Jared didn't argue. What was the point of arguing with someone who was right?

Nodding agreement, he stumbled into the bathroom. It was a bit primitive, but it had running water and indoor plumbing. He fit the plug into the bottom of the bathtub, turned the single faucet, and stifled a yelp when cold water gushed out.

He sank to his knees and stared at the rising water, wondering how he was going to convince himself to get into that tub of cold water.

He scrubbed his hands over his face, trying to clear away enough of the fatigue to think. If the innkeeper wasn't supplying hot water, that meant the guests were expected to make their own.

Jared lowered his hands. Of course. This wasn't an aristo inn where servants would be responsible for the warming spells that would keep tanks of water hot for the guests. He'd have to use Craft to heat the water. A small thing, really. Certainly nothing a Red-Jeweled Warlord would have to think twice about.

It took several tries before he got the water to the temperature he wanted, too mentally and physically drained to get even the simplest spell right the first time.

Finally, he got in the tub and let the hot water soak away the sweat and grime, the ache in his muscles, and the tension that had ridden him hard since he'd seen the brass button among the boulders.

By the time he returned to the bedroom, a square wooden table and two straight-backed chairs were positioned in front of the fire. The table held two steaming bowls of beef stew, a small loaf of bread, a dish of butter, cheese, fruit, a bottle of wine, and two glasses.

Daemon sat comfortably in one of the chairs, smoking one of his black cigarettes. "You're almost recognizable now," he said as he flicked the cigarette into the fire. "Come and eat."

Jared went to the bed first to check on Lia. He noticed a cup on the bedside table.

"A healing brew," Daemon said.

"She woke?" Jared leashed the emotion that bubbled up before he had a chance to identify it. Before he had to acknowledge it.

"No. I brought her up out of the healing sleep enough for her to drink, but she wasn't aware of anything."

So she didn't know he hadn't been in the room. Didn't know it had been Daemon who had held her and coaxed her to drink.

Feeling his body relax, Jared joined Daemon at the table.

"Eat," Daemon said, picking up his spoon.

They concentrated on their food for a few minutes.

"Will she be all right?" Jared asked, carefully buttering a thick slice of bread.

"You'll know by morning."

Jared forced a mouthful of bread past the lump in his throat. Right now, he couldn't bear kindness or understanding from Daemon. "Could you tell anything else?" he asked.

One of Daemon's eyebrows rose. "Do you have something specific in mind?" He sounded amused. "Could I tell she's still a virgin? Considering how many centuries I've been playing bedroom games, it's a little insulting if you think a detail like that would slip past me. Or did you mean, could I tell that she's recently injured her knee and hasn't stayed off it enough to let it fully heal? Or that she hasn't made the Offering to the Darkness yet? Is that what you meant?"

Jared dropped his spoon. His body went ice cold. "What?"

"She hasn't made the Offering to the Darkness yet."

"You can't—" Jared raked his fingers through his hair. "You can't be sure of that."

"Jared," Daemon said patiently, "you wear the Opal and the Red. I can sense both levels of strength in you. I only sense one level in her—the Green—and the . . . potential . . . for a much darker strength. If nothing interferes when she makes the Offering, my guess is she'll wear the Gray."

"No one can tell beforehand what Jewels a person will wear after the Offering," Jared protested.

Daemon mopped up the last of his stew with a piece of bread. "She carried off the masquerade of being Grizelle so successfully, no one had doubted they were seeing a Gray-Jeweled Queen." Mild irritation flickered across his face and was gone.

"She had good illusion spells," Jared argued.

"An illusion spell wouldn't have hidden the truth from someone who wears a Jewel darker than the Gray."

There was something in Daemon's voice that told Jared that was as far as he would go toward acknowledging the rumors that he wore the rare Black Jewel.

"Which means," Daemon continued, "that there must be something in *her* that resonates with the Gray in order to complete that illusion. That's why I think Lady Arabella Ardelia is a Gray-Jeweled Queen who hasn't taken the final step necessary to actually wear the Gray Jewels." He paused, gave Jared a considering look. "But you had sensed the illusion before she revealed the truth. How?"

Frowning, Jared ate a spoonful of stew. It was a guess that hit the target. Since he didn't want to admit it was his body not his brain that had picked up the signals, which he then dismissed as being wrong, he mumbled, "Maybe it's because of the Invisible Ring."

"Yes, I imagine it is," Daemon replied dryly. Before Jared could say anything, he added, "Why don't you tell me how you ended up here."

So Jared told Daemon everything that had happened since he left Raej. Well, almost everything. He couldn't bring himself to mention the Fire Dance and the rut. But he told Daemon what he knew about the others. He told him about Thera's tangled webs. He told him about Blaed's romantic interest in the young Black Widow. He told him about the brass buttons and Garth . . . and about the fight that had ended with a half-Blood boy dead and Lia desperately ill.

Using Craft and his thumbnail, Daemon delicately pealed an apple. "Why didn't she buy passage on another Coach and head for the Tamanara Mountains as fast as possible?"

A bite of cheese stuck in Jared's throat. He took a large swallow of wine to force it down. "After she sensed the wrongness, she didn't know whom she could trust, and she wasn't willing to bring an unknown enemy into Dena Nehele. Traveling cross-country was the only way she could bring everyone with her and give herself the time to find Dorothea's pet." He struggled to take a deep breath. "And she didn't have enough marks to buy a second passage for all of us because she bought me."

Daemon stared at Jared. Then he swore softly, viciously.

Jared's eyes widened. "*You* put the compulsion spell on her."

"Nothing so crude," Daemon snapped. He drained his wineglass, filled it, and drained it again. "I didn't force her to buy you, Jared. I nudged her toward that part of the auction grounds, and that's all I did. I knew if she was the Queen she seemed to be, she wouldn't let a Red-Jeweled Warlord like you be destroyed in the salt mines of Pruul. Not if there was a chance of winning your loyalty." He swore again. "It never occurred to me that she might not have brought enough marks with her."

Jared cut two more slabs out of the half wheel of cheese and offered one to Daemon. "Apparently, everything was more expensive than the Gray Lady's court had anticipated, from the guard escorts to the slaves. There's no way you could have known that. There's no way you could have known she'd spend more than she could afford in order to get one more person out of Raej."

"Perhaps not," Daemon agreed. "But, Hell's fire, if I'd suspected she was cutting it that tight, I'd have slipped her enough marks to cover the extra expenses when I had that note delivered."

"You—" Jared's voice cracked. He hastily swallowed some wine. "*You* sent that note? But you were in Raej. How could you know?"

Daemon smiled indulgently. "Let's just say that, after the attack on the Gray Lady last spring, I wondered what might be waiting for her at the Coach stations she'd be most likely to head for and made arrangements to be informed. Unfortunately, my source arrived too late to help the men who walked into that trap. But she sent the warning—and I'd guess there were fewer males who saw the sun rise than saw it set." He paused. "Would you like some coffee?"

Jared pushed his plate to one side and nodded. He toyed with the silverware and watched Daemon smoke another cigarette while they waited. "You said 'she.' " Jared's hand curled into a fist. "Knowing it might be dangerous, you still sent a witch to check out a trap?"

"Yes."

"She could have been hurt. How could you be so careless, so—"

"Cruel?" Daemon said too softly. His face changed subtly when Jared didn't answer.

Jared recognized that cold mask. He winced when Daemon's deep voice lost every hint of color. That bored tone could cut someone as mercilessly as a sharp knife.

"Have you ever heard of Surreal?" Daemon asked, lighting another black cigarette.

Jared swallowed. Oh, yes, he'd heard about the most expensive whore in the entire Realm of Terreille. When he was seventeen and trying to gather up enough nerve to ask Reyna's permission to visit a Red Moon house, he'd spent several sweaty nights fantasizing that Surreal would come to Ranon's Wood for some reason and find him interesting enough to waive her usual fee.

"She's a whore," Jared said tightly. Had Daemon ever . . . ? "What was she supposed to do? Distract an entire troop of guards?"

"I'm sure she could have if she wanted to," Daemon said with such dismissive casualness it made Jared clench his teeth.

A chime sounded. A moment later a tray floated beside the table. The dirty dishes vanished. Daemon transferred the pot of coffee, mugs, cream, and sugar to the table and vanished the tray. He poured the coffee, making a small sound of approval after his first sip.

"However," Daemon continued as Jared spooned sugar into the other mug, "she's also a first-rate assassin. So gracefully vicious when she's holding a knife." His eyes narrowed. "Puppy, do you have any idea how much sugar you've just dumped into your coffee?"

Because his mind had stuttered on the word "assassin" and he really didn't know, Jared poured the heaping spoonful of sugar back into the sugar bowl. He stirred carefully, trying not to disturb the half inch of sugary sludge at the bottom of the mug. He raised the mug to his lips and hesitated.

Daemon coughed politely. Several times.

Jared took a sip. Shuddered. Set the mug down.

Daemon's shoulders quivered. He pressed a fist against his mouth.

"Good coffee," Jared murmured. Hell's fire, his teeth itched.

Daemon bolted for the bathroom.

Listening to the muffled laughter behind the closed door, Jared considered switching the mugs but decided he wasn't up for whatever Daemon's response might be after choking on the first mouthful.

Jared's mug vanished.

Daemon returned a couple of minutes later, placed the cleaned mug in front of Jared, sank into his chair, and grinned wickedly.

Jared fixed another mug of coffee. "This is fine."

"I'm so pleased."

Jared almost gave in to the urge to give Daemon one hard kick. "They're rather opposing professions," he said, his thoughts circling back to the woman who, it was said, had exotic looks and enough bedroom skills to melt a man's bones.

"Not really." Daemon sat up, gave Jared a sharp look, and then drank his coffee. "Especially when one profession is part of the tools used for the other."

Jared choked.

"Did I just ruin a long-held fantasy?" Daemon asked innocently.

"Of course not."

"She doesn't kill *every* male she beds."

"Wouldn't matter if she did."

"Your Thera would like her."

Mother Night, banish the thought. "She's not my Thera."

"Blaed's Thera, then."

"Haven't you got the possessive turned around? Shouldn't you say Thera's Blaed?" He thought about that for a second, then set his mug down with a thump.

"Thera's blade." Looking too much like a cat that has one paw firmly on the mouse's tail, Daemon poured more coffee. "Which is something you shouldn't forget, Warlord."

The dinner that had tasted good a few minutes ago swam greasily in Jared's stomach. "You think—"

Daemon made an exasperated sound. "If I didn't know you're too tired to think straight, I'd knock some sense into you. Listen, and listen well. Blaed's a good man and a good Warlord Prince. In a few years, when he matures, he'll be an even better one—and a dangerous one. From what you've said, Thera's a strong-willed young woman who's been on a battleground for far too long. A Green-Jeweled Black Widow with that kind of fire in her isn't the kind of witch Dorothea would allow to stay whole no matter what sort of games were being played. Because that kind of witch is a serious rival."

Jared sipped his coffee. "Thayne?"

"Why? Because he protected some innocent, terrified animals that were caught in a battle? Because, no matter how he feels about them, he might have realized how much harder the rest of the journey would be without them, especially if any of you were injured?"

"I hadn't thought of it that way." And now, remembering Thayne's burned face, he wished he *had* thought of it. He rubbed his eyes, fighting to stay awake. "Who, then?"

"It doesn't matter," Daemon said gently. "You're too deep into the game, Jared. Your presence—and Blaed's and Thera's—combined with Lia's wonderfully erratic actions, tangled up what was probably supposed to be a quick kill. Besides, how can a bargain to kill the Gray Lady be fulfilled if she isn't there?"

"We still need to know who the enemy is," Jared insisted.

"You do," Daemon countered. "Dorothea SaDiablo—and her Master of the Guard. The rest doesn't matter anymore." He stood up and stretched the muscles in his back. "You can stay here tomorrow. The owner and I have an understanding."

Jared shook his head. "If anyone puts together the Shalador Warlord who was in that fight and the one staying here . . ."

"No one will put it together. No one will remember seeing a Shalador Warlord walk into the tavern room—at least, no one will remember until he's been away from this place for a day."

Even dulled by fatigue, Jared understood. Daemon had cast a spell around this place, a kind of psychic fog that hid one specific memory.

Daemon rolled down his sleeves, fastened the ruby cuff

links, and shrugged into his black jacket. "I have to return to the court. I'll be leaving before dawn. Stay in the room. Get some rest. The owner or his wife will make sure you have everything you need. I've left a change of clothes for you. We're about the same size, so they should fit well enough. Something will be found for Lia tomorrow."

"Thank you. For everything."

Daemon slipped his hands into his trouser pockets. "Get some sleep. In the bed. A warm body next to her will be more comforting—for both of you—than a pile of blankets."

"If she snarls about it, I'll blame you." If she was still alive to snarl.

Daemon smiled gently. "Fair enough." As he opened the door, he looked back at Jared. "By the way, you wear the Silver."

Jared wasn't sure how long he stared at the closed door. By the time he got his legs to move and got the door open, the hallway was empty. No point searching. He could spend the rest of the night turning this place inside out with Daemon, fully shielded, standing nearby the whole time, and he'd never know.

After Red-locking the door, Jared pulled off the dressing robe and slipped cautiously into the bed. He felt Lia shivering despite the warming spells on the blankets. He settled beside her, tucked the covers around them, and slid his arm around her waist. Slowly her chilled skin warmed. She made a sleepy, contented sound.

Jared dimmed the candle-lights in the room. But sleep didn't come for a while.

Maybe being able to sense the Invisible Ring depended on whether a man wore a Jewel lighter or darker than the Gray since Grizelle had probably created it. He still couldn't sense it, but Daemon had been able to tell which kind he wore. And Daemon wouldn't lie to him. Not about something like that.

He wore the Invisible Ring. He wore the Silver.

Whatever that meant.

CHAPTER EIGHTEEN

Krelis stared at the male organs neatly arranged on a thick pad of blood-soaked cloth. There were wounds on all of them, which meant the agony had begun long before the barber had used the knife.

His vision grayed. He swallowed hard against the sickness clogging his throat.

Gliding behind him, Dorothea brushed the back of his neck with the tip of a large, white feather, and purred, "Recognize anyone?"

Krelis squeezed his eyes shut. Sweet Darkness, he hoped those *things* had belonged to landens or slaves. Something expendable. Something that required no thoughts, no feelings.

"I want you to choose five guards, men you value," Dorothea said. "I understand one of your cousins recently became one of my guards."

Krelis took a few steps away from the table. "Yes, Priestess. A distant cousin from the distaff side of the family."

"He'll be one of the five."

"For a special assignment?" Krelis asked. His cousin was only Sixth Circle. Being noticed so quickly would please the family.

"In a manner of speaking. You'll also include the young guard you've been personally training as well."

"As you wish, Priestess." Krelis narrowed his eyes, trying to remember who was immediately available in the First Circle who could balance the two less-experienced men. "What will be required of them?"

"Very little." Dorothea brushed her chin with the white feather and smiled malevolently. "You've been something of a disappointment, Lord Krelis. Difficulties with the Gray Lady were one thing. But having this little bitch elude you . . ." She shook her head. "It troubles me. It makes me wonder if your loyalty is as strong as it should be. It makes me wonder if I made an error in my choice of Master of the Guard."

Krelis felt light-headed. "Priestess . . ."

"So I've decided to give you a bit more incentive."

As she moved toward him, Krelis wondered how he'd ever mistaken that predatory walk for something enticing, inviting.

"Do you remember your predecessor, Lord Krelis?" Dorothea purred. "You're going to bring those five men to me. And every day that little bitch runs free, one of those men will pay for your failure." Her eyes slid to the blood-soaked cloth. "Since you're the one selecting them for this, the last four, at least, will understand who's responsible for their suffering. You may choose whether your cousin or your protégé is the last. I hope you find her before then, Krelis. I truly do." She waved the feather, tickling his lips. "I expect them here within the hour. Do you understand?"

Krelis wanted to lick his dry lips, but he was terrified his tongue might touch that feather. Since there was no chance of handing over the little bitch-Queen tomorrow, he knew how that feather would soon be used. "I understand, Priestess," he choked. "I understand."

How could it have gone so wrong? Krelis wondered a couple of hours later as he leaned back in his chair, a half-full bottle of brandy cradled to his chest. He'd anticipated so much, had taken such care.

How could it have gone so wrong?

With the bounty he'd offered, every marauder band in that part of the Realm was hunting her, and they'd *still* found nothing but cold trails and the buttons his pet had left.

And his pet hadn't even left those lately.

His fault for believing the bastard hadn't had something vital snipped out of him when the Ring of Obedience had been placed around his cock. The fear of the pain changed most of them. They never again felt the arrogant assurance that honor and Protocol would protect them. Warlord Princes became savage over time. Warlords shriveled up inside.

But his pet hadn't been a slave that long, only long enough to feel desperate, and bitter enough about the betrayal that had sent him into slavery that the offer of service without a Ring sounded sweet enough to rape honor and justify betrayal. He'd been intelligent enough to realize the quality of his life would rest on Hayll's whims, and doing such an extensive favor for the High Priestess would almost guarantee that he'd never feel the pain of the lash or the agony of the Ring again.

Almost.

Krelis laughed bitterly. The bastard had believed that by killing the one Queen who had successfully stood against Dorothea over these past decades, he'd earn a promise of safety.

Except there was no promise. And there was no safety. Krelis had finally understood that when he watched five pairs of eyes fill with terror when he left them in that barren room.

He'd always been ambitious. He'd thought it was because he wanted the kind of power that could only be attained by serving in the First Circle of a strong court. Now he knew it was because he'd wanted to be safe. And he *was* safe. Safe from the minor Queens who didn't believe a strong male could be trusted at all unless he was Ringed. Safe from the petty abuse inflicted on males by any witch who wore a darker Jewel. Safe from torments designed to soothe a bitch's ego.

Safe from everything except Dorothea.

Which meant he wasn't safe at all.

But she was all he had now. He'd realized that, too, when he'd seen how carefully the guards who were posted outside that barren room had shuttered their expressions, closing him out. He'd betrayed the unspoken understanding that the Master would protect his men from the whims of the witches in the court. They would obey him to escape punishment, but they would never respect him.

With one order, Dorothea had isolated him from everyone but her First Circle—and he'd even be isolated from them if he didn't succeed brilliantly enough to erase his failure up to this point. If his cousin was subjected to that gruesome maiming, his family would tolerate his presence when he joined them but would never welcome him. His dream of a pretty, placid, broodmare wife would wither and die with his unborn children. He'd be left mounting the whores who worked in the Red Moon houses.

Krelis raised the bottle of brandy to his lips and kept swallowing until he needed to breathe.

He'd find the little bitch before his cousin felt Dorothea's knife.

And his pet would learn the price of failure.

CHAPTER NINETEEN

"Would you like to play chess?" Jared asked as he set up the game board the innkeeper had provided and tried—hard—not to throw a fine fit of male hysterics. That's what Lia had called his reaction when her legs had buckled while she'd been pacing the room earlier in the day. Working the stiffness out of them, she'd said. Scaring the shit out of *him,* he'd shouted.

Then his wobbly-legged little Queen had threatened to dump the hot soup that had been part of the midday meal into his lap if he didn't stop pestering her to take a nap.

He didn't pester. He never pestered. He was *concerned.* Couldn't she tell the difference?

"One game," Jared coaxed, grinding his teeth so he wouldn't yell at her to sit down. "Just to pass the time."

Looking much too fragile and very young in the too-large sweater and snug trousers that had belonged to one of the innkeeper's sons, Lia crossed her arms and gave Jared a stony stare that would have made him nervous if it hadn't been accompanied by a hint of a pout. "You snarled the last time we played."

Jared placed one hand over his heart. "I promise not to snarl." About the game, anyway. "Of course, if you don't want to play, we could just turn in for the night."

She snarled at him.

"She who snarls shouldn't comment on someone else's little grumbles," Jared said virtuously.

Her hands balled into fists.

Jared watched her, fighting against the desire to provoke her a little more. In her weakened condition, if she threw a punch at him, she'd probably end up on the floor and would be even madder when he had to help her up.

After he'd finished setting up his red pieces to his satisfaction, Jared reached for the black pieces.

"Mine!" Lia said, sitting down too abruptly for the movement to have been completely intended.

While she set up her pieces, Jared poured a glass of fruit juice for her and a glass of wine for himself.

He'd wrapped himself around her last night, more out of a need to feel each reassuring breath she took than any belief that his presence would help her. This morning, he'd been rudely awakened when her elbow jabbed his belly and she started swearing to do vile things to his most valued body parts if he didn't let go. When his still-sleepy brain had finally understood the reason for the desperation that laced her curses, he'd made her madder by carrying her into the bathroom.

He'd chuckled at her muttering when he tucked her back into bed and climbed in with her, so pleased to have her alive and well enough to be angry that he never gave a thought to how she might react to having a naked male beside her. He'd cuddled her for an hour.

And he'd held her and cried with her when she asked about Tomas.

He'd tried to spoon-feed her at breakfast.

He'd tried to give her a bath.

He'd mentioned taking a nap every hour or so, politely pointing out that she'd been very ill the night before and needed a lot of rest.

So maybe he'd fussed a bit too much, but he was entitled to fuss. She'd scared him. She'd more than scared him.

But he had *not* pestered.

"You're muttering already," Lia grumbled, watching him through narrowed eyes. She tossed her hair over her shoulders and picked up the glass of fruit juice.

Her hair was like a soft, dark cloud, Jared thought, sipping his wine. She'd let him brush it after her bath—had to let him brush it because, after a few strokes, her arms had felt too heavy to lift. Daemon had drawn most of the venom out of her, but her body still felt the deep fatigue of fighting to survive on top of the demands she'd made of it during the ambush. While he'd brushed her hair, he'd woven a soothing spell around her that Daemon had taught him during the year they'd been in the same court. It had put her to sleep for a couple of hours.

Remembering that, he grinned.

"What?" Lia said. "Did you put something in the fruit juice?"

"Of course not," Jared huffed. "Roll the dice. Let's play."

She rolled a five for a Summer-sky Queen. He rolled a three for a Tiger Eye. Giving her a sassy grin, he opened by moving one of his Black Widows.

Several moves later, he began to worry about the change in her game. Her Queen remained in the background while her stronger pieces—especially the Black Widows and Warlord Princes—were doing most of the defending, supporting the weaker pieces who only captured one of his when there was no possibility of an exchange. Again and again, she retreated, giving up more ground and growing more timid each time he captured one of her pieces.

And all the while, her Queen did nothing.

Her brash courage might have enraged him when the instincts bred into Blood males howled to defend the female, but seeing her act timid and uncertain produced a deeper anger—and a deeper kind of fear.

Losing Tomas had produced an emotional wound that would heal in time, but she'd carry the scar of it the rest of her life. And there would be more scars. Dena Nehele's continued freedom would be paid for in blood.

Her mind knew it, but her heart couldn't accept it yet.

And he couldn't allow her the luxury of thinking retreat would keep her people safe.

He moved one of his Warlords to threaten a Blood male pawn. If she moved her Queen to challenge, he'd let the pawn go. If she didn't . . .

It felt like half the night had passed before she hesitantly moved her Queen. Her hand trembled a little, and her face lost the little color she'd gained throughout the day.

Wanting to distract her and give himself time to choose

a move that would seem a logical alternative to capturing the pawn, he said, "Does your grandmother really look that intimidating?"

Lia had just taken a sip of juice when he asked the question. She clamped a hand over her mouth until she managed to swallow. "Gran?" she finally gasped. Then she started laughing.

Jared moved a Priestess nearer to the protection of his Sanctuary.

"Hey!" Lia huffed, sitting forward. "No fair moving a piece when I'm too teary-eyed to see you do it." She frowned when she figured out his move.

Before she could comment, he gave her another nudge. "Is she?"

Lia caught her lower lip between her teeth. "Well, those *are* the clothes she wears when she has to travel outside our borders. And she *does* look impressive when she wears her Queen clothes, but—"

"Queen clothes?" Jared interrupted. He held up a hand. "Move first, then explain Queen clothes."

Lia scooted a Warlord Prince across the board.

Not sure if that was meant to do something besides move a piece, Jared studied the board for a minute but didn't make a move.

"That's what Gran calls the fancy gowns and things she wears once or twice a month to keep her First Circle happy," Lia said. "She says, if males really don't notice female fashions the way they swear they don't, then why do they start drooling like a dog with a large soup bone whenever women wear evening gowns?"

Jared choked on his wine. "We don't drool."

"No? Oh. Well, that's good. One of my cousins had this big dog who drooled buckets and always wanted to put his head in your lap. She—my cousin, that is—wanted to train the dog to put his head into just the boys' laps so they'd have to explain why the fronts of their trousers were wet, but she only got to the lap part and not the boy part before the adult males in the family found out about it and roared. So we all got drooled on."

Wondering if he'd had a game plan when he started,

Jared moved a Prince to support a Healer. "If she only wears Queen clothes once or twice a month, what does she wear the rest of the time?"

"Um." Lia moved her other Warlord Prince. "Well, clothes like this." She pinched a bit of sweater between her thumb and forefinger. "Papa says that if you enter a large room full of people and there's one woman there who looks like she should be out weeding the garden, she's probably the Queen. Prince Harland—"

"Who?"

"Gran's lover. He says—"

"Her *what*?"

"Lover. He's also her Consort. Anyway, he says a Queen is a Queen no matter what she wears—"

"Or doesn't," Jared added under his breath, not quite able to picture the Gray Lady as part of an elderly couple having a tickle and tussle in a rumpled bed—even if he *had* been able to picture it quite clearly when he'd imagined himself as the lover. But that was different. Somehow.

"—and that it's more important for her to be comfortable and happy than it is to have her measure up to someone else's idea of proper dress, and if *he* didn't have any complaints, Papa shouldn't either."

"Your papa should listen to an elder."

"Harland's not Papa's elder. They trained together." Jared wheezed.

Lia leaned forward. "Are you coming down with something?"

A terminal case of curiosity.

"How—" Jared bit his tongue. There were some things a man did not ask a twenty-one-year-old virgin about her grandmother.

Lia shook her head and tsked sadly. "Someone your age really should know about these things. Didn't your papa ever talk to you about that?"

"He talked to me at great length about a great many things. Including that."

Sniffing primly, Jared added, "He even demonstrated once."

Lia almost spilled the juice all over her lap.

"Not like *that*," Jared growled. He made a circle with his left hand and brought it toward the pointing forefinger of his right. When his hands were half a hand apart, he noticed how huge Lia's eyes had gotten—and quickly lowered his hands.

Lia gulped some juice. "That's it?"

"That's the gist of it." And if he had to explain any more of it, he wouldn't be putting a warming spell on the bathwater. Which reminded him of why he *shouldn't* have to explain it. "Didn't your mama ever talk to you about that?"

"Of course she did," Lia huffed. Then she added, giving him a speculative look, "But she never said anything that looked quite like that."

This conversation was going to kill him. He just knew it. "Your move," he said a bit desperately, wanting to distract her.

She looked at the game board. "No, it isn't."

"Is."

"Isn't."

"Is."

"Isn't."

"Move anyway."

She moved a Blood male pawn.

He pounced on it with a Warlord.

Her pained gasp broke his heart.

He caught her as she stumbled away from the table. "I'm sorry," he said, wrapping his arms around her. "Lia, I'm sorry."

"He'd still be alive if it wasn't for me," Lia sobbed. "If I hadn't bought him, he'd still be alive."

"Maybe," Jared said. He gently stroked her back.

"He would." She clutched his shirt and pressed her face against his shoulder. "He would."

"Listen to me, sweetheart." Jared gave her a little shake. "Listen to me. You may have heard the women the Gray Lady brought out of Raej talk about being enslaved and the brutality they endured, but you don't know what it's like for the males. You can't."

"I've heard—"

"You've heard nothing," Jared said, sharpening his voice enough to prick her pride and make her raise her head and look at him. "You've heard what they would admit to, what the scars on their bodies won't allow them to deny. But they aren't going to tell you about the other kinds of wounds or the deep scars you can't see. *No* man would tell a young Queen about the kinds of twisted games that are played in those courts. We're all scarred, Lia. We're stripped of our honor and our pride. We're punished when we act like Blood males and punished when we don't. Dorothea SaDiablo and the Queens who dance to her tune don't just rape a man's body, they rape his soul. They take what's good in a man and twist it out of all recognition."

Jared captured Lia's face between his hands. "As bad as it is for a Jeweled male, it's ten times worse for a Blood male whose inner barriers can be pried open by any Jeweled female who wants to toy with him. And half-Blood males, who have no barriers at all, don't have any kind of a chance. Unless they're sired by an aristo male, most of them never reach maturity. They're used until they start showing signs of becoming men, and then—" Jared stopped. Took a deep breath. "Tomas might have lived another year or two. But if you hadn't bought him, he never would have known kindness, never would have known what it was liked to serve a Lady who cared about him."

Fresh tears spilled down Lia's face. "He didn't know he wasn't a slave," she choked out.

Jared wiped away the tears with his thumbs. "He served, Lady Ardelia. He was too bright not to understand the difference whether you actually said the words or not. He deserved more time. He deserved a better life. But he didn't die because of you, Lia. He died because of Dorothea's greedy ambition to devour the entire Realm of Terreille. If you want to avenge Tomas, continue to be the strong Queen you are. Don't let Hayll's shadow fall over Dena Nehele."

Lia leaned against him, wrapping her arms around his waist.

Jared swayed back and forth, rocking her as he softly

sang an old song that Reyna used to sing when he needed comforting.

"That's nice," Lia murmured.

Jared sank the fingers of one hand into her hair. "Yes, it is."

"You've got a pleasing voice. Deep but smooth."

Jared smiled. "My father always said I got my mother's voice but an octave lower." His arms tightened around her. "Lia, we have to leave in the morning, and I've been thinking . . ."

Lia raised her head and studied his face. "Why does that sound like something I should worry about?"

Jared frowned at her. "There's nothing wrong with my brains."

"That's true," Lia agreed thoughtfully. "Your being so bossy when you start fussing has nothing to do with your brains."

"What?"

She smiled at him.

His frown deepened. "Tomorrow we'll go to Dena Nehele."

"No."

"Once you're safely home, I'll go to Ranon's Wood—"

"No."

"—and bring the others—"

"NO!"

Lia shoved him hard enough to break his hold on her. She stumbled back a couple of steps before she regained her balance.

"Don't be stubborn about this, Lia," Jared growled.

Her gray eyes darkened. "You're a fine one to accuse anyone else of being stubborn."

Jared gritted his teeth. "You'll be safe."

"I knew the risks when I agreed—"

"You knew nothing!" Jared shouted. "You were supposed to meet an escort at a Coach station who would get you safely home. *You*, Lia. Despite what you may want to believe, those men weren't there to make sure the rest of us got to Dena Nehele. So get it into your stubborn little head that you're going home tomorrow."

"I'm going to Ranon's Wood—"

Jared spewed every obscenity he could think of.

"Those people are my responsibility, Lord Jared. *Mine.*"

Jared bared his teeth. "My Jewels are darker than yours, which makes me stronger. If I have to, I'll truss you up in enough psychic restraints it'll take your granny half a day to undo them all and dump you on your father's doorstep. He may have yielded about letting you go in the first place, but if his balls still work, he won't let you go again no matter what your grandmother says!"

"How dare you say that about my father! What right do you have to make demands of me?"

"I serve you."

Lia shook her head. "No, you don't. The others, yes, until the journey ends. But not you."

It felt like a large fist had just punched him under the heart. Jared stared at her, trying to get his breath. "I serve you," he said hoarsely. "I wear the Invisible Ring." The Silver Ring.

"There is no Ring!" Lia raked her fingers through her hair. "There never was a Ring! It was only a bit of Craft my mother calls lightning and smoke to fool them so they wouldn't question my not using the Ring of Obedience."

"I wear your Ring," Jared insisted.

"Listen to me, you feather-brained mule. *There is no Ring.* I made it up. All of it. Whoever heard of an Invisible Ring?"

Daemon Sadi.

But he didn't say that. He took the verbal blows, unwilling to consider why they hurt so much. "Why?"

Lia took a couple of wobbly steps and made it to the chair before she fell down. "You're a good man, Jared. And you're a strong Warlord."

"You couldn't have known that about me."

"I'm a Queen," she said wearily. "I knew. But as you just pointed out, your Jewels outrank mine, and there was a lot of hate in you that day. I couldn't leave you there, and I couldn't control you."

"You could have used the Ring of Obedience."

Lia paled. "Do you—" She swallowed hard. "Do you think I could have used that—"

Either she couldn't think of a word obscene enough or couldn't bring herself to say it.

No, Jared thought as he carefully sat on the edge of the bed. She couldn't have used the Ring of Obedience.

"I knew I couldn't control you," Lia said. "And I couldn't afford to fight you. I thought you'd escape as soon as your body healed. Then you folded up inside yourself and I didn't know what to do. I kept thinking you'd go. As soon as you realized there was nothing holding you, you'd go."

But something *had* held him back.

Jared rubbed the back of his neck as he stared at his feet. Had she really counted on him going at the beginning of the journey? Had she counted on one less male to feed? Or . . .

He looked up. She watched him so carefully, as if she were trying to gauge the impact of her words.

"I wear no Ring," Jared said, watching her with equal care as he remembered how well she could put on an act when she felt it was necessary.

"You wear no Ring," Lia agreed. She looked away.

"You have no claim on me."

"None."

"If I walk out of this room, what will you do?"

"Meet the others in Ranon's Wood and take them to Dena Nehele."

"Why?"

When she looked at him again, he saw a Queen with shadows in her eyes.

"I took them out of Raej. I hold their lives in my hands because of that choice. So until we stand within the borders of Dena Nehele, they're my people, Lord Jared."

And he wasn't? Oh, no, she wasn't getting away with that.

Smiling, Jared walked up to her and held out his hands. "Time for bed. We need a good night's sleep if we're heading for Ranon's Wood at first light."

She looked wary, but she slipped her hands into his.

"You know," he said pleasantly as he helped her to her feet, "I'm going to have to remember how good a liar you are when your back's against the wall."

"What?" Lia said weakly.

He kept a firm grip on her hands. "I've spent this entire journey chasing my own tail because I couldn't sense the Ring in order to confirm that it existed. If you'd told me a couple of days ago that you had made it all up, I would have believed you."

"Why won't you believe me now?" Lia wailed.

Jared gave her a sharp smile. "Because we had help last night. A Warlord Prince I know did the healing. Just before he left, he confirmed that I wear the Invisible Ring. The Silver Ring."

Lia tried to tug her hands free. "Why would you believe *him?*"

"He had no reason to lie. You, on the other hand, didn't mention it until I threatened to drag you back to Dena Nehele. If you were in my place, what would you think?"

"That you're an idiot."

Slipping an arm around her waist, Jared led her to the bed. "I don't think you're an idiot. It was just bad timing on your part."

She muttered something that sounded nasty.

"Come on, Lady Grumpy. Put your nightgown on, and I'll tell you a bedtime story. Unless, of course, you're like me and prefer to sleep in nothing but your skin."

Her face had a lot of color now.

"Maybe you could sleep somewhere—"

"Not a chance."

"Oh. I . . . I'll change in the bathroom."

"You do that." He waited until she was at the bathroom door. "Oh, Lia. Just in case you get any ideas about slipping out of here without me, you should know that I've put a Red shield around the bathroom as well as this room and a Red lock on the door that leads to the adjoining bedroom."

The mutter that got cut off by the bathroom door closing was *definitely* nasty.

Her brains were still as wobbly as her legs, Jared decided

as he undressed. Why bother to tell him now, even if it
was true? He'd just go to Ranon's Wood, and *she* was going
to Ranon's Wood, may the Darkness protect the stubborn
little idiot. She thought she could push him out of her life
before he was ready to go? Well, she could think again.

And he *would* go as soon as he got her safely to Dena
Nehele. He'd said nothing less than the truth when he'd
told her all male slaves carried scars. Nine years as a pleasure slave had carved some deep ones into his soul.

He had no future in Dena Nehele. Or maybe it was more
honest to say that he wouldn't allow his heart to show him
something that could never be more than a wistful dream.

Jared settled into bed and waited for Lia.

But he'd keep her safe until then. Safe so that, someday,
a man without scars on his soul would be able to love her
the way she deserved to be loved.

CHAPTER TWENTY

Krelis pressed his palms against the desk to keep his hands from curling into fists.

Don't believe too quickly, he reminded himself as he stared at the Second Circle guard standing in front of him. *Don't hope at all.*

"Are you sure the man wasn't selling you a lie for a few silver marks?" Krelis finally asked.

"The bastard had no reason to lie, Lord Krelis," the guard replied with a feral smile. "And I paid him nothing. Whenever I take leave time outside Hayll, I find it more . . . lucrative . . . not to travel as a guard. These loose-tongued merchants and traders from other Territories are much more willing to complain and gossip with a fellow trader trying to make a little profit. They say things they wouldn't even dare think in the presence of a Hayllian court guard."

A clever man, Krelis thought as he leaned back in his chair. A dangerous man. A man who knew how to fashion lies to look like bright truths. A man who, one day soon, would find a way to speak to the High Priestess directly. And if he, Krelis, wasn't very careful, he'd find himself condemned by compliments. "This loose-tongued merchant is sure he saw a Shalador Warlord at a traveler's inn?"

The guard nodded. "A Red-Jeweled Shalador Warlord who looked like he'd been doing some hard traveling lately."

"He was alone?"

The guard shrugged. "The bitch didn't walk through the front door with him. Maybe he slipped the leash."

"Or maybe she slipped in the back way." Krelis rubbed his chin. The bitch-Queen had been traveling north or northwest since his pet had left the first message. So what was that Shadalor bastard doing so far south? Where were the others? If the bitch really wasn't with him, if he *had* slipped the leash, why wasn't he heading for his home Territory to hide for a few days?

Unless he was deliberately showing himself to lay a false trail. Or had the fool gone to that inn hoping to strike a bargain?

"This merchant. He was sure about the rest of it?"

The guard shifted his feet. He pressed his lips together. "It's hard to mistake *that* one for any other."

A chill started in Krelis's lower back and crept up his spine. "Yes, it is." Hell's fire, he needed a drink! "Your diligence to your duty is highly commendable, Warlord. You may be certain I'll keep it in mind. Inform Lord Maryk that his presence is required." Krelis gestured toward the door.

Accepting the dismissal, the guard bowed and left.

Krelis called in a bottle of brandy, but Maryk knocked on the door before he could consume enough of it to settle his nerves. Smothering a curse, he vanished the bottle, and snapped, "Come in!"

"Lord Krelis."

Maryk's bland expression was a subtle insult, but he hadn't been able to completely extinguish the contempt from his eyes.

"I've received some information about the little bitch-Queen who's been such an annoyance to the High Priestess," Krelis said. "I'm going to look into it personally. Until I return, you're in charge. If the High Priestess summons, you'll have to answer her."

Maryk swallowed carefully. They both knew what could happen to males when Dorothea was annoyed.

"I understand, Lord Krelis. Is there anything that will require special attention?"

Krelis shook his head. "You have the assignment roster. I've been informed of nothing else."

"Then, may the Darkness grant you a safe and speedy journey."

Yes, Krelis thought, as Maryk escorted him to the land-

ing place. The guards—especially the First Circle guards—
might despise him, but they'd rather have him standing between them and the High Priestess of Hayll than nothing
at all.

And not one of them would envy him this journey.

Krelis didn't bother to knock before he opened the door
of the small receiving room. Men didn't have to extend any
kind of courtesy to pleasure slaves. Even this one. Besides,
he'd already used up his courtesy on the pouty Queen who
ruled this forsaken Province. Hell's fire! What had the High
Priestess been thinking of to loan the Sadist to a witch
who'd had half of her brains bred out of her?

Daemon Sadi stood with his back to the door, looking
out a window.

Krelis closed the door hard enough to make anyone else
jump. Daemon didn't even twitch.

"Sadi," Krelis said, coming into the room far enough to
see the beautiful face in profile.

"Lord Krelis."

The boredom in that deep voice grated on Krelis's
nerves. That Sadi didn't bother to look at him grated
even more.

Krelis's hands curled into fists. "Do you know why I'm
here?"

"No."

If Sadi's voice and face were any gauge to measure by,
he also didn't care.

"It seems your Lady grants you a lot of liberties,"
Krelis said.

"She has a low threshold for pain."

Not knowing how to respond to that, Krelis said nothing
for a minute. "You were seen at a traveler's inn a couple
of days ago."

"Was I?"

"You met a Red-Jeweled Shalador Warlord named
Jared there."

"Did I?"

"Did you arrange to meet him?"

"That would have required effort. He's not that interesting."

"After he rented a room, he wasn't seen again. You left the common room shortly after he arrived and weren't seen again either."

"It appears someone else was as bored as I was if keeping track of everyone else's movements was the best entertainment available."

Krelis clenched his teeth. "You met with him. Why?"

"We were in the same court a few years ago. When he showed up at the inn, having dinner together seemed like a way to pass some time."

"What did you talk about?"

"Nothing interesting enough to remember."

"Was there a woman with him? A witch?"

"I'd gone to that hovel to get away from the stink of witches. I wouldn't have stayed in the room if one of them had been present."

Krelis took a deep breath and forgot what he was going to say. The air in the room felt soft, heavy. An elusive scent drifted past him, a scent that warmed the muscles in his groin at the same time it melted the tension from the rest of his body.

He took another deep breath. What had they been talking about? The Shalador Warlord. Now he remembered. "You talked all evening and remember nothing?"

"We talked during dinner."

"Did he mention the Gray Lady?"

"He wasn't quite that boring."

"What—" Krelis bit his lip. The pain cleared his head a little. "I want to know what the two of you did that evening."

Daemon turned and looked at him. "Do you?" he asked too softly.

Krelis nodded slowly.

Daemon smiled that cold, cruel smile.

Krelis shuddered and then gasped.

Long-nailed fingers whispered down his back, over his buttocks, down the backs of his thighs. They were still drifting over his calves when another pair of phantom hands brushed the back of his neck and began the journey.

"He bored me." Daemon took a couple of graceful, predatory steps toward Krelis. "It left me feeling mean, so I seduced him."

Another pair of phantom hands whispered over Krelis's chest and belly, separating just before they reached his groin to travel down the front of his legs.

"He was begging by the time I began to feel amused," Daemon crooned, taking another step toward Krelis.

Krelis opened his mouth to protest.

The tip of a phantom tongue delicately licked his upper lip.

Another tongue licked the inside of his thigh, moving upward.

Warm breath washed over his balls, over his hard organ.

"He was sobbing by the time I left the room," Daemon crooned, coming just a little closer, but still not close enough to touch.

A phantom mouth brushed against Krelis's throat. Sucked gently.

"Do you want me to show you what I did to him?"

Krelis couldn't think. Didn't want to think about anything but that beautiful face, about the moment when that real mouth would glide over his hot skin, when that real tongue would—

Daemon smiled. "I thought not."

Everything stopped. Instantly.

Krelis swayed. His vision blurred. Every breath made his body throb. In that moment, he would have promised anything, done anything to make Daemon finish it.

Knowing that revolted him.

He bit his lip until it bled. By the time he could think again, Daemon was looking out the window as if nothing had happened.

Krelis wanted to lash out, wanted to threaten some kind of dire punishment that would make up for his body's screaming need for relief.

Daemon turned his head and smiled that cold, cruel smile.

Krelis staggered out of the room.

A few steps away from the door, he leaned against the wall while he waited to get some strength back in his quivering legs.

Now he understood why Queens and favored witches from aristo families paid Dorothea such exorbitant fees for the loan of Daemon Sadi. Now he understood why they were willing to endure his cruelty, why they were willing to risk his temper. To have that exquisite pleasure brought to completion . . .

Krelis pushed away from the wall, desperate to get away from this place. Maybe, with distance, he could deny the terrible feeling that, no matter how skilled the whore or how much relief he took between her thighs, he would never again experience the kind of pleasure he'd felt with the Sadist.

CHAPTER TWENTY-ONE

Lia stopped abruptly at the edge of the official landing place outside Ranon's Wood.

Jared grabbed her, drawing her back against him while he absorbed the significance of what he was seeing—of what he *wasn't* seeing.

The section of the Coach station roof that had been torn away.

The broken windows.

The empty corral where the horses for hire would have been kept during the day.

The pieces of the stable door that were scattered around the yard.

The absence of people.

And the deeper feeling of emptiness.

"The land's been wounded," Lia said in a hushed, aching voice. "Oh, Jared, the land's been deeply wounded."

Hay fields that should have been thick with stubble from the harvest had small islands of yellow grass growing out of a sea of barren ground. Trees that had been landmarks for generations scarred the morning sky with their dead branches.

"The Blood fought here," Lia whispered. Her hand shook as she wiped a tear from her cheek.

Hearing her unspoken question, Jared chained his grief, leashed his growing fear. "This didn't happen because of our coming here. Look at the land, Lia. This happened during the growing season, not the harvest. When we got the supplies at the landen village, the old woman warned me that there was trouble in Shalador." He took her hand.

"Come on. Ranon's Wood is about a half a mile from here."

It would have been easy to probe the village, would have been easy to reach for the familiar minds of his family. He didn't do either.

The second time Lia stumbled because he'd increased the pace beyond her ability to keep up, she planted her feet and refused to move.

"You go on, Jared. Find out what's happened to your people."

"I'm not leaving you."

"I'll be fine. There's nothing here that will harm me."

"I'm not leaving you."

As they stared at each other, the words seemed to echo.

Jared swallowed. Tasted bitterness. Silently acknowledged the lie beneath the sincere words. As much as he didn't want to, he *would* leave her—as soon as he saw her safely home.

"Jared!"

Jared whirled, putting Lia behind him. Hell's fire, where were his wits? No one should have gotten this close to them without his sensing it, especially someone cantering toward them on horseback.

"It's Blaed!" Lia said, stepping around Jared and waving.

Reining in a few yards away from them, Blaed slid off the roan mare's bare back and dropped the reins to ground-tie her. He spared one quick glance for Jared before focusing on Lia with a hunger that made Jared tense.

Not a sexual hunger, Jared realized as Blaed's eyes traveled over the body that was covered from neck to mid-thigh by the bulky sweater, but the hunger a strong Blood male feels when he's bonded to a Queen.

"You're well?" Blaed asked hesitantly.

Lia gave him a dazzling smile. "I'm fine. I—"

Blaed pulled her into his arms. "Thera's been frantic about you."

Thera's not the one hugging her hard enough to crack her ribs, Jared said on a spear thread.

Blaed let go too fast.

Jared lunged to catch her. Blaed grabbed the front of the sweater.

A minute later, Lia was standing out of reach of both of them, eyeing them warily. "Whoever said males were sensible obviously never met either of you," she grumbled.

Blaed grinned at Jared. "She *is* well."

"Don't encourage her too much," Jared said dryly. "She needs more rest than she thinks she does."

Lia straightened her sweater. "Let's go to the village. I'd like to talk to someone sensible. Someone *female*."

"I thought you wanted to talk to someone sensible," Jared said.

Blaed coughed.

Lia looked at the sky and threw up her hands.

The gesture, so like Reyna's, stabbed Jared. As he turned away, he met Blaed's now-solemn hazel eyes.

Feeling the prickle between his shoulder blades, Jared chose each word as if it were a step he had to take on a trail filled with hidden traps. "When did you get here?"

"Last evening," Blaed said in a neutral voice. "Thayne's always been able to call animals to him. Enough of the marauders' horses survived, so we each had a mount."

"My mother's a good Healer. She'll take care of the witchfire burns for him."

"Jared . . ."

"My father got you settled in all right? Did you talk to him about getting a Coach to the Tamanara Mountains?"

"Jared . . ." Blaed's hand closed on Jared's arm.

Feeling the sympathy that flowed out of that touch, Jared jerked away, circling Blaed cautiously as he moved toward the roan mare.

"Go home, Jared," Blaed said quietly. "I'll escort Lia."

Torn, again, between two needs, Jared froze.

"Go home, Jared," Lia said.

Because it was the woman and not the Queen who said the words, he found himself galloping down the road to Ranon's Wood. His mind refused to see the images his eyes collected, and he was grateful. There would be time enough to deal with the destruction later.

It didn't take long to reach the lane that ended at the

weathered, rambling house that had been in Reyna's family for generations. The Healer's House, passed on, not from mother to daughter, but from the old Healer to the strongest, or only, Healer in the next generation. Year after year, the land had been tended by and yielded its bounty to the women of that bloodline. Generation after generation, strong Blood males had sought out those women, settling for a long-term contract as a consort if they weren't able to win the coveted title of husband.

Jared tied the mare's reins to the hitching post near the path that led to the front door.

Every spring, all the women in the family gathered for a few days to help plant the gardens at the Healer's House. The males of all ages divided their time between helping with whatever repairs might be needed after the winter and watching indulgently while the women laughed and squabbled over the planting.

Jared opened the gate. It didn't hang true and got stuck. He went sideways through the narrow opening.

"Mother?"

No one had planted this year. He felt the absence of laughter as keenly as he felt the land's wounds. Flower beds that had dazzled him with color when he was young held a few wind-seeded flowers that looked spindly and faded.

Jared took a hesitant step toward the house. Took another. He raised his voice. "Mother?"

Another step.

He saw the smears of old blood around the front door.

Hurrying now, he flung the door open. "Mother!"

Sweating and freezing, he rapidly explored the downstairs rooms the family used. Then the healing rooms. Then the stillroom. Out the back door to the greenhouse. He didn't notice anything except that there was no one there.

"MOTHER!"

Inside again, he took the stairs two at a time, checking his brothers' rooms first.

Davin's room was bare of personal belongings. Janos's looked as if someone had hurriedly searched through it and had left the clothes and books where they'd fallen.

No one in the second-floor guest rooms.

No one in the third-floor rooms.

Back to the second floor.

His clothes no longer hung in the wardrobe, but his books still filled the low bookcase next to the writing desk that had stood in front of the window for as long as he could remember. The same quilt covered the bed that had once felt so huge and that he now knew would be a snug fit for two people.

One room left.

His hand shook as he opened the door to his parents' room.

Pain and grief entwined with love hit him at the threshold.

He closed his eyes and clung to the doorframe, unable to step back, unable to go forward.

Walls remembered. Over time, wood and stone absorbed the feelings of those who lived in a place and could be sensed by anyone with power.

This was different. Stronger. As if . . .

Jared opened his eyes and looked at the large double bed that Reyna had shared with Belarr—the bed that a male child, no matter how young, didn't climb into without his father's permission.

At first, he thought Reyna had bought a new quilt for the bed, but he couldn't figure out why she, who loved bright things, would choose such a dull color.

Then he saw a patch of blues and greens at the bottom corner, and then he realized the quilt had been soaked with blood.

Jared staggered toward the bed, fighting the sickness that churned in his stomach.

Blood sings to blood. That's why the feelings were so strong. They weren't in the wood and stone, they were in the blood.

His hand shook violently as he reached for the quilt.

The blood was old, but there was so much of it. All he had to do was open his inner barriers and touch it, and he'd know.

"Jared," a gravelly voice said.

His hand hovered over the quilt. Another inch. Just another inch.

His hand wouldn't move.

"Jared."

Jared spun around, his heart pounding wildly.

An old man stood in the doorway. Unkempt gray hair hung to his shoulders. Grief and pain had carved deep lines into his face. His left sleeve was pinned above where the elbow had been.

Jared stared at the old man. His eyes widened. "Uncle Yarek?"

"Uncle Yarek," the old man agreed, smiling sadly. "Reyna said you'd be coming home this autumn."

"Mo—" Jared's voice broke. In a rush, he crossed the room and hugged his uncle. Terrified of the fierce grief rising inside of him, he choked it back, chaining it down.

"Come away, Jared," Yarek said softly as he stepped back into the hallway, drawing Jared with him. "Come away from this room. It's too painful to look on. We'll go outside. We'll go out and sit in the garden, and we'll talk."

Saying nothing, Jared followed Yarek to a stone bench at the far end of the garden. Near the bench was a small, covered well.

"Would you like some water?" Jared asked.

Grimacing a little, Yarek settled on the bench. "Sure."

Jared lifted the cover and lowered the wooden bucket. When he looked around for the dipper, Yarek said, "Here," and called in a mug.

Jared filled the mug and handed it to Yarek. "Whenever my friends and I spent the afternoon playing in the woods, we'd all end up here because this well had the sweetest water in Ranon's Wood."

"Yes, it did." Yarek drained the mug and handed it back to Jared. "Now it's as bitter as a woman's tears."

Jared hesitated, finally dipped the mug into the bucket and drank.

As bitter as a woman's tears. Or was it the land's tears he was tasting now? For the Blood, was there really any difference?

Because he was thirsty, he drank another mug of water before settling on the bench next to his uncle.

"What happened here, Uncle Yarek?"

Yarek looked at the sparse garden and sighed. "War's what happened, Jared. War between the tribes."

"But we've been united since the time of Shal."

"If everyone had remembered Shal's warnings about the long-lived races, we might have stayed united and strong. But that slut who controls Hayll has a way about her. It's like finding a weed in the garden. You know it doesn't belong there, but it looks small and pretty so you let it stay, not realizing that, although it looks small and pretty above the ground, underneath it's sinking a tap root so deep you can never cut out all of it, and it sends out all these other runners that choke out everything but other weeds.

"That's what happened to Shalador. One by one, place by place, we lost our strong Queens, our good Queens. Some to age. Some to 'accidents.' One by one, until all that was left were the weeds."

Jared rubbed his forehead. "And even a good man will eventually yield to a bad Queen if the hunger for the bond gnaws at him long enough and hard enough."

Yarek nodded. "A strong love bond eases that hunger, too. A Blood male needs one or the other. I guess that's why the warriors who came to demand we yield to the new Queen did what they did."

Unable to look at Yarek, Jared focused on the cracked, barren ground in front of him. "Did what?"

Yarek shuddered. "They slaughtered the witches. They butchered our hearts. They didn't give a call to battle and wait for the ones who chose to fight to come to the killing field. When every family in Wolf's Creek refused to yield and every male told them what they could do with their damned Rings of Obedience, the delegation left. Thirteen men. That's all we saw until the next day when hundreds of them surrounded the village and attacked. They weren't after the men. Our wounds and deaths happened because we were in the way. It was the witches those bastards wanted. Little girls, old women, Ladies in their prime, the darker-Jeweled girls on the verge of womanhood . . .

"They raped some of them, just like they raped the land. Left some alive, broken and mutilated. Some of the lighter-Jeweled young witches were captured and taken away. A few—very few—escaped the breaking and slaughtering, but they weren't old enough or strong enough for the males to bond to comfortably."

"Is there anyone left at Wolf's Creek?" Jared asked, carefully circling around the questions that needed to be asked.

Yarek shook his head. "Only a couple of houses were left standing by the time it was done. They took most of the livestock, and we knew the land couldn't yield enough for us to eat even if we were able to tend it and could find a Queen to heal it—and there was nothing to get us through from a new planting to the harvest.

"Belarr arrived that evening with forty men . . . and Reyna. She did what she could to keep us alive. Then Belarr and the other men brought us to Ranon's Wood. There's always been strong family ties between Wolf's Creek and Ranon's Wood, so Reyna didn't have to look far to find hands to help her." Yarek cleared his throat. "I told her to take the arm. It wasn't hanging on by much anyway, and I'd managed to stop the bleeding before they arrived. I told her to put her strength into the young ones. She cried but, may the Darkness embrace a true daughter, she did what I asked.

"A week later, the bastards came to Ranon's Wood. Belarr had set up a watch, so they didn't come in without warning, but they came, and it was Wolf's Creek all over again—except they didn't even give Belarr or anyone else a chance to refuse to yield.

"He fought. Mother Night, how he fought! But . . ."

"He wasn't trained as a guard," Jared said quietly. "He wasn't trained as a warrior."

"No. He was a strong man and a fine administrator and he'd served his Queen and Ranon's Wood well, but he wasn't a trained warrior."

Belarr had had the strength of the Red, but hadn't had someone like Randolf to show him how to use that strength to kill, hadn't had a Warlord Prince like Blaed with him who would surrender to instinct and find the killing field within himself.

"They had to kill him, you see," Yarek continued in a low voice. "They had to. They couldn't let a Red-Jeweled Warlord live after they'd torn his wife's body apart enough to make her scream but not enough to let her die quickly."

Jared made a choking sound.

Yarek didn't notice. "They paid dearly, Jared. The bastards paid for Reyna with their own blood. And they didn't really win in the end.

"She was in the village when the attack started. Janos died trying to reach her. And she went down fighting to protect a young girl.

"I don't know how Belarr reached her or where he found the strength to get her away from them. They were both dying by the time he got her home, and she . . . she kept trying to heal him. He asked me to leave them be, to look for Janos when the fighting was over. Then he carried her up to their room and lay down with her on the bed. Wasn't my place to be there, so I closed the door."

Yarek pulled out a handkerchief and wiped his nose. "I left the house and hid in the woods. Sounds cowardly . . ."

Jared shook his head. "You'd already fought one battle. You weren't strong enough to fight another."

"I did have another reason," Yarek said slowly, tucking the handkerchief into his pocket. "On and off all through the winter, Reyna kept saying you were coming home this autumn. I didn't have much hope for Janos. I figured someone from the family should be here to meet you, and I was the only one left."

"The only one?" Jared whispered. "Those bastards killed *all* of them? All the aunts and uncles? All the cousins?" He put his head between his knees and tried to breathe. "Aunt Janine?"

Yarek rubbed Jared's back. "My Lady died at Wolf's Creek."

Jared squeezed his eyes shut. "Shira and Mariel? Mother Night, they didn't take Shira and Mariel, did they?" He sat up too fast.

Yarek pushed Jared's head back down. "No, they didn't get Shira and Mariel. My girls crossed the Tamanara Mountains last autumn, with Davin as their escort."

"Davin?" Jared braced his hands on his knees and pushed himself upright. "*Davin as escort?* But he's—"

"Old enough," Yarek said firmly. He rubbed his chin. "Reyna was fretful last autumn. One day she showed up and talked to Janine. The next thing I knew, the girls were sent off with Davin and some travelers who were resting up in Ranon's Wood before heading west, hoping to serve that Queen on the other side of the mountains."

"They went to Dena Nehele." Jared sighed. "Thank the Darkness."

"You know something about the Gray Lady?" Yarek asked sharply.

"She's a Queen worthy of the best a man can give. If she took Davin into her court, he'll do well."

"Then she may be the only Queen left who *is* worthy of it."

"No," Jared said softly, "there's one other."

Yarek gave his nephew a considering look. "You rode in alone. What happened to the witchling?"

Jared blinked. "The witchling?"

"The one bitten by the viper rats. The one the little Black Widow's been fretting about so much."

Jared blinked again. "Little Black Widow?" He rubbed the back of his hand over his mouth. "What did she say about Lia?"

"Ambush. Viper rats. You taking off with the witchling to find help. The rest of them hightailing it here." Yarek shook his head and huffed. "Poor thing was making herself sick with all the fretting, and that young Warlord Prince knew about as much as an ant can piss about soothing a witch who's got herself fretted. Now, me"—he waved his hand—"I *know* something about soothing a fretting witch. Janine wasn't much of a fretter. All I had to do for her was keep some cheap clay pottery around that she could smash whenever she got really annoyed. That and a long, hot ride between the sheets usually eased her mood."

"What?" Jared said weakly.

"Can't settle things the same way with a daughter—"
Jared choked.

"—so I had to learn other ways of soothing, didn't I?
Wasn't Janine who got Shira to stop fretting when Tavi
performed the Fire Dance and then turned down her invitation to be her lover, was it?"

"What?"

" 'Sweetheart,' I said, 'a young Warlord's got a right to
choose his lover same as a young witch.' "

"What in the name of Hell was she doing inviting *anyone*
to her bed?" Jared shouted.

"She'd had her Virgin Night. She was free to try out a
man if it pleased her."

"Shira's not old enough—"

"She's twenty-five now," Yarek said, looking fierce.

"Then why didn't her lover escort her over the
mountains?"

"She didn't find one she wanted to keep. Damn shame,
but there it is. I wanted Mariel to have her Virgin Night
before she left—have a Shalador male take care of it so I'd
know it was done right—but there was too much upset at
the time, and it would have been too risky with her emotions all stirred up like that."

Jared braced his head in his hands and moaned. He'd
been able to picture Janos and Davin grown—up to a
point—but Shira and Mariel? Shira, with lovers. Mariel,
ready for her Virgin Night and probably spending her eve-
nings dreamily thinking about which consort she'd like to
request for that night.

Lia, who wasn't thinking about any of it.

He moaned again.

Yarek narrowed his eyes. "You acting so prudish about
Shira and Mariel for a reason, or are you just trying to
dodge my question about the witchling?"

"The witchling." Jared rammed his fingers through his
hair. What would Lia say about being called a witchling?
What would *Thera* say about being called the *little* Black
Widow? "She's—"

They both tensed when they heard a horse approaching

at an easy pace, but they couldn't see the road from that part of the garden.

The roan mare whickered a greeting. Minutes later, Lia and Blaed came around the side of the house.

Jared ground his teeth. "She's supposed to be resting."

"That's the witchling?" Yarek asked, jumping to his feet. He whistled silently. "Even dressed like that, she's a lovely woman."

Pleased to feel his blood simmering and more than willing to let grief find its release through anger, Jared stood up more slowly. "She's also the Gray Lady's granddaughter."

Yarek gurgled a bit, but didn't have time to say anything before Lia and Blaed reached them.

"Warlord," Lia said politely, smiling at Yarek. "Jared," she added cautiously.

Yarek bowed low, then grinned. "Lady. I hope my nephew's remembered his manners while he's been serving you."

"Did he have any?" Lia murmured, a hint of mischief in her eyes.

"Why don't you just keep pushing yourself until you collapse?" Jared shouted at her. "Watching you crawl in the dirt will certainly make us all feel better."

Lia paled.

"JARED!" Yarek clouted Jared's shoulder. "You shame your mother to say such a thing!"

Jared closed his eyes and hunched his shoulders. He stood there, trembling, saying nothing.

"If you'll excuse me, Warlord," Lia whispered.

As soon as she was out of earshot, Blaed turned on Jared. "Damn it, Jared. What's wrong with you?"

Jared glared at Blaed. "What's wrong with *me*? What's wrong with *you*, bringing her out here?"

"*I* didn't bring her *anywhere*. I managed to climb up behind her before she went looking for *you*."

Jared's hands curled into fists.

Blaed took a wider stance and braced his feet.

"Youngsters," Yarek said firmly. "Enough blood's been spilled on this land."

Jared swayed. He resisted Yarek's embrace for a moment before giving in and clinging. "I'm sorry," he whispered. "I'm sorry. I've been sitting here, becoming incensed because the cousin I still remember as a girl is old enough to have lovers. I lash out at you. I lash out at Lia. Mother Night, will I ever stop lashing out at people who don't deserve it?"

"It's the grieving pain, Jared," Yarek said softly. "It's something too big to give in to all at once. I know, boy. I know."

Jared stepped back. Took a deep breath. "Blaed—"

Blaed shook his head. "I understand." He looked at the garden. "I shouldn't have let you come without some warning, but I didn't know how to tell you about this. Any of this."

The three men turned and watched Lia enter the greenhouse.

"I don't want to leave Thera alone too long," Blaed said. "She's still too edgy." He looked at Yarek. "I could give you a ride back to the village. Jared and Lia can ride double on the gelding."

"You can take the gelding," Jared said.

"Not if Lia's staying I can't," Blaed replied sourly. "Damn horse caught a whiff of her and has been acting like a stallion who's caught the scent of the only mare in season."

"I appreciate the offer, young Prince." Yarek squeezed Jared's shoulder. "Don't stay too long. The bastards shouldn't come back, but it would be too easy to get cut off out here."

"One thing," Jared said, drawing Yarek a few feet away. "What . . . What happened to the bodies?"

Yarek rubbed his chin. "That's why I said the bastards didn't win in the end. They hadn't been interested in the bodies at Wolf's Creek. Just left them there. But they took the time to look for Belarr. I guess they wanted to make sure he was dead. It was after sunset before they came here. I could hear them smashing things while they searched. They came out again, cursing for all they were worth, shouting at each other that they'd find him, and the Healer, too.

"I waited a while before going inside.

"Belarr and Reyna were gone, Jared. Just gone. There was that quilt soaked with their blood, but that was all."

Jared watched the clouds move slowly across an autumn-blue sky. "Do you believe in the Dark Realm, Uncle Yarek?"

"The place where the Blood's dead go before their power fades enough for them to return to the Darkness? Myself, I always thought stories about the demon-dead were just that—stories. Now I'm not so sure. Belarr would have done anything to stop them from taking her. If going to such a place would have given him a little more time with her, he would have found a way." Yarek paused. "I never found Janos, either."

"I hope it does exist," Jared said quietly. "I hope they found the way to get there, and they're still together."

"Me too, Jared. Me too. Now make your peace with the witchling and try not to fret her."

"Another male flaw," Jared grumbled. "I fuss. I pester. Now I'll be accused of fretting her."

Yarek gave Jared a long look before patting his shoulder. "They all say that. And they all get used to it. Eventually."

Jared waited until he heard the mare's hoofbeats before he approached Reyna's greenhouse.

She'd found a bucket of water and the specially shaped dipper Reyna had used to water the seedlings.

"Lia." Jared waited for her to acknowledge his presence. She didn't.

Feeling awkward, he shifted his weight from one foot to the other as he watched her move from pot to pot, speaking so softly he couldn't make out the words that weren't meant for him anyway.

She held the dipper in her left hand. Two fingers of her right hand rested just above the soil in the pot. She poured the water over her fingers and murmured a phrase. The same movements, the same words, over and over.

It wasn't until he really looked at the seedlings in the first pots and saw how much stronger and greener they looked than the rest of the plants that he realized what she was doing.

Queen's magic.

According to their oldest legends, the Blood had been created to be the caretakers of the Realm, to use the awesome power they'd been given to maintain the balance between the land and all its creatures. As the caretakers, they became the rulers of everything that walked upon Terreille or flew above it or swam in its waters.

The price of power was service. Or so the legends said.

The Blood had a deep respect for the land. Many had a special gift for nurturing it.

But only a Queen could heal it once it had been wounded. Only a Queen's blood and a Queen's strength could turn barren ground back into fertile soil.

They were, after all, the land's heart.

Coming up behind her, Jared lifted her right hand and poured water from the dipper over it to clean the cuts she'd made on her fingertips.

"No, Lia," he said gently, turning her around.

She stared at his chest. "Let me do this. I need to do this."

Jared shook his head. "There's nowhere to plant them. There's nowhere for them to go." Was that true for the Shalador people as well? he wondered. Would they, too, wither and die?

Since she didn't pull away from him, he slipped his arms around her and nudged her closer. He sighed when her hands touched his waist.

"I used to help her in here," Jared said in a hushed voice. "She always said I had to make myself useful if I was going to—"

"Going to what?" Lia asked when he didn't continue.

Jared grimaced. "If I was going to pester her."

Lia chuckled. "No wonder you're so good at it. You've been in training your whole life."

Jared made a rumbling sound, which amused her even more.

Drawing her closer, he rested his cheek on the top of her head. "I saw her once, a few months after I was Ringed.

During the training time. I don't know if she was in that particular Territory for another reason and just happened to be walking in that plaza that day or if she'd somehow found out where I was and had come to see me.

"I saw her. It would have been hard to miss a golden-skinned woman with shining black hair that flowed to her waist and those rare green eyes." He paused. "I have her eyes."

Lia stroked his back.

"The witches in charge of the training saw her, too. They didn't know, or care, who she was, only that her presence there was important to me. One of them walked over to me and fondled me through my clothes. And there was nothing I could do about it. There was nothing they'd done to me up to that point that had humiliated me quite that much. In a way, it's ironic that I felt so much shame because Shalador boys look forward to the day when we're old enough for the Fire Dance, for the time when we'll step into the dance circle and display ourselves to every woman in the village. I wouldn't have been dancing for my mother, but I would have danced in front of her and never given it a thought."

"That's different," Lia murmured. "That would have been your choice, and it was part of the male rites among your people."

"Yes," Jared whispered, not sure he could bear her understanding. "So I went up to her, and I told her it was her fault. That all of it was her fault. That it was because of her that I was Ringed and would never know any pleasure with a woman. That if she'd been a different kind of woman, this wouldn't have happened to me.

"Then I told her I hated her, and I walked away.

"I looked back just once. She was on the ground, curled up in a tight ball. No one stopped. No one touched her or tried to help her."

"Oh, Jared."

"I blamed her for a long time because it was safer to blame someone else. But I couldn't forget the look in her eyes when I said those things. I couldn't forget seeing her on the ground.

"When I stopped blaming her, the only thing I wanted to do was go home. I even made a couple of timid attempts to escape, but I was too terrified of the agony the Ring can produce to manage it. So I used to lie in my bed and imagine that I'd gotten home somehow. Just for an hour. Just long enough to see her, to talk to her. Just long enough . . . And now I'm home, and it's too late. I'm too late, and I'll never be able to take back the words."

Lia held him while he cried. He had no tears yet for his father and brother. There would be time enough to mourn them later. There was no room in him to grieve for anyone but Reyna.

She held him long after the last tear.

"What was she like?" Lia asked softly.

Jared wiped his face on his coat sleeve. "Compassionate. Generous, stubborn, strong, loving, patient, courageous." *Like you.*

Lia took his hand. "There's something I want to show you."

She led him to the back of the greenhouse and pointed to three large, glazed pots. Each one was divided into two sections and contained two seedling trees. "Someone must be caring for them. They're the only healthy plants here."

Love formed a lump in Jared's throat that was sharper than grief. "Those are our luck and love pots," he said, his voice husky. "And these"—he brushed a leaf with his fingertip—"are honey pear trees."

Lia leaned over, brushing her fingers over the leaves and thin trunks while she crooned to the little trees.

"Reyna gave each of us one of these pots on our sixth birthday. Luck and love, she called them. There's a hollow in the base. In the spring, we'd write down a wish or a dream or a desire and then fold the paper and pass it through the base into the hollow. Then we could plant any seeds or seedlings we wanted in the pot. They were ours to care for. Some years they grew. There were a lot of years when the seedlings started out well enough, but then we'd forget about them.

"She never touched them. I planted honey pear seedlings

one year because I wanted a honey pear tree that I didn't have to share with anyone. I drenched them whenever I remembered and then forgot to water them for weeks at a time. When they died, I got mad at her. She waited through my undignified tantrum and then quietly told me that the plants were a symbol, a way for me to learn that no one else could nurture my wishes or dreams or desires. If I wanted them to thrive, I had to take care of them myself."

"These seedlings can't be more than a year old," Lia said. "So she must have planted them and tended them for you."

"Yes." Two honey pear trees for each of her sons—even the son who had walked away from her.

"What happened to the papers you tucked in the hollows?" Lia asked.

"We'd take them out after the harvest to compare what had happened during those months to what we'd written."

"Did you get your wishes if the plants thrived?"

"Sometimes." Jared smiled crookedly. "Although one year I had to wait until the next horse fair to get the pony I'd admired so much because it wasn't for sale until then."

Lia smiled with him. "Is your last wish still in the hollow?"

Jared's smile faded. It had been years since he'd thought about the luck and love pots. "I don't know." He took a couple of deep breaths before using Craft to pass his fingers through the pot's base.

His fingers brushed against paper. Touched sealing wax.

Frowning, he drew the paper out of the hollow. When he turned it over, he saw his name written in a feminine hand.

"I'll wait outside," Lia said.

"No, you—"

Lia touched his arm. "I won't go far."

Jared watched her until he felt convinced she wouldn't wander out of his sight. Then he settled on the stool Reyna had kept in the greenhouse and broke the letter's seal.

Jared,

A few weeks ago, a Black Widow came through Ranon's Wood with her brother and his Lady. They were exhausted and the Warlord had been wounded in a fight. After the healing, they stayed with us a few days to recover their strength. Since whatever marks they had between them would be needed for the rest of their journey, I had refused payment. The Black Widow offered to trade a skill for a skill, so I asked if she could make a tangled web that could show how you fared.

When she approached me several hours later, I knew she didn't want to tell me what the web of visions had revealed.

She told me you would return to Ranon's Wood this autumn.

Then she told me I wouldn't be here to see you.

At first I thought she meant that I'd be away from the village or committed to a healing and you wouldn't be able to wait. But I've been a Healer too long not to understand words that are left unspoken. I didn't ask if it would be an accident or illness or if I could do something to prevent it. What matters is there are things to be said, and this may be the only chance I'll have to say them.

I won't insult you by saying that your words didn't hurt or that I didn't cry. They did hurt. I did cry. But I understood even then why you needed to say them. Since that day, Belarr and I have had to accept the bitter truth that, in some ways, you were right. Because of our mistakes, no matter how well intentioned, a son lost his freedom and a precious part of his life.

The Blood survive on trust, Jared. We trust that everyone will follow the Laws and Protocol that keep the weaker safe from the stronger. We trust that males won't use their strength against a female except in self-defense. We trust that every witch who is served will respect the males who hand over their lives into her keeping. When the code of honor we've lived by for thousands upon thousands of years is broken, fear seeps in, and no man trusts what he fears.

Despite the risks of the Virgin Night and the vulnerable days of our moontimes, yours is the more vulnerable gender. The need to serve has been bred into Blood males for so long, you can't be emotionally whole without it. Driven by the most intrinsic part of yourself to need what you fear—I can't imagine a deeper, more personal nightmare.

We wanted your ability to trust to be deeply rooted before you had to see the dangers that were the other side of the bond. We waited too long. For that, we're both sorry.

Having lost one son, Belarr didn't wait with your brothers. Sometimes it hurts to see the wariness in their eyes. Sometimes I fear that they'll never be able to give their hearts fully to a woman because of it.

The night the Black Widow told me you'd be coming home, I had a dream. I've wondered since if she'd cast some spell that allowed me to see the visions in her tangled web that she couldn't bring herself to tell me. I couldn't remember the dream, but I woke up terrified.

The next day, I talked to Janine, and we arranged for Shira, Mariel, and Davin to travel over the Tamanara Mountains with the Black Widow and her family. I tried to get Janos to go with them, but the distrust of unknown witches runs too deep in him. He feels safe in Ranon's Wood.

I received one letter from Davin before the snow closed the mountain passes. He and the girls are serving in a District Queen's court in the Territory called Dena Nehele. He misses his home and family, but I think he'll be able to put down roots and be happy.

There are two more things I have to tell you.

Before they left, the Black Widow asked that you deliver a message when you reached Ranon's Wood. I'm to tell you that she and her brother and his Lady are going to Dena Nehele and hope to serve the Gray Lady. She said she wouldn't say more than that because they were being hunted, but you would know who the message was meant for.

The second thing. There were many things Belarr regretted that he didn't get the chance to tell you. One night he said if he could tell you just one thing, it would be this: that he'd known since you were a boy that you would wear the silver, but if you ever had a chance to wear the gold, you should grab that chance and hold on to it with everything that's in you. It upset him, so I didn't ask him what he meant. I simply give you his words in the hope that they have mean-ing for you.

If you feel you need my forgiveness, you have it. You've always had my love.

May the Darkness embrace you, my son.

Reyna

Jared carefully folded the letter and vanished it.

The Silver and the Gold.

Belarr had known about the Invisible Ring.

Was that why he'd felt sure he'd heard of it before? Was it the echo of something Belarr had said that had kept him from doubting its existence? On one of their rambles through the woods, perhaps. Maybe it had been the kind of comment an adult made in passing and then forgot, but a child never did.

Belarr had known he'd wear the Silver and had hoped he'd have a chance to wear the Gold.

Jared paused at the greenhouse door.

Looking a little guilty, Lia wandered through the herb garden, touching each plant as she passed.

Shaking his head, Jared went to join her.

He'd pretend not to see the drops of blood on the leaves. This time.

But he wouldn't pretend the Invisible Ring didn't exist. It didn't matter if she denied it with every breath. He wasn't going to give up this last tie to his father.

Lia stuck her fingers in her mouth as soon as she saw him.

"Prick yourself?" Jared asked.

She pulled her fingers out of her mouth, and mumbled, "Yes."

Jared put his arm around her shoulders and guided her toward the lane, ignoring her attempts to slow down and touch another plant. "The letter was from my mother."

That distracted her long enough for them to reach the lane.

"I thought it might be." Lia studied his face. "She knew you wanted to take the words back."

"Yes, she knew." He helped her mount the gelding and

then swung up behind her. "It's time we got back to the village. My mother left a message for Thera."

It did his heart good to have her pester him all the way back to the village to explain what he'd meant.

CHAPTER TWENTY-TWO

Krelis stared at the bloody, quivering thing kneeling in front of him. Three days ago, it had been a man. One of his guards.

Now it was missing so many pieces, he couldn't identify it.

It looked at him without really seeing him and made harsh, pleading sounds. Bloody spittle leaked from one corner of its mouth.

Krelis swallowed hard.

It was better this way. It would have hurt to recognize it enough to be able to call it by name.

Krelis turned away. The blood-streaked white feather that was inserted into the stub of flesh kept moving with each jerky breath, as if it were waving at him.

Or mocking him.

This was why the witches called it the Brotherhood of the Quill.

Dorothea came out of the adjoining room, slowly rolling the handle of a curved, thin-bladed knife between her hands. She spared him one withering glance before going to the table that held the rest of her sharp, bloody toys. She set the knife gently in its place.

"Lord Krelis."

The way she said his name told him that he'd done nothing but disappoint her lately, and she didn't expect this report to be any different.

Cold-blooded, malevolent bitch, Krelis thought fiercely.

A moment after the thought formed, marrow-freezing fear swept through him.

He hadn't meant it, would never think it again. She was

the answer to everything he wanted, the answer to centuries of work and sweat. As her Master of the Guard, he was one of the most powerful men in Hayll. Respected. Feared.

He turned that thought over and over. He'd worked hard to gain enough status to keep the fear at bay. Now he was in the position of being feared.

Krelis felt some of the tension ease.

Now he was one of the males the witches couldn't strike against, couldn't Ring. Unless they, too, served in Dorothea's court, they had no safety from him.

He smiled. His smile widened when he caught Dorothea's sudden, arrested look.

"There's something you wish to say to me, Krelis?"

Her voice had gone a little breathy, like a woman at the beginning of arousal.

"I've found them, Priestess," Krelis said. "They've gone to ground in a Shalador village called Ranon's Wood."

"All of them?"

Krelis clenched his teeth. "The Shalador bastard disappeared with the little bitch-Queen, but they're supposed to meet the others there."

Selecting a short-bladed knife, Dorothea glided over to one of the large, potted, flowering bushes that sat near her playroom windows and cut off two overblown yellow flowers. "There's no reason to assume he'll take her to that village. He could just as easily take her to Dena Nehele and claim whatever rewards he can for his brave service," she added with a sneer.

Krelis had thought of that, had sweated over that. It pleased him that he'd worked out an answer he felt sure would suit her. "Ranon's Wood is his home village. It had been softened this spring when the new Shalador Queens wisely decided to bring the Territory into Hayll's shadow. He'll find little help there, whereas we'll have an entire village of hostages."

"Tell me more," Dorothea purred as she cut the flower stems until they were barely an inch long.

"We'll offer a trade. His village for the little bitch Queen. If she's turned over to us, we'll let everyone else go."

Dorothea looked up from her stem trimming. "Will we?"

Krelis smiled, feeling more sure of himself than he'd felt in days. "No, Priestess. The useful ones will be taken as slaves. The rest will be eliminated."

"All well and good if the bitch is there."

"We'll also have the slaves she bought at Raej. They must have some bargaining value for her to be so determined to get them to Dena Nehele. There's no reason Hayll can't bargain more keenly and get further concessions from the Queens or aristo families in the slaves' Territories." He wanted to laugh. His pet could tell his fellow travelers a good many things about being part of a bargain with Hayll. "If she's not there, we can demand a trade—the slaves for the bitch-Queen. Some of them aren't worth much, true, but if the children are aristo, their families are going to think hard about believing any promises the Gray Lady makes if she doesn't trade her kin for theirs since it was her buying them that put them in this danger. And the Shalador Warlord isn't willingly going to sacrifice his family for a witch he's only known for a short time."

Walking up to the quivering thing, Dorothea tucked the flowers into the holes where its ears had been. "What are your plans?"

"I'll take a thousand Hayllian guards to Ranon's Wood and—"

"So many?" Annoyance crept back into Dorothea's voice. "Surely there can't be *that* many Jeweled Blood left in that privy hole of a village. You'll have the courts thinking the Gray Lady's an enemy to be respected, even feared, if you need that many Hayllian warriors to subdue the little bitch who serves her."

Did she *want* them to fail? Krelis wondered. Why deny a fierce enemy when the denial fooled no one? Taking that many men was a sound fighting decision.

He hesitated, almost tempted to explain this to Dorothea. Instead he said, "It's not unusual for guards to be called from various stations throughout a Territory to participate in a specific training exercise or a special assignment. The Masters of the Guard in the minor courts won't give it a second thought. And the guards themselves won't think past having an opportunity to be observed by the Masters in the stronger courts in the hopes of being offered a contract. There's no reason they have to know this isn't a chance for them to show off their skills. And there won't be anyone else to say differently."

Dorothea began her slow, hip-swaying pacing. "How long?"

Krelis swallowed carefully, keeping his eyes away from the thing. "A couple of days, Priestess, before I'll be able to hand the Gray Lady's bitch into your keeping."

"A couple of days," Dorothea murmured.

He caught a flash of amusement in her eyes. He held his breath and waited. By tomorrow evening, his cousin or the young Warlord whose training he'd been overseeing would look like that quivering thing. His pet's information had come two days too late, which was something Krelis wasn't going to forget when he got to Ranon's Wood.

"A couple of days," Dorothea murmured again. Pausing at the table, she selected a knife and looked at the quivering thing.

It whimpered. Tried to shift its position.

Dorothea put the knife down and approached Krelis. "This has been a difficult time for you, hasn't it, darling?" she said as she stroked his cheek. "And I do understand how wearing it can be when a person's concentration is split between business and family. Since you've obviously taken my incentives to heart, I'll tell you what I'll do. Your cousin and protégé will remain confined but untouched. We'll discuss their future upon your return."

Krelis turned his face just enough to kiss her palm. "Thank you, Priestess." When she lifted her hand, he stepped back and bowed low. "If you'll excuse me, there's a great deal to do."

"Of course."

He took a step toward the door. Stopped. Turned back. Cutting off his ability to feel anything, he carefully studied the thing that had been a man.

Dorothea eyed him curiously. "Is there a problem, Lord Krelis?"

Krelis's lips curved in a small smile. "My pet has not

fulfilled his duties satisfactorily and will, I fear, require discipline."

Dorothea's eyes filled with glittering pleasure. "Yes, fear is always a useful tool. Something your predecessor didn't understand."

Krelis almost reached the door when she added quietly, "But then, *he* was an honorable man."

CHAPTER TWENTY-THREE

Jared poured another two fingers of whiskey into his glass. Raising it to eye level, he studied it.

A liquid cloak to cover the heart and protect it from lethal shards of pain. A fluid wall to keep grief at bay.

He turned away from such thoughts. If he kept his mind harnessed to practical matters, he didn't really have to think at all.

And right now, he couldn't afford to think.

"Jared." Yarek sipped his whiskey, hesitated.

Jared leaned back and waited. He and Yarek were the only ones left in the inn's dining room. Lia, Thera, and Blaed had gone for a walk after the midday meal. He suspected Lia needed a little time away from the pulsing needs everyone in the village was trying so hard to keep reined in. He'd seen the hunger in the males' eyes, the relief in the witches'. And he'd seen the way Lia had quietly accepted and eaten the full bowl of stew that had been placed before her—the *only* full bowl that had been served. She hadn't shamed the village by refusing the food offered, hadn't denied them the honor of serving a Queen.

She must have choked on every mouthful with all those eyes anxiously watching her, but she never showed it.

Sitting beside her, his heart had swelled with pride . . . and something more.

He would never burden her with his feelings. Having been a pleasure slave—having his self so divided and debased—made it impossible for him to have what he wanted most.

But he would love her for the rest of his life.

"Jared," Yarek said again.

Jared pulled his attention back to his uncle. "What is it?"

Yarek cleared his throat. Took another sip of whiskey. "The witchling . . . the Lady. She's got a kind heart, but . . ."

"If she says there's a place for all of you in Dena Nehele, then there is," Jared replied.

"A land can only give so much, can only hold so many before the scales tip and we take too much."

"I think Dena Nehele can absorb a hundred of Shalador's own." A hundred survivors out of two thriving villages. Jared took another swallow of whiskey.

"More and more people are going over the mountains," Yarek said worriedly. "Plenty of them settle in the other Territories, but—"

Jared laid a hand over Yarek's. "You were the one who always told me not to plant troubles where there aren't any."

"Suppose I did."

"So Dena Nehele will gain Shalador's best and be better for it."

Naked grief filled Yarek's eyes before he looked away.

Jared leaned back, unable to offer any words of comfort that wouldn't shatter his own fragile control.

Shalador's best would never leave Shalador—unless they found their way to the Dark Realm. The war had seen to that.

"The Coaches are intact?" Yarek asked after a moment.

Jared nodded. The two Coaches that belonged to the destroyed Coach station hadn't been damaged in the attack, but he still hadn't figured out how they were going to fit everyone who couldn't ride the Winds on their own into two Coaches that comfortably held thirty people between them. And he didn't know who would handle them. The three Warlord brothers who had run the Coach station hadn't survived the attack, and no one else had the training.

Yarek frowned, gave Jared an uneasy glance, frowned harder. "Didn't have a Black Widow in Wolf's Creek."

"Not every village has one, any more than they have a Priestess or a Queen," Jared said, wondering where this was leading.

Yarek rubbed his chin. "The Hourglass covens have different ways. Stands to reason considering the kind of Craft they do."

Nodding, Jared waited.

Yarek shrugged, and asked hesitantly, "Do they eat different?"

Jared narrowed his eyes. That hint of fear hadn't been there a few hours ago when Yarek talked about Thera fretting.

"The women asked about it, you see, and I said I'd ask you."

"About what?" Jared said cautiously.

"Well, they butchered the two pigs and the chickens that were left." Yarek held up a hand as if Jared had protested. "No room to take them with us and no point leaving them to fill someone else's belly. But a cool box filled with cooked meat won't take up much room in the Coaches and would make everyone feel a little easier having a bit of their own for the first day or two. So we'll eat hearty tonight and tomorrow morning."

"What's that got to do with Thera?"

"Seems she came along early this morning and saw what they were doing. Came back a few minutes later carrying a couple of wash buckets and insisted on having all the offal she could fit in them. Soon as they were filled, she vanished the buckets and left."

"I don't—"

"I told you how she was fretting last night, remember?"

Jared nodded.

"Well, after I got her calmed down a bit, she went up to the room she's sharing with the young Warlord Prince. He went up with her, then came down a few minutes later in a snarling mood. At the time, I just thought she wanted to be alone for a little bit and had shown him the door. Now I'm thinking she wanted some privacy to spin one of those tangled webs. When she came back downstairs a couple of hours later, she was troubled but a lot calmer—and very hungry. Didn't have much to offer her last night. That's why the women started wondering—"

"Lord Yarek! Lord Yarek!" A boy barreled into the dining room. "Riders coming," he gasped. "Thirteen of them."

Jared jumped to his feet, knocking the chair over.

"Mother Night," Yarek whispered. "They've come back."

The descent to the Red was swift but controlled. By the time Jared stepped into the street, he was centered in his strength and ready, almost eager, to rise to the killing edge.

He looked east.

Lia and Thera, returning from their walk with Blaed, slowed down when they saw him.

Blaed gave Jared a swift look, then dragged the two women into the nearest building.

Jared turned and began walking down the street.

Brock and Randolf came out of one building, but neither of them stepped into the street to join him.

It was his uncle Yarek and Thayne—and Garth—and the Jeweled Warlords and witches who were left who formed a wall at his back.

The riders turned into the main street and rode forward slowly. Six pairs of Warlords behind a Sapphire-Jeweled Warlord Prince.

The Warlords stopped.

The Warlord Prince kept coming. He reined in a few yards from Jared, dismounted, and closed the rest of the distance on foot until he stood a man's length away.

"Warlord," he said with deceptive pleasantness.

"Prince Talon," Jared replied, keeping his face and voice neutral.

"We need to talk, Warlord. Privately."

Jared jerked his head at the building to his left. "This will do."

He barely got into the room before Talon slammed him into the wall.

"What in the name of Hell were you thinking—*if* you were thinking?" Talon roared as he jammed his tunic-filled fists under Jared's chin. "You've been staggering around in a hostile Territory like a drunken landen! If we hadn't come across that slaughter and followed the tracks, we'd *still* be searching."

Jared bared his teeth. He clamped his hands around Talon's wrists. "Maybe your tracking abilities are at fault."

"I'm the best tracker around!"

"Then think how much trouble the second-best tracker has had."

Talon's eyes glazed with fury.

Remembering how easily a Warlord Prince rose to the killing edge, Jared leashed his own anger. "Talon—"

Talon just shook him and roared.

"What do you care?" Jared snarled. "You got your niece back. Lia's not your concern."

Talon slammed him into the wall again. "*I'm* the one who taught her to ride. *I'm* the one who taught her how to use a bow. *I'm* the one who taught her how to fight with Craft. Don't you *dare* tell me she's not my concern."

Jared stared at Talon. Finally, he said, "Have you ever played chess with her?"

"What's—" The glaze of fury slowly faded from Talon's eyes. Releasing Jared, he stepped back. After a minute, he shook his head, and said dryly, "I think I just did."

Now that Talon's anger had passed, Jared felt the sting of the accusations. "If you were so concerned, why didn't you stay to escort her to the Tamanara Mountains?"

There was no way to describe the look in Talon's eyes. "Warlord," he said quietly, "even a rogue knows when to yield to a Queen."

Jared squirmed a little, like a boy chastised by an elder. "But you came back. You've been searching for her."

"Well," Talon said with a genuine smile, "I *am* a rogue." He gave Jared a rough clap on the shoulder. "Let's go see the witchling. She deserves a good scolding."

"Can I watch?" Jared asked, falling into step beside Talon.

"Of course," Talon replied, laughing. "How else will you learn how to do it right?

Jared knocked on the bedroom door but didn't wait for Lia to answer before he slipped into the room.

"You wanted to see me?" he asked, studying her with some concern. She seemed subdued and a little pale. He understood her feeling subdued. Talon's skill at scolding far exceeded any instructor *he'd* ever had. "Are you feeling well?"

"I'm fine," Lia murmured, twisting the bottom of her sweater. She wasn't quite pacing, but she also couldn't seem to stand still. "Jared, I have a favor to ask."

"All right."

Lia pressed her lips together and stared at the floor. Finally, she sighed. "One of the reasons—the main reason—I haven't had my Virgin Night is that I never wanted to ask one of the males in the court to do something so intimate out of a sense of duty."

Jared thought the males in the court would be appalled to hear her say that, but he could understand how Lia might think of it as some unwanted "duty."

"I—" Lia took a couple of deep breaths. "Would you do it?"

Jared's mind went blank. To have this much. To give this much. To know that she trusted him this much.

Lia flicked a nervous glance at him.

Jared ran a hand through his hair. "Yes. Of course. When we get to Dena Nehele—"

"No." Lia scraped her teeth over her bottom lip. "It has to be now. Before sunset."

Jared took a step back. His legs hit the edge of the bed. He sat down abruptly. "Now? *Right now?*"

Lia nodded. "Thera says if I don't have my Virgin Night before sunset, I never will."

Jared opened his mouth, sure that he'd been about to express a reasonable opinion, but nothing came out.

If only it hadn't been Thera, who had heeded a similar warning and had survived because of it. *That* he couldn't dismiss.

"Lia . . ."

"If you're not comfortable with it, I can ask Talon—"

Jared shot to his feet. "I'll kill him first."

Lia blinked. Frowned. Finally said, "If you kill him first, won't that make the rest of it . . . awkward?"

"It will make it impossible," Jared replied, spacing out each word.

"Oh."

Jared rubbed his hands over his face. His body remembered what it felt like to hold her, kiss her, and it *wanted*. His heart yearned to make love to her. His mind kept squeaking the words "Virgin Night" like some terrified mouse.

Jared lowered his hands. "I'll be back shortly. You stay right here." He gestured toward a chair. "Sit down. Relax. Concentrate on breathing or something."

He bolted from the room.

Out in the corridor, Jared sagged against the wall.

He'd have to find Talon and ask him. Hell's fire, he had to ask *someone*. Being a pleasure slave didn't qualify him for seeing a witch through her Virgin Night. He'd seen plenty of witches who'd been broken during that first intimacy. They all had a lost, slightly vacant look in their eyes. Any fire that had burned in their hearts had been snuffed out under a man's body.

If something went wrong, he didn't think he could bear seeing Lia's eyes filled with that lost, vacant expression.

Oh, witches adjusted to the loss of their Jewels and their Craft. The ones from aristo families were sent into arranged marriages. He wasn't sure what kind of life the others endured. They adjusted. But they were never again whole. Many of them just faded away until there was little more than a husk left going through the motions of living. Some of them slipped into madness. None of them could be seeded more than once after being broken, and more than half of those pregnancies ended with an early miscarriage.

When he was younger, he thought it was unfair that broken witches should be stripped of their ability to have children as well as being stripped of their Jewels. But after having lived in the Territories that stood in Hayll's shadow, he doubted any of them regretted that barrenness. It was not in a witch's nature to become a breeder for the gender she would consider as the enemy.

Jared pushed away from the wall. He and Talon had spent the early afternoon removing the seats in the two small Coaches so they could fit more people in, while Yarek oversaw packing the storage spaces—and finding a safe place for the six honey pear trees Lia insisted come with them.

Thank the Darkness, some of Talon's men knew how to handle a Coach, so there was no problem now about finding drivers.

With luck, Talon would be checking on something else that had to be readied for their departure, and it would take some time to find him. Maybe by then, Lia would have reconsidered.

He shook his head. Not with Thera's warning riding her.

Before he took two steps, Talon turned the corner.

Groaning, Jared sagged against the wall again.

"She still upset?" Talon asked, eyeing the bedroom door.

"Not exactly," Jared muttered.

Talon's eyes narrowed. "She feeling all right?"

"She's doing fine." Jared looked Talon in the eyes. "She wants her Virgin Night."

Talon gaped at him. *"Now?"*

"Yes. Now. I was just coming to look for you."

Watching Talon sag against the wall made Jared feel better.

Talon rubbed a hand over his chest. "She wants me to—"

"No," Jared said too quickly.

A slow, wicked smile curved Talon's mouth. "In that case, Warlord, since the woman and the bed are in there, why are you out here?"

Jared's face heated. He shifted so that his back was fully pressed against the wall. "I've been a pleasure slave since I was eighteen."

Talon nodded in understanding. "That's a long time to know the bed without ever knowing intimacy or pleasure. And at that age . . . Hell's fire, you can probably count the number of times you were *really* with a woman."

"I could count it on one hand and not use all my fingers."

Talon rubbed his forehead. "Mother Night, you're almost a virgin yourself. Are you sure you want to do this?"

Jared stared at the opposite wall. "She asked me." He paused. "Would you consider seeing a witch through her Virgin Night a duty?"

Talon stiffened. "I'd call it an honor."

Satisfied, Jared nodded. "You've done it?"

"A few times. It's safer when the male wears the darker Jewel."

Talon settled more comfortably against the wall and crossed his arms. "It's not that difficult, really."

"It's dangerous," Jared argued.

"It can be if you forget why you're in the bed—or if she panics."

Well, that helped.

It took less than five minutes for Talon to explain what he had to do for the Virgin Night.

"That's it?" Jared asked.

Talon shrugged. "That's it. Just take it slow. Let her get comfortable with each step before you go on to the next, and you'll do all right."

Jared glanced at the end of the hall.

"Go on," Talon said with a smile. "I'll stay here and make sure she doesn't bolt."

Jared took a deep breath, blew it out, and then walked to the bathroom at the end of the hall.

After cleaning his teeth, he paused and sniffed himself. He shook his head and stripped. Halfway through the fast bath, he realized he'd accepted what he was about to do and felt steady.

More than steady.

He dried off, vanished the sweaty clothes he'd been working in, then called in the trousers Daemon had given him and put them on. No point wearing anything more, he thought as his hand closed over the Red Jewel around his neck. He ran his other hand over the trousers. Did clothes retain something of the person who had worn them? Right now, he wouldn't mind absorbing some of Daemon's bedroom skills.

Jared closed his eyes and took a couple of deep, quiet breaths. He thought of the way Daemon's hands glided over a woman's body, coaxing, caressing. It became a slow, delicious dance that a woman was helpless to resist. It changed so subtly from cool water to fire she never had a chance to see the blaze before it consumed her in pleasure.

Smiling, Jared returned to the bedroom door.

Talon gave him an assessing look, returned the smile, and walked away. At the corner, he raised his hand. A Sapphire shield blocked the hall.

"That will make sure you're not disturbed," Talon said. He gave Jared an easy salute and left.

Taking one last deep breath, Jared opened the bedroom door.

Lia sat in the chair, fretting the sweater.

Jared leaned against the door and smiled when she peeked at him through her lashes.

"It's not as if you haven't seen me before," Jared said, charmed by the shyness.

"That was different," Lia muttered, focusing on his bare feet.

Jared took another breath . . .

. . . and heard the drums.

Heard the Priestess's voice rising out of the twilight to call the men to the dance.

His nostrils flared. His blood heated. Tension flowed out of him as desire saturated his body.

He flicked a glance at the hearth. The wood that had been readied to take the evening chill out of the room began to burn.

A flick of his hand closed the curtains. Only the young fire lit the room, smudging all the sharp lines until there were no lines, until the walls seemed to disappear and go on forever.

Another flick of his hand vanished all the furniture except the bed and the small tables on either side of it.

Lia yelped when she landed on the floor. "Jared, what—"

He walked toward her. Her eyes widened.

"Can you hear the drums, Lia?" he asked softly.

"I—"

"Can you hear them? Like the land's heartbeat. Or the heartbeat of the Shalador people." He held out his hands. "Let me show you the Fire Dance."

He lifted her up and pulled her against him. Her heart beat a staccato rhythm. Her cold hands pushed at his waist.

He did nothing but hold her, letting his eyes wander over her face.

When she stopped trying to push him away, he slowly lowered his head, his lips parting for a kiss.

She arched back to escape his lips. He smiled because it only pushed her hips tighter against his.

Since she wouldn't give him her mouth, he took her throat. Soft kisses. Gentle sucking.

He licked her jaw.

Her hands clamped on his waist.

"Do you hear them, Lia?" he asked as he licked the corner of her mouth with the tip of his tongue.

"I—I hear something beating." Her voice had gone husky.

"The drums." Jared brushed his lips over hers.

Her eyes were dark smoke. "Is there someone singing?"

"Yes," he whispered into her ear. "Listen to her. Follow her. The Fire Dance lies at the end of her voice."

He covered her mouth with his and let them both sink into the drums and the voice and the musky twilight.

Stepping back, he drew her into the center of the room.

Lia plucked at the sweater. "It's warm in here."

"Take it off," Jared suggested quietly as he slowly circled her, his feet automatically following the set pattern of steps.

Lia tossed the sweater aside. She puffed out her cheeks. "Maybe we should open a window."

"Maybe you should take off the shirt." His fingertips brushed down her arm as he moved past her. "The Fire's supposed to be hot."

She reached for the first button. Her hand froze. Her eyes locked on the golden chest that glistened from more than one kind of heat.

"Let me help." Jared gave her a feathery kiss while he used Craft to undo all the buttons. His hands brushed the shirt aside, brushed it over her shoulders, brushed it down her back.

She made breathy little sounds.

"Watch me." He stepped back into his circle. "Watch the Dance."

"Aren't—" Lia puffed out her cheeks again. "Aren't you supposed to be naked when you do that?"

He vanished the trousers.

She gulped and tried to stare at her feet, but he'd already drawn her in too deeply. She raised her head and watched him dance, watched the muscles flex, watched him smile as he moved his hips, watched the shadows form into other dancers.

Listening to the drums, Jared increased the tempo, stepping close enough to brush against her, stepping back to widen the circle.

She pivoted in the center of the circle, her eyes following him, no longer shy enough to look away from a male celebrating his maleness.

As the drums began to fade, Jared wrapped an arm around Lia's waist and whirled her around the room until they reached the side of the bed.

Cupping her face in his hands, he kissed her long and deep.

"Let me show you the rest of the Fire Dance," he said hoarsely.

She didn't answer. But the look in her eyes was answer enough.

He undressed her slowly, coaxed her into the bed, and stretched out beside her.

She shifted a little to move her hips away from his throbbing cock.

He shifted with her.

"It'll be all right," he said as his hand glided down her arm and back again. "It'll be all right."

While he brushed his lips against hers, he reached with his mind and brushed lightly against her inner barriers.

She recoiled with a gasp.

Jared murmured soothing nothings while he kissed and caressed her.

Always before, he'd given pleasure in order to escape the pain of punishment. Now he gave pleasure for the pleasure of giving it. He explored her body, fascinated by the muscles that quivered, and finally relaxed, under his light touch. He tasted her, rubbed himself against her so that her scent would be on his skin and his on hers. He laughed silently when her fingers dove into his hair to hold his mouth to her breast. He enjoyed the way her body both pulled away from and reached for the finger lightly brushing between her legs.

And all the while he slowly seduced her body, he stroked her inner barriers until she was so used to his presence she didn't react at all.

Then he began the journey into the abyss. Down, down, down while his mouth and fingers made her quietly desperate, while her grasping hands made him burn.

Down, down, down until he slipped under her inner barriers and saw the shining green web of herself.

Jared flowed upward. Carefully, delicately, he brushed a strand of her inner web.

Her body tensed. Thrashed.

His rolled, half-covering her to keep her still.

It's all right, Lia. He brushed the strand again.

Yes, she said, but her body shuddered, and she didn't sound at all convinced.

Following Talon's instructions, Jared carefully flowed his Red strength between the strands of her web, then formed a shield above her. That, Talon had explained, was why it was better for the male to wear the darker Jewel. If the witch panicked for some reason and tried to descend into the abyss, she wouldn't be able to get past the shield and inadvertently rip through her own inner web.

When he was done, he kissed her—and jerked back in surprise.

"What . . ." Lia said, her eyes wide with shock.

Jared caressed her breast, and felt the caress.

She pulled his head down and kissed him with a hunger that, when added to his own, left him reeling.

This was the seduction and the danger, Jared realized as he kissed her again. When a man was inside a woman's inner barriers, he could become so tangled up in the physical sensations of being both the giver and receiver that he wouldn't be able to distinguish his body from hers.

He covered her. Felt his body pressing her down. Felt

the bed under her back. Felt himself press into the opening until he met the physical barrier.

Jared buried his face against her neck.

Breathing hard, Lia gripped his shoulders. "Do it."

"Lia . . ."

"Do it."

He thrust.

And took the pain as well as the pleasure.

For a moment, the world turned end over end, whirling them in a storm of sensations.

He wanted to thrust again, to feel that pleasure.

He was terrified of the blood that covered him.

Lia dug her nails into his shoulders hard enough to break the skin and cried out in pain.

Sheathed inside her, the impaled and the impaler, Jared forced his body to remain still while they rode out the storm.

And realized that he could have stepped away from it. That he could have kept himself disengaged enough not to be swept away.

That's how a Jeweled male broke a witch. He mired her in the duality of sensations while staying in the eye of the storm. And then he gave pain instead of pleasure. The witch became her own enemy, feeling as if she were inflicting the pain upon herself. Unbalanced by the conflict, she would try to flee, but the pain would follow, driving her to her own destruction.

The knowledge made him shake.

"Jared." Lia wrapped her arms around him. "Jared?" She shifted under him.

He struggled to find the self-control that would let him pull back enough not to get swept away by the physical sensations, not to lose control completely.

"Jared," Lia murmured, stroking his back urgently. "Please."

Even if he could have distanced himself from her body, he couldn't bear to pull away from *Lia.*

So he wrapped her in his strength—body, mind, and heart—and surrendered both of them to the pleasure of the Fire.

CHAPTER TWENTY-FOUR

Leaning against his desk, Krelis slowly twisted the Sapphire-Jeweled ring on his right hand.

Darker than the Green Jewel, lighter than the Red.

But skill and training counted for something, didn't they? What was a pleasure slave's raw strength compared with centuries of learning how to fight? What difference did it make if the bastard wore the Red? He didn't really know how to use it.

Except the Shalador Warlord *had* held off the marauders who had banded together to capture the Green-Jeweled bitch-Queen. Had done a lot more than hold them off.

Had his pet been partially responsible for that? Krelis wondered as the Sapphire Jewel appeared and disappeared with each turn of the ring. Had he used his own training to support and guide the Red? It could have ended with that ambush. *Should* have ended with it.

His pet had been a serious miscalculation. He hadn't expected loyalty. No Hayllian expected *real* loyalty from these here-and-gone races. But a man who allowed himself to be bought should have the good sense to *stay* bought.

Well, that was one other thing he'd take care of when he got to that privy hole called Ranon's Wood.

"Come in," Krelis snapped in response to a knock on his office door.

Lord Maryk stepped into the room just far enough not to be noticeably still in the corridor. "All the supplies have been gathered, Lord Krelis. The guards from the last two southern Provinces are expected within the hour."

"I'd thought my instructions were simple enough to be clear," Krelis said, keeping his eyes on his Sapphire ring.

"We don't need a lot of supplies. We'll be back here by tomorrow night."

"Our men will need to eat after a fight," Maryk replied stiffly.

A fight, Krelis thought, resisting the urge to laugh in Maryk's face. How much fight would a village that had already sustained an emotional belly wound have left?

"We're not fighting other warriors," Krelis said curtly. "Whoever is left in that village already lost a battle with their own people. How much of a challenge can they be to a thousand Hayllian warriors?"

"Closer to fifteen hundred."

Krelis finally looked up.

Maryk shrugged. "Because this was a special request from the High Priestess's court, every Master sent along a few more than we'd asked for."

The other Masters had undoubtedly added a few to keep tempers from flaring as well—not only in the guards' quarters but in the manor houses of the Hundred Families. What young, ambitious male serving in a lesser court *wouldn't* resent being kept from an assignment that might bring him to the notice of the most powerful witch in Hayll?

He'd felt that way himself not all that long ago.

Some things, however, were best seen from a distance.

"We've already wasted enough time waiting for these young bucks to finish buttoning up their pants and shining their boots," Krelis said. "We leave in one hour. If the southern guards aren't here by then, they can stay behind or catch up to us."

"I understand, Lord Krelis." But Maryk didn't leave. "Have you decided who will take command of the men?"

Krelis rounded the desk, opened a drawer, and took out a large, white feather. Tucking it inside his leather vest, he said, "I will."

CHAPTER TWENTY-FIVE

Shivering, Jared gratefully accepted the mug of coffee Blaed handed him. The night air had a sharp bite to it, but worry seemed to bleed more heat from his body than the elements could.

"Everything's packed," Blaed said quietly. "We were ready to leave hours ago. Even riding the White Wind, it won't take more than a few hours to reach the Tamanara Mountains. Couldn't this have waited?"

Jared sipped his coffee and wondered the same thing— and tried not to resent that Lia had asked Thera to stay with her instead of him.

Talon silently came around the corner of the Sanctuary that was located a mile outside of Ranon's Wood. He'd made a circle around the building every hour since Lia and Thera had entered it, getting personal reports from the men who were standing guard and rotating the watch often enough to make sure everyone had a chance to warm up by the fire and eat a bowl of stew. Four of his men had stayed in Ranon's Wood to keep watch. The other eight had come with Talon, taking their turns in the rotation.

"Is there a problem?" Talon asked softly when he joined them.

"We're ready to leave," Blaed said, his voice ripe with impatience and nerves.

"The Queen isn't," Talon replied.

"Why is it taking so long?"

"The Offering to the Darkness takes from sunset to sunrise."

Blaed's jaw dropped. "She's—" When Talon hissed in anger, he looked back at the men warming themselves around the fire and lowered his voice. "She's making the Offering to the Darkness? *Now?*"

"Sometimes you choose the time to make the Offering. Sometimes the time chooses you," Talon said.

Blaed made a frustrated sound.

Jared understood exactly how Blaed felt.

"You're free to go back to the village or go on to the mountains," Talon said curtly.

Blaed glared at Talon before retreating to the fire.

"Don't jab at him," Jared said quietly. "You know Thera won't leave without Lia, and Blaed won't leave without Thera."

"I know," Talon said just as quietly. "But he needs to learn now that there are times when a man can, and should, argue about a Queen's choice of action and there are times when he should keep silent and do what needs to be done. Lia understands the risks she's taking by staying here to make the Offering. She must have felt the need outweighed the risks."

"It would have been safer if she'd waited until we reached Dena Nehele, until she'd had time to recover from her Virgin Night."

"Of course it would have been safer—*if* we can reach Dena Nehele without another fight. If we can't . . . The Green Jewel is still vulnerable in a one-on-one attack by a darker Jewel, but there are only two Jewels that can overwhelm a Gray."

The Ebon-gray and the Black. And only two Blood in the entire Realm of Terreille wore them: Lucivar Yaslana and Daemon Sadi.

Jared didn't think Dorothea SaDiablo would be foolish enough to let either of *them* be part of a welcoming committee.

But thinking of Daemon reminded him of something else.

"Have you ever heard of the Invisible Ring?" Jared asked.

Talon looked startled, then thoughtful. He blew on his hands to warm them before slipping them into his coat pockets. "It's been quite a few years since I've heard anyone mention the Invisible Ring," he said a little sadly, a little bitterly. "Seems like once the Ring of Obedience starts being used in a Territory, men shy away from any mention of a Ring of any kind."

Jared let his breath out slowly. "I wear the Silver."

"I thought you did." Talon looked at him and smiled. "So do I."

Jared didn't know what to say.

Talon looked up at the sky. It had been drizzling a couple of hours ago, making everyone uncomfortable. Now the clouds had passed. and the star-filled sky was clear.

Talon said quietly, "These two things a man may choose as long as stars shine up above. For the Silver Ring is Honor, and the Ring of Gold is Love." He smiled ruefully. "Not good poetry, but that's how I was taught it."

Jared leaned against the Sanctuary. "Not a tangible Ring, then, but real all the same."

Talon nodded. "Very real. And sometimes it weighs heavily enough on a man to almost feel tangible."

"Yes," Jared said softly.

Talon nodded again but continued to look at the stars. "I was about your age when I turned rogue. I still had two years left to the contract I'd signed to serve a Province Queen, but things started happening in the court. She started to change, started showing a little too much deference to the Hayllian ambassadors and aristos who visited the court. One day I realized that the only way I could continue to serve her was to give up the Silver Ring." He paused. "I wasn't willing to give it up. Not then. Not now. So I used the first excuse I could find to be away from the court for a couple of days . . . and I just kept going. I promised myself then that I'd never serve in another court, that I'd never put myself in the position of having to choose between breaking a solemn vow or giving up my honor."

"That's why you don't formally serve the Gray Lady."

"I made no vows, so I'll break no vows. But make no mistake about it, Jared. In my own way, I do serve her."

Thinking of a mistake made by the boy he had been, Jared sighed wearily. "How many men become ensnared by what they think is love and then find that they've sacrificed something precious?"

Talon rested a hand on Jared's shoulder. "The Gold doesn't ensnare, Warlord. The Gold doesn't demand the Silver in exchange. That's how you know it's the Gold."

Jared studied the older man. "Have you ever loved?"

Talon hesitated. "No," he finally said. "I've never worn the Gold. Come on. Let's warm up by the fire for a bit. We've still got a few hours before sunrise."

Thoughtful, Jared followed Talon to the fire.

Maybe it was because he was cold and tired and concerned about Lia that he had thought he'd heard something that hadn't been there.

Or maybe there really *had* been a touch of wistfulness—and envy—beneath Talon's words.

The sky was starting to lighten when Lia and Thera walked out of the Sanctuary.

Jared strode toward the two pale, exhausted women who had their arms around each other as if they needed the support. But he stopped abruptly before he reached them, too shocked to continue moving.

Lia's psychic scent hadn't changed.

It *should* have changed. He should have been able to sense the deeper, richer power of the Gray in her. But all he picked up was a solid, unmistakable Green.

Lia glanced at him but wouldn't meet his eyes.

Jared struggled to breathe.

What had he seen in her eyes before she looked away? Sorrow that her attempt to descend to her full strength had failed? Regret that she'd tried to make the Offering to the Darkness when she was physically, mentally, and emotionally tired, and, because of it, had failed that ultimate test of Self?

No second chances. The Offering could be made only once. Whatever potential depth of power a person might have reached was lost forever if it wasn't won during that one grueling night. Whatever Jewels a person came away with after the Offering were the darkest Jewels he or she could *ever* wear.

Which is why a witch who should have been a Gray-Jeweled Queen had ended up wearing the Green Jewels of her birthright. She might hone her Craft and gain more skill with the power she had, but because she'd gambled on one night, she wouldn't be strong enough to protect her Territory or her people against Dorothea SaDiablo.

Thera looked at Blaed and Talon before focusing on him. "We'd like to return to the village and leave as soon as possible," she said.

Jared clenched his teeth until the muscles in his jaw began to jump. "Whatever you Ladies wish."

Lia flicked an uneasy glance in his direction before hurrying toward the horses.

Watching them, Jared pivoted slowly until he could see the men around the fire. How many of them knew he'd given Lia her Virgin Night?

Most of them, judging by the way they kept their expressions carefully blank and politely looked around or through him.

Only Randolf didn't look away, and his eyes held something that might have been sharp regret.

Even Brock just shook his head and turned his attention to smothering the fire and preparing to leave the Sanctuary.

As resentment began to burn through the shock, Jared walked away from them, needed to get away from them. They blamed him for diminishing a Queen, blamed the inexperienced pleasure slave for daring to perform a service that should have been left to a strong, seasoned male.

Talon's hand closed on Jared's arm, forcing him to stop.

"It's wrong," Jared snarled. "It's all wrong. Talon, I swear by the Jewels and all that I am, I did everything I was supposed to do."

"No one's saying differently," Talon replied calmly.

"No?" Jared looked over his shoulder at the other men. "A pleasure slave isn't considered a man. How would he—"

"Shut up."

Jared tried, but the resentment kept building. "It's wrong," he insisted. "Even if she wasn't able to descend to the Gray, she shouldn't have ended up with just her Birthright Green. She should have at least come away with the Sapphire or the Red."

"Hold your tongue," Talon snapped. "This isn't the time or place to chew over what happened or why. It's done, and there's nothing we can do about it, so we'd better all start accepting it."

With his hand still clamped on Jared's arm, Talon headed for the horses. "Once we've got everyone tucked safely in Dena Nehele, why don't you spend a few months in the mountains with me?"

"Why?" Jared said, feeling the guilt that he should have done something different, something *more*, coil around his heart and squeeze.

Talon bared his teeth in a feral smile. "Because, Warlord, after you spend a winter with me, all that shit you spew about pleasure slaves will be knocked clean out of your head."

"Well, that's something to look forward to," Jared grumbled as he mounted the bay gelding.

Lia, Jared noticed with a fresh stab of resentment, was surrounded by Talon's men—and they didn't make room for him to ride beside her.

"Let's move," Talon said. "Jared, take the lead. I'll watch our backs. Everyone in the village will be waiting for us at the Coaches."

The Sanctuary was only a mile from the village, but it was the longest mile Jared had ever ridden.

The sky got lighter.

Feeling a prickle between his shoulder blades, Jared urged the gelding into a canter.

He probed the road ahead of him, looking for a trap. He probed the village and lightly touched the minds clustered together.

He expanded his probe outward . . .

. . . and found a blank spot.

And another.

And another.

And another.

The kind of blank spot a dark Jewel would notice when a lighter Jewel was wrapped in a psychic shield.

Mother Night.

Hold steady, Talon said on a spear thread. *We're almost there. If they were ready to attack, they would have done it by now.*

Jared acknowledged the message and kept his eyes on the road. Thank the Darkness they had moved the Coaches into the village instead of leaving them near the landing place. Otherwise, they would likely have been destroyed.

By the time they cantered up the main street of Ranon's Wood, a circle of psychic blank spots surrounded the village.

Jared turned the gelding to one side, letting the others pass.

Talon reined in next to him.

"Can we make a run for it?" Jared asked quietly.

Talon shook his head. "At a quick guess, I'd say there's several hundred of them out there, including a handful of Warlord Princes. They've cut us off from the Winds, and we haven't got a chance of breaking through and outrunning them overland."

"So we fight as well as we can."

"So we fight," Talon agreed, urging his horse toward the Coaches.

"And we die," Jared said, moving with him.

Talon stared straight ahead. "If the Darkness is kind."

Lia moved toward them as soon as they dismounted. Before she could say anything, a Craft-enhanced voice thundered over the land.

"Warlord! Shalador Warlord! I am Krelis, Master of the Guard for the High Priestess of Hayll! Your village is surrounded by Hayllian warriors, the finest warriors in the Realm. You have two hours, Warlord. If you hand over the Green-Jeweled Queen, I'll let the rest of you go. If you don't, there will be nothing left of you or your people but dust."

Jared slipped a protective arm around Lia's shoulders. He felt relieved when Blaed stepped behind her to protect her back and Thera moved a little closer to her other side.

"Well," Talon said, turning to face them, "it looks like the bastards have declared war."

CHAPTER TWENTY-SIX

Krelis leaned against the stable of the damaged Coach station outside Ranon's Wood. From there, he could keep an eye on the landing place, the road leading to that privy hole of a village, and the station itself where a few of his men were clearing out the debris in a couple of rooms to turn it into a temporary headquarters.

One of the Hayllian Warlord Princes approached him, and said, "All the men are in position."

"Fine," Krelis replied. "Pass the word that they're to do nothing but keep watch and make sure no one tries to slip between them."

The Warlord Prince paused. "There's no reason to give these—people—two hours."

"There's every reason," Krelis snarled. "I want that Shalador bastard to sweat. If I'd demanded that the bitch Queen be handed over immediately, the Jeweled males left in the village probably would have fought out of instinct. So we give them a little time to think, to worry. Give *him* a little time to look at his family and the people he grew up with and weigh the pain that will come to them against protecting a Queen he barely knows. Give the rest of them time to think about their own skins and weigh their children's lives against the life of one stranger. During the first hour, the villagers will split themselves into two camps. Before the second hour ends, the Shalador Warlord will either bundle her up and deliver her himself, or he'll yield to the rest of his people and not stand in their way when *they* deliver her to me."

The Warlord Prince made a sound of disgust "And we let the others crawl back into their lair?"

Krelis's lips curled in a sneer. "Once I have the bitch-Queen, the men can do whatever they please with the rest of them. The females can be passed around for as long as they survive. The children will be sold as slaves. The males can be broken, then hobbled and used for training exercises. That should give everyone a chance to show his skills."

A queer gleam filled the Warlord Prince's eyes. "Yes, it should."

Krelis waved his hand in dismissal.

He'd give the Shalador bastard time to sweat because it would also give *him* time to figure out what to do about the two Warlord Princes in the village—especially the Sapphire-Jeweled one. He hadn't expected them. Another oversight his pet would have to account for. *They* might have to be eliminated before the bitch-Queen was handed over.

Well, that was the Red-Jeweled bastard's problem.

Krelis called in a small wooden box. Inside was the brass button he had used to get past the traps spelled into the other ones in order to read the private messages, the brass button that had an extra spell woven into the metal—a spell his pet didn't know about.

Krelis triggered the spell that yanked the psychic leash wrapped around his pet.

Then he made himself as comfortable as possible, and settled down to wait.

CHAPTER TWENTY-SEVEN

Jared, Talon, Blaed, Yarek, Thera, and Lia sat in a circle inside one of the Coaches.

Or two half circles, Jared thought uneasily. Blaed and Yarek flanked Thera the same way he and Talon flanked Lia.

He almost wished someone besides Yarek had been chosen to represent the survivors of Ranon's Wood and Wolf's Creek. He didn't want to be separated from his uncle during the last hours he had left.

But that would depend on Yarek. Jared's choice was already made.

"I'm going to surrender," Lia said softly.

Thera's green eyes turned icy. "Don't be a fool. Do you really think those bastards are going to let the rest of us live?"

"He said—"

"He's *Hayllian*, and that bitch's Master of the Guard. What did you expect him to say? 'Make it easy for us because we're going to kill you anyway?' Once they have you, there's nothing to stop them from unleashing their Jewels and tearing this place apart."

"If I surrender, they might spare the children," Lia insisted.

Thera gave her a withering look. "Have you ever seen a young girl after a few males get done with her? Especially Hayllian males? Or what they do to a boy? I'd rather slit Cathryn's throat than let her be handed over to what's waiting out there. And Corry's and Eryk's, too. At least that would be quick and kind."

Lia made a distressed sound. "These people have endured enough."

"These people are going to die," Thera said harshly.

"Because of me."

Thera expelled a vile string of obscenities. "You really
turn into an idiot when you don't get enough sleep."

Gray eyes met green.

Feeling Talon's attention sharpen, Jared watched the two
women who balanced and complemented each other's
strengths so well. They didn't move, hardly seemed to
breathe.

A minute passed.

Two minutes.

Finally, Lia said quietly, "Queen's gamble."

"Yes," Thera said just as quietly. "It's the only way
now."

Yarek cleared his throat. "What's this Queen's gamble?"

Lia's eyes held Thera's. "Something my grandmother
taught me."

Talon's eyes narrowed as he studied the two of them.

Since Talon had the most fighting experience, Jared
waited for the Warlord Prince to say something, but he
wasn't surprised when Talon remained silent and thoughtful.

Yarek cleared his throat again. "Meaning no disrespect
for your grandmother, Lady, but I doubt anything's going
to get us through an attack from that many warriors."

"This will. If everyone does what he's supposed to do,
this will."

"Is there enough time for us to prepare?" Talon asked
respectfully.

"There's time," Lia said, as Thera nodded slowly.

Talon rose to his feet. "Then I'll tell my men."

"No," Thera said, her voice taking on an eerie quality
that made Jared shiver. "Go with Blaed and Jared and tell
the others who came with us from Raej." Her mouth
curved in a malevolent smile. "Tell *all* of them. Yarek,
inform your people. They'll need some time to accept having to face another battle. But do it quietly."

With some effort, Yarek got to his feet. "Doesn't matter

if they have time or not. They'll accept it. What choice do they have?"

Thera looked up at him. "None."

Not sure if he wanted to give reassurance or get some, Jared leaned toward Lia.

She leaned away from him, avoiding even that much contact.

It didn't matter, Jared told himself as he and the other men left the Coach. He didn't blame her for not wanting to be near him. He *wouldn't* blame her for not feeling for him even half of what he felt for her. It wouldn't have come to anything anyway.

But, Mother Night, how he wished she'd let him hold her once more.

CHAPTER TWENTY-EIGHT

Leaning back against the bales of straw his men had arranged into a tolerably comfortable seat, Krelis delicately tested the knife's edge against the ball of his thumb.

"What is it?" Krelis growled at the Warlord who kept shaking his head as he stepped into the stable.

"One of the villagers came down the road a minute ago."

Satisfied with the edge, Krelis sheathed the knife. "I'm expecting one of them. Did you put him in the Coach station?"

"No, Lord Krelis." The Warlord's mouth curled in a vicious grin. "And it's not likely you were expecting this one. He came around the curve in the road, saw us, and stopped. I thought he might be trying to spy on us, but he started grinning like a half-wit, unbuttoned his trousers, and watered the road. Then he turned around and headed back to the village. Didn't even tuck himself in."

Krelis leaned forward. "What did he look like?"

The Warlord shrugged. "Big male. Pale skin. Short hair. He wasn't close enough to see anything else."

Krelis snorted. "We don't have to worry about that one. The High Priestess already took care of him. I'm surprised he still has brains enough to unbutton his trousers in the first place." He stood up and stretched. "No, we don't have to worry about that one. But keep an eye out for my pet. He should be here anytime now."

Once the Warlord had returned to his position, Krelis

slipped his hand into his coat pocket. His fingers curled around the brass button.

He gave the psychic leash another yank.

His pet still needed one or two lessons in obedience.

Teaching him would pass the time—until it was the Shalador Warlord's turn.

CHAPTER TWENTY-NINE

Jared studied the people gathered in the tavern's small back room.

Eryk and Corry stood on either side of little Cathryn. Each of them held one of her hands.

Thayne, looking exhausted and obviously still suffering from the witchfire burns, leaned against the back wall, close to Blaed.

Brock leaned against the opposite wall, near the door, which was casually blocked by Talon. His face had that pained look of a man who badly needs to answer a call of nature but doesn't want to miss anything.

Pale and sweating heavily, Randolf restlessly paced the width of the small room, staying on the far side of the round table and chairs that were the room's only furniture.

Thera had said to tell all of them, but they hadn't been able to find Garth, and Jared decided not to waste time looking for him.

"We're going to fight," Jared said.

Brock muffled a groan.

Thayne nodded once.

Randolf swore fiercely. "We're slaves. Slaves don't fight."

Jared watched Randolf closely. "You fought during the ambush."

"There wasn't much sense in sitting back when the rest of you were tearing the place apart, was there?"

"There isn't much sense in sitting back now, either."

Randolf slapped his hands down on the table hard enough to make it rock. "Yes, there is. Do you know what happens to slaves who fight? What they'll do to any of the villagers who survive the first strike will be a slap on the wrist compared to what they'll do to us."

Jared's control snapped. *"We're not slaves!"* he roared. "We haven't been slaves since we left Raej."

Randolf stared at him.

Brock tried to suppress a pained laugh.

"We're not slaves," Jared said, struggling to leash his temper. "That's why the Gray Lady's so dangerous, even if that bitch Dorothea hasn't realized it. For the past few years, she's bought slaves at the auction and *set them free.* They go home, Randolf. Or they make a new home, a new life for themselves in Dena Nehele."

Randolf groped for a chair and sat down, his eyes never leaving Jared's face. "Why didn't Lady Lia tell us? Why this game?" He shook his head. "You're wrong. You have to be wrong. We're *Ringed.*"

"The Rings don't work," Blaed said. "Just enough power was put into them to make us think they were still connected to a controlling ring. But they aren't. Besides, Lia has no idea how to use one."

Randolf rubbed the back of his hand across his mouth. "Why didn't she tell us?"

Jared felt two light psychic touches. Talon's and Blaed's signals that they were descending to their full strength—and ready to rise to the killing edge.

"Because," Jared said quietly, "once she brought us all together, Lia sensed something was wrong, but she couldn't find the source. So she continued the pretense of bringing slaves to Dena Nehele, and she made things as difficult as she could for whichever one of us serves the High Priestess of Hayll while trying to get the rest to safety."

"One of us serves that bitch?" Randolf's hands curled into fists.

Jared rested his hands on the table. "If Lia had told you in the beginning that you were free, that you could catch the Winds and go home, would you have gone?"

Randolf's head moved slightly before he stopped himself from looking at the children.

"No," Randolf said after a thoughtful silence. "No, I wouldn't have. I've got too much pride as a Warlord and a guard to let a young Queen wander around without an escort." A dangerous gleam filled his eyes. "Do you know who it is?"

"It's Garth," Brock said, wincing as he straightened to his full height and tucked his thumbs into his wide leather belt. "It's Garth."

Jared turned to face Brock at the same moment Randolf exploded out of his chair.

"I warned you!" Randolf shouted, throwing himself at Jared with enough force to send them both to the floor. "I told you that bastard was tainted! Damn you, why didn't you listen to me? We might have gotten her home if you'd listened to me!"

Randolf threw a couple of punches before Blaed and Talon pulled him off Jared.

By the time Jared got to his feet, Brock had disappeared.

"Hold him," Jared said as he rushed out of the tavern.

Spotting Brock walking purposefully down the road in the direction of the landing place, Jared ran to catch up to him. "Brock! Brock!"

When Brock turned around, Jared stopped abruptly, stunned by the bitterness in the other man's face.

"Even now, when he's barely half of what he used to be, you choose to believe him, to trust him," Brock said. "Even now."

Regret cut deep into Jared's bones. "I trusted you."

"Not enough to be useful," Brock snapped. "You trusted the Warlord Prince whelp and the Black Widow enough to tell them we weren't slaves, but not me. It might have been different if you'd trusted me."

"It wouldn't have made any difference," Jared said coldly. "You'd already chosen whom you serve."

"It might have," Brock insisted. His face twisted with conflicting emotions. "Do you know how I came to be a slave? My *Queen* sold me to Hayll. The Territory Queen is getting old, and the bitch I served wants to rule more than a small Province. So she traded twenty of her best males for Hayll's influence in choosing the next Territory Queen. She sold our freedom, our *lives* for ambition."

"When a male serves, he puts his life into his Queen's

hands," Jared said. "It's hers to do with as she pleases. That's the risk we all take, Brock." Remembering Talon, he added, "His life, but not his honor. You had that much choice."

"Who are you to talk about honor? You're a pleasure slave, a nonman pretending to be a Warlord. *A Queen killer.* Where were you hiding your honor when you butchered *her*?"

"I was owned by her. I didn't serve her." But the verbal thrust hurt as much as a knife in the gut.

"You're splitting hairs, Jared," Brock said harshly. "But if that's how you want to split it, then as far as I knew, I was owned by the Gray Lady. What's the difference between you killing the bitch who owned you and me buying some kind of freedom for myself by helping the High Priestess get rid of a rival? All I had to do was lead the marauders to her if she escaped the trap at the Coach station."

Brock's lips curled into a sneer. "Hayll didn't want her killed by a newly purchased slave because it would make all the other witches nervous about going to Raej to buy their pretty toys. *I* wasn't going to have a Queen's blood on *my* hands."

Jared felt a weight settling in his chest. "Who was Garth before Dorothea did that to him?"

"The Province Queen's Master of the Guard. A leader. Men trusted him, listened to him. Even our father always listened to him," Brock added bitterly.

"Garth's your *brother*?"

"My older brother. Always stronger. Always better at everything. After the High Priestess broke him back to his Birthright Purple Dusk and sealed him up inside himself, he wasn't stronger or better anymore, was he? No one was going to listen to *him* anymore, were they? But they still didn't listen to me, either." Brock looked at Jared with eyes full of hatred. "The others would have listened to me if *you* hadn't been there. *I* would have been the dominant male in the group if it hadn't been for *you*. She would have trusted *me*."

Jared studied Brock. How could the strong man he'd

known on the journey become this whining boy? "The link with Garth," Jared said slowly. "It not only hid your true nature, it also helped you act as Garth would have acted, say what he would have said."

Brock nodded, his mouth curving in a sly, nasty smile. "I'm the one who thought of that after the Priestess put the compulsion spells around me that would make sure the Gray Lady bought me. Being brothers, it was easy to make a link that would meld our psychic scents so that the bitch-Queen couldn't separate one from the other. I even made him place the first couple of buttons, since no one paid any attention to the mind-damaged male. But he started fighting me, defying me. After a while, all I could do was keep enough of the link so that I wouldn't be discovered."

Hold it back, Jared told himself. *Leash it. Save this rage for the fight ahead.* "You brought them to Ranon's Wood. You brought these carrion-eaters from Hayll down on my people."

"If she'd been captured at the ambush like she was supposed to, we wouldn't have come to your precious village at all. If anyone brought them here, it was *you.*"

"Get out of here," Jared said too quietly. "Get away from my people. You belong with those Hayllian bastards."

Brock pouted. "If I'd known she was going to give us *real* freedom, it would have been different."

"Get out."

The pout twisted back to nastiness. "You're going to die, Jared. All of you are going to die, and all the words in the Realm aren't going to change that." Brock bared his teeth in a smile. "Maybe once the High Priestess is done playing with Lia, they'll let me have her for a while. I'd like to take a long, hard ride between her thighs."

Jared clenched his fists and his teeth.

Hold it back. Keep it leashed. Striking out now would bring the Hayllians in faster, and Thera and Lia needed as much time as they could get to prepare this Queen's gamble.

Looking a little disappointed at getting no reaction from Jared, Brock raised his hand in a mocking salute. Then he flinched and put a hand to his head.

"Have to answer," he mumbled. "Have to . . . summoned." He turned and continued down the road to the landing place at a fast walk.

By the time Jared got back to the tavern, Thayne had taken the children away—but Garth had returned.

Blaed and Talon held Randolf back while the guard snarled threats and obscenities at the large man standing on one side of the room.

"Damn you, Jared," Randolf shouted. "Tell them to let me go. Let me get rid of the bastard before he does any more harm."

"He's already gone," Jared said fiercely. "It was Brock, Randolf. All the time, it was Brock. His Queen sold him into slavery. *He* sold himself to Hayll." Weary, Jared rubbed his hands over his face. "You had the wrong man, but you were also right—Hayll's pet *is* tainted."

Looking past Jared, Randolf studied Garth as if seeing him for the first time. "He was a guard."

A fierce intelligence filled Garth's pale blue eyes. A huge fist thumped the large chest. "Mmmaster."

"He was a Master of the Guard," Jared said.

Randolf swore, but there was pain, not violence, in the words. "To do that to a Master . . ." he said softly.

"Let's not waste time," Jared said. "We've got to help Lia and Thera plan a defense against—"

"Jared—" Talon warned.

Before Jared could turn, Garth's hand landed on his shoulder hard enough to make his knees buckle.

"Lllisten to Queen," Garth said, giving Jared a little shake. "Queen sssmart. Confuses mmmales."

"Confusing us is helpful?" Talon asked dryly.

Garth waved his other hand. Blaed prudently ducked.

"Hayll. All mmmales out there. Confuse mmmales here. Confuse mmmales there." Garth gave them all a deadly smile. "Confuse Brock always. Sssmart Queen. You lllisten."

Giving Jared a friendly whump on the back that tumbled him into Talon and Randolf, Garth left the room.

"Well," Talon said after a moment, "he's got a point.

It's damn hard to block someone's moves if you can't figure out how she thinks."

"Yes," Jared replied thoughtfully. Something Brock had said about links and psychic scents and Jewels kept teasing him, but its significance stayed just out of reach. "Let's find out a little more about this Queen's gamble our Ladies are planning."

"Even if it confuses us?" Blaed said with a hint of a smile.

Something. Something. "Especially if it confuses us."

CHAPTER THIRTY

Krelis leaned back against the table, crossed his feet at the ankles, and studied the surly man before him. "You disappointed me, Brock. You didn't live up to your side of the bargain."

"I did," Brock replied belligerently. "I did what I agreed to do. Wasn't *my* fault there were problems that even *you* didn't anticipate."

Krelis crossed his arms to keep his hand away from his knife. "What kind of problems?"

When Brock took a step toward Krelis, two Opal-Jeweled Hayllian guards grabbed his arms and hauled him back.

Brock struggled uselessly for a moment.

Krelis caught a whiff of fear and found himself aroused by it. "What kind of problems?"

"A broken Black Widow who wasn't broken," Brock said, pouting. "A Warlord Prince who'd disguised what he was until we were well into the journey. Garth still having brains enough to figure out what the buttons were for and picking them up after I'd left them for the marauders to find. That damn Red-Jeweled nonman deciding to play Queen's stud. You can't blame me for any of that."

"Perhaps not," Krelis said. "But the fact is your inability to perform your task greatly inconvenienced the High Priestess—and there are penalties for inconveniencing the High Priestess of Hayll."

"I did my part," Brock insisted, trying to shake off the guards. "You've got the little bitch-Queen now."

Krelis looked at the other four guards who had quietly entered the room. At his nod, the guards restraining Brock tightened their hold.

"But the inconvenience, Brock." Krelis shook his head. "Some compensation has to be made for the inconvenience." Smiling, he withdrew the large white feather from his leather vest and unsheathed his knife. "I have one more small task for you, and then our bargain will be complete."

CHAPTER THIRTY-ONE

"**W**e're going to build a psychic web," Lia said in a voice that had all emotion washed out of it.

Jared glanced at the other men crowded into the tavern's back room. Blank faces. Confused eyes. Talon rubbed the back of his neck and frowned at the chalk circle Lia had drawn on the table. Blaed looked at the ceiling, his eyes filled with wry humor.

Since Garth was the only one nodding as if that statement made sense, Jared wondered if he'd feel less confused if he banged his head against the table a few times.

Then he looked at Lia, and the trickle of amusement faded.

The Queen and the Black Widow who sat across from each other were suddenly strangers to him, filled with a wild unknown. There was something dangerous about the way they sat so still, so quiet.

"Jared, since you wear the darkest Jewel, you're going to be the web's focal point," Lia said.

Great. Wonderful. *Mother Night.*

Jared shifted uneasily. "What's it supposed to do?"

"It will give the weakest of you the protection of the strongest," Thera said in that voice that made all the men shiver. "Through the strands of the web, all of you will be connected. A strike against any one of you will be absorbed by all of you. The Red Jewel will feed the web and keep it strong."

"It sounds fine as a defense," Talon said, "but Jared won't be able to hold it long if they start unleashing their own Jewels."

"They want Lia alive," Thera said, staring at the circle

drawn on the table. "They won't risk a full attack until they have her."

"Even if they do nothing, he still can't hold it forever," Talon argued. "And they're not going to get bored and just go home."

"Ten minutes," Lia said. "Once the signal's given, he only has to hold it for ten minutes."

Only.

Jared wanted to laugh, but he was very afraid it would come out sounding hysterical. Didn't they realize how many Hayllians were surrounding Ranon's Wood?

Thera slashed a look in his direction—as if she'd heard the laughter. "You held Red shields against the marauders for that long."

"There weren't as many of them," Jared said testily.

Thera shrugged. "They were fighting, always draining the shields. The Hayllians won't be attacking with any strength. Alive, Lia is a valuable hostage. If they'd wanted her destroyed, the village and everyone in it would be gone by now."

"When the Hayllians start to advance, everyone wearing the Jewels will provide a token resistance, gradually retreating toward the Coaches," Lia said. "Jared will remain here in the tavern, where he can watch the road."

"I can—" Jared began.

"Your task is to defend," Lia said sharply.

"I don't like it," Randolf said, shaking his head. "We're not going to achieve anything. Gaining a few more minutes won't change the outcome of the battle."

Thera's eyes were ice with a hint of green. "You don't have to like it, Warlord. You just have to obey."

After silencing Randolf with a searing look, Talon fixed his gaze on Lia. "With respect, Lady, I say again—this web you and Lady Thera devised is an admirable protection, but it won't get us out of here."

Lia raised her chin. "Yes, it will."

Frustrated, Jared raked his fingers through his hair. "How?"

They said nothing.

Seeing his own hurt mirrored in Blaed's eyes, Jared pushed aside bruised feelings.

Blind trust. In the end, it always came down to blind trust because it was the ultimate test of the bond between a Queen and the males who serve her.

"It's time to start," Thera said, rising.

Silent, all the men except Jared, Talon, and Blaed left the room. When Lia rose, the three men formed a triangle around the two women, Talon automatically taking the point while Blaed and Jared each flanked his own Lady.

"Prince Talon, your presence is required," Lia said when they stepped outside. She moved out of earshot and waited for the Sapphire-Jeweled Warlord Prince to join her.

Jared's muscles quivered at the formal request. Before he could decide whether or not to insist on being part of that private conversation, Thera dragged him back inside the tavern.

She gave him a brittle smile that was probably meant to reassure him but, instead, turned his guts to water.

"I need some of your blood," Thera said, holding up a small pewter cup. "For the web."

Power sang in the blood. Life sang in the blood.

And trust, like love, was one of the heart's songs.

Jared pushed up his sleeve and offered his wrist.

She was quick, gentle, and far more careful about healing the nick in his wrist than he would have been.

Giving him another brittle smile, Thera put the cover on the cup and dashed to the Coach she and Lia were using to prepare this Queen's gamble.

Stepping outside again, Jared eased closer to where Lia and Talon were still standing.

"If that's what you want," Talon said grimly, "a fast—"

"I told you what I want from you," Lia replied. "Exactly what I want. Will you do it?"

Jared eased closer. The fierce unhappiness in Talon's face made his heart beat strangely, as if it couldn't decide to pound until it burst or just fade until it stopped.

"Promise me, Talon." Lia gave Talon's hand an urgent squeeze.

Talon looked at their clasped hands. His fingers curled

around hers. When he finally spoke, his voice was heavy. "I swear by the Jewels and all that I am that I'll do exactly as you asked."

Leaning forward, Lia swiftly kissed Talon's cheek. "Thank you."

Then she noticed Jared and stepped back, blushing.

Still watching Lia, Talon's eyes narrowed thoughtfully. Then his attention shifted to Jared for a moment. "If you'll excuse me, Lady, I have some preparations to make."

"Of course," Lia murmured.

As Talon walked past Jared, he muttered, "May the Darkness have mercy on me," and kept going until he reached his Warlords.

"Lia," Jared said quietly, taking a couple of steps toward her.

Lia retreated. "I—I have to help Thera."

There were shadows under her eyes from lack of sleep. There were shadows *in* her eyes, hiding so many things.

And there was that *something* he should understand about Jewels and psychic links that was still teasingly just out of reach.

"Lia, what is the Queen's gamble?"

"What it's always been." Lia licked her lips. "That the males she's assigned certain tasks to will perform those tasks exactly as requested. That they won't allow themselves to become distracted by whatever else is happening—or whatever else they *think* is happening."

"Lia . . ."

Her hand clamped on his forearm. "Jared, you must hold the web. You *must*. Everything depends on it."

Jared swallowed hard. "I'll hold it."

What he saw in her eyes took his breath away.

Lia tried to smile. "I have to help Thera."

When she tried to move away, he reached out and gathered her in his arms. "Once more," he whispered, lowering his head. "Just once more."

He kissed her gently, deeply.

Confused, he released her and stepped back. "Go help Thera."

Jared watched as she hurried away from him. There was

a tartness to her psychic scent that shouldn't have been there. It didn't fit her. Wasn't like *her*.

"Jared."

Putting that puzzle aside, Jared turned at the sound of Talon's voice. "What did she ask of you?" Jared demanded.

Talon gave him a considering look. "You know better than that."

Yes, he knew better than to ask another male about a private request made by a Queen, but that didn't stop him from wanting to know the answer.

Talon looked around, as if to make sure there was no one near enough to overhear them. Moving closer, he said quietly, "You've played chess with her?"

"A couple of times."

"Does this fit her pattern?"

Fool, Jared thought. *You should have thought of this yourself.* He closed his eyes and pictured the game board. "If her stronger pieces aren't acting as the main defense, they're supporting minor pieces in an attack. She tends to pair strong pieces. A Warlord Prince with a Black Widow, for example."

"How appropriate," Talon murmured. "What about the Queen?"

"She—" Jared felt the blood drain out of his face. "Mother Night, Talon, what are they planning?"

Talon shook his head. "I don't even want to guess. Something or someone put a nasty edge on Thera's temper, and Lia's always had the kind of courage that scares a man right down to the bone."

"They work well together," Jared said as he stared at the street without really seeing it.

Talon, too, stared at the street. "Yes, I imagine they do."

CHAPTER THIRTY-TWO

An interesting way to spend an hour, Krelis thought as he picked up the discarded tunic and carefully cleaned his knife. A useful exercise.

Sheathing his knife, he studied his work.

A crude effort compared to the High Priestess's, but he hadn't had the time nor the practice to equal her skills.

At least, not yet.

Krelis smiled at his pet. "I think it's time for you to fulfill the rest of our bargain."

CHAPTER THIRTY-THREE

"Warlord! Shalador Warlord!" Krelis's Craft-enhanced voice thundered over Ranon's Wood. "Come to the curve in the road, Warlord. There's something I want to show you."

Jared took a couple of steps away from the Coach and stopped abruptly, surprised by Blaed's and Talon's hard, restraining hands.

"Don't be a fool," Talon growled quietly.

"Warlord! I want to show you something. No one will harm you."

Lia and Thera came out of the Coach. Both pairs of narrowed eyes stared in the direction of the landing place.

"Is the little pleasure slave afraid to act like a man just once before he dies?" Krelis's voice taunted.

Thera twitched a shoulder. "The web's ready. It's keyed to Jared. If anything happens to him, there's no time to make another."

"I'm going," Jared said firmly.

Thera turned on him. "If you're going to let a little cock-waving ruin everything we've planned—"

Jared cut her off. "He wants to show me something. I want him to keep his distance until this last game is ready to be played. If I don't go out, he'll come in."

"Jared won't be going alone," Talon said.

Before Jared could object, Talon leaned closer and quietly added, "I know a few moves that would have you walking bowlegged for a month. So why don't you make the Ladies happy and graciously accept the escort?"

Jared bared his teeth in a feral smile. "To please the Ladies."

Talon returned the smile. "We live to serve, Warlord."

The unhappiness under the words kept Jared from arguing. If whatever Lia had asked of Talon went wrong, the man would welcome whatever the Hayllians did to him.

Knowing that, Jared rested a hand on Talon's shoulder, and said softly, "We live to serve."

"You didn't have to threaten me," Jared growled a few minutes later as he, Talon, Blaed, Randolf, and three of Talon's men walked to the curve in the road. "And I'm not a child who needs his hand held."

"No, you're not a child," Talon agreed. "You're just the only one of us who's essential to the Ladies' plan."

Unable to argue with that, Jared clenched his teeth.

"You're damned thin-skinned whenever anyone mentions pleasure slaves," Talon continued. He grinned. "A winter up in the mountains will give you a tougher hide. It's colder than Hell up there. Nothing like a cold night to knock some sense into a man."

"I haven't said I was going with you."

"You haven't said you weren't."

Jared grunted.

They came around the curve in the road.

Jared took one more step before his legs froze.

Six Hayllians waited about two hundred yards down the road. One of them was a Sapphire-Jeweled Warlord.

Jared managed one glance at them before his eyes focused on the mutilated thing that was walking unsteadily toward him.

Talon sucked air through his teeth and let it out in a slow hiss.

Blaed shuddered.

Randolf whispered, "Mother Night."

How could a man live when that much of him had been cut away? Jared wondered as his stomach twisted.

Halfway between the two groups of men, Brock raised his arms, his fingerless hands reaching, reaching.

"Warlord!" Krelis shouted. "Take a good look, Warlord! If you don't bring the little Queen to the landing place in one hour, that's what every male in the village will look like before we're done. Do you understand me?"

Thank the Darkness his uncle Yarek hadn't come with him, Jared thought. The next hour would be hard enough for the villagers without their knowing what would come at the end of it.

"Do you like the feather, Warlord?" Krelis taunted. "Even a nonman should have something between his legs, don't you think?"

"Let's go," Talon said. "We're wasting time here."

Blaed's throat worked convulsively. "What about Brock?"

Snarling, Randolf raised his right hand. A bolt of power from his Purple Dusk ring struck Brock in the heart.

Brock jerked once, and then collapsed.

Randolf wiped the back of his hand over his mouth. "Not even a bastard like Brock deserves to have that done to him."

Jared didn't protest when Talon's men hurried him back to the village. He didn't argue about Talon, Blaed, and Randolf following after them, guarding their backs.

But he promised himself that, if Lia's plan failed, his people wouldn't suffer at the hands of that Hayllian bastard.

Even if he had to kill them himself.

CHAPTER THIRTY-FOUR

Krelis watched the retreating men and smiled.

At first, he'd felt disappointed that the Shalador Warlord hadn't had the balls to come alone. Now he was pleased that there had been other witnesses. Alone, the bastard could have denied what he'd seen. But those other males . . .

It wouldn't take long for it to be whispered through the village. Once the males heard what was planned for them, they'd hand over the Queen. Only a fool wouldn't try to buy a little mercy.

Maybe he'd bring the Shalador bastard back with him. It would cost a few men to drain the Warlord's power enough to smash through the inner barriers and contain him, but it would be worth the cost.

He'd like to hand Lord Jared over to Dorothea. She would know just what to do with a male who'd caused her so much inconvenience.

Maybe she'd even let him watch.

CHAPTER THIRTY-FIVE

Keeping his own fears and uncertainties locked away, Jared worked to send out a feeling of confidence to the villagers patiently waiting for Thera to add them to the psychic web she'd created within a tangled web.

No one spoke. No one even whispered to the person behind them. No one dared be the one to break Thera's fierce concentration.

She pricked each villager's finger, placed one drop of blood on a specific thread of the web she'd built, and then, using Craft, froze the blood in position so that the web began to look like a delicate silver necklace dotted with red beads.

Over and over again, moving swiftly as the minutes slipped away.

And each time she placed a drop of blood in its chosen place, Jared felt another mind added to the web. If he let his eyes unfocus, he could see it in his mind. But the web he saw with his inner vision didn't have drops of blood, it had little Jewel stars—or clear beads for the Blood who weren't strong enough to wear the Jewels. Some he could still recognize by their Jewels—Eryk and Corry, his uncle Yarek, Thayne—but as more and more people were added, their psychic scents began to blur and blend together.

The Hayllians would sense something odd, but they wouldn't be able to find the source because *everyone* would become the source.

Which was basically the same trick Dorothea had used to hide Brock from Lia.

As he took a moment to admire Thera's cunning, he also

realized most of the Shalador witches were wearing tunics and trousers and had loosely braided their dark hair.

His pride in his people swelled at their courage.

Without being able to separate one psychic scent from another, there was no easy way to tell what Jewel each witch wore, and if the Hayllians didn't get a good enough look to notice the golden skin, the witches could play "hide the Queen" for hours—or at least long enough to prevent the Hayllians from unleashing a full attack before everything was ready.

He estimated they had a quarter of an hour left when Blaed and Talon stepped up to the web, the last two to be added. Everyone else had dispersed to various points in the village.

"There," Thera said, rolling her shoulders as she stepped back from the web. She took a couple of deep breaths. Then she detached the two bottom tether threads from the wooden frame. Holding the web by the top tether threads, she lifted it from the frame and looked at Jared. "Take off your shirt."

Exchanging a puzzled look with Talon and Blaed, Jared stripped to the waist.

"Take a breath and hold still," Thera said. "This is the safest way to protect it."

Still puzzled, Jared watched as she laid the web over his chest and belly. Then he felt the spidersilk threads and beads of blood melt into his skin. He gasped.

Thera studied his chest for a moment before nodding. "Don't worry," she said with a knowing smile. "You're not stuck with everyone permanently. Once the power in the web is gone, the spidersilk and blood will pass back through your skin and fall off."

"Can I get dressed now?" Jared growled. He shivered, but it wasn't just because it was too cold to be standing around half-naked.

"Yes, you can get dressed."

"Is it done?" Lia said quietly as she joined them.

"It's done," Thera replied.

They turned toward the Coach.

Jared hastily pulled on his shirt. He wanted a minute with Lia while he had the chance.

"Wait a minute," Blaed said sharply. He pointed at Thera. "You and Lia aren't connected to the web."

"What?" Jared and Talon said in unison.

"They're not part of the web. I waited until the end, but I got here when Thera added the first person." Blaed stared at the two women, his eyes filled with hurt and fury.

Lia studied the three men. She took a deep breath. "Thera and I can't be part of the web." She held up a hand to stop their protests. "We can't be. But I swear to you, we're well protected."

"Come on," Thera said. "We have to take care of the last of it."

"What last?" Jared demanded, taking a step toward them. "You didn't mention anything else."

Lia's eyes stopped him from taking another step.

The three men watched Thera and Lia hurry to the Coach.

Jared pressed his hand against his chest. He wanted to rub the area over his heart to try to ease the deep, growing ache, but he was afraid he might damage the web.

Talon nudged Blaed. "Let's get into position." He started up the street, then turned back. "Jared? Are you all right?"

Jared lowered his hand. "I'm fine."

A minute later, he stood alone in the street. Everyone else was hidden. The Coach's door remained closed. A few minutes from now, Krelis would realize they weren't going to hand Lia over to him, and the battle would begin.

Too late, Jared thought as he walked to the tavern, where he would remain hidden until the very end. He should have told Lia while he had the chance, should have let her know how much she meant to him. The regret he felt about not being able to talk to Reyna should have taught him not to wait to say what was in his heart. But shame for the way he'd lived for the past nine years had prevented him from saying three important words to Lia.

And now it was too late.

CHAPTER THIRTY-SIX

K relis slid his knife in and out of its sheath.
He liked the rhythm.

Almost time to teach that Shalador bastard what happens to anyone foolish enough to defy Hayll.

The knife slipped in and out, faster and faster.

Maybe he'd have the Black Widow bitch's legs tied apart and let her compare the rhythm of both of his knives.

She'd scream. Oh, how she'd scream.

Maybe he'd make the little bitch-Queen watch.

What did it matter that no one, including the Priestess he served, thought he was an honorable man anymore? He had something better than honor now.

He had power.

CHAPTER THIRTY-SEVEN

From his position at the tavern window, Jared saw Thera slip out of the Coach and dash for the nearest building.

What was she doing? he wondered as he watched her dart from building to building, moving up the street. If she had further instructions for Talon, why didn't she send them on a psychic thread?

He shifted position to keep her in sight. Why was she heading east? The only things in that direction were the dance ring and the Sanctuary. She couldn't reach either of those without trying to slip past the Hayllians. Even Thera wouldn't be that foolish.

And why had she left Lia alone?

He looked in the other direction. He could just see the closed door of the Coach Thera and Lia had been using.

Jared hesitated a moment, then stepped outside. He looked east.

Thera had vanished.

He looked at the Coach.

He shouldn't be out here. But surely they had a minute left, didn't they? A minute to check on Lia, make sure she was all right. A minute to silently tell her what he wouldn't say out loud now because he didn't want to distract her.

He took a step toward the Coach.

"Warlord!" Krelis's Craft-enhanced voice thundered. "Your time's up, Warlord!"

Jared looked longingly at the Coach before retreating into the tavern. He took a deep breath, let it out slowly. Took another. Following Thera's terse, final instructions, he began to fill the psychic web with his Red strength. Slow and steady. No pulses of power that could overwhelm the non-Jeweled Blood in the web. Slow and steady.

Randolf. Blaed. Talon.

He used them as touchstones because they had been the last three added to the web and he could still recognize them. He used them because feeling Talon strongly through the web let him know the web was fully engaged.

They were as ready as they could be.

Any Hayllians coming up from the landing place would have to pass the Coaches, would have to pass by him.

Jared bared his teeth. "Come on, bastard. Let the battle begin."

CHAPTER THIRTY-EIGHT

Hearing Lord Krelis's voice thunder over the village, one of the Hayllian guards who was watching the east end of the village rubbed his hands in anticipation.

Now Hayll would teach another of these inferior races what it meant to be Blood. Now he'd have a chance to bring himself to Lord Krelis's—and the High Priestess's—notice.

Maybe he'd even have a chance to show one or two of these Shalador bitches what it was like to be mounted by a *real* man.

He glanced over his shoulder at the slope that led down into that dirt circle. His grin faded. He shuddered.

What had they used that circle for? Some kind of witches' celebration? Some bestial rite that the males feared?

He'd thought of exploring that circle, maybe even dropping his pants and taking a squat to defile it. But when he'd reached the top of the slope, he'd hit a wall of cold air that made him certain that any male who walked through it would end up with shriveled balls and a permanently limp cock.

So he was here, at the bottom of the slope, waiting for the signal to move forward. The bloodletting would have to wait. The commanders had been very firm about that. Full psychic shields to protect themselves and controlled strikes to wear down the Jeweled Blood and drive them all to the center of the village.

However, once the little bitch-Queen was caught . . .

Something passed by him, a few yards to his left, and headed up the slope.

Immediately, he extended his psychic probe and started searching.

The answer that came back from that probe was more subtle than a thought: *Nothing there.*

Uncertain, he sharpened his probe. If any of the villagers managed to slip past the Hayllians surrounding this privy hole, it wasn't going to be near *him.*

For just a second, he thought he felt something, touched something.

Something female. Something fiercely violent and powerful.

A cold fist settled against his lower back.

Then: *Nothing there.*

Shaking his head, he turned back to face the village.

When the order finally came, he moved forward eagerly.

That damn circle was making him jump at shadows, was making him feel odd things, hear odd things.

Because, for just a moment, he could have sworn he heard drums.

CHAPTER THIRTY-NINE

Jared clenched his teeth, squeezed his eyes shut, and concentrated on feeding his Red strength to the web.

Damn you, he thought when he felt Randolf take a hard strike. *Tap the strength that's offered. Use it.*

They wouldn't use it. He'd realized that after the first couple of minutes. The males who had decided to be the main diversion would sip the strength he was providing to maintain their protective shields, but they were draining their own Jewels to strike at the Hayllians and keep the bastards from closing in too quickly.

With his inner vision, he could see the web, its spidersilk threads now colored a strong red from his Jewel. He could see the Jewel stars flare with each strike. They were all winking, constantly flaring and dimming as the fighting continued.

Another strike.

Another.

Talon's Sapphire Jewel star flared wildly for a moment.

Jared held his breath until it steadied.

How long could they hold out? What were Thera and Lia waiting for?

He wanted to be out there, fighting with his friends, his people.

The Silver Ring kept him chained inside the tavern.

A cold gust of wind rushed over his skin, the kind of wind that made the changing leaves sound like rattles. The kind that was always a prelude to a violent autumn storm.

Jared opened his eyes.

He was inside the tavern. He shouldn't be able to feel

the wind. He was dressed. He certainly shouldn't be able to feel it on his skin.

Then he heard the drums.

The sound singed his blood and froze it at the same time.

These drums weren't calling the males to the dance. *These* drums were calling the witches to war.

And they answered.

Through the web, he felt the temper of the fight change, felt it grow colder, more savage. Merciless.

He looked out the window, trying to focus on the point where the Hayllians at the landing place—and Krelis— would enter the village.

But he didn't see any of those things. As the wind swept over his skin again, as his blood pounded to the rhythm of the drums, he saw the web with its bright beads. He saw a dark circle surrounding it, slowly constricting as the Hayllians advanced.

He saw another circle appear beyond the dark one. Light, dark. Silver, gold. It was all those things—and it held all the answers if he could just stay quiet enough to hear them.

He raised his hand. Reached out to touch it.

A warning shout broke his concentration and the vision disappeared.

Jared tensed when he saw Randolf retreating up the road. The Warlord didn't even glance at the Coaches. Jared silently applauded that self-control. If they could draw the Hayllians far enough into the village, Lia still might be able to get away.

Moments later, several Hayllians appeared. One of them, a Sapphire-Jeweled Warlord, wore the badge of a Master of the Guard.

Krelis looked around, then focused on the tavern, as if he could see, or at least sense, Jared standing inside. He smiled and gestured lazily.

Three Hayllian guards headed for the tavern.

The Coach door burst open.

Lia dodged the Hayllians' grabbing hands and raced up the street.

"Lia, no!" Jared shouted. Desperate to protect her, he used Craft to blast the tavern door open.

That startled the Hayllians enough to buy her a couple of seconds.

"Lia!" Jared shouted.

"Go after her!" Krelis roared.

Before any of them could move, a bolt of Sapphire power hit Lia in the belly. Her body burst, spraying blood and guts over the street. Her mouth opened in a silent scream as she flew backward.

Jared reached her first. He forgot the Hayllians. Forgot the web. Forgot his promise. Forgot everything but the woman lying on her back in the middle of the street.

"Lia." Jared dropped to his knees. One of his hands hovered over her ruined body. The other gently stroked her hair.

Hearing footsteps, Jared raised his head and bared his teeth.

Krelis stood a few yards away.

Jared saw no regret in those hard gold eyes. Disappointment and anger, yes, but not regret.

"Jared," Lia said weakly.

Dismissing Krelis, Jared gave her all his attention. "Hush, Lia," he said softly. "Don't try to talk."

"Jared," she gasped. "The web. Nothing else matters but the web. Everything's keyed to you."

"Hush, Lia."

Her hand flailed. Her fingers found his hair. Curled. Tightened. Yanked hard.

Jared grunted in surprise.

"Hold the web," Lia said in a voice that had an eerie quality to it.

Jared lowered his forehead until it touched hers. It didn't matter now. It was too late now. He wouldn't tell her that. But now, when they only had a few moments left, he would tell her something else.

"I love you, Lia," he whispered. "I'll always love you."

"Remember to say it when it counts," she replied tartly.

Stung by her tone of voice, Jared raised his head.

And watched gray eyes change to frosty green, watched the illusion of Lia's face disappear.

He felt something gathering, gathering. Heard a roaring.

"Mother Night," he whispered.

The link between Garth and Brock had worked so well because Garth's Birthright Jewel was the same as Brock's Jewel of rank.

Like Lia's and Thera's.

Now he understood the tartness in Lia's psychic scent when he'd kissed her, why she and Thera had stayed so close to each other, why Lia had tried to avoid physical contact as much as possible.

Thera had linked their psychic scents together to hide the fact that Lia . . .

The roaring grew louder.

Power gathered, gathered, gathered *beneath the Red.*

Everything keyed to him. Keyed to his blood.

He looked at Krelis and knew the Master of the Guard heard the roaring, too. Felt the power gathering.

He looked at Thera.

She bared her teeth in a smile that was pure malice. "Checkmate."

"Mother Night!" Jared whimpered. He threw himself on top of Thera, pressed his face against her neck, and closed his eyes.

The inner part of the web was still a strong red color, but the outer threads had faded, the power had retreated.

How much time? Jared wondered as he began sending the Red back into the web. He'd forgotten Lia's warning about ignoring what he thought was happening and letting himself get drawn into the trap she and Thera had laid for the Hayllians, letting himself get distracted from his task.

Steady. Steady. If he flooded the web with power, he might shatter the minds it was meant to protect. But if he wasn't in time, his carelessness would cost them the strongest.

The roaring got louder.

Almost had them all. Almost.

Louder.

Steady. Steady. There! He had Randolf. Blaed. *Talon!*

Unleashed in one wild, raw, uncontrolled blast, Lia's Gray strength hit his inner barriers hard enough to make him scream before it flowed around him and the psychic web keyed to him.

He heard men scream.

He heard sharp cracks, like tree limbs snapping.

He heard squelchy sounds, like overripe melons being dropped on a hard floor.

With his inner vision, he saw the web glowing bright red in the eye of a violent gray storm. He saw the dark circle of Hayllian minds flare and flare and flare until it shattered. He saw that other circle change to solid Gray.

Gasping, he poured more strength into the web.

A circle of Gray to contain the storm of power. When the unleashed Gray hit that Gray wall, the backlash would be as bad as the initial strike.

The thought had barely formed when the backlash hit him. He held on, drawing everything he could out of his Red Jewels.

It would return to its source. Whatever wasn't absorbed as it roared through the Hayllians' minds and crashed against their Jewels would return to its source.

Hell's fire, Mother Night, and may the Darkness be merciful! Did Lia know enough to shield herself? She would be as vulnerable to the backlash as the rest of them.

The ground shook.

Wind howled through the streets of Ranon's Wood.

Lightning tore the sky apart.

He felt the land embrace the power of a Queen that was being fed into it as what was left of the Gray flooded back to its source.

And then he felt the silence.

Thera punched his shoulder weakly. "Get *off* me. I can't breathe."

Jared's head jerked. What had he been thinking of, lying on her like that? He rolled off her but immediately reached for her belly.

Nothing to do for her. Even a Healer as good as Reyna had been couldn't have helped her.

Groaning, Thera sat up. She looked over his shoulder. What color there had been in her face fled.

"Mother Night," she gasped before she got to her hands and knees, crawled a couple of feet away from him, and became violently sick.

Jared twisted around to see what had frightened her.

He recognized the badge worn by a Master of the Guard. That was all he recognized.

Too numb to look away, he stared at the torn, pulped mess.

It would have been all of them. Without the web protecting everyone connected to it . . .

He shook his head, breaking the trance.

He wouldn't think of it. *Couldn't* think of it.

Thera's continued retching brought him back to the immediate.

He crawled to her, slipping in the trail of intestines.

Gathering up the hair that had escaped the loose braid, he put one hand on her forehead to support her, closed his eyes, and tried with all sincerity to convince his stomach to stay put.

Then he frowned. How could she be retching when chunks of her stomach were strewn all over the road?

Thera finally sat back on her heels. "Shit," she said weakly, "it smells."

She fumbled with the torn tunic, trying to widen the tear. "Help me get it off. It smells."

"Thera . . ."

"Help!"

Swearing under his breath, Jared ripped the tunic in half.

Thera immediately swiped at the remaining guts and started tearing at the gauzy material wrapped around her middle.

Jared stared for a moment. He pushed her hands away and ripped the material. Tossing the gauze aside, he gingerly wiped her belly with a piece of her tunic.

No shattered bones. No torn flesh.

Jared leaned back. His hands curled into fists. "You sneaky little—You tricked us!"

"I tricked *them*," Thera snapped. "*You* were supposed to ignore it."

"I was supposed to ignore it?" Jared said mildly as anger started to heat his blood.

She eyed him. Grabbing the tunic, she scrubbed at her belly. "We figured you were going to be a little upset about this," she muttered.

Even his teeth felt hot. "Upset? I thought I saw Lia get ripped apart right in front of me, and you figured I'd be a *little* upset?" He paused. Thought. Exploded. "YOU IDIOT! Do you realize how lucky you were that whoever unleashed that Jewel didn't go for your heart or your brain?" He shook her hard enough to make her squeal. "You could have been killed! Who—"

She didn't have to answer.

Talon strode down the street, stepping over Hayllian bodies, kicking pieces out of his way.

Did Talon even see them? Jared wondered as he leaped up to intercept the furious Warlord Prince.

"Damn you, Lia, I did as you asked!" Talon roared. "A strike to the belly. Not even a fast, clean kill, *but a strike to the belly!*" His eyes filled with tears. "Damn you for cutting out my heart, I did as you asked!"

Jared grabbed Talon's shoulders. "It was a trick, Talon. This is Thera, and she's all right. *It was a trick.*"

Talon made a slashing gesture with his hand. "Then what's all that spewed in the street?"

"Pig guts," Thera muttered, scrubbing harder.

They stared at her.

She cringed.

Maybe it was mean-spirited, but after the scare she'd given him, Jared relished being able to intimidate her.

"Pig guts?" Talon said in disbelief.

"Pig guts," Jared said, nodding slowly. "When they butchered the pigs yesterday morning, our little Black Widow toddled away with two large buckets of offal." He smiled at Thera.

She whimpered.

Talon's soft snarl grew to a roar. "I should take you over my knee and wallop some consideration into you!"

"Once the Hayllians surrounded the village, this was the only way we could win the fight," Thera said with a bit of her normal fire.

"You could have told us," Jared snarled.

"You would have yelled at us, and we didn't have time for that."

He and Talon did more than yell. With their arms locked around each other, Jared wasn't sure if he was holding Talon back or if Talon was holding him.

"Why are you blaming just me?" Thera wailed. "I saw the warnings in the tangled web, but I'm not the only one who planned this."

That stopped them cold.

"Lia," Jared said softly. Releasing Talon, he turned in a slow circle and finally looked, *really* looked at what a Gray-Jeweled Queen could do.

"She mustn't see this," Talon said grimly. "She hasn't had time to become comfortable with the power she carries inside her now. This could cripple her. Someday she'll have to unleash the Gray again, and if she won't because of this, it could cost Dena Nehele dearly."

Jared turned back to Thera and saw the exhaustion and how hard she was holding on to some emotional control. "Where?" he asked quietly.

"The dance ring," Thera said wearily. "She's in the dance ring. We put a cold spell around it when we went for a walk the other day so that no one would want to go into it."

Jared ran.

He saw his uncle Yarek and Thayne and a few other villagers come out of the buildings and look around, dazed.

He heard Blaed shouting Thera's name.

He heard someone running behind him and knew it was Talon.

Please, he thought as he ran. *Sweet Darkness, please don't let her walk out of the dance ring and see this.*

He leaped over a body and ran up the slope. He hit a wall of air cold enough to make his breath hitch, but it vanished as soon as he went through it.

Reaching the crest, he skidded to a stop.

Talon joined him, breathing hard.

Lia sat near the center of the ring, her legs spread wide, her hands clutching her chest.

"Lia," Jared breathed.

He rushed down to the dance ring and dropped to his knees between her legs. "Lia?" Cautiously, he reached out to touch her but didn't quite dare. "Lia?"

Her blank eyes stared at him.

Talon went down on one knee beside her.

Lia blinked. Blinked again.

Hesitantly, Jared rested his hand on her thigh. "Lia?"

"It knocked me down," she said, pouting.

She sounded like a little girl whose best friend had snatched her favorite toy.

"It knocked me down," she said again. She lowered her hands.

Jared looked at the Gray Jewel smeared with blood. His blood. That's how she had keyed her Gray power to recognize the psychic web and not destroy everyone connected to it.

And the Blood shall sing to the Blood—and through the blood. Thank the Darkness.

"It's mine," she pouted. "It shouldn't knock me down."

"It was the backlash, sweetheart," Talon said gently.

"Oh."

Did it damage her? Jared asked on a spear thread.

Talon hesitated, then shook his head. *I think she's just dazed. Even with a Gray shield around her, she must have taken a vicious hit.*

Humming softly, Lia caressed the Jewel.

Jared could almost feel her fingers sliding over his skin.

When she looked up again, her eyes were no longer blank.

"Your men?" she asked Talon.

He turned his head toward the village, his attention focused inward. After a moment, he said, "A couple of them were injured, but not seriously."

"Your people?" she asked Jared.

"They're fine."

She hesitated. "Thera? Did all the Gray shields I made hold around Thera?"

"They held just fine. She was brilliant. She scared the shit out of us. After that little performance, I think Blaed deserves a month of fussing without any objections." He glanced at Talon. "Don't you?"

"At least," Talon said dryly.

Lia hesitated again. Longer this time. "I killed them, didn't I?"

Jared didn't answer.

"They're dead," Talon finally replied.

Lia burst into tears.

Shifting position, Jared pulled her into his lap and rocked her.

The sobs ripping through her unnerved him.

"Let her cry it out," Talon said, resting a hand on Lia's head. *I'll go back to the village and bring a couple of horses.* He grimaced. *If any of them survived. I know how to make a brew that will sedate her for several hours. I'll bring that, too.*

Rising slowly, Talon left the dance ring. When he reached the top of the slope, he turned back. *You did well, Warlord.*

Resting his cheek on Lia's head, Jared rocked her until her tears finally stopped. "So did you, Lady," he whispered. "So did you."

CHAPTER FORTY

Dena Nehele.

From the rogue camp that protected the middle pass through the Tamanara Mountains, Jared looked at the rolling hills, the sweeping forests, the rivers and lakes. He saw the cultivated fields, the pastures dotted with animals, the villages and towns.

This high up in the mountains, the autumn air already held the taste of winter. The change came more slowly to the land below him.

To the south, the trees were still holding on to the green of late summer. But as his gaze swung to the north, the green gave way to golds, oranges, and reds.

A beautiful land. A healthy land. A thriving people.

Jared looked back at the Coaches. Lia was still inside, still sleeping off exhaustion and the brew Talon had made for her.

It was better this way. During the hours it had taken to reach this camp, he'd made his choice and believed it was the right one—for both of them. But he felt grateful he wouldn't have to be the one to tell her. And he hoped with all that was in him that he wouldn't look back on this day and regret the decision.

After they finished the simple meal the camp had provided, the others would make the last leg of the journey. By sunset, they'd be in Grayhaven, the town that took its name from Lia's family estate.

His uncle Yarek and the rest of the villagers would be all right. Shalador's seeds would thrive in Dena Nehele's soil.

What would the former slaves do? Most likely, Eryk and Corry would return home. Little Cathryn would remain, probably with Lia's family. So would Garth—at least until a Black Widow helped untangle the rest of his mind. Randolf and Thayne might choose to return to their own people.

Blaed would not.

Like Thera, the young Warlord Prince had made his choice. He might send a message to his family, but he had chosen the land he would now call home—and he had chosen the Queen he would serve.

Jared blinked against the stinging in his eyes. Just the wind, he lied to himself.

But, sweet Darkness, he was going to miss those two.

They broke away from a group of villagers and joined him, almost on cue.

It was tempting—and worthy of an "older brother"—to tease Thera about leaning on a man, but it didn't seem fair to rile her and spoil Blaed's contentment.

"I'd like to ask a favor," Jared said.

"Of course," Blaed answered instantly.

Thera said nothing. Her eyes held a hint of anger.

"My youngest brother, Davin, now lives in one of the southern villages. I'd appreciate it if you'd locate him and give him the two honey pear trees our mother planted for him."

Blaed nodded cautiously.

"The ones meant for Janos . . ." Grief for the boy he remembered jabbed at him. "I'd like you to have them. As a wedding gift."

"We haven't even handfasted yet," Thera grumbled.

Jared smiled. "But you will." His smile faded. "The ones she planted for me . . . I want Lia to have them."

Tensing, Blaed's eyes flicked to the Coaches and back to Jared.

Thera just watched him. "You're leaving."

It was hard enough to tell Thera. He wasn't sure he would have survived telling Lia.

"I'm going with Talon," he said, his voice suddenly husky.

"Then what you said meant nothing?"

This time, when tears stung his eyes, he didn't lie to himself. "It means everything."

After a moment, Thera nodded. She stepped away from Blaed, put her hands on Jared's shoulders, and kissed his cheek. "What should I tell Lia?" she asked quietly.

Hugging her, Jared pressed his cheek against hers and replied just as quietly, "Tell her I'll be back in the spring."

CHAPTER FORTY-ONE

Jared stepped off the landing place.

The abandoned traveler's inn looked rougher than it had six months ago when he had brought Lia there to be healed. Yet the call that had been more subtle than a thought had come from there, as it had before.

He entered the inn. Coming farther into the room, he looked at the table tucked near the stairs, at the bottle of wine and the two glasses, at the beautiful, golden-eyed man who sat waiting for him.

"Will you join me for a drink, Lord Jared?" Daemon asked.

Jared smiled. Unbuttoning his heavy winter coat, he approached the table. "Thank you. I will."

Daemon studied him for so long, Jared lifted a hand self-consciously to his hair. He'd shaved off the beard that had kept his face warm through the cold mountain winter, but he'd let his hair grow long enough to tie back and hadn't decided to cut it yet. His clothes, by even the kindest stretching of the truth, couldn't be called anything but sturdy and warm.

Compared to Daemon's sleek elegance, he felt like a grubby child.

And resented it.

Daemon's eyes filled with amusement.

Jared lowered his hand and sighed. Daemon knew, damn him.

"You've shed your slave skin," Daemon said with quiet approval.

Jared sat down and poured a glass of wine for himself. It surprised him that the approval meant so much.

But wasn't that one of the reasons he had come?

Daemon toyed with his wineglass. "I'm glad you responded. I expect I'll be kept on a short leash for quite some time, so it's unlikely that we'll meet again."

Jared tensed. "Dorothea can't link you to what happened." Mother Night, he hoped not. He didn't want to think about what Daemon's life would be like if she did.

"Krelis did." Daemon's mouth curved in a vicious smile. "But I doubt he mentioned our little discussion." He took a couple of swallows of wine. "No, she just wants to be sure I'm held in a Territory closer to Hayll. She has enough problems right now. It seems no one's eager to be her new Master of the Guard. And the efforts to soften the Territories bordering those already under Hayll's control have been seriously undermined by the stories that have spread about how a young Queen and a handful of former slaves defended an entire village against Dorothea's Master of the Guard and five thousand Hayllian warriors."

"There weren't that many," Jared mumbled.

Daemon shrugged. "Well, you know how stories grow with the telling. Especially with a little help."

"You cut the ground out from under Dorothea in any way you can, don't you?" Jared said.

"In every way I can," Daemon agreed solemnly. "But there's only so much I can do. And it's not enough."

Jared felt the sadness he'd been fighting all winter well up inside him. "Dena Nehele will fall, won't it?"

"Not while a Gray-Jeweled Queen rules there. Not while the strongest and the best serve her and remain vigilant against Hayll's subtle cultural poisoning. But, yes, eventually Dena Nehele will live in Hayll's shadow."

"Then all our efforts are pointless."

"No, Jared, they're not. Even in the most rotted Territories, there are still overlooked places where the Blood remember what it means to be Blood, what it means to honor the Darkness. Where males remember what it means to serve and witches remember that the bargain isn't one-sided. Those who remember may lose control of their lands, may have to live careful, hidden lives, but they must survive in order to restore their people when the time comes."

"When what time comes?" Jared asked, sitting forward.

Daemon hesitated. "When a Queen far more powerful than Dorothea can imagine walks the Realm. She's coming. That much I know. That much I was promised," he added quietly.

They drank in silence.

"Why did you call me here?" Jared finally asked.

"To say good-bye. And to tell you not to be a fool."

"About what?" Jared waited. Hoped. All the talks he and Talon had had during the long winter nights hadn't eased his doubts because Talon didn't really understand what it meant to be a pleasure slave. But if there was anyone who could understand how deeply that kind of slavery wounded a man, it was Daemon Sadi.

"There are many shades and flavors of love, Jared," Daemon said quietly. "Not all of them have the richness and the depth to be Gold. You have a chance at something many men only dream of. Don't let the Gold slip through your fingers."

Jared carefully refilled their glasses. "Is it fair to hinder a strong Queen with a Consort who has a degrading past?"

"Is it fair to deny the woman a man who loves her with everything that's in him?" Daemon countered.

"I was a pleasure slave for nine years."

"Nine years," Daemon snarled impatiently. "What's nine years compared to *centuries*?"

"Would *you* ask a Queen to accept you as her husband?"

"In a heartbeat."

Jared sat back, awed and a little frightened by the terrible yearning that filled Daemon's eyes.

"You love someone," he whispered. "Who?" He bit his tongue, instantly regretting the question.

Daemon's smile was gentle and a little self-mocking. "I don't know. She hasn't been born yet. But I've loved, and served, her all my life. I'll love no other. And I'll serve no other willingly." Reaching across the table, he laid his hand over Jared's. "Don't let the Gold slip away, Jared. Don't spend the rest of your life regretting that you didn't take the risk."

Daemon drained his glass and rose. "I have to go."

Jared stood, too. There were so many things he wanted to say, but words weren't enough. Taking a deep breath, he gripped Daemon's shoulders, opened his inner barriers, and let his feelings flow through his hands—his gratitude, his friendship, and the sincere hope that Daemon would someday find his Lady.

A little embarrassed, he stepped back. "May the Darkness embrace you, Prince Sadi."

Daemon cupped Jared's face in his hands and kissed him softly on the mouth. "And you, Lord Jared. And you."

Jared remained long after Daemon had gone. He picked up his glass, then set it down untouched.

Taking one last look around, Jared left the traveler's inn.

It was time to go to Grayhaven.

It was time to take the risk.

CHAPTER FORTY-TWO

"Excuse me," Jared called. He urged the bay gelding closer to the kneeling woman and bit back his impatience. He'd spent the past hour wandering around the Grayhaven estate, following the vague directions he'd been given. Lady Lia, he'd been told, was out gathering a few plants. Just follow the path there and he'd come to her by and by.

He'd followed that path and several offshoots. Every person he'd seen along the way had cheerfully pointed him in a different direction.

Well, the woman who hadn't answered him seemed intent on the same task so, hopefully, he was getting closer. Maybe she was a servant who had accompanied Lia. A lower servant, he decided, raking his eyes over the shabby clothes and the wide-brimmed straw hat that looked as if it had been run over by a couple of heavy wagons.

"If I could have a moment of your time." Hell's fire, any servant accompanying a Queen should dress better—

The woman stood, pulled off her hat, and turned around.

Jared stared at the flowing gray hair, at the gray eyes, at the Gray Jewel hanging from the gold chain around her neck.

Dismounting, he said meekly, "I beg your pardon, Lady. I didn't mean to disturb you."

The air around him chilled. The gelding snorted, and backed away as far as it could.

"You must be Lord Jared," Grizelle said coldly.

Jared swallowed hard. "You've heard of me?"

"You're the Warlord whose courage and honor helped a young Queen survive a dangerous journey." Grizelle's voice became knife-sharp. "And you're the ass who made my granddaughter cry."

Jared hunched his shoulders, but his heart leaped in hope. He kept his eyes focused on the ground between them. "I needed time, Lady. I needed to shed my slave skin." He glanced up.

Grizelle studied him from head to toe. "It seems you succeeded."

There was no softening in her expression or her voice.

Jared felt a shiver start in the soles of his feet and work its way up his body. This was the Gray Lady, who was still the Queen of Dena Nehele and who could banish him from her Territory.

And this was the family matriarch who would decide if he could even try for the future he hoped for.

"Why are you here, Warlord?"

"I—" Jared took a deep breath. "I came to see Lia."

Grizelle narrowed her eyes. "Are you planning to leave again and add a few new bruises to an aching heart?"

"No!" He forced himself to meet her eyes. Better to know now before he hoped too much. "I was a pleasure slave, Lady."

Grizelle's eyebrows rose. "Oh?" she said mildly. "I gather that means you know how to keep a bed warm on a cold winter night."

Jared opened his mouth. When his tongue started to dry out, he closed it.

Grizelle tipped her head to one side and eyed him curiously. "It's very tempting to ask you to recite your qualifications as a consort, but I've noticed that young men can be rather prudish about discussing their sexual skills. They either look like they're about to faint or they start babbling nonsense. Fortunately, Harland is mature enough to be more forthcoming."

Afraid his legs would buckle, Jared locked his knees. Fainting sounded like a very good idea right now.

"You're not this shy with Lia, are you?" Grizelle asked.

"No, but I—" Jared clamped his teeth together. In another minute, he'd start babbling. He knew it. He raked his hand through his hair, pulling it out of the leather thong. "Hell's fire," he muttered, stuffing the thong into his coat pocket. "Facing the Hayllians was easier."

Grizelle laughed. "Yes, I suppose it was."

"Gran!"

Jared spun around at the sound of Lia's voice.

"Gran, I've got everything . . ."

Lia came over the top of a slight rise and saw him.

A wave of joy, filled with her psychic scent, washed over him, quickly followed by uncertainty.

She was wearing trousers, muddy boots, and the too-large sweater she'd gotten at the traveler's inn.

His heart ached because he didn't see a young Gray-Jeweled Queen who most people now would treat with cautious respect. He saw Lia.

"I have one question for you, Warlord, and I want an honest answer," Grizelle said quietly, as Lia started down the rise.

It took all of his self-discipline to take his eyes off Lia and face the Gray Lady.

"If you come back into her life, what Ring will you wear?"

It didn't surprise him that a Queen like Grizelle would know about the Invisible Ring.

He wished he'd been there when Lia had found out that the Ring she'd insisted she'd made up to fool the guards at Raej really existed.

Lia.

He turned to watch her walk hesitantly toward them.

"Warlord? What Ring do you wear?"

"The Gold, Lady," Jared said softly. Lia was close enough that he could see the hope—and the love—shining in her eyes. "I wear the Gold."

SHADOWS AND LIGHT

by

Anne Bishop

SECOND IN THE TIR ALAINN TRILOGY

"Plenty of thrills, faerie magic, human nastiness,
and romance." —*Locus*

An encroaching evil threatens the lives of every witch,
woman, and Fae in the realm. And only the Bard,
the Muse, and the Gatherer of Souls possess the
power to stop the bloodshed.

0-451-45899-0

Praise for *Pillars of the World,* Book I in the
Tir Alainn trilogy:

"Bishop only adds luster to her reputation for fine fantasy."

—*Booklist*

"Reads like a beautiful ballad involving two humans who
believe love is the ultimate magical force in the universe...
Fans of romance and fantasy will delight in this engaging tale."

—*Book Browser*

Available wherever books are sold or at
www.penguin.com

R421

Fantasy from
ANNE BISHOP

Return to the world of **The Black Jewels**

TREACHERY AND TREASON

*Edited by Laura Anne Gilman and
Jennifer Heddle*   0-451-45778-1

Celebrate the worst in human nature with this
anthology that unveils the darker side of the soul. It
includes tales of trickery, deceit, treachery, and betrayal
by some of the best minds in science fiction, fantasy,
and horror, including: William C. Dietz, Dennis L.
McKiernan, and a story from The Black Jewels universe
by Anne Bishop.

Available wherever books are sold or at
www.penguin.com

(0451)

The Black Jewels Trilogy

by Anne Bishop

"Darkly mesmerizing...fascinatingly different."
—*Locus*

This is the story of the heir to a dark throne, a
magic more powerful than that of the
High Lord of Hell, and an ancient prophecy.
These three books tell of a ruthless game of
politics and intrigue, magic and betrayal, love
and sacrifice, destiny and fulfillment, as the
Princess Jaenelle struggles to become that
which she was meant to be.

Daughter of the Blood
Book One
456718

Heir to the Shadows
Book Two
456726

Queen of the Darkness
Book Three
456734

Available wherever books are sold or at
www.penguin.com

R420

Penguin Group (USA) Inc. Online

What will you be reading tomorrow?

Tom Clancy, Patricia Cornwell, W.E.B. Griffin,
Nora Roberts, William Gibson, Robin Cook,
Brian Jacques, Catherine Coulter, Stephen King,
Dean Koontz, Ken Follett, Clive Cussler,
Eric Jerome Dickey, John Sandford,
Terry McMillan...

You'll find them all at
http://www.penguin.com.

Read excerpts and newsletters, find tour
schedules, enter contests...

Subscribe to Penguin Group (USA) Inc. Newsletters
and get an exclusive inside look
at exciting new titles and the authors you love
long before everyone else does.

PENGUIN GROUP (USA) INC. NEWS
http://www.penguin.com/news

Classic Science Fiction & Fantasy

2001: A SPACE ODYSSEY by Arthur C. Clarke
Based on the screenplay written with Stanley Kubrick, this novel represents a milestone in the genre. Now with a special introduction by the author.
0-451-45799-4

ROBOT VISIONS by Isaac Asimov
Here are 36 magnificent stories and essays about Asimov's most beloved creations—Robots. This collection includes some of his best known and best loved robot stories.
0-451-45064-7

THE FOREST HOUSE by Marion Zimmer Bradley
The stunning prequel to *The Mists of Avalon*, this is the story of Druidic priestesses who guard their ancient rites from the encroaching might of Imperial Rome.
0-451-45424-3

BORED OF THE RINGS by *The Harvard Lampoon*
This hilarious spoof lambastes all the favorite characters from Tolkien's fantasy trilogy. An instant cult classic, this is a must read for anyone who has ever wished to wander the green hills of the shire. This is a must-read for fans and detractors alike.
0-451-45261-5

To order call: 1-800-788-6262

SHADOWS AND LIGHT

by

Anne Bishop

SECOND IN THE TIR ALAINN TRILOGY

"Plenty of thrills, faerie magic, human nastiness,
and romance." —*Locus*

An encroaching evil threatens the lives of every witch,
woman, and Fae in the realm. And only the Bard, the Muse,
and the Gatherer of Souls possess the power to stop
the bloodshed.

**Praise for *Pillars of the World*, Book I in the
Tir Alainn Trilogy:**
"Bishop only adds luster to her reputation for fine fantasy."
—*Booklist*
"Reads like a beautiful ballad involving two humans who
believe love is the ultimate magical force in the universe...Fans
of romance and fantasy will delight in this engaging tale."
—*Book Browser*

To order call: 1-800-788-6262

R421